Race to Death

Leigh Russell

W F HOWES LTD

This large print edition published in 2015 by
W F Howes Ltd
Unit 4, Rearsby Business Park, Gaddesby Lane,
Rearsby, Leicester LE7 4YH

1 3 5 7 9 10 8 6 4 2

First published in the United Kingdom in 2014
by No Exit Press

A CIP catalogue record for this book is available
from the British Library

ISBN 978 1 51000 967 7

Typeset by Palimpsest Book Production Limited,
Falkirk, Stirlingshire

Printed and bound in Great Britain
by TJ International Ltd, Padstow, Cornwall

MIX
Paper from
responsible sources
FSC
www.fsc.org   FSC® C013056

To Michael, Jo, Phillipa and Phil

CHAPTER 1

Downing the dregs of his third pint, Adrian fell into conversation with an official in a uniform green jacket and matching tie.

'This is our first visit to York Races.' Adrian waved his free hand in the direction of the Knavesmire Racetrack. 'I once had a girlfriend who came from York but that's as close as I've been to the place. We've been to Kempton Park, but we've not been here before.'

The other man paused in his stride and nodded, apparently paying attention. Adrian tried to size him up. As a local, familiar with the track, he might be able to offer a few useful hints, if Adrian could gain his confidence. It would have been easier to judge the situation if he was sober. He wished Vivien was beside him. With her good looks they might have stood a chance of coaxing a decent tip out of the bloke, but Vivien had gone on ahead with Adrian's brother.

'I mean,' Adrian went on expansively, 'we're no experts, far from it. We like a bit of a flutter though. My brother just won a tidy little sum. Lucky bastard. So,' he leaned forward, swaying slightly, 'you're in the know. Any tips for a beginner?'

He winked at the steward who just smiled and wished Adrian luck before turning away.

Another man came and hovered beside him, wearing the same uniform green jacket. He was studying the crowd up ahead so Adrian couldn't see much of his face, only a light bushy beard and the frames of his gold-rimmed spectacles.

'Your first visit here?' the steward asked.

Adrian said it was.

'You after a tip, sir?'

Adrian laughed and said it would be nice. The official suggested Adrian check out the view from the Shirley Heights Bar.

'Take the lift up to the fifth floor of the Ebor Stand and look out from the balcony. It's well worth a visit. You won't regret it.'

He knew that wasn't the kind of tip Adrian was hoping for.

Disappointed, Adrian hurried off to catch up with his wife. Eventually he found her standing outside one of the champagne bars. He paused to admire her for a moment.

'Where's Charles?'

'He's gone to blow some of his winnings on a glass of champagne. You'd better go after him if you want one. He'll probably get a bottle. He said we should have the best.'

'You've got the best right here,' Adrian replied, thumping his chest with one hand.

He threw his other arm round her white shoulders, grumbling cheerfully that his brother was showing off again. 'Him and his money,' he added a trifle enviously. It was all right for Charles. He didn't have a wife to support.

It was no surprise when Vivien refused to accompany him up to the Shirley Heights Bar.

'In these shoes,' she protested, laughing, 'you must be joking.'

She tossed her head, flicking her long blonde hair across her bare shoulder. Adrian could never understand why his wife chose to wear uncomfortable shoes, the heels so high she struggled to walk at all. It was amazing she hadn't done herself an injury.

'I'll stay here and wait for Charles. But you go up if you want to. I'd rather keep my feet on the ground, and drink champagne.'

'Suit yourself. I'll be back before he gets through that queue.'

Adrian walked past a list of former winners displayed on a glass board beneath a sign in huge chrome letters: 'Ebor Stand'. He looked back when he reached the entrance of the elegant glass and brick construction that towered above the walkway. He couldn't see Vivien or his brother in the mêlée. Facing the entrance was a cabinet packed with trophies, photographs and other memorabilia of famous horses. To his right images of jockeys on horseback had been etched onto a glass wall. He crossed a smart hallway. As he made his way round the corner to find the lifts, the sense of luxury continued. The lift had carpeted floor, wooden walls and a large mirror. Vivien would have liked that.

Shirley Heights Bar was packed. There was a queue of people for the bar itself, which was all wood and chrome and shiny black surfaces, modern and classy. He had drunk too much already, and the day had barely begun. Turning, he made his way out through large glass doors onto a spacious balcony. People were seated at small chrome tables, enjoying the view. It was a cheerful scene, everyone in their Sunday best intent on having a good time. Which was what he should have been doing, downstairs with Viv and Charles. Still, now he was up here it would be daft not to look at the view. He might catch a glimpse of his wife, far below. He wondered if she was looking up, hoping to see him, high above the ground.

Leaning on the thick chrome bar that ran around the edge of the balcony, he gazed down at the forecourt. To his left the brick wall of the Ebor building obscured the view towards the racetrack. A few inches in front of him a chest high reinforced glass barrier surrounded the balcony. Below that, pots of flowers masked the view immediately beneath him. He looked up across the car park

4

and the Knavesmire to the city, a mile or so in the distance, where he thought he could make out the Minster rising above the rooftops. Looking to his right he saw a tall clock tower looming over the vista. There was a flurry of movement behind him as everyone on the balcony began making their way inside. In the bar ubiquitous screens displayed the action. The next race was about to begin. Above the cacophony an excited commentator was shouting from the monitors.

Turning, Adrian found his way blocked by the steward who had recommended the view to him.

'I'm going to the bar,' he said. 'If I can just get past you—'

The other man didn't budge. 'If you go to the corner, you get a great view of the clock tower.'

'I saw it,' Adrian muttered.

All the same he looked round, not wishing to be rude. As he did so, he felt a sharp prick on his neck.

'Ouch! I've been stung!'

He turned back. The face in front of him looked fuzzy. His throat felt as though it was closing up. Fumbling to loosen his tie, he realised he had drunk far too much. His fingers wouldn't work properly. He opened his mouth to cry out, but his lips seemed to be frozen. His tongue felt thick. He tried to move his head. It was fixed, his neck rigid. Barely conscious, he felt someone grip him tightly under his arms.

★　★　★

His relief at being helped turned to anger. The steward was wasting valuable time. Adrian needed urgent medical attention. He had suffered a stroke, or an anaphylactic reaction to an insect bite. Moments before, he had been enjoying a day out at the races. Now he could be dying. Someone he dimly recognised was lifting him off the ground. With eyes stuck wide open, he registered a beard and gold-rimmed glasses. He was being held upright, propped against the railing. With a jolt he felt himself hoisted upwards and pushed forwards, in danger of slithering helplessly over the edge. He wanted to scream, but he couldn't move or call out.

As he fell a loud wind roared past his ears, indistinguishable from the roar of the crowd. The race was over.

CHAPTER 2

People were milling about chatting, laughing, queuing and drinking. Women in party frocks and smart suited men mingled with grave punters, all there to chance their luck on the horses. Adrian had gone to look at the view from the fifth floor, leaving Vivien with Charles who had gone to buy a bottle of champagne. The two brothers had left her on her own for ages, standing alone in the chattering crowd. At first she didn't mind. With so many gorgeous dresses to look at, it was like watching a fashion show. After a while she grew anxious, afraid that Adrian and Charles would never find her again. Nervously she searched the assembled throng, looking for a familiar face. Everyone seemed to be enjoying themselves except her. At last she spotted Charles pushing through the crowd towards her. She looked away to hide her relief. Although she was pleased to see him, she was embarrassed watching him barge past other people to reach her, as though he was afraid to leave her by herself. He hadn't minded abandoning her earlier.

★　　★　　★

He joined her, red-faced and out of breath. Three champagne flutes jiggled precariously in his grasp as he wiped his damp forehead with his sleeve, grumbling about the toilets and the queue for drinks. Raising her glass to take a first sip, she was vaguely aware of a commotion behind her. A shrill scream rang in her ear, reverberating painfully inside her head. At the same time, people started jostling one another violently all around her. Someone jogged her arm and she dropped her glass. It shattered on the ground. She barely noticed its contents fizz and splash her shoes, because by then Charles had grabbed her by the elbow to drag her away from the disturbance. One of her shoes fell off as she stumbled after him. Pausing only briefly in his stride, he heaved her bodily off the ground, with one arm. Carrying her at his side, he forged his way through the crowd that was surging past them towards the source of the tumult.

'Don't look round!' he yelled at her.

Nearby she heard someone sobbing.

Reaching the edge of the crowd he put her down. Everyone around them seemed to be talking at once. An authoritative voice was yelling above the din. Vivien couldn't make out what he was saying. Other voices nearby clamoured in a disjointed chorus.

'Oh my God!'

'Did you see that?'

'From the balcony on the top floor.'

'Dropped like a stone.'

'He needs help.'

'Is there a doctor here?'

'It's too late for that.'

As if losing a shoe wasn't bad enough, Vivien noticed for the first time that her frock was spattered with champagne. She swore. Straightening up, she felt her face blush with shame. A man had fallen from a balcony. There was no need for her to see past the crowd of onlookers to know he must be dead or at least badly injured. Blood was probably still oozing from his shattered skull, and she was concerned about having her dress dry cleaned. With a shudder, she glanced around. No one was paying her any attention.

In the mêlée, security guards began shepherding spectators over to the side of the terrace where Vivien was standing behind Charles. Holding his arm for support, she pulled off her shoe. The area where the man had fallen was speedily cordoned off, watched over by a team of security guards. Unceremoniously corralled together, the crowd all seemed to be talking. Once the initial shock had worn off, the mood of the onlookers became irascible.

'How long are we going to be kept here like this?' a drunken voice yelled.

A chorus of complaints broke out.

'We paid good money to come here today.'

'I'm sorry, sir, but there's nothing we can do about it right now,' a policeman answered firmly. 'I'm afraid no one is allowed to leave until we've had a chance to speak to you all.'

'Well, go on then, speak up.'

'We need to speak to each of you individually, sir,' the copper replied stolidly.

Vivien moved to one side of Charles, but there was nothing to see. Several uniformed police officers had gathered around the body, masking it from view. A burly man was running and bellowing, waving his arms vehemently to intercept two security guards who had almost reached the entrance to the Ebor building. Above the sporadic din, Vivien could just about make out the orders he was barking.

'Don't go in. No one is to go inside the building until we get the green light. Guard all the exits. Don't let anyone in.'

A security guard started forward as two men emerged from the building. Just then, several people surged forward in front of Vivien, blocking her view.

Adrian had been gone for about an hour. She searched the crowd in front of her but it was impossible to find anyone in this scrum. At her side, Charles leaned down and yelled in her ear.

'Are you all right?'

'I'm fine. Have you seen Adrian?'

Instead of answering, he seized her by the arm and began pulling her towards the front of the crowd. Awkwardly she hobbled after him, worried about broken glass, or her toes being trodden on.

'Stop pushing,' a man growled.

Other voices joined in. 'We all want to see what's going on.'

Ignoring the chorus of protests, Charles carried on shouldering his way through the throng. He dragged her over to a uniformed policeman, where he loosened his hold on her. The two men had a hurried conversation. As Charles was speaking, the policeman turned to stare at Vivien. Unnerved by the intensity of his gaze, she felt a tremor of fear.

The two men fell silent when she stepped forward to hear what they were saying. Charles stared fixedly at something over her shoulder. The constable shifted uneasily from one foot to the other.

'What's happened?' The words rose hysterically in her throat. 'Something's happened to Adrian, hasn't it? Has he – did he – is it him? I want to see.'

'Are you sure?' Charles asked gently. 'You don't have to do this, you know. I'm his brother. I can do it.'

'Do what?'

He hesitated before answering. 'They need someone to have a look at the man who fell from the balcony and confirm if it's Adrian or not.'

He couldn't meet her eye. They both knew.

CHAPTER 3

The narrow street was packed with tourists, rubbing shoulders together, enjoying the crowded walk along The Shambles, York's well preserved medieval street. Half closing his eyes, Ian could almost have believed they had stepped back to the fourteenth century, if it weren't for the modern shoppers, girls with cropped hair and tattoos, boys wearing anoraks and earrings, and everyone in trainers. He looked up at quaint wooden shop fronts, which he could see over the top of his wife's head. It was one of the advantages of being over six foot tall. Bev's delicate beauty made him smile, but although he looked robust beside her apparent fragility, the reality was inevitably more complex. He watched her eyes flit from one side of the narrow street to the other, taking in displays in the shop windows: jewellery, silverware, chocolates, tearooms, and all manner of knick knacks and confectionery. From time to time she gave an excited cry, but for the most part she stared, wide-eyed, at bow windows with their squared panes, interspersed with white walls and black timber. If they had been in York on holiday she would have been in raptures over the displays, but her pleasure was restrained.

Although she was putting a brave face on it, Bev wasn't happy about their move to York, hundreds of miles away from her family and friends. Having worked his way up from a detective constable to his recent post as detective inspector, there had never been any doubt in Ian's mind that he would accept promotion, wherever it took him. As it happened, it wasn't entirely chance that had taken them so far from Kent. Keen to make a success of his marriage as well as his career, he wanted to put some distance between himself and his in-laws. Despite his rapid promotion, Bev's parents had never thought him good enough for their daughter and he wanted to take her as far away from their stifling influence as he could.

At lunch time they walked through a park to a small café from where they had an impressive view of an historic monument. Clifford's Tower stood on top of a high mound. Ian smiled at the sight of kids clambering up the steep slopes and rolling down again. They had just started eating when Ian's work phone rang. Bev's neat features puckered with annoyance. 'Can't you ignore it? We're eating. We can't just get up and go.'

They both knew the answer to her question. If

the call was a summons to a crime scene, the sooner Ian set off the better.

After listening intently for a moment, he gave an apologetic grimace.

'It looks like I'll be paying a visit to the races sooner than I planned.'

'Don't tell me you've got to go to work right now. What about lunch?'

'Why don't you finish your lunch, then go and have a look round the market and get a taxi home?' He pulled out his wallet. 'You wanted to go to the market—'

Although she smiled at his clumsy attempt to placate her, he could see her eyes were glistening with disappointment.

'I'll ask them to pack it up for us. We can have it later,' she said, although they both knew he might not be home for dinner.

'Come on,' he said, standing up. 'Let's sort out the food and get back to the car and I'll drop you home.'

He gave a guilty grin, doing his best to hide his impatience. He didn't want to abandon his wife, but his thoughts were already on the brief report he had just heard.

'What do we know?' Ian asked the sergeant who was waiting to drive him to the races.

Ian had been introduced to Detective Sergeant Ted Birling, but this would be the first time they worked together. The sergeant was in his mid-twenties. Ian found it strange to think that there was nearly ten years between them. He didn't feel any older than his colleague. With black hair and very dark eyes, Ted looked Italian or Spanish. He would have been classically handsome if his eyebrows weren't so thick. The lower half of his face was covered in stubble and the backs of his hands were covered in coarse black hair. While Ian wanted to find out as much as he could about the death they had been called to investigate, he was also keen to discover what sort of officer Ted was. The sergeant's wiry physique gave an impression of physical power in spite of his relatively short stature.

'It's a simple case really, sir. A man fell to his death from a fifth storey balcony at the racetrack.'

'So are we looking at suicide?'

'It appears that way, on the face of it, although the constable on site says there's a question over how he came to fall.'

Ian sighed. If they had been dealing with a murder case, the detective chief inspector would have attended the scene herself. As it was, his boss had chosen to ruin Ian's Saturday by sending him to check on a man who had jumped off a balcony.

'Selfish cow,' he muttered.

'What's that, sir?'

'Nothing. Do we know why we've been called out?'

The sergeant shrugged. 'It's not very clear, but

several witnesses reported seeing a second person on the balcony with the victim just before he plunged to his death, and apparently a race official found someone lurking on the balcony shortly after the incident.'

They turned off the main road. Ahead Ian could see the sweep of the white fences of the racecourse.

'Lurking, eh? Let's not go jumping to conclusions before we have all the facts. This is probably a suicide, or an accidental death. The dead man had probably had a few too many.'

'Yes, sir.'

Despite his cautious words, Ian felt a rush of excitement. The incident might be suspicious, in which case he was about to embark on his first investigation as a detective inspector – and he was going to be the first senior officer on the scene.

CHAPTER 4

A long straight avenue took them past more signs. They turned right towards the racetrack. To their left a stunning art deco clock tower soared high above the other buildings in view. 'Terry York' was written in large lettering on the clock face. As they drew closer, Ian was disappointed to see many of the window panes were broken. The building was derelict.

'That clock tower's amazing,' he said aloud.

'Yes, it's a listed building.'

'I wonder what'll happen to it?'

Ted didn't answer. A moment later they drew up beside a triangular porch on their right bearing a sign, 'Welcome to York Racecourse'. Ahead of them a white arch spanned the road bearing the same inscription. Before they were out of the car a uniformed constable appeared, striding towards them.

'This way, sir.'

They followed him through the turnstile.

The walkway that led to the racetrack was broad enough for a white forensic tent, with room to stand around outside it. Behind the tent, two uniformed officers guarded the entrance to the five storey Ebor building. Sending Ted to find out whether anyone had accompanied the victim to the races, Ian spoke to a portly grey-haired sergeant in charge of a team providing a police presence on site.

'That's where he jumped from, sir.' The sergeant squinted up at a vertical series of balconies. 'All the way from the top, five floors up.'

'Jumped or was pushed,' a constable beside him added, in a voice high-pitched with excitement.

'He didn't stand a chance,' the portly sergeant said, shaking his head. 'Lucky he didn't land on top of anyone. The place was heaving before we cleared the area.'

Ian looked up at the balcony. Once the man had fallen, it looked as though a fatality was inevitable.

'It must be a drop of over fifty feet,' he said.

'Something like that, sir.'

It seemed a very public way to commit suicide. But if the man had thrown himself off the balcony, presumably he hadn't been thinking straight. Ian turned back to the sergeant waiting patiently at his side.

'There must have been any number of witnesses?'

'Yes, there were hundreds of racegoers here. Hundreds.'

'Had most of them been drinking?'

'Not all of them, sir. There's many are serious about the horses.'

'We've got a list, sir,' the uniformed constable piped up.

Ian gave a brisk nod.

'This could have been an accident,' he said, speaking more to himself than to his colleagues.

'An accident, sir?'

'I'm just wondering whether he could have gone too close to the edge of the balcony because he was too drunk to appreciate the danger he was in. Or he might have been high, having a good time on his day out, and misjudged the risk.'

'I couldn't comment on that, sir,' the sergeant answered impassively. 'But I understand there was something suspicious about it.'

Ian felt his heart begin to race, but before he could ask any questions Ted joined them. He looked animated.

'Several witnesses claimed they saw a second figure up on the balcony with the victim, and we've got the other man in custody,' he announced triumphantly. 'One of the race officials brought him down shortly after the incident. It looks as though they were having an argument up on the balcony, and the suspect pushed the victim over the edge.'

'We don't know he was pushed, and if he was, we don't yet know it was deliberate,' Ian pointed out.

'There are several witnesses—'

'Let's not start making assumptions, Sergeant.'

Ian turned and thanked the grey-haired sergeant in uniform before walking away with Ted.

'It's a long way up there,' Ian said as they approached the entrance to the Ebor Stand. 'No one down here could have seen exactly what happened. Things are not always what they seem. The suspect might have been trying to stop the victim jumping. That could have looked from down here like he was pushing him. Don't confuse speculation with conclusions based on clear evidence.'

'Yes, sir.'

Meticulous forensic scrutiny of the balcony and lifts was under way. Ian and Ted pulled on protective suits and shoes and entered the lift. On the fifth floor, white-suited photographers and scene of crime officers were at work, examining every inch of the bar and balcony. There was nothing to suggest that a struggle had taken place. Crossing to the perimeter, Ian glanced over the barrier. As a rule heights didn't bother him, but he felt slightly giddy looking at the ground far below. A stout metal bar ran round the balcony, roughly waist height on a tall man. Less than a foot beyond that a thick barrier of reinforced glass ran around the outer limit of the terrace. There was no way anyone could have slipped past the protective barrier by accident.

★　★　★

'I can't see how there could have been anyone else involved,' Ian said to a nearby scene of crime officer, 'not without someone up here noticing a struggle. It's odd, don't you think?'

The other man barely glanced up from his work.

'Unless everyone else was inside watching a race.'

Ian frowned. He should have thought of that himself, it was so obvious. A race had been due to start. Everyone enjoying the view from the balcony had gone inside to watch the screens, while outside a man had been pushed over the barrier. It wouldn't have been easy, but it would certainly have been possible, especially if the victim had been caught off guard. It was fortunate the other man involved had been apprehended at once. Not only were they investigating a murder, but the killer was already behind bars. The detective chief inspector had done Ian a favour, after all. Within a day of arriving in his new post, his reputation seemed assured.

CHAPTER 5

Still in their protective suits and shoes, Ian and Ted took the lift back down to the ground floor. A team of uniformed officers had been drafted in to question race officials and security guards. Yet more uniformed officers were moving along a line of spectators noting down contact details, in an atmosphere of chaotic organisation. Members of the public had been corralled there for over an hour. Dressed in garish finery, they were subdued, talking in muted tones, as though attending a funeral. Meanwhile, the next race had been delayed while the police took down details of potential witnesses.

A woman with dyed blonde hair was sitting just inside the cordon, sobbing. At her side, a man in his early thirties stared disconsolately at the forensic tent.

'That's the victim's wife and brother,' a constable told Ian. 'They're here from London.'

'When are they leaving?'

The constable shrugged.

'I don't know, sir.'

'I'll speak to him,' Ian said.

He didn't think he would get much sense out of the woman.

'This is the dead man's brother,' the constable said clumsily, by way of introduction.

Dealing with the bereaved was difficult under any circumstances. To make matters worse, the man was pale and shaky, obviously suffering from shock. Ian was loath to intrude on his grief, but the job had to be done. He spoke as gently as he could.

'I'm very sorry about your brother, sir. Is it all right if I ask you a few questions?'

The two men man stepped away from the weeping widow. Once they were out of earshot, the victim's brother leaned forward and began talking in an earnest undertone. Beneath cropped light brown hair he had a broad forehead above widely spaced blue eyes, a thick fleshy nose and square chin.

'I knew my brother, Inspector.' He stared fiercely at Ian as he spoke, his blue eyes intense. 'I knew him well.' He broke off for a second, his chest heaving in a deep sigh. 'They're saying he jumped, but he would never have done that. Someone's responsible for this and I'm going to make damn sure they pay for what they've done. They won't get away with it.'

Ian concealed his surprise. 'Are you telling me you know who pushed him off the balcony?'

★ ★ ★

23

It was the other man's turn to look surprised.

'Pushed him?' he repeated. 'Good God, no. Why would anyone want to kill Adrian? No, what I'm saying is, someone's responsible for this. With all the bloody health and safety they're so obsessed with these days, how could they allow it to happen? There should have been a proper safety rail up there. The place was a death trap. As soon as I get home, I'm seeking legal advice, and I'm going to screw this place for every penny they've got. I owe it to my sister-in-law to get compensation for this. And I'm going to see to it this racetrack is shut down. I'm not an idiot, Inspector, and I'm not going to let this rest.' His face flushed with anger, and his hands clenched into fists.

Ian didn't point out that there was a sturdy thick metal rail around the balcony, supplemented by a strong reinforced glass barrier. Instead he asked where the victim's brother was staying. He didn't recognise the name of the hotel, but Ted knew the location. It was in the city centre and easy to find.

'It's five minutes walk from the station,' the sergeant added.

'We need to speak to you both,' Ian explained, turning back to the victim's brother. He glanced over at the distraught widow. 'It can wait till tomorrow.'

'We have to get back to London tomorrow. Our train tickets are booked. We've got seats reserved.'

★   ★   ★

Ian shrugged. The man had just lost his brother and he was worried about missing a train.

'We'll do our best to accommodate you, sir, but you might find your sister-in-law isn't ready to travel so soon.'

'She'll be better off away from here . . .' A worried look crossed the brother's face. 'And I have to get back to the office.'

'What time is your train?'

'Around two. We thought we'd have lunch – Adrian wanted . . .'

'Fine. We'll meet you in the reception area of the hotel in the morning. Shall we say ten o'clock?'

Muttering condolences, Ian moved away. He was keen to view the body before it was moved.

After glancing up at the balcony, he entered the forensic tent. The victim looked as though he was in his mid-thirties, about the same age as Ian. He was lying on his back, where he had fallen, arms and legs awkwardly splayed. He had a large oblong face with a prominent nose, and light stubble. His hair was cut very short above his square face. If it wasn't for his extreme pallor, and a pool of blood on the path beside his head, he could have been sleeping. Apart from his flabby torso, the resemblance to his brother was marked, even in death. A doctor was carefully feeling the dead man's limbs with deft fingers. About forty, plump and brown-haired, she looked thoughtful.

'There are a few broken bones,' she said in

answer to Ian's question, 'but I can't be sure of anything right now, except that he's dead. At least his face is intact,' she added. 'Not that it makes any difference to him.'

'He landed on his back then?' Ian asked.

The doctor paused before answering.

'Yes, the position of the body is certainly atypical.'

With a tremor of anticipation, Ian asked her what she meant.

'Accidental falls from a significant height usually result in injuries to feet, legs, pelvis, vertebrae, because instinctively the victim will turn in the air to land feet first. But when the person is unresisting – dead, drugged or otherwise uncon-scious – the body shifts to a horizontal position during the descent, ending up either flat on its back or flat on its front.'

'So you're saying he was already dead when he landed?'

'He bled from an injury to the back of his head which looks as though it was sustained when he landed on the ground.' She frowned. 'I'm sorry, Inspector, but it's not clear-cut. I won't be sure exactly what happened until the body's been prop-erly examined, and the results of the toxicology report are back. There's something not quite right about it, and that's all I can say for now. I might be wrong,' she added with a complacency that belied her words, 'but I'm going to recommend the coroner requests a home office forensic pathologist to do a post mortem.'

Ian decided not to risk irritating the doctor by pressing her to say more. Her co-operation could make his work a lot easier.

'Yes, it looks as though that's the way it's heading,' he agreed. 'But in the meantime it would be really helpful if you could tell me the probability of anyone surviving a fall of – what, fifty feet?'

Her response was so pat he suspected she had researched the information before coming out.

'With a fall of a distance more than twice an individual's height there's more than a fifty per cent probability of serious physical trauma. Falling over fifty feet onto a hard surface is almost certain to prove fatal.'

The doctor had nothing more to tell him.

Ian didn't merely dislike viewing corpses; it actually made him feel physically sick. He had learned to control his feelings enough to hide his queasiness from his colleagues, but he was constantly on his guard. It shouldn't make any difference, but he always felt particularly distressed when he viewed victims who had been around the same age as him. This body was somehow especially disturbing as Ian had spoken to Adrian's brother a moment before entering the forensic tent. The family resemblance was strong. He could have been speaking to the dead man just before he saw his body. Eager to escape into the fresh air, Ian hurried out of the tent with its morbid interior.

As they walked back to the car he and Ted discussed what the victim's brother had told them. Ted thought the brother's statement bore out the theory that a third party had deliberately pushed the dead man off the balcony.

'I can't see any reason to question it,' he insisted. 'We've got the man who did it.'

'Have we questioned the steward who found him?'

Ted shook his head. 'He's only given an informal statement so far.'

'Chase that up, Ted. He should be easy enough to find. Now, what do we know about the suspect?'

'The guy who pushed him?'

'You're assuming the suspect's guilty before we've even spoken to him.'

'Do you think he might not have done it, sir?'

Ian suppressed a smile. Apart from his personal passion for justice, it wouldn't do his reputation any harm to have his first case as an inspector wrapped up so promptly.

'Let's see what the suspect has to say,' he replied impassively.

CHAPTER 6

A murder incident room had been set up in the police station in York. There was a business-like atmosphere in the entrance hall. A couple of officers were chatting as they heaved on stab vests. Apart from the fact that all the faces he saw were unfamiliar, Ian could have been back in his old police station in Kent. Passing two officers, he smiled at their Northern accents. Behind his back they would refer to him as the Southerner, even though his family originally came from the North and he still retained a slight accent. Entering the incident room, his excitement was dampened by the sombre mood. It formed a stark contrast to the cheerful atmosphere that characterised the station as a whole.

'It's a straightforward case,' Detective Chief Inspector Eileen Duncan was saying as Ian entered.

A hefty woman in her late forties, with dark hair already greying at the temples, she had a sharp nose, thin lips, and a square chin. On balance he felt reassured by her air of fierce determination. Despite her forceful air, she was attractive. He wondered whether she had a family, or if she had dedicated herself to her career to the exclusion of everything else. He knew it could be hard for a woman to rise up through the ranks if she took career breaks in order to have children.

'Adrian Curtis died as a result of falling from a five storey balcony,' she was saying. 'We have a suspect in custody, so we should be able to wrap this up quickly, and be done with it before the papers get busy. We need to play it down, hopefully as an unfortunate domestic, with no hint of blame landing anywhere else. If possible, avoid any criticism of the safety measures in place at the racetrack.'

A murmur of agreement greeted her announcement. Even a newcomer like Ian was aware that the races were worth millions in revenue to the local area. Everyone was twitchy about any potential bad press. Eileen turned to Ian.

He cleared his throat. 'It certainly doesn't look like an accident,' he said. 'The coroner's calling in a home office forensic pathologist to conduct the post mortem. The circumstances are suspicious, ma'am.'

'Are you sure?' Eileen asked, 'or does it just look that way at the moment?'

Everyone turned to stare at Ian.

'We've just come from the racetrack, ma'am. It could have been suicide or murder, but it definitely wasn't an accident. The rail round the balcony can't have been easy to climb over. I don't know if you've been up to Shirley Heights Bar on the fifth floor.'

A couple of officers muttered something.

'There's no way anyone could have fallen off that balcony by mistake.'

'The victim's insurance company are going to love you,' someone muttered.

'The racetrack will be pleased,' someone else said.

Convinced Adrian hadn't plummeted from the balcony by accident, they urgently needed to discover whether anyone else had been with him when he fell. If his death had been murder, the faster they established that fact, the sooner they could begin their investigation.

'Is there anything to suggest he might have been at risk of suicide?' Eileen asked. 'However difficult it might have been for him to climb over the railing, there's no telling what a man might do if he's desperate enough.'

'It's a selfish way to go, if it was suicide,' Ted said. 'Why would anyone want to inflict that on other racegoers, strangers enjoying a day out?'

'There might have been one particular person he wanted to be there to witness his dramatic death,' Eileen replied. 'If there's a connection between the victim and anyone else at the race-course this afternoon, we need to follow it up.'

'His wife was there,' Ted said.

* * *

Ian repeated what Adrian's brother had said. He wasn't surprised when Eileen discounted that statement with an impatient wave of her hand. Adrian's brother was hardly a reliable witness. He must have been in shock. Besides, he had already admitted he intended to sue the racetrack for negligence. Any suggestion Adrian had deliberately clambered over the rail would damage the chance of compensation.

'I appreciate it's in the family's interest to deny there's any chance the death was suicide, but I believed him, ma'am. He was so adamant about it.'

'As you'd expect if he was lying.' The detective chief inspector gave a tolerant smile. 'Sometimes the more certain a witness seems, the less he should be believed.'

There was a mutter of agreement in the room. Ian felt uncomfortable at her patronising tone, but he held his tongue. He didn't really mind. He was a newcomer on an established team. His colleagues were sizing him up, just as he was making his mind up what he thought of them. So far he was cautiously pleased with what he had seen.

The man who had been brought down from the balcony by a race official had been taken to a cell to sober up. He woke up after a couple of hours and began shouting for attention.

'Is he in a fit state to answer questions?' Ian asked.

'He's awake enough to demand to see a lawyer,' the custody sergeant replied. 'He wasn't that drunk in the first place, and whatever ill effects he had, he's slept it off now.'

Ian hesitated. If he attempted to question the suspect while he was still under the influence of alcohol, anything he said would be deemed inadmissible in court. On the other hand, the longer they delayed speaking to him, the more time they were wasting. With a nod at the custody sergeant, Ian had the suspect brought to an interview room.

In his twenties, Harry Moss was slender, with straw-coloured hair. A snub nose and round cheeks gave him a boyish appearance, but the effect of his youthful looks was spoiled by a surly expression. He launched into a rambling response to Ian's opening question, 'What were you doing at the races today?'

He claimed to have gone to the races for a day's outing, only to be abruptly swept along in a wave of accusations culminating in his being locked in a cell. His voice rose in a crescendo of indignation as he demanded to see a solicitor. Ian sent for the duty brief. It was growing late when at last they were ready. The suspect had been read his rights, and the duty solicitor was seated bolt upright at his side. Ian wondered if it was her first case. She looked very young, with short dark curly hair and sharp eyes. After going through the preliminaries, Ian began to question Harry in earnest. He said he didn't often go to the races, but he enjoyed a flutter.

'It's a nice day out, but I don't take it as seriously as some.'

When Ian asked what he had been doing on the fifth floor balcony, he laughed, passing freckled hands nervously over his chin.

'Me? Catch me up there? You are joking. Scared of heights, me. You ask anyone. It was never me up there.'

'Are you saying the steward lied?'

'What steward?'

'The one who found you on the balcony.'

'I told you, I wasn't there.' He threw an appealing glance to the solicitor who sat listening intently. 'Look, I keep telling you, you've got this all wrong.'

'The steward was quite clear about it.'

'Well *he*'s got it wrong then.'

'We'll be speaking to the witness.'

'Speak to who you like. I'm telling you the truth.'

'What were you doing in the Ebor building?'

'I went in for a look around, a few drinks, you know.'

'By yourself?'

'Yes. That is, I went to the races with a couple of mates, but they were only interested in the betting. I like a flutter, don't get me wrong, but I'm not obsessed with the horses, not like some. There's plenty more to see there.'

'You mean women?'

★   ★   ★

Harry seemed to have relaxed and spoke readily about his day at the races. He looked Ian straight in the eye, with no appearance of unease.

'Look, it was just a day out. I like a bit of a chat. What's wrong with that? I'd paid for my ticket, same as everyone else. I wanted to have a good time.'

'We know you went up to the fifth floor.'

'So I was there. I never said I wasn't. I went to the bar, had a few drinks, nothing wrong with that, is there? Jesus, it's not illegal for a bloke to have a day out, is it? I was having a good time until you lot showed up and before I knew what hit me I was being bundled into a police van.'

However hard he was pressed, Harry insisted he had never been out on the fifth floor balcony. At last Ian gave up and the suspect was escorted back to the custody suite, grumbling.

Ian thought Harry might be telling the truth, but Eileen dismissed his reservations. He hesitated to contradict his new detective chief inspector. She had already questioned his judgement once. He listened in silence as she continued firmly.

'We've got our suspect secure, and we've got a witness. You can get a formal statement tomorrow. There's nothing more needs doing tonight. You can go home, Ian. You look all in.'

'Thank you, ma'am.'

He couldn't think of anything else to say. He

knew she was being considerate, but he was riled. He wanted respect, not kindness. As a sergeant he had been used to having attention paid to his views, even if his senior officer hadn't always agreed with him. As an inspector, he had expected to be given at least as much credence as before. He dropped his gaze and stared down at his shoes, carefully polished the previous evening, now dusty from the racetrack. He had arrived determined to make a good impression. Eileen had seemed happy for him to join her, but it was clear he was going to have to work hard to earn acceptance on the team.

Worn out with the demands of his first investigation since his promotion, he was pleased to escape the claustrophobic atmosphere of the police station. Picking up his own car in the police station car park, he put his foot down. Guilt at leaving his wife alone in an unfamiliar city was an added strain. Bev was doing her best, but he knew she was finding it difficult to cope without the support of her family and friends. He wanted to be there for her. When he arrived home, she was sitting at the kitchen table, flicking through a book of wallpaper samples. Looking up, she held up a page and asked for his opinion.

'I think I've narrowed it down to the lemon or the pale green,' she added.

There was no need to decorate, but he understood she needed a project to occupy her mind.

'You know you're much better at things like this than I am,' he replied, kissing the top of her cropped blonde head.

'And then there's the floor,' she went on. 'Carpet would be warmer, but I'm not altogether sure I like the idea of carpet in the kitchen. They say it's fine, that special kitchen carpet, but I'm not sure. What do you think?'

He nodded, reluctant to respond in case he said the wrong thing.

It was late and he was tired.

'If you want carpet in the kitchen, that's fine with me.'

'But what do you think? You go into lots of people's houses. You must've seen kitchen carpet in some of them . . .'

'Do you know, I'm not sure I ever have?'

As if he would have noticed something like that when questioning a witness in a murder investigation.

'Then maybe it's not such a good idea, if no one else has got it. Honestly, to listen to the salesman, you'd think everyone had it and we'd be odd if we didn't go for it.'

'Well, you decide. Whatever you want. I'm sure you'll do a great job.'

He hoped he didn't sound patronising.

They had both eaten but it wasn't too late to sit down together over a glass of wine. When he told her they had a suspect behind bars, she clapped her hands.

'That's great. Your first case as an inspector, and you've solved it already!'

He smiled, hoping she was right. But he had an uneasy feeling the truth would prove more complex, and more terrible, than anyone else yet suspected.

CHAPTER 7

Ian went into work early on Sunday morning, leaving the house before Bev was stirring. At the bedroom door he looked back at the mound of her sleeping figure with a faint flicker of regret; it might have been guilt. Driving through residential streets that were almost deserted at that hour, he dismissed thoughts of his wife and turned his attention to the coming day. After grabbing a coffee, he went straight to his desk, impatient to start work. A race official had apprehended Harry on the balcony. The police constable who had taken the official's name and address was on duty that morning. Ian decided to quiz him in person, hoping he had something useful to add to the information he had recorded.

All the constable could remember was that the official had been an odd-looking man aged anything from late twenties to early forties, with a mop of fair hair. The constable was balding. His uniform was stretched tightly across his barrel-shaped chest. He didn't give an impression of incompetence.

'What do you mean by "odd-looking"?' Ian asked. 'Odd in what way, exactly?'

'I'm not sure, really, sir. I didn't pay him much attention, to be honest. Seeing as he was a race official, I assumed he'd stay around to help. I was more interested in the suspect. But I seem to remember he had an awful lot of blond hair.' He frowned. 'Of course there's nothing to stop a bloke dyeing his hair, but it didn't look natural.'

The official's name was Barry Gordon. He lived in Newton Terrace, near the centre of York. The sat nav directed Ian along Fishergate and past Clifford's Tower. He barely had time to glance up at the ancient edifice before his route took him across the river. With Clifford's Tower behind him, he turned into Cromwell Road, then followed the base of the city wall along a narrow street of terraced properties with large bay windows. Ignoring the parking restrictions, he drew up outside a small house. A willowy woman opened the door. She had pale blue eyes and very fair straight hair that fell in a long fringe.

'Is Barry in?' he asked, after introducing himself.

'What's he gone and done now?' the woman asked with a weary sigh. Turning, she yelled down the hall. 'Dad! Dad! Get out here now!' She turned back to Ian. 'He does his best, but he's such hard work. I don't know what I'm supposed to do with him. I'm not that young myself and – oh, here he comes.'

*   *   *

40

She broke off as an elderly man came into view, hobbling towards them. He blinked short-sightedly at Ian.

'What?' he called out in a quavering voice as he approached. 'What is it?' Before he could say anything else his slight frame was shaken by a chesty cough.

When he was finally able to speak, he confirmed that his name was Barry Gordon.

'Barry Alfred Gordon,' he announced, and commenced another coughing fit. His daughter muttered under her breath about smoking.

Ian checked the address. There was no doubt he had come to the correct house. He pressed on with his enquiry, although it was hard to believe that this frail old man could conceivably have wrestled with Adrian, let alone lifted him off his feet and heaved him off the balcony.

Ian enquired whether there was another Barry Gordon living there, a son or grandson of the old man who shared his name, but the two people in the hall were the sole occupants of the house.

'She moved back in with me when she lost her husband,' the old man explained.

From the shrewish expression that crossed the woman's face, Ian guessed her husband had left her. Barry confirmed that he had been at the races with his daughter the previous day. She nodded her head, her anxious face relaxed into a smile.

'He likes a bit of a go on the horses, don't you dad?'

It didn't take much to prompt them to reveal they had been outside the Ebor building when Adrian had fallen from the balcony.

'We saw it all,' Barry said with a malicious grin. 'We were that close to it. There was such a fuss. People rushing about all over the place, and police and ambulances and the security guards, and all those young women in their fancy get ups.' He cackled.

'Show some respect, dad,' his daughter admonished him with an embarrassed glance at Ian who stood, stony-faced, hiding his disappointment behind a mask of indifference.

Ian didn't stay long. The constable who had taken down people's details at the races must have muddled up Barry Gordon's contact details with those of the official who had apprehended Harry. A call to the station confirmed that no one else called Barry Gordon lived at the property Ian had just visited. There was nothing else to do but return to the station where the Criminal Intelligence Unit set to work examining the other witnesses' details. They all checked out. There were two other Barry Gordons and a Bartholomew Gordon listed on the York electoral register. None of them worked at the racecourse. Looking further afield, they discovered a Barry Gordon living in Leeds who had worked for the security firm employed by the racetrack. He hadn't been a race official in a green blazer, but at least he had worked there when the races were on, checking no one was drinking too much or otherwise risking causing a disturbance.

CHAPTER 8

Taking Ted with him this time, Ian set off. The A64 took them west to Leeds, where they found Barry Gordon at home. A gigantic man, he towered over the two detectives. Their hopes of gathering information leading to an arrest were quickly dashed when Gordon told them he had been visiting his wife in Leeds General Infirmary the previous afternoon. Ted scowled. Even Ian's characteristic optimism faltered. Unlike the rest of the team, he hadn't been convinced Harry was guilty, but he was still disappointed that their key witness continued to elude them. Apart from Barry's wife, nurses would be able to confirm his story, plus there would be CCTV footage showing he had been at the hospital while Adrian was falling from the balcony. Back at the police station in York, a telephone call confirmed that the Leeds Barry Gordon's alibi checked out. They still hadn't found their missing witness.

'So where the hell is he?' Ted muttered irritably.

Ian shrugged. He could be anywhere by now,

virtually impossible to trace, even if Barry Gordon was his real name.

'Damn him,' Ted muttered angrily, 'the time we've wasted on this wild goose chase. That PC should be shot.'

Along with the rest of the team, Ted assumed the constable at the races had been inept in confusing the steward's details with those of Barry Gordon, an old man who had happened to be at the races. They had all heard Eileen bawling at the constable for his careless record keeping. Remembering what he had heard about the official's fake-looking hair, Ian couldn't help wondering whether the constable had been unfairly censured. Masquerading as a race official, it would have been easy for the killer to have overheard old Barry Gordon giving his name to a police officer. It was perfectly feasible that the disguised killer had repeated the other man's name and address when he was asked for his own details by a different officer. The more Ian thought about it, the more likely the idea seemed. All the same, he held back from telling anyone what he was thinking. As a newcomer, it would be politic for him to prove himself before he challenged the detective chief inspector's opinion with a theory that might turn out to be totally wrong.

Meanwhile the race officials' manager had obliged them by going to the police station to study CCTV images taken just after the fatality. He arrived promptly, a thin, nervous looking man, who hesitated before speaking.

'We've never had anything like this before,' he said several times.

He leaned forward, squinting at the screen for a moment, before shaking his head. All at once he sat up, watching Harry emerge from the Ebor building.

'That man with him isn't one of ours.'

'Are you sure?'

'Positive. I've never seen him before and besides, he's not wearing our uniform. His jacket's very similar but it's got the wrong buttons. And that's not an official tie. Look.'

It was Ian's turn to stare. The differences were fairly subtle between the jackets of the two stewards on the screen. Neither face was clearly visible. But only one of the jackets had metal buttons.

He turned to the manager.

'So if he's not a steward, what's he doing there? How did he get in?'

The manager shook his head. 'Anyone can buy a ticket to the races.'

'So you're saying anyone could turn up at the racetrack wearing a green jacket, and pretend to be a steward?'

'Well, yes, in theory there's nothing to stop someone wearing a green jacket. There's no rule against it. And if there was, he could have concealed it under a coat, couldn't he? He would have had to pay to get in, of course. But if a member of the public was caught deliberately impersonating a steward, they'd risk a ban and possibly criminal charges, depending on the circumstances. And they'd be spotted fairly promptly. Someone would notice.'

'How?'

'Well, the stewards work in teams.'

'Do they ever work alone?'

'Of course they're free to walk around by themselves, and some of them do, so if someone wanted to pretend to be an official, I suppose they might get away with it for a short time.'

'Long enough to kill someone,' Ian thought. Out loud he said, 'Anyone could turn up in a green jacket and pretend to be a steward?'

'We've got three hundred stewards. We couldn't watch all of them all the time. But they operate in teams of four or six, and supervisors go round every half hour to check everything's OK.'

'The DCI won't be pleased,' Ted said when the manager had gone. 'She thought the case was all wrapped up.'

Ian shrugged. 'We were all hoping that.'

He wasn't interested in his senior officer's statistics just then. They were investigating a murder in which the key witness had not only vanished, but had turned out to be an imposter.

'He was the murderer, wasn't he?' Ted went

on, increasingly animated, 'the man who was pretending to an official. He must have been up there on the balcony with Adrian. He was the one who pushed him over the edge, and then he brought Harry down to take the rap. Harry probably wasn't even up there on the balcony at all. Bugger. He said he didn't like heights, didn't he?'

Ian nodded. Chancing to bump into Harry on his way down, the murderer could have seized on him as a useful diversion.

'We had him,' Ted went on. 'He was talking to a constable, right there. And now Christ knows where he is, or who he is.'

While the police had been preoccupied with Harry, and Adrian's body had still been lying on the tarmac where he had fallen, the murderer had vanished.

'We had him and we let him slip through our fingers,' Ted repeated angrily. 'How long is it going to take us to track him down now?'

Ian didn't answer. It looked as though the killer could be too intelligent to have left any clues. They might never find him.

CHAPTER 9

Chilling out in front of the television with a cold beer, Richard was tempted to ignore the phone. No one ever called him on the landline. It was usually only Emma's parents who used that number, and she was in the shower.

'Is that Richard?'

'Yes.'

He didn't recognise the voice, couldn't even tell if it belonged to a man or a woman.

'Richard Western?' the caller continued.

'Yes,' he repeated, mildly irritated. 'Who's that?'

'You don't need to know who I am. All you need to know is that I'm going to kill you.'

'Who are you?'

The faint hum of the dialling tone answered him.

There was no point reporting it to the police as a threatening phone call. Nothing had happened. It was a prank, that was all. It was odd, because the house and the landline were registered in Emma's name. He had only been living there for about six months. In any case, even if he *had* decided to take it seriously, he wouldn't have been able to describe the voice, other than to say it sounded oddly husky. But he couldn't risk any fuss. The caller had most likely been a disappointed woman pursuing him after a casual fling. He was careful never to give out his name or number, or to leave any other means of tracing him, but any one of the women he had met could have nicked a business card from his wallet. He might even have dropped one by mistake while he was wriggling out of his trousers. There had been so many women over the years, it was hardly surprising if one of them had taken it into her head to stalk him. It was her hard luck that he was in love with his girlfriend.

He had honestly tried to ignore other women now that he was living with Emma, but the temptation had sometimes proved too strong to resist. It wasn't his fault. Women threw themselves at him all the time. That was one of the many reasons he had fallen for Emma. She hadn't jumped into bed with him at the first opportunity. It wasn't as if he was doing anything wrong, not really. Emma would be upset if she found out, but he never screwed other women while she was around. She would never know. She was going to stay with her parents soon and would be away for a whole week, enough time for one last casual fling. He had resolved to give up his infidelities more than once, but this time he seriously intended to stop. Emma going away was a sign. He would indulge in one final clandestine affair before proposing to her. As long as she remained oblivious to his escapades, where was the harm if he went out for a few drinks and picked up a willing bit of skirt from time to time? He was conscientious about going for regular check-ups. This would be his last chance to have some fun before he finally settled down.

Emma had intimated that she would like a big wedding, and he intended to give her whatever she wanted. He had glanced in the windows of a few jewellery shops as he walked past. The diamonds all looked the same to him, but Emma was going to have the most expensive engagement ring he could afford. While he remained single his occasional dalliances had been innocuous. Once he was married his conduct would constitute adultery. That was not on. So he was going to wait until after her trip before asking her to marry him. If he hadn't found a stream of willing women, he would probably have turned to gambling or fast cars, or even drugs, anything to satisfy his craving for thrills. In a way he was doing Emma a favour. At least his encounters with women were free. There were no strings, and no consequences.

Until the phone calls started.

The second call came only a couple of hours after the first one. This time Emma was in the kitchen.
    'Get that, will you?' she called out.

He obliged without a second thought.

'Richard? It's me.'

He recognised the voice at once. This time it sounded more businesslike.

'What do you want?'

'Have you heard about the death at the races?'

'What?'

'You'll read about it in the papers tomorrow.'

'What are you talking about?'

He kept his voice down so Emma couldn't hear.

'Who is it?' she called from the kitchen.

'No one.'

He almost hung up, but the caller was speaking again.

'A death at the races.'

'That's got nothing to do with me. I wasn't there.'

'A death at the races,' the voice repeated. 'It'll be in the papers soon. You'll be next.'

Before he could respond, the phone went dead.

CHAPTER 10

The hotel where Adrian had been staying with his wife and brother was situated in Toft Green, close to the town centre and the railway station from where buses ran to the Knavesmire on race days. Parking outside, Ted led Ian down a flight of steps into a smart reception area furnished with large comfortable chairs and sofas set around low tables. A heavily made-up young woman behind the desk gave a bright smile when Ian approached.

'Are you checking in, sir?'

'I believe you have a Mrs Curtis and a Mr Curtis staying here? They're expecting me.'

'Who shall I say is asking for them?'

Her painted eyebrows lowered when she saw Ian's warrant card.

'That's the woman whose husband jumped off a balcony at the races, isn't it? I'll call her room for you.'

Ian wasn't averse to people believing Adrian had killed himself. The truth would be in the papers soon enough. In the meantime, public misunderstanding might buy the police more time before the killer was put on his guard.

At the races, Ian hadn't seen Vivien's face clearly. Now, in spite of her puffy bloodshot eyes, he could see she was good looking as soon as she entered the manager's office. She had long straight hair with blonde highlights, dark at the roots. Her oval face had heavy dark eyebrows, a long straight nose, and a full bottom lip beneath a thin top one, while a pointed chin gave her an elfin look. The skin on her prominent cheek bones flushed dark pink as her brother-in-law took a seat beside her, shifting his chair until he was sitting very close to her. Throughout the interview he glanced at her repeatedly. His concern was understandable. She had just lost her husband in a sudden and shocking manner. Even so, Ian couldn't help speculating about the nature of the relationship between the man and woman sitting in front of him. He wondered whether the widow was disturbed by her brother-in-law's striking resemblance to her dead husband, or whether there was another reason why she avoided looking at him.

'Mrs Curtis, please tell me in your own words what happened on Saturday,' he invited her gently.

Somehow he wasn't surprised when her brother-in-law promptly answered for her.

'I can tell you that, Inspector. Vivien and I were together the whole time.'

'Go on.'

Ian listened closely to Charles' account of their Saturday afternoon. After a brief account of how they had arrived at the races, Charles reached the point where his brother had decided to make his way up to the balcony.

'Why didn't you go with him?'

'I wish I had now, but I was too busy getting in drinks. Vivien stuck with me,' he added, glancing at her. 'To be honest, neither of us fancied the idea of traipsing all the way up to the fifth floor just to look at the view.'

'What gave your brother the idea of going up there in the first place?'

Charles shrugged. His eyes flicked sideways again.

'A steward recommended the view,' Vivien replied in a low monotone.

Ian turned to look at her, aware that her next words might prove a key moment in the investigation.

'What did the steward look like?' he asked. 'Anything you can remember about him would be helpful.' He paused. 'Anything at all.'

But Vivien hadn't seen the official herself. She had only heard Adrian mention him. She didn't seem to understand Ian's next question. He repeated it slowly. The sedative she had been given seemed to be kicking in again.

'Enemies?' she echoed, bemused. 'Adrian didn't have any enemies.'

'Inspector, my sister-in-law's in shock,' Charles interrupted, waving his hand in an impatient gesture. 'She needs to go home.'

'I'm very sorry to have to ask these questions, sir, but we are investigating the circumstances of your brother's death.'

Charles sat forward with a frown, suddenly alert. 'What circumstances?'

Beside him, Vivien stirred. 'What does he mean, Charles? What's going on?'

Her brother-in-law sat back, draping his arm across the back of her chair in a proprietorial gesture as Ian explained that there was reason to suspect Adrian's death hadn't been accidental.

'That's a lie. Adrian would never have killed himself,' she said dully.

'My brother didn't kill himself,' her companion repeated forcefully.

Ian watched them both closely as he told them the police were aware of that fact.

'You mean . . .?' Charles said.

Vivien didn't respond but sat staring dully at Ian while Charles glared at him.

'We have reason to suspect Adrian may have been the victim of an attack.'

'You mean – there was a fight of some sort?'

'There was no sign of a struggle.'

'You can't mean you think he was murdered?'

'We're investigating the possibility,' Ian said gently. 'We can't rule it out.'

'That's preposterous! No one would have wanted him dead. My brother was an inoffensive man, Inspector. People *liked* him. To suggest he was the sort of person who might have provoked hostility is – it's a preposterous suggestion. I can assure you there's no truth in it. No truth in it at all.'

Ian shrugged. 'We can only deal with evidence, Mr Curtis. And the evidence points to an unlawful killing. I'm sorry.'

Without warning, the widow flung herself forward on her chair with a protracted wail. Her shoulders shuddered as she sobbed.

'Stop it, Vivien,' her brother-in-law urged. He turned to Ian, red-faced with anger. 'Now look what you've done. You've got her all worked up again, just as she was beginning to calm down. She lost her husband yesterday, for Christ's sake. You've got a lot to answer for, Inspector.' On his lips the title sounded like an insult.

Ian could only reiterate that he was sorry. He had a job to do.

'I appreciate how difficult this must be for you, but if the circumstances of Adrian's death were suspicious, we need to find out what happened, and the faster we can act on any information, the sooner we are likely to find out who's responsible.'

'I can tell you who's responsible.'

Red-faced with anger, Charles launched into a tirade against the racetrack, blaming its safety officers for his brother's death.

Although Ian had established to his own satisfaction that no one could have fallen from the balcony by accident, he let the victim's brother have his say. Sometimes people let down their guard when they were angry, disclosing information they would never reveal when they were in control of their feelings. Finally, Charles fell silent. He had given nothing away. Meanwhile his sister-in-law continued to sob quietly at his side.

'Vivien's very upset by all this,' Charles announced, rising to his feet. 'She doesn't want to talk about it anymore. If you have any further questions, you can ask me.'

'Do you think there's something going on between them?' Ted asked as they drove back to the police station.

'Between Adrian's wife and his brother?'

'Yes. I just thought there might be something going on.'

Ian considered. While he had to agree the two mourners were obviously on intimate terms, it was impossible to judge whether they had been drawn close by grief or if their closeness was part of an ongoing deeper relationship.

'I mean,' Ted pressed his point home, 'do you think they could have been having an affair?'

'Let's not go jumping to conclusions.'

Ian was quietly impressed by Ted's astuteness in recognising that it might have suited Adrian's brother to be rid of him. It was possible Adrian had discovered his brother was having an affair with Vivien. If something *had* been going on between them, Charles might have had a motive for getting rid of his brother. Charles had been at the races that day. His alibi had been provided by Vivien. Perhaps her apparent grief had actually been prompted by guilt. Cautiously he agreed with Ted that questioning Charles and Vivien had certainly opened up new possibilities.

'Good thinking, Ted.'

The sergeant beamed and Ian smiled back, remembering how pleased he had been to receive validation from his inspector when he had been a sergeant.

CHAPTER 11

'Let's open another bottle,' Richard enunciated his words with care. '*Another* one? Are you sure? I think you've had enough, and I certainly have. It's Monday tomorrow.'

'Always sensible,' he muttered, 'sensible Emma.'

'What?'

'Nothing.'

He wondered if that was why he was going to marry her, because he knew she would be a sensible wife. Of course that didn't explain why she wanted to marry him. That wasn't a sensible choice. Far from it. Miserably, he poured the dregs of the bottle into his glass and drained it.

After supper he had gone online and searched the news. A headline had screamed at him from the home page of a national news website. A man had fallen to his death at York Racecourse the previous day. The nuisance caller had promised a death at the races would be in the news. He had warned that Richard would be next. It was too much of a coincidence to be chance. Breathing deeply, he had lain back in his chair and closed his eyes to hide his anxiety from Emma. It had to be a practical joke. The caller must have read about the death before Richard had heard about it. People at the races would have witnessed the tragedy first hand. Reporters, police officers, and staff at the racetrack would all have known about it. Racegoers might have seen it happen. A lot of people could have known about it, before it had even been reported by the media.

But it was possible Richard had spoken to the killer. Apart from the fact that he might have information that could help the police, he couldn't help wondering whether he should genuinely be worried for his own safety. He did his best to put such speculation out of his mind. Not a man prone to fanciful imaginings, he managed well enough for a few hours. But by late evening, dizzy with alcohol, he was finding it hard to control his thoughts. He couldn't face the prospect of lying in bed, in the darkness, the phone a physical presence in the house. Emma was bound to notice something was wrong.

'You know we've got through two bottles, and I haven't had much,' Emma said as she extricated herself from his embrace. 'I'm going to clear up and then I really want an early night. Monday morning tomorrow.'

Sprawled on the sofa, he watched her rise to her feet in one graceful motion, admiring the way her slender frame uncurled until she was standing upright. He shook his head and was surprised to feel the room spinning slightly. He couldn't remember how much he had drunk. Emma had said something about two bottles.

'I'm going for a walk,' he announced without moving.

'A walk? Are you serious? It'll be dark soon. You've got work tomorrow. And you're pissed.'

'I won't be long,' he assured her. 'I just need to clear my head.' The room swayed as he stood up. 'And I'm not pissed.'

She laughed and leaned forward to kiss him gently on the lips. 'All right, you're not pissed, if you say so. But don't be long.'

He nearly sat down again, but he had said he was going for a walk and he needed to prove to her that he was a man of his word. She had to trust him. He couldn't remember exactly why that was so important, but it was.

By the time he realised he wasn't wearing a coat he was already outside. It was chilly, the air bracing after an earlier downpour. The cold wind sobered him up. He remembered why he had deliberately drunk himself into a haze that evening. He couldn't recall much about the psycho on the phone, and regretted not having written down the exact wording of the threatening calls. At the time he hadn't given them much thought. He wracked his brains now, trying to remember exactly what had been said. The caller had definitely issued threats. He was sure of that. 'I'm going to kill you,' and more of that kind of nonsense. When he had mentioned a death at the races it had meant nothing to Richard. He had dismissed it as crazy talk. The news had made him feel very different.

Although it was May, it didn't feel like spring. The evening was cold enough for winter, so he walked quickly. Feeling a sense of power in his legs as he strode along the pavement, his fears began to dissipate. Some tosser with a grudge against him had read about the incident at the racecourse and decided to use it to scare him. That was all. There was no reason for him to be unduly bothered by the prank calls. Nothing had changed. The papers had been stuffed with eyewitness accounts from people talking about the death at the racecourse before Richard read about it. There was no reason for him to suppose he was in danger. He walked briskly past the school and the brick church, and on to a path that led alongside the river. The pedestrian walkway opened out onto a wide area of grassland. He screwed up his eyes looking for the river through the trees. The railway bridge was dimly visible and beyond that Lendal Bridge, a dark outline in the gathering dusk. He swore as a cyclist sped silently past, almost knocking him off balance. Unnerved by the narrow escape, he spun round and retraced his route. Although he hadn't walked far, by the time he reached home again he was no longer cold, but he was exhausted and ready for bed.

When he opened the front door, the phone was ringing. He froze, but the shrill summons stopped almost at once. Too late for Emma's parents to be calling, it must have been a wrong number. Before he could let out his breath in relief, he heard Emma's voice. In a panic, he dashed into the living room. She looked up with a puzzled expression as she held out the phone.

'It's for you. Who the hell is it, calling at this time? He wouldn't give me his name.'

He shook his head. Unwillingly he took the phone and raised it to his ear. His arm seemed to be moving by itself.

'Hello, Richard.'

'What the hell do you think you're doing, calling at this time of night?'

'I hope you enjoyed your walk, Richard,' the voice crooned softly. 'I thought I should ring and make sure you got back home safely. You never know what might happen to you if you go out alone in the dark.'

Before Richard could reply, the caller rang off.

CHAPTER 12

Ian drove to the mortuary alone on Monday morning, leaving Ted to organise a team to follow up witness statements. With a death at the races, there were a lot of them to get through. Avoiding the centre of town, he took the ring road along Gillygate, past narrow side turnings of houses interspersed with a few rows of shops: hair dressers, nail parlours and cafes. In each of those properties, people would have heard about the death at the races. Many of them were probably talking about it as he drove past. Out of all those people, at least one person knew who was responsible for Adrian's death. Passing the main car park, he drew up near white metal up and over doors where a ramp led directly to the mortuary. Almost as soon as he pressed the buzzer the door was opened by a smiling young blonde woman who introduced herself as Avril, the pathology technician. She led Ian along a hushed passageway. Doing his best to suppress his customary nausea, he introduced himself to the home office forensic pathologist who had been called in to examine the body.

★   ★   ★

The pathologist was a plump man in his forties. With ginger hair and pale freckled skin, he contrived to be ugly yet endearing, with a snub nose and twinkling blue eyes. He smiled cheerfully at Ian.

'Forgive me. I won't shake hands.' He held up a bloodstained gloved hand, his shrewd eyes seeming to register Ian's discomfort. 'Jonah Hetherington.' He placed his other hand on the victim's head in a proprietorial gesture. 'This was a suspicious death—'

'Let's not start jumping to conclusions,' Ian interjected, with a quick glance at the body.

Feeling queasy, he raised his eyes to the pathologist.

Jonah continued speaking, ignoring the interruption.

'The victim had no chance of survival.'

'He fell over fifty feet. No one's likely to survive that,' Ian agreed.

'Of course not, but you'd expect his landing to fracture the upper spine and tear open the aorta, putting an end to the flow of blood from the heart.' He looked directly at Ian. 'And that didn't happen.'

'I don't understand.'

'What it means is that this man didn't throw himself off the building.'

'You can't be sure of that.'

'Well, actually, I can, because it would have been physically impossible.'

'Physically impossible? Why?'

'He would have been incapable of moving before he died.'

'I'm still not sure I understand.'

'The toxicology report shows traces of Pentaketaphine in his bloodstream.'

'What does that mean?'

'It means he had been injected with the drug shortly before he fell. Traces of metabolites, the breakdown products, were found in his blood. Pentaketaphine is a neuromuscular blocker. It blocks electrical impulses across the brain, causing paralysis and unconsciousness. Basically, it's an anaesthetic paralytic, causing full body paralysis.'

Ian shook his head. He understood enough to grasp that the victim had been heavily sedated, even anaesthetised, before his death. He still wasn't clear about the significance of this new information. From what the pathologist was saying, it seemed clear that Adrian's death hadn't been accidental. But it still could have been suicide.

'Are you saying his death wasn't accidental?'

'I'm saying he was murdered.'

'What about suicide? Presumably he could have taken the drug himself?'

Jonah shook his head. 'No. He can't have administered the drug himself, unless you found the syringe on the roof.'

'Someone could have removed it afterwards,' Ian suggested, although that would imply an accomplice to suicide, at best.

The pathologist shook his head again.

'There's no way around it, Inspector. Unless you can find a syringe, this man was murdered.'

Ian couldn't understand his insistence.

'He could have injected himself before going out on the balcony,' he suggested, 'and then disposed of the syringe—'

'No, there's no way he could have done that. He would never have made it up to the fifth floor unaided. Pentaketaphine causes almost instantaneous muscular paralysis of all the muscles in the body, including those used for breathing. Without ventilatory support, he would have died from asphyxia within minutes. The bad news is he would have been conscious of what was happening to him as he was falling, because the drug causes paralysis but it's not a sedative. But I doubt he would have been fully compos mentis by then. In answer to your question, it's physically impossible for him to have injected himself before he went up on the balcony. He was visible up there for a few minutes before he fell, wasn't he? As I said, Pentaketaphine takes effect very quickly. Within seconds he would have been too weak to climb over the railing unaided, and fully immobilised soon after that.'

★   ★   ★

The detective chief inspector watched Ian with a puzzled expression as he reported the significance of the Pentaketaphine discovered in Adrian's bloodstream.

'What the hell's that?' someone asked.

'Horse tranquilliser,' another voice answered.

'It's a drug that paralyses the muscles,' Ian explained.

'It's used in operations to prevent involuntary movement,' someone else added, 'in very small doses.'

'It works by blocking messages from the brain to the muscles, causing paralysis and preventing the subject from moving, even breathing,' someone else read aloud from an iPhone.

'The point is,' Ian went on, 'the drug acts very quickly. If Adrian had injected himself before entering the building he wouldn't have made it up to the balcony on the fifth floor. Even if he managed to reach the lift, he would have collapsed on the way, fallen unconscious and stopped breathing.'

'Is it possible he could have injected himself on the balcony and then somehow managed to throw himself off?' Eileen asked.

'If that's what happened, we would have found the syringe,' Ian pointed out. 'The search team have been over the whole building and the walkway below, the bins and the flower beds, everywhere, and found nothing. In any case, why would he inject himself with a drug that inhibits movement just before committing suicide? But the fact is, he would have been paralysed within seconds of being injected, so he wouldn't have been able to throw himself off the balcony. And he couldn't have fallen over the edge. There's a chest high rail and a glass barrier, with a gap in between. It wouldn't be easy to climb over, even for someone who's fit and able. For a man injected with Pentaketaphine it would be impossible. Someone else must have taken the syringe away, which means we're looking at murder.'

There was a pause. Everyone turned to gaze at the photograph of the dead man. Adrian had been carrying several credit cards in a wallet stuffed with cash. If he had died anywhere other than on a racetrack, the amount of cash in his wallet might have raised eyebrows. He had evidently been prepared for a good day out. The detective chief inspector broke the silence.

'Right,' she snapped briskly. 'That confirms what we already suspected. We're investigating a murder. Have the next of kin been told? We need to get the body formally identified, and we need a confession from Harry Moss.'

CHAPTER 13

Ian phoned the hotel early on Monday morning and arranged to drive Charles and Vivien to the mortuary. Impatient to return to London, Charles had insisted on dealing with the identification as soon as possible. He reminded Ian that he and his sister-in-law had missed the train on which they had booked their return journey on Sunday morning, and that he should have been back in his office already. At ten o'clock Ian picked them up from their hotel and they drove in silence to the hospital, parking in the public car park near the main entrance. As they climbed out of the car, Vivien broke down in tears, insisting she couldn't go through with it. Ian reassured her that she would be able to stay in the waiting room while Charles identified the body. He led them along a series of corridors, following signs to the mortuary. No one took any notice of Vivien who sobbed all the way there. Charles kept his arm round her, half supporting her as though she might have fallen if he hadn't kept hold of her elbow, propelling her forwards. Her show of grief was convincing. Ian wondered if it was genuine.

★　★　★

After traversing several corridors, they went through a wooden door into a hushed area with grey doors and dark red flooring. While they waited, a couple of young nurses went by chatting in low voices, a tall grey-haired woman pushed a trolley of buff folders along the corridor, and a middle-aged man strode past with an air of self-importance, his white coat flapping around his sturdy legs. Ian was pleased when Avril joined them. With a few quiet words of condolence to the widow, she escorted them through a grey door marked 'Mortuary – Visitors Suite'. The waiting room had been sensitively furnished with two sofas and two armchairs, accommodating mourners in need of comfort of physical company, and those wanting their own space. Boxes of tissues were placed on low tables within easy reach of all the seats. The room was pleasantly scented, the decor enhanced by a series of innocuous water colours hanging on the walls. A vase of flowers on one of the tables added to the welcoming atmosphere. Vivien made straight for a sofa where she sat, dabbing her eyes delicately. Ian wasn't surprised when her brother-in-law sat down beside her and put his arm round her shoulders. In the context, there was nothing inappropriate in his gesture. Nevertheless, it wasn't the first time Ian had wondered about the nature of their intimacy.

Vivien was shivering. Charles offered her a cup of tea and was rising to his feet to investigate the drinks machine provided for visitors, when Avril returned.

'You can come and see him now,' she said gently.

Vivien shook her head and buried her face in her hands.

'Don't worry,' Charles was quick to reassure her. 'I'll go. You stay here.' He nodded at Avril before turning to Ian. 'You'll keep an eye on her, won't you? She's taking it all rather badly, I'm afraid.' He lowered his voice. 'A doctor here put her on Diazepam, but the sooner I get her home the better. She ought to see her own GP, don't you think?'

He spoke about Vivien as though she wasn't in the room with them. She didn't appear to care, ignoring his remarks if she registered them at all. Charles stooped over her and muttered in an urgent undertone. Ian strained to catch what he was saying, but couldn't hear. He wondered if Charles was warning her to keep quiet.

This was the first time Ian had been alone with Vivien. He was determined to make the most of the opportunity to pump her about Adrian, without Charles at her side controlling her responses. She sat with lowered head, her face concealed by a veil of blonde hair.

'Mrs Curtis,' he began.

She didn't stir.

'Mrs Curtis, Vivien,' he tried again.

This time he was rewarded with a response. She raised her head and gazed mournfully at him.

'I don't want to see him,' she whispered. 'I don't want to look at him. I never want to look at him again. It wasn't meant to be like this. We should have gone back to London, and left him here.'

She dropped her head in her hands again.

Ian prompted her to carry on, before her brother-in-law returned.

'Who should have been left here?'

'What?'

'You were saying you and your husband should have gone back to London—'

'God no,' she burst out. 'We should have gone back to London and left him here to rot.'

'Left who here?' Ian pressed her. 'I don't understand. Who should have gone back to London?'

Leaning back on the sofa, she closed her eyes and appeared to drop off to sleep. As Ian wondered whether to try again, the door opened. Avril entered, followed by Charles who looked anxiously at Vivien.

'She's been asleep the whole time,' Ian lied.

Vivien wouldn't remember what she had said, but Ian intended to quiz her about it as soon as he could. And he would question her without her brother-in-law breathing down her neck.

CHAPTER 14

On his return to the station, Ian found Eileen waiting for him. He started to tell her about his visit to the mortuary, but she wasn't interested in hearing about Vivien. When he wanted to touch on his concerns, she dismissed his suspicions about the widow and her brother-in-law with a wave of her hand.

'That's all very well, Ian, but what's happening about Harry Moss? I've got an extension, but you know we can't keep him in custody for much longer without charging him. He's been sitting here for nearly forty-eight hours. We need evidence.'

'We're looking into it, ma'am.' He paused, then realised she was waiting for him to continue. 'Sergeant Birling's checking into his background right now, and we've got a team looking at CCTV, trying to plot his movements at the races before the time of Adrian's death.'

'Good. We've got our suspect. Now we need to make sure we don't let him slip away. That's all. Let's not make things any more complicated then they need to be. Time is of the essence, Ian. Time is of the essence.'

Clearly the high profile location of the murder was putting the detective chief inspector under pressure. There was a danger her judgement might be affected by her impatience to achieve a quick result, but Ian hadn't known her long enough to risk challenging her decision. While there were occasions when obstinacy could prove an asset in a senior investigating officer, it could cause problems for Ian if he were to get off on the wrong foot with her. He would have to proceed carefully. In the meantime, she seemed to have made up her mind Harry was responsible for Adrian's death, before they had even finished gathering evidence. That struck him as rash. At the same time, he had to consider the possibility that Harry really was guilty. Working with Eileen was one of the reasons he had accepted the post in York. She had a first rate reputation. Pitting his own instincts against hers might turn out to be a huge mistake.

'All I'm saying is, we can't be sure yet,' he replied.

'We may be pursuing a false lead,' she conceded, 'but until we know otherwise, let's focus on Harry as our most likely suspect for now. We have to start somewhere.'

Ian nodded, relieved that her approach was more reasoned than he had first supposed.

★　★　★

He found Ted chatting to another young sergeant. They both looked round and smiled as Ian joined them. For the first time he began to feel comfortable about his move to York. His fellow officers weren't all like Eileen, whose determination to make an early arrest was making her impatient. He asked Ted what he had found out about Harry. On the face of it, the account was straightforward. Harry lived in a small terraced house which he rented with a friend. He worked for City Rents, a local estate agent dealing with short lets. Ian decided to visit his workplace first, as Harry's flatmate would probably be at work during the day anyway. City Rents was situated along Fossgate. Parking was difficult so Ian left his car in a side street and walked back to the estate agents past shops and a few cafes.

A sharp-faced young woman greeted him from behind a desk. Sitting on a padded chair, he gratefully accepted the coffee she offered him, before introducing himself. If she was disappointed that he wasn't looking for a property to rent she didn't show it as she leaned forward on her desk, looking attentive. Cautiously Ian questioned her about her colleague, doing his best to give nothing away. She seemed surprised.

'Has something happened to Harry?'

'He's helping us with our enquiries.'

'Is he in trouble?'

'All I can tell you is that he's helping us with our enquiries,' Ian repeated quietly.

She told Ian that Harry had worked for City Rents for about eighteen months, and that he was a cheerful and obliging colleague.

'Off the record, would you have any criticism of him at all?'

She hesitated. Ian leaned forward expectantly, but her response was disappointing.

'He doesn't always turn up for work on time. I mean, he's been as much as twenty minutes late. And it's always on a Monday.'

'Does he lose his temper when you raise the issue of his lateness?'

'Harry lose his temper?' She burst out laughing. 'I'm sorry, it's just that Harry's the most easy going guy you could ever wish to meet. In some ways, he's fabulous to work with only—'

'Only—?' Ian prompted her.

'Only he can be impossible. I mean, he's a genuinely nice guy, wouldn't hurt a fly, but it can be so frustrating trying to get him to do anything. I mean, he's so apologetic when he gets something wrong, or when he's late, but you know he's going to do it again, because he can't help it. He's so disorganised.'

Harry lived on the ground floor of a Victorian property off Gillygate. Cars were parked nose to tail at the kerbside, but Ian managed to find a space a few doors along from Harry's house. A low brick wall bordered the small front yard, which contained one desiccated tree. The door was opened by a young man with straggly black hair who stood blinking stupidly as Ian introduced himself. Suddenly animated, the young man demanded to know where Harry was. Ian trotted out his usual bland response about helping the police with their enquiries. At first, Harry's flat-mate was reluctant to answer any questions. After a few minutes, he grudgingly acknowledged that his refusal to co-operate might not be helping.

Like Harry's colleague at work, he seemed amused by the idea of Harry losing his temper.

'Harry in a temper? You're having a laugh. He's so laid back, he's almost asleep most of the time. He's a good bloke, though,' he added quickly.

'What about when he's been drinking? Does he ever get angry then?'

'No. He just laughs a lot. He's just a bit soft, if you know what I mean. Other people are always taking advantage of him. He's too nice, that's his trouble. I've tried telling him.'

Ian wondered if Harry's flatmate had ever taken advantage of his good nature.

CHAPTER 15

A day at work calmed Richard's weekend jitters. Anxious about coping with marriage, yet fearful of losing Emma if he didn't propose soon, he had panicked about a few prank phone calls. It was a classic case of displacement. There was nothing suspicious in the caller having mentioned the death at the races. Everyone knew about it. Richard's colleagues at work were obsessed with it.

'Here in York,' he overheard people saying. 'I can't believe it.'

'And it was so public.'

'Those poor people who saw him fall. How terrible.'

'My neighbour was there. She said it was awful.'

'I'd be traumatised.'

The chatter went on all day. As for mentioning Richard's walk, anyone could have spotted him down by the river. It didn't mean anything. By the time Richard left the office at the end of the day, the killer's threatening call seemed transformed. No longer based on sinister inside knowledge, it was reduced to mere gossip.

★   ★   ★

It didn't cross his mind that there might be another crank call when the phone rang that evening, so he didn't remonstrate when Emma reached out to answer it. No one he wanted to speak to used the landline. He stretched his legs out in front of him, watching her face relax into a smile as she listened. There was something almost unbearably touching about her at such moments, when she wasn't aware of being observed.

'I don't think so,' she said, bursting into laughter, her face slightly flushed. 'Yes, he's right here,' she added, looking round at him.

He shook his head, frowning. If Emma's parents were asking to talk to him, it meant they wanted to put pressure on him to accompany her on her visit to them. It was awkward to keep refusing them, but he didn't enjoy seeing his future in-laws, and he had already made his excuses. He had said he couldn't take the time off work, which was true. There was no reason why he couldn't make it for the weekend, but he had his own plans, and they didn't include visiting Emma's parents.

'I don't want to speak to your parents again,' he muttered crossly.

'It's not them.'

'Who is it then?'

She shrugged. 'He wouldn't say. He just asked for you and said you'd asked him to call. He says he knows you. Whoever he is, he's a bit of a charmer.'

Watching her soft lips mouthing words he was irritated, remembering her easy laughter down the phone. He snatched the phone from her grasp. Her eyebrows rose in mock surprise. Holding her gaze he gestured as though raising a glass, and nodded at the kitchen. To his relief she understood at once and stood up with a ready smile.

'I put a bottle in the fridge earlier,' she called out over her shoulder as she trotted off to fetch two glasses of white wine.

'I enjoyed talking to Emma. That was an unexpected bonus. I look forward to talking to her again very soon. I wonder how she's going to manage when you're gone.'

Richard was instantly alert. This time he was fairly certain he was talking to a man. As soon as Emma left the room he began speaking rapidly into the phone, watching all the time for her return. He could hear her clattering around in the kitchen, opening a cupboard for glasses, and shutting the fridge door.

'If you touch a hair on her head you'll be sorry,' he muttered urgently. 'You'll never get away with it. Wherever you are, I'll find you. You won't get away with this.'

There was a guttural, choking noise. The caller was laughing.

'But you won't be able to find me when you're dead,' the voice teased softly. 'And what about the girls you work with, the ones you took out for lunch. Are they going to miss you?'

82

The nuisance caller's knowledge about Richard's life was more unsettling than his death threats.

'Who are you? What do you want? How do you know about my work colleagues?'

'So many questions!' The caller chuckled. 'All you need to know is when you're going to die, but I can't tell you that, because I haven't made up my mind yet.'

There was a faint click as the line went dead.

The phone trembled in his hand. The stalker knew about Emma, and about the girls in his office. He must have been spying on Richard. The realisation made him feel nauseous with fear and disgust. He wondered what else the caller knew about him. A sour taste of vomit rose in his throat. Rage bubbled behind his eyes until he couldn't see clearly. The side table seemed to shimmer as he stared at it. He couldn't move to replace the receiver.

'Are you all right?'

Emma's question jolted him out of his shock. He blinked and realised his eyes were moist. Hot with embarrassment, he looked down, shifting awkwardly in his seat.

'I'm fine,' he mumbled.

'Are you sure?'

'I said, I'm fine. Why wouldn't I be? Now, where's that wine?'

He forced a smile but she wasn't fooled. She sat in a chair opposite him so she could see his face.

'Who was that on the phone?'

'What? That? Oh, no one. Just an old friend from work.'

She knew he was lying, but his mind seemed to have frozen. All he knew was that he couldn't tell her the truth. She wouldn't understand why he couldn't report the threats to the police. The caller must be associated with one of the women Richard had encountered, a friend or a brother who was feeling aggrieved. Nothing else made any sense. He had no enemies. Apart from some harmless sexual encounters, he had never stepped out of line in his life. His relations with women had all been totally innocent, taking place between consenting adults. It wasn't as though he had ever forced himself on a woman. But if the police investigated he would have to tell the truth and Emma would learn all about his affairs. He dreaded to think how she might react. Even if she forgave him, she would never trust him again.

Emma put two glasses of wine down on the low coffee table in front of him. She leaned forward and put one hand on his knee.

'Are you sure you're all right?'

'I said, I'm fine.'

He no longer tried to hide his irritation. Lowering his eyes, he reached for a glass and raised it in salute. As he did so, the phone rang. In his agitation he let the glass tip in his grasp, spilling wine over the table. He swore loudly and winced at the desperation he could hear in his own voice. Emma threw him a worried glance as she stood up to answer the phone. He could tell from her tone of voice that it was her mother. He breathed deeply, doing his best to calm down.

'That was my mother,' she said as she hung up.

'Come here,' he urged her, patting the sofa beside him.

She joined him and he sat with his arm round her, sipping wine, and struggling to hide his fear.

CHAPTER 16

Ian remained at his desk long after he should have gone home. Eileen's attitude worried him. There was nothing specific he could identify, but he couldn't help wondering if she looked down on him as a Southerner. It was ironic, considering he was a Yorkshireman by birth. Born in Scarborough, he had lived in the area until his mother had died shortly before his twelfth birthday. When his American stepfather had moved back to the USA, Ian and his brother had gone to live with their natural father in Kent. After completing his education in the UK, Ian's brother had followed their stepfather to the States. Ian had remained in England. It was his home, he had a good relationship with his father, and he wanted to join the police. Apart from all of that, he had already met Bev and his teenage crush had developed into love. They had lived together, married, bought a house, sold it, moved and bought a second house. After all that, he still felt like a sixteen-year-old boy, trying to impress his girl. It was pathetic to live in fear of her displeasure, but he couldn't help himself.

'I love you too much,' he told her once.

She had laughed. 'There's no such thing as too much love.'

Bev paused the television and looked up when he walked in. He smiled weakly, knowing how she hated being left on her own in the evening. He could see her eyes shining with emotion but, despite years of training and experience in dealing with people, he could never interpret his wife's expressions. Looking at her beautiful face, he had no idea if she was angry with him for coming home so late, or pleased to see him.

'Where have you been all evening?'

'I've been working.'

'And you were too busy to call and let me know?'

He sighed. To hear that he was at his desk rereading statements would hardly have placated her. He could easily have come home earlier. The truth was that he had stayed at work late in the forlorn hope that he might crack the case. He hadn't, of course. The investigation had advanced no further than it would have done if he had gone home hours earlier.

'I was busy,' he echoed lamely.

She turned back to the screen and he wandered into the kitchen. Hungrily he salvaged what he could from a plate of congealed dinner which he ate alone in the kitchen. Bev was watching a film. If he went and sat beside her while he was eating, he would only annoy her even more. It was hardly the homecoming he would have chosen. Fortified by his dinner, he waited until the film ended before going back to the living room armed with two bottles.

'Fancy a beer?'

She grunted.

'How was your day?' he persisted.

He sat down on a chair, smiling easily, as though everything was fine between them. Perhaps it was. It was so difficult to tell with her. An awkward pause followed his question. He didn't know whether to be relieved or dismayed when she began moaning about her tedious day.

'And it's only Monday,' she concluded. 'I don't know how the hell I'm going to get through the rest of the week.'

To be fair, she didn't know anyone in York. They didn't have any friends there. On Sunday Ian had driven her to a large designer outlet shopping centre on the outskirts of town where she had spent the afternoon browsing the clothes stores, but he couldn't spend every afternoon taking her out. He had work to do. That was the problem. He was likely to be at work all day, and often during the evening too. Bev had spent all day on her own, and she was bored. She needed to get out and find something to do. Tentatively he suggested she look for a job.

'What am I supposed to do?'

In Kent she had enjoyed working in a recruitment agency. The answer to her question was obvious.

'Why don't you go around some recruitment agencies tomorrow? If they can't find you a job, maybe one of them can take you on.'

Bev looked pained. Used to being paid to interview other people who were looking for employment, now she would be on the other side of the desk, struggling to find work.

'What if I can't find anything?'

'We'll manage,' he reassured her.

That wasn't the point. Bev sitting at home growing increasingly bored and miserable was a dreary prospect.

She looked so wretched, he went and sat beside her on the sofa and put his arm round her, muttering to her not to worry. Something would turn up. Any office would be pleased to recruit her.

'It's all right for you,' she replied, resting her head comfortably on his shoulder. 'You've got a proper job. I mean, you're a somebody. You've got a career. You're a DI. I'm just someone who had a job in an office.'

'You're an experienced recruitment agent.'

'Whatever. It's hardly skilled work, is it? Anyone could do what I did. It's not like a career. It's just a job. You've been trained. You're worth something to the force. They've invested in you. Someone else will be doing my job now in Tunbridge Wells. Seven years I sat at that desk, and it's like I was never there.'

'Someone else is doing my job back on the Kent force now,' he pointed out. 'It's not as if they're all sitting around at the station saying things have changed since I left. The station's carrying on just the same, as though I was never there.'

It would have been a depressing thought if he didn't have his new post to occupy his thoughts. He leaned down and kissed the top of her head, breathing in the familiar scent of her shampoo.

'Something'll turn up,' he whispered. 'You'll see. It'll be all right. It just takes time.'

CHAPTER 17

Charles insisted she take the pills the doctor had given her to make her sleep. They didn't help. Within seconds of waking up, the reality of her life as a widow overwhelmed her, only now she had to deal with it through a horrible fog in her head. Although the site of Adrian's death made no real difference to anyone, certainly not to him, it was terrible to think he had died in a public place with so many people looking on. She couldn't ignore her mental image of him lying on his back, surrounded by a host of strangers, his face rigid, his eyes staring straight up. His death was public knowledge. She was the widow of the man who had fallen off the fifth floor balcony at the races. The eyes of the hotel staff slid past her, embarrassed. She could see speculation as well as sympathy in their faces.

Unwilling to see anyone, she stayed in her hotel room as much as possible, only going out when she had to visit the mortuary with Charles. He had insisted she move to a room with a view of the city wall.

91

'You'll be better off here,' he had said. 'Don't worry about the bill. I'll take care of it.'

As always, she was grateful for his consideration. She would never have been able to sleep in the bed she had shared with Adrian just before he died. All the same, she was beginning to feel hemmed in by Charles' attention.

The day after Adrian's death Charles had been eager to get back to his office, but he had changed his mind as soon as the police became involved.

'You're in no state to go home,' he told her, solicitous as ever. 'And I can't leave you here by yourself, not after what's happened. You wouldn't cope. Not on your own.'

'What about your work?'

He shrugged, cupping her shoulder in his large hand. His stubby fingers caressed her skin. Uneasily, she avoided looking at him, silently willing him to leave her alone.

'Work can manage without me for a while. You can't.'

And that was the end of the discussion. She had learned the futility of trying to resist Charles once he had made up his mind. One way or another, he always got what he wanted. And besides, he was right. She couldn't manage without him.

Apart from their physical similarity, the two brothers were very different. On first meeting Adrian, Vivien had been struck by how gentle he was. That was the characteristic that had initially attracted her to him. When he had introduced her to his older brother, she understood that his confidence must have taken a knock growing up in his brother's shadow. She wasn't sure if Adrian realised how powerful his brother's influence had been in his life. Certainly he would never tolerate any criticism of Charles, whom he hero-worshipped. Two years older than Adrian, Charles outshone his brother in almost every way: his good looks, his charm, his lucrative career. While Adrian worked for an estate agent, Charles had a well-paid post in a London hospital. Compared to Charles, Adrian didn't seem quite so attractive, but by the time Vivien met the older brother, she had already agreed to marry the younger one. It wasn't an unhappy marriage. Adrian was kind to her. He used to tell her that making love to the most beautiful woman in the world was the only area of their lives where Charles could never outperform him; even that turned out to be untrue.

It had been easy to keep their affair from Adrian. It would have been upsetting enough for him to have learned she was cheating on him. Discovering she was sleeping with his brother would have destroyed his confidence completely. For the best part of a year she and Charles had carried on a furtive affair, meeting discreetly at small hotels. Without Adrian, she wondered what plans Charles might have for a future with her. It had always been easy to find out what her husband was thinking; another difference between Adrian and his brother.

Charles encouraged her to take the sleeping pills. He said they would help her relax and cope with the stress. But she didn't want to stay calm any longer. The three days since Adrian had died had passed in a haze. She wanted to clear her head so she could think. She had a niggling suspicion that Charles wanted her sedated for his own reasons. The circumstances in which Adrian had died worried her. Witnesses at the scene had noticed a second figure on the balcony with Adrian. All Vivien could recall was Charles going off to the champagne tent to get a drink, leaving her waiting around outside. He had been gone for a long time. She told herself it was a coincidence that Charles had disappeared just at the time of Adrian's death. She didn't think there would have been enough time for Charles to reach the balcony and return again without being seen. The problem was, she couldn't be sure.

The police had spoken to her at the racetrack. She recalled crying a lot, and seeing people bustling about, issuing orders. Her memories of that time were confused, but she thought she remembered hearing Charles telling the police he had been with her at the time of Adrian's fall. That wasn't true. There could only be one reason for Charles to lie

94

about his own whereabouts at the time Adrian was up on the balcony. The trouble was, she couldn't be sure he really had said they had been together. Her memories were so confused. If she shared her suspicions with the police they were bound to arrest Charles, leaving her on her own, and he might not have said he had been with her at all. Yet witnesses had seen someone on the balcony with Adrian. Strangers would have no reason to lie about it. And if someone had been on the balcony with Adrian when he fell, it could only have been Charles. The more she thought about it, the more obvious it seemed. Adrian didn't know anyone in York. No one else would have any reason to want him dead. She was used to the guilt that had weighed her down since the affair had started. It was degrading enough to have an affair with her brother-in-law. But to suspect he had murdered her husband was devastating.

After slotting the bolt down on her door to stop Charles walking in, she went into the bathroom. Sitting on the toilet, sobbing softly to herself, she pushed the next capsule out of its foil sheet and flushed it down the toilet. She would tell Charles she was still taking the sleeping pills. He would never know it wasn't true. She had lied to Adrian for so long, it couldn't be difficult to lie to Charles as well. Climbing back into bed, she lay there, staring at a faint crack that had been painted over on the ceiling. She had to wait for her head to clear and then she would decide what to do. It didn't help that she couldn't stop thinking about Adrian. It was a cruel irony that Charles resembled him so closely. Sometimes when he came into her room, for a second she forgot what had happened and thought Adrian had returned. Charles had been forgiving the first time she had called him Adrian. The second time he had allowed a flicker of irritation to cross his face. Since then she had been more careful. It might be dangerous to upset Charles.

CHAPTER 18

On Tuesday morning they had to let Harry go. Ian watched the young man walking quickly down the avenue away from the police station towards the road, back to the outside world. The atmosphere in the Major Incident Room was tense. Eileen stalked around like a predator sizing up the herd. Everyone else kept their eyes averted, reluctant to attract the detective chief inspector's attention. As soon as she left the room the atmosphere lightened slightly, but the fact remained that they had an unsolved murder on their hands, and their main suspect had just walked free. Harry had been warned not to leave the area, but the only evidence they had against him was circumstantial. Worse, it relied on the statement of a witness who had vanished leaving nothing but a fake identity behind him. The investigation which had started so well was degenerating into chaos.

Ian stared morosely at the details of the man who had called himself Barry Gordon. Everything about the missing witness had turned out to be false, starting with his name and address. With hindsight, even his appearance had obviously been created for the occasion: green blazer, glasses, beard. It was all a disguise. They had no idea who he was, or what he looked like, other than that he might not really wear glasses, and he probably didn't have a beard or fair hair. As far as Ian was concerned, discrediting the witness raised serious doubts about Harry's guilt, yet Eileen was convinced they had let Adrian's killer slip through their fingers. She was fuming. To be fair, if Harry *was* responsible for Adrian's death, she was right to feel frustrated at not being able to nail him. But Ian wasn't convinced Harry was guilty.

The day passed slowly. There were so many un-answered questions. It still wasn't clear exactly what the victim had been doing on the balcony. The police hadn't traced the steward who had recommended the view from the fifth floor to Adrian while Charles and Vivien had been queuing for champagne. Ian wondered if the man calling himself Barry Gordon had himself directed Adrian up to the balcony, before escorting Harry out of the Ebor building, claiming to have discov-ered him up on the fifth floor. It was possible the whole scenario had been orchestrated by that one man, disguised as a race official – a man who had now gone missing, leaving behind no clue to his identity. The more Ian thought about it, the less far-fetched the idea seemed. If it was true, then they were dealing with an ingenious killer who had planned ahead, working patiently to achieve his goal.

Eileen was sceptical when Ian suggested Adrian's wife and brother as possible suspects. She said the pair had been together at the time the murder took place. Ian pointed out they had no other witnesses for that.

'It may be a sensible theory, but where's the evidence?' she replied. 'Just because Vivien was his wife doesn't mean she was involved in his murder. We've got nothing to implicate her, or his brother. We need to stick to the facts, Ian. Work with what we know. Firstly we have statements from several independent witnesses who saw a second figure up on the balcony with Adrian just before he fell. Then there's the race official who found Harry Moss in the act of leaving the fifth floor—'

'If he *was* a race official.'

'Until we can prove otherwise, let's assume he was.'

'He gave us a false name and address,' Ian reminded her.

'The constable who took down his details admitted he might have been confused. There was a lot going on. We need to find that witness, Ian. And we need to find the connection with Harry, and put pressure on him to make him talk.'

★　★　★

Checking through their statements, Ian realised that Vivien had never actually confirmed that she and Charles had been together while Adrian was on the balcony. Too sedated to say much, she had left it to Charles to do the talking. They only had his word for it that he and Vivien could provide one another with an alibi. Remembering how close the two of them appeared to be, Ian couldn't help speculating. They might both know a lot more about the circumstances of Adrian's death than they would admit. They could have been in it together. Abandoning Vivien and Charles, he spent several hours searching for a link between Harry and Adrian, without success. He turned his attention back to Vivien and Charles. They had both told him this was their first visit to York. While questioning them at the hotel, Ian had shown them a picture of Harry. If they were telling the truth, neither of them recognised him. Harry had denied knowing Adrian, Vivien or Charles. He could find nothing to connect Harry with the dead man.

He decided to investigate Adrian, and began by looking into his childhood, contacting his secondary school and then his first employers. Few people remembered Adrian. He only uncovered one potentially interesting snippet of information from the dead man's history when his first employer thought he recalled that Adrian had once struck up a fleeting friendship with a girl who came from 'somewhere up North.'

'We don't need to prioritise following up a tenuous lead from nearly twenty years ago,' Eileen said when he told her what he had discovered.

Reluctantly, Ian agreed. He turned his attention back to Charles. Far more successful than Adrian, Charles seemed unlikely to have resented his younger brother. But sibling relationships could be complicated, especially where sexual jealousy was involved. The more he found out about Charles, the more instinctively uneasy Ian felt about the dead man's brother.

CHAPTER 19

Bev woke up on Tuesday morning alone in bed. Half asleep, she called out and wasn't surprised when there was no answer. Kicking off the duvet, she rolled out of bed and shuffled downstairs. In some ways she didn't mind that Ian had already left the house, although it was early. Whenever he was involved in an investigation he became obsessed with it, permanently on edge when he was at home, snapping at her, and impatient to return to work. At least she could relax with him out of the house, and plan her day without interruption. She shouldn't have been thinking about hunting for a job yet. They had only recently moved, and there was a lot still to do. Thinking about her situation rationally, she ought to have been pleased to have time to sort out the house. The problem was that she was lonely. If she could have arranged to meet up with a friend, or call in on her mother, it would have been different. As it was, she faced another day stuck at home all by herself with nothing to look forward to but the late return of a husband too tired to talk.

★　　★　　★

Predictably enough, Ian was preoccupied with his work.

'Just let me get through this investigation,' he said whenever she wanted to talk about herself. 'You know it's my first case here. I have to do well, establish myself as competent and reliable.'

Bev didn't answer, but she felt let down. Before the move, Ian had insisted on prioritising his career in order to secure his promotion. He had promised her things would be different once he was an inspector, but nothing had changed. Not content with dragging her off to the north of England, he was still putting himself and his own career first. The only thing that had changed was his excuse.

'Once I'm established, things'll be different,' he told her.

She didn't answer.

Slamming the front door on her chores, she went out to look for a job. Ian was right. She had been a fool to want to take a break from working. Some people were happy in their own company. It was driving her crazy. Mixing with other people helped to fill up the emptiness of her life. She wished she could feel content. She had everything she could possibly want. Young, fit and healthy, she lived in a beautiful house with an attractive and devoted husband. But she was bored and miserable. She had to take control of her life and find herself something to do. The additional income wouldn't go amiss either. While they weren't desperate for money, they still had to pay for the belated honeymoon Ian had booked. On top of moving, that was yet another expense. After walking to Heslington Road she didn't have to wait long for a bus, and was soon bowling along into town. It wasn't far. There were a couple of recruitment agencies near Lendal Bridge so she started there.

In the first agency a well groomed young girl recorded her details, assessed her typing skills, and took a copy of her testimonial from her previous boss, before saying the agency would be in touch as soon as anything appropriate turned up. It had taken nearly an hour to establish there was nothing for her on their books at present. The second agency took down her details and promised to contact her if they could find anything suitable. It was depressing, but she comforted herself that it was only her first day of job hunting. Something would turn up. In the meantime, it wasn't as though she was struggling to make ends meet. That afternoon, she was surprised to receive a call inviting her for a job interview. The agent explained that a local supermarket was looking for someone to support their human resources manager, with particular responsibility for recruitment. Bev hadn't worked for a retail organisation before, but working in a different environment might be useful for her CV and, in any case, it wasn't as though she was in a position to pick and choose. The supermarket was a short bus ride from where she lived. It would do no harm to go along for an interview.

On arrival she was greeted by a lanky man in his thirties. He was quite good looking, with blue eyes and straggly dark hair that exaggerated the pallor of his skin. Smiling, he ushered her to a chair and asked her about her previous job.

'I'm sure your experience is going to be relevant for our position,' he said with an encouraging nod.

Bev forced a smile. She had used similar phrases herself, many times, when interviewing job seekers. It meant nothing.

'I see you you're married, Mrs Peterson.' He looked up at her. 'May I call you Beverley?'

He fiddled with her application form as Bev explained that she had moved to the area on account of her husband's promotion. Her interviewer's eyes narrowed, as though he was considering how to respond.

'That must be exciting,' he said at last, sounding anything but excited.

'I suppose so.'

Her voice revealed her feelings too clearly. He smiled, leaning forward with a show of interest in what she was saying. Used to men paying attention to her, she began to relax.

'What exactly does your husband do that has brought you all the way here from—' He glanced down at her form, 'from Kent?'

'He's a detective inspector.'

The supermarket manager dropped his eyes and smoothed out the sheet of paper on his desk with long thin fingers.

He asked about her previous job and then, after a pause, said that he thought she might suit their requirements very well.

'It's quite a junior position with a low basic salary,' he added apologetically, 'and I won't pretend we're very busy right now, but it's bound to pick up soon.'

'Bound to,' she agreed, echoing his professional bluster.

He offered her the job on the spot, and she accepted straight away. Having recently moved into the area she didn't want a complicated work-load, and she certainly didn't want to take on any responsibility, at least not for a while. Her new manager grinned. He must have realised he had recruited an experienced agent for a pittance. For as long as she stayed, she would be good value.

CHAPTER 20

Jocelyn had a frustrating day. First of all her alarm didn't go off. That had never happened before. She must have forgotten to set it the previous evening. She woke up, comfortable and relaxed, stretched her legs and glanced at her phone. On seeing the time she was momentarily confused, thinking it was the weekend. Waking properly, she swore as she stumbled out of bed and threw on the clothes she had been wearing the day before. James wasn't in the bedroom.

'Why didn't you get me up?' she complained when she found him in the kitchen.

'I thought you were having a lie in.'

'A lie in? It's Tuesday!'

He shrugged, cheerfully munching toast.

'I'm going to be late now,' she grumbled.

'Should've set your alarm,' he said unhelpfully as he took a gulp of coffee. 'Oh well, must dash.'

He bent down to kiss her before hurrying away. In a panic, she sprinted to the bus stop and barely made it in time.

★　★　★

Her head was thumping when she reached work. She was really annoyed with James for leaving her to oversleep. Since they first met she had wanted to spend the rest of her life with him, but there were times when she wondered whether she had made a mistake jumping into bed with him so soon. She still fancied him like mad, but since she had moved into his flat he had started to bug her. Having begun badly, her morning didn't improve. Her boss blamed her for an order that had been overlooked, although it hadn't been her fault.

'You should have checked,' the boss snapped when Jocelyn protested.

After a stressful morning, she walked round the block to the supermarket to get something for lunch. Having missed breakfast, she was starving. Scanning the shelves, she selected a variety of goodies, instead of her usual economical 'Meal Deal'. Spotting a cashier idle behind a till, she hurried towards her. Just as she reached the check out, a blonde woman shoved a trolley right in front of her. Normally Jocelyn would have fumed in silence, but today she was in no mood to be pushed around. Reaching forward she tapped the other shopper smartly on the shoulder.

'Excuse me! I was here first.'

The woman in front turned her head. Huge blue eyes stared blankly at Jocelyn.

'I'm sorry?' It wasn't an apology.

'I was here first. You just pushed in front of me.'

The woman turned away and began to unload her shopping.

Jocelyn raised her voice. 'Hey, you pushed in!' She looked over at the cashier who was watching with a bored expression. 'She pushed in front of me.'

The cashier shrugged and started to ring up the other woman's items.

Not only was it infuriating to be overtaken in the queue, but to make matters worse the trolley in front was piled high. Jocelyn was only buying four items. Just because the other woman was blonde and beautiful, she assumed she could do whatever she wanted. The thought made Jocelyn even angrier. Squeezing past, she dumped her own items down on the counter.

'I was here first!'

The cashier didn't look up.

'You need to get in the queue,' she said in a bored monotone.

'I *was* in the queue. She pushed in front of me.'

The cashier raised thin eyebrows and stared morosely at Jocelyn for a second, before turning back to her till.

'You need a basket for those.'

'I don't need a basket,' Jocelyn spluttered, 'this is all I'm getting.'

'You need a basket,' the cashier repeated doggedly.

The blonde woman stood watching silently.

'Oh for Christ's sake, just forget it,' Jocelyn snapped.

She stalked away, without buying anything.

She was still smarting from her aggravating day when she reached home that evening. James made conciliatory noises, but she could tell he wasn't listening.

'And as if that wasn't bad enough,' she persisted, determined to gain his sympathy, 'after putting up with so much crap from the boss from hell, I didn't even have lunch.'

'Poor you,' he replied, glancing at his watch.

'James, are you listening to me?'

'Of course I'm listening. You're standing right in front of me. How could I not hear you? Come on, cheer up.' He kissed her. 'Tell me about it.'

'Why should I bother? You're not listening to me.'

'I said I'm listening. You were telling me you didn't have time for lunch.'

Jocelyn explained how a woman had barged ahead of her at the check out.

James looked faintly puzzled. 'How did that stop you getting your lunch?'

'I was so mad at her for pushing in front of me that I walked out. And by then it was too late to go anywhere else.' She didn't add that she had run to the toilet to cry. 'I didn't dare risk being late, not after the morning I'd had.'

'You can hardly blame someone else if you walked out.'

'Oh, take her side.'

'I'm not taking anyone's side,' he objected. 'Poor you,' he repeated more gently, finally realising she was upset. 'Come on, don't let it get you down. She was just some unhappy old spinster.'

Jocelyn couldn't help laughing. 'I don't think so.'

Once again, James had cheered her up just when she was beginning to feel he was a big disappointment.

CHAPTER 21

Feeling guilty, Ian popped home at lunchtime on Tuesday. It wasn't far. Intending to surprise Bev, he found the house empty. He called her mobile, but she didn't answer. On balance he was pleased she had gone out. It was better than sitting at home feeling sorry for herself. Leaving a note to say he would be home in time for supper, he drove straight back to the police station to continue researching Adrian's family. So far he had nothing to substantiate his suspicion that Vivien and Charles were having an affair. There was plenty of evidence that they saw a lot of one another, but there was no reason why Adrian's wife and brother shouldn't be friends. Only seeing them together suggested their relations might be more intimate than was appropriate. He spent a dreary afternoon rifling through documents and bills. They had gone out for dinner together, sometimes with Adrian, occasionally without him, but it all meant nothing.

Eileen wasn't excited about the idea that Vivien might have been having an affair with her brother-in-law.

'Lots of married women have affairs,' she said, a trifle sharply. 'It doesn't mean they want to kill their husbands.'

'I'm just getting the background,' Ian mumbled.

'Concentrate on the suspect for now, Ian. Let's see if we can find a connection between Harry and Adrian. And if there isn't any connection, could it have been a random attack by a stranger? They were both drunk. Did anyone see them fall out? Could the attack on Adrian have come about as a result of a sudden drunken rage?'

'I don't think so, ma'am. By all accounts, Harry wasn't a violent man. Plus Adrian was drugged before he was killed which suggests the murder was premeditated.'

She pulled a face. 'Then we're back to looking for a connection between Harry and Adrian.'

'Harry only denies he was ever on the balcony, and his flatmate seems to corroborate his claim that he didn't like heights.'

'Find the missing witness, the man who masqueraded as a steward. He's the key to this.'

If Eileen hadn't been his senior officer, Ian would have retorted crossly that he had been advocating doing just that, right from the start of the investigation. As it was, he merely muttered in agreement.

'We're doing our best.'

Ian was pleased when he returned at the end of the day to find Bev busy in the kitchen. He sat down with a cold beer, watching her. She grinned when he asked how her day had gone.

'I thought you were never going to ask.'

Her eyes were shining with excitement. Ian hadn't seen her looking so cheerful since they had left Kent.

'I've got a job!'

Ian hid his surprise. 'That was quick,' he said, adding hurriedly, 'congratulations! I knew it wouldn't be long before some lucky employer snapped you up.'

He stopped, wary of overdoing his show of enthusiasm, but it had been enough simply to prompt her to tell him her news. As she prepared the supper she told him how the first recruitment agency where she had registered had fobbed her off with vague promises. At the second agency she had visited, she had been offered an interview almost immediately.

'I'd only just got home when they rang. Of course they're going to check my references, but he could tell I knew what I was talking about. You don't work in the profession for seven years without learning a thing or two about recruitment.'

Ian asked when she was going to start.

'They want me to go in on Monday. That gives them a few days to get things set up. I can't wait! It'll be so good to get back to work.'

'You don't have to take the first job that comes along—' He faltered, seeing her expression darken.

114

'But of course you know what you're looking for, and – well, if this is it, then good for you. I'm really pleased for you.'

'The thing is, it may not be exactly what I was looking for. It's hardly my dream job. But working there will get me back in the swing of things. I can't just sit around here all day doing nothing. It's driving me nuts. And I don't have to stay if I don't like it there.'

Ian nodded. What she was saying made sense. He offered to go out and buy a bottle of champagne to celebrate her new job, but they agreed it wasn't necessary. They had already opened a bottle of red wine. Nevertheless, Bev thanked him. He could tell she appreciated the suggestion. Smiling sheepishly she confessed to feeling relieved. She hadn't been sure how he would take her news and was happy that he was pleased. They passed an enjoyable evening, finishing the red wine and opening a second bottle, and going to bed early. For a while Ian forgot all about the murder investigation. Lying in bed half asleep he wondered, not for the first time, why he continued driving himself to succeed in such a stressful job. He was tempted to mention his reservations to his wife, but she was already asleep. As he sobered up, he was glad he hadn't raised the matter with her. She hated him working for the police. If he ever admitted to having doubts, she would never let him hear the end of it.

★　★　★

Bev woke up early the following morning to have breakfast with him. Instead of gulping down a quick coffee as he was on his way out, he sat down at the table and was treated to poached egg and beans on toast. He would have preferred to sit at his desk with a roll from the canteen, quietly planning his day's work, but it was a relief to see his wife looking so cheerful. One hour more or less at work made no difference when he was at a loss about what to do with his time anyway. He didn't mind listening to Bev chattering about her new job. It took his mind off his own.

'It might not be much, but it's a start,' she said, 'and it's convenient, but I'm not getting too excited. It's all a bit up in the air right now. Anything could happen.'

Ian nodded. She could have been talking about his investigation.

CHAPTER 22

Richard pulled himself up short and hung his head, pressing his teeth together until the tension made his jaw ache. He hated himself for snapping at Emma. It wasn't her fault he was finding it increasingly difficult to control his temper. Without meeting her eye, he sloped off to the kitchen where he opened another beer and took a swig before returning to the living room, mumbling vaguely about pressure at work.

'I've not been sleeping well,' he added. It was a lame excuse.

'If something's bothering you, tell me about it.'

She meant well but her sympathy irked him. He shook his head, smiling to conceal his hostility. As he expected, she wasn't fooled by his pretence.

'Do you want me to stay here and not go and see my parents next week?'

He shook his head more vigorously and burbled about how disappointed her mother and father would be.

'Come with me then. You need a break—'

He interrupted her roughly. 'You know there's no way I can take any time off right now,' he lied.

'We've got a huge deal pending. It's more than my job's worth to blow it.'

'Come for the weekend then. You can get the train back on Sunday night. You need to get away. You're working too hard.'

He didn't bother to answer. The prospect of escaping the constant threat of menacing phone calls was certainly appealing, but spending the weekend with Emma's parents was hardly his idea of a relaxing break.

'I won't stay the week then,' she said firmly, when he didn't answer. 'I'll come back on Friday morning so I can get all the washing done and clean the house and then we can spend the weekend together.'

He nodded without really listening. She was trying to be nice, but nothing she said could possibly help him. Visiting her parents was no guarantee of a respite. His nuisance caller must be watching the house. Unless it had been a lucky guess, he had known when Richard had gone out for a walk. He might have Richard's mobile number and call him on that. Worse, it was impossible to be sure how much he knew about Emma. He might trace her parents and call their landline if Richard went to stay with them. The thought made him tremble.

'I've got a lot on my mind right now,' he said, truthfully. 'It won't be for much longer.'

He desperately hoped that was true.

★   ★   ★

He hadn't been asked for money yet, but it was only a matter of time. That was the obvious conclusion, given that the caller knew about Emma. The suspicion surrounding the death at the races must have been a godsend for the stalker. Having heard about it, he had taken advantage of it to put the wind up Richard. The more anxious Richard became, the more likely he was to agree to the demands of a blackmailer. Already he was so nervous, he was prepared to pay a substantial sum to be shot of the whole affair. If he refused to pay up, Emma would be given details of at least one of his affairs, no doubt in disgusting detail. Probably there were photos. Under such circumstances, he was actually pleased she was going away. He needed time to himself so he could think of a way out of this mess. He didn't care how much it cost. He just wanted it to be over.

He had some savings Emma knew nothing about, but that didn't amount to much. If it came to it, he might have to confess to an imaginary addiction to gambling to explain away the debt he would incur in paying off a blackmailer. Wild thoughts spun around his mind. He imagined suggesting a meeting so he could silence his stalker, once and for all. He would explain to the police how he had been attacked and inadvertently killed his assailant in self-defence. But he would never get away with it. The police were bound to trace the phone calls, which would prove that Richard's alleged mugger

119

hadn't been a random stranger. His stalker wasn't stupid. In the meantime there hadn't been any calls for a couple of days. Briefly he allowed himself to hope the situation had resolved itself. It wasn't far-fetched to suppose his stalker had been playing a similar game with other people, in which case someone else might have done away with him, or exposed him to the police. But that was probably a vain hope. The reality was that Richard had been wound up into a state of almost unbearable anxiety. Now his nuisance caller was leaving him alone to sweat. Emma's expressions of concern only exacerbated his agitation. Where once it had seemed exciting to keep his escapades a secret, he was starting to despise himself for his sordid affairs. Yet all the time, at the back of his mind, he was waiting for Emma to go away so he could seek out some uncomplicated carnal relief.

Fortunately Emma was preoccupied by her trip, or it might have been impossible to conceal his unrest.

'I've filled up the freezer,' she told him as they sat down to supper.

Before moving in with her he used to eat off a tray in front of the television, takeaways or microwave prepared meals. Emma liked to cook what she called 'a proper meal' for him every evening, and expected him to sit at the table with her. He suspected she only did it to impress him, but he played along with it.

'And don't worry,' she went on, 'they understand you can't get away from work right now. Oh, and don't forget the car's booked in for a service on Tuesday.'

While she chattered on, he grunted and nodded without taking in what she was saying. After supper, he offered to load the dishwasher so she could do her laundry in preparation for her trip. He watched her bustle away, relieved to be free of her fussing. Clearing the table, he stacked the plates neatly in the rack, finding the mindless domestic chore curiously relaxing. He had almost finished when the phone rang.

A plate he was holding slipped from his grasp and smashed on the stone floor. Shards of white china flew across the room. Ignoring the splinters crunching underfoot, he dashed to seize the phone before Emma could reach it. Breathlessly he struggled to cast his words into the oppressive silence on the line.

'Richard? Is that you?'

His mother-in-law sounded surprised. Restraining himself from crying aloud in relief, he said he was pleased to hear from her. For once, he meant it.

CHAPTER 23

By the following morning Ian had forgotten his reservations about his job. He went into work early as usual, determined to keep going until he found what he was looking for. Somewhere in all the statements he had read, there had to be a new lead. He was seated at his desk scrolling through documents on his screen when Eileen put her head round his door. Without pausing to greet him, she asked him to join her.

'Now, please, Ian,' she added sharply when he didn't stand up straight away.

'Yes, ma'am.'

He leaped to his feet and followed her along the hushed corridor to her office. Eileen was keen to have the area of the racecourse searched yet again for evidence, and she wanted all the CCTV footage from the races watched once more.

'We're missing something. We need to pinpoint the moment when Adrian first met that man who was masquerading as a steward, and then see where they both went after that. We have to identify this phoney official.'

'That may not be possible, ma'am.'

Eileen stared at him. 'Make it happen, Ian. We have to find this man.'

'Yes, ma'am.'

He knew she was only passing on pressure from higher up, but it still rankled.

Ian sat fidgeting at his desk. He would have liked to pace up and down his office with his hands behind his back, but there wasn't enough room. He had been allocated a first floor office. Decorated in white and powder blue that was almost grey, the room would have been perfect if it hadn't been so small, but that had its advantages. If the room had been a decent size he would doubtless have shared it. Although it could be dull sitting there by himself, he was pleased to have his own office at last, with his name on the door. He was a detective inspector, after all, even though the detective chief inspector treated him like a rookie constable. After a few minutes he stood up and stretched his legs. From his window he had a view out over a grassy plot dotted with small trees. Looking down to his right he could see the end of the low red brick custody suite, its square windows crisscrossed with white bars. He sat down again and reread the information they had on Adrian. Aged thirty-five, he had been married for nearly three years to a wife five years younger than him. He was an estate agent who had apparently been doing well in spite of the recession, perhaps because he worked in commercial lettings not private property sales. He had lived with his wife on the outskirts of London.

Ian scanned through the answers his brother, Charles, had given to questions about their trip to York.

'Whose idea was it to come to York?'

'It was my idea. I thought it would be fun – it *was* fun, until this happened.'

'Why York?'

'For the races. A friend of mine came last year and he had a great time, won some money as well, so that's what gave me the idea. I suggested it to Adrian and he jumped at the idea. He's always enjoyed a bit of a flutter. Vivien was keen as well. Any excuse for her to dress up and all that. It was a kind of birthday present. Did you know it was his birthday?'

'Did Adrian know anyone in the area who might have wanted to harm him?'

'Not that I'm aware of.'

'Did he have any connection with York at all?'

'Nothing he ever mentioned to me.'

'Did he ever meet anyone from the area?'

'No. Well, actually, he might have mentioned a girl who came from around here, but that was years ago, and it wasn't anything serious. There were a few girls before Vivien. Apart from that, I wasn't aware he had any connection to the place at all, and I don't think he'd ever been here before.'

*   *   *

Since Harry had been released, a search team had spent two days scrutinising every inch of the pedestrian walkway where Adrian's body had landed. Another team was searching through all the buildings on the site, looking for a lead to the identity of the missing official. The likelihood was that he had taken his disguise with him, but there was a chance he had chucked it away before leaving the site. Ian sat down at his desk again and closed his eyes, picturing a scene of crime officer discovering a green jacket with non-regulation buttons that would provide a DNA sample for which they had a match. Shaking himself free of idle wishful thinking, he went to see if any real progress had been made.

In the Visual Image and Identification Detection Office, constables were watching hours of CCTV footage from the races. They had identified Adrian arriving with his wife and brother, and were watching them hanging around outside the track before the first race. Along with the rest of the racegoers, the three of them were drinking and chatting in the sunshine. His arm draped around his wife's shoulders, Adrian threw his head back and laughed at some quip his brother had made. His simple pleasure was indescribably poignant. Within an hour he would return to almost exactly the same spot, dead. After losing sight of him for a while, they saw him enter the Ebor building. Upstairs in the Shirley Heights bar there was a mêlée of racegoers. Adrian appeared for a second in the doorway before disappearing once more in the crowd. There was a brief glimpse of him passing through the glass doors out onto the balcony, then nothing. A patch of green weaving among the racegoers was all they could make out of his suspected killer. No one else took any notice of the two men, one in pursuit, the other cheerfully oblivious of his approaching death.

When the next race was announced, virtually everyone who was outside drinking on the balcony rushed indoors to watch the race on the big screen. Only one woman stayed behind. Ian watched her closely, wondering if she could be implicated in the murder. She didn't look like a woman who could easily hurl a grown man off the balcony. All the same, fanciful notions flitted through his mind until she gathered up her bag and hurried back inside to watch the race with everyone else. Not quite everyone – the killer and his victim remained in a corner of the balcony, just out of sight of the camera. Ian peered over colleagues' shoulders to study the images as closely he could. Other people carried on drinking and enjoying their day out, unaware of the attack taking place just a few yards away from them. The quality of the film wasn't bad. Nevertheless, they didn't have a clear view of the killer's face. By focusing on what they *could* see of him, and enhancing the image as much as possible, they were able to catch a fleeting glimpse of the side temples of the frame of a pair of glasses, and the profile of a bearded face half concealed beneath a mop of fair hair, before he moved out of sight again. What they saw tied in with what witnesses at the scene had reported, but it brought them no closer to finding out the identity of the possible killer. They watched the footage again. After the second viewing it became pointless yet Ian stayed, mesmerised by the image of a dead man drinking, chatting, laughing, and generally having a good time with his arm around his beautiful wife, apparently swapping jokes with his brother.

At the end of another frustrating day, Ian went home early. Eileen had put his back up and he was disinclined to put in extra hours that evening, going over old ground. He cheered up when Bev was pleased to see him. They decided to go out for a meal and walked down towards town until they found a reasonable Indian restaurant. Gazing at his beautiful wife, Ian tried to feel happy. He had achieved his promotion, Bev was settling into her new life in York. Everything was turning out fine. Just for a few hours he wanted to relax with his wife and forget that an anonymous killer could be prowling the streets of York, hunting for his next victim.

CHAPTER 24

When he came close, Jocelyn's legs felt like jelly and she had a dizzy turn.

'Go on ahead, and stop talking to me.'

'But I want to—'

'Just leave me alone, will you?' she snapped. 'One of us is going to trip if we don't concentrate.'

She needed to focus all her attention on the paving slabs in front of her. Once, she made the mistake of glancing between the battlements to her right, all the way down to the road below. The scene wavered before her eyes. For a few seconds her legs wouldn't move. She felt lightheaded and nauseous. It required a huge effort of will to move forward again, left foot, right foot, left foot again, edging forwards.

'No one's going to trip,' he laughed.

He walked on, past several couples who were strolling hand in hand along the city wall. They weren't very high above the steep grass slope on their left, but telling herself she was being irrational made no difference. Sick and giddy, she knew she wouldn't recover until her feet were on the ground. James strode on ahead making no attempt to hide his irritation. He didn't once look back to see how she was coping.

'I can't help it,' she muttered crossly.

They walked along the top of the wall for nearly a mile. It felt much longer.

At last they reached the steps by Clifford's Tower, where James had booked a table at a nearby restaurant. The food was good, but Jocelyn had lost her appetite and it wasn't long before they were bickering again.

'You can never just enjoy yourself, can you?' he grumbled. 'I'm spending a lot of money bringing you here to an expensive restaurant, and all you've done is complain. I might as well not have bothered. This is supposed to be a treat.'

She did her best to relax but it was hard to shake off the memory of her terror on the wall. James wasn't helping. The more he drank, the more belligerent he became. She turned away from him and gazed at the view through the large window of the restaurant. Daylight was fading slowly over the tower, picking out grey stones in the high yellow brick wall. On the steep slope daffodils had closed up for the night, and a solitary goose perched on the grass. Above the floodlit tower a luminescent sky glowed, shining through a cricket bat-shaped hole in the wall.

She was probably as taken aback as James was when she stood up without warning.

'I'm going home.'

She was on her feet, pulling on her jacket. It would have been humiliating to sit down again unless he begged her to stay. He didn't remonstrate, but carried on drinking his wine. That decided her. The flat wasn't far away, just across the bridge and a short walk along Bishopsgate. Leaving him to settle the bill, she stalked out of the restaurant. Once out on the street, she turned right and walked quickly along the road and into a small park that led to the bridge. Quickly she traversed a grassy area that led to a low obelisk where four paths met. It was raining and she didn't have an umbrella. Hearing footsteps behind her, she looked over her shoulder. James was hurrying after her. She stopped, shivering in the chilly wet air.

As he caught up with her she could see his eyes glaring angrily in the dim park lighting.

'What the hell are you playing at?' he demanded.

All at once she didn't feel safe in the park where the sound of traffic was muffled by a screen of trees, and the area was poorly lit. She told herself she was being daft. James wasn't going to hurt her.

'I had to get away.'

'You mean you wanted to get away from me.'

Without warning he raised his hand and slapped her on the side of her face. The unexpected impact made her reel. The sound reverberated inside her head like a gun shot.

'Come with me,' he growled, swaying drunkenly.

Shocked by his violence, she began crying hysterically. 'Leave me alone,' she managed to blurt out. 'It's over. I don't ever want to see you again.'

'You'll be sorry you said that.'

Abruptly he turned on his heel and strode away.

Trembling, she hurried along the path and up the steps onto Skeldergate Bridge, careful not to slip on the wet steps. The street lights and noise from passing cars reassured her. Far below the river flowed blackly but up on the bridge she felt safe. By the time she reached the far side of the bridge, James had vanished. She was alone. It had been a hard winter and there was still a bite in the air as she scurried down the stone steps on the other side of the bridge, back towards the flat a few hundred yards further along the street. At the bottom of the steps an unlit tunnel on her right led back under the bridge. Turning left, she hurried on towards Bishopsgate. Through the trees on the other side of the river she could see Clifford's Tower, floodlit. She intended to go there one day and read about its history, but she hadn't got around to it yet. All she knew was that hundreds of people had once died in the tower in some terrible tragedy. She shivered as a drop of rain slid under the collar of her jacket and down between her shoulder blades.

★　　★　　★

A hand seized her roughly by the throat making her choke. The smell of leather filled her nostrils, and she felt the smooth rigidity of the material as a second hand was clapped over her mouth, gagging her. Before she could react, she felt herself being lifted off her feet. With her hands flailing helplessly in the air, she was dragged backwards onto a wide paved area that ran alongside the river. To her left she could see the vast black emptiness of the water. Over to the right, on the other side of road, there was an empty patch of grass, dotted with a few trees. Only a few hundred yards further along the road were distant lights from a block of flats. There were people in there, eating and drinking, watching television, preparing for bed at the end of the day, oblivious to her terror. With a burst of energy she tried to prise his fingers off her face so she could scream out for help. His grip was too strong. She was afraid he was going to push her off the path into the freezing water. Her writhing was futile. With a powerful jerk he twisted her neck as he tugged her along, parallel to the river.

Panic and exhaustion threatened to overwhelm her. She was powerless to stop him hauling her towards a disused Victorian warehouse that stood right at the water's edge. She rolled her eyes wildly, desperately seeking for help. On the far side of the river she could see a red traffic light through the trees, where cars were being driven along the roads. She could see their lights. There were people in the cars who could raise the alarm if they only knew what was happening, but they were too far away to witness the attack. Dazed with pain and fear, she felt her heels bump along the cobbled edge of the paved area. She was hauled down stone steps, alongside the high brick wall of the warehouse. One of her shoes fell off. She would have collapsed but her assailant was holding her, squeezing her neck so tightly she could barely breathe as he pulled her down towards the water.

Desperately she lunged at an orange life belt attached to the wall. Her fingers scraped uselessly across its smooth surface without dislodging it. A sign on the wall said: 'Gibson's of York', with an emergency phone number. It was no use to her. Endeavouring to gain some leverage on the ground, she stumbled sideways, cracking her head against the wall. Stunned, her brain pounding, she struggled to remain conscious as he shoved her down onto the wide bottom step. One of her arms twisted awkwardly beneath her as she fell, wrenching her shoulder. Sharp flakes of stone and hard traces of dried pigeon excrement pricked her legs. A car zoomed past, just a few feet away up the steps. It could have been a hundred miles away. The fleeting glare from its headlights lit up ugly black graffiti on the wall above her.

★　★　★

He was above her now, kneeling on her chest, his fingers tightening their grip around her neck, his face hidden in shadow beneath an overhanging hood. All she could see were glassy staring eyes as she lay on the ground, trembling and fighting for breath. She kicked out feebly with her legs, scrabbling helplessly at hard gloved fingers pressing down on her throat. It was too late for resistance. She couldn't breathe. Someone was talking to her. Little wisps of vapour floated past her line of vision as he spoke, briskly and cheerfully.

'Soon be over. It'll be quicker if you keep still.'

Somewhere a car engine revved. His head jerked up, alert to the sound. That was her chance, only she was too weak with terror to move. His fingers didn't loosen their grip. The starry sky spun past her out of control as her chest exploded with pain.

CHAPTER 25

Charles stared at himself in the mirror. He would return to his post in London soon, but first he had a few issues to sort out, one of which was deciding exactly what to do with Vivien. Idly he brushed his hair. Not far off forty, he could easily pass for thirty; late twenties if you didn't look closely. Admittedly he drank far too much, but other than that he looked after himself. He was sufficiently good looking to be attractive to women, and he worked out regularly. Until recently he had been content to carry on in the same way as he had been doing for years. With his looks and personality, he certainly wasn't single for lack of opportunities. He had simply never had time for a serious relationship. Not that he had ever felt he was missing out, until Adrian had brought Vivien into the family. At first she had been just one more in a series of affairs; one more 'conquest'. He had conducted affairs with married women before. Several of them had been seriously wealthy, and generous, especially the older ones.

★ ★ ★

Starting the affair with Vivien hadn't been difficult. The opportunity had arisen, and he had taken advantage of it. Since she was married to his brother, he came into contact with her frequently. He wasn't proud of himself for cheating on his brother, but he hadn't been able to stop himself, and she hadn't exactly rejected his advances. She was culpable too. Everything changed with Adrian's death. Charles' guilt exploded into a terrible anguish. He could hardly bear to look at Vivien any more, let alone touch her. There were too many painful memories. He did his best to hide his feelings from her, insisting he wanted to look after her. Nothing could have been further from the truth.

When his brother had first introduced Vivien to the family, Charles had been surprised by the strength of his own resentment. Adrian had always been a source of aggravation to him. At school, while Charles had slogged away to achieve top grades, his brother had been happy to mess about with his mates. They were a bunch of time wasters, drinking beer and playing computer games, chasing girls and getting into pointless scrapes. Charles could have lived with that. What had bugged him more than his brother's relaxed approach to life was that no one else seemed to care. Teachers who were aloof with Charles laughed and joked with his brother. When he complained, his mother had warned him not to be spiteful. He had never understood how it had turned around so that he was the one in the wrong with his mother. That was just typical.

'Granted he's not academic,' she had said, 'but he's a nice boy and he's popular. Not everyone's as bright as you are, Charles.'

'As hard working as me, you mean. He's a dosser. He's just taking the piss. You ought to ground him, make him do some work for a change.'

Younger than Charles, it didn't feel right when Adrian had married first. Not only that, he somehow managed to bag himself a gorgeous wife. Charles simply couldn't understand what she saw in him. By no means the most beautiful woman he had ever seen, there was something irresistibly seductive about her voluptuous curves. The first time, they both agreed it had been a stupid mistake. It would never have happened if they hadn't been drunk. Charles' remorse had been genuine. Until the next opportunity presented itself. After that, Adrian had seemed to go out of his way to throw Charles and Vivien together. One evening they had gone out for dinner. Charles had brought one of his girlfriends along. When Adrian had gone home early, feeling queasy, he had insisted Vivien stay.

'Have a nice evening,' he had urged her. 'You can get a taxi home, or perhaps Charles won't mind—'

Charles had called a taxi for his date, and had

driven Vivien home himself. They had taken a detour, stopping off at a small hotel on the way.

After that, they had planned their assignations. It had never been difficult for Vivien to deceive Adrian. On reflection, Charles blamed the affair on his brother's gullibility. He had it coming. He had always been a fool and, like an idiot, he had married a woman with loose morals. If anything, Charles had done his brother a favour. If he hadn't embarked on an affair with his sister-in-law, she would have ended up sleeping with someone else. At least Charles had the decency to be discreet about it. Not only had he saved his brother the pain of discovering his wife was a slut, but Adrian might have contracted any number of nasty infections if Vivien had gone around picking up other men. She certainly needed someone to lean on now Adrian had gone; her helplessness irritated Charles almost beyond endurance. It was hard not to let his feelings show. But he owed it to Adrian to take care of his widow, because he was responsible for his brother's death.

CHAPTER 26

James' anger was intensified by disappointment. He had been seeing Jocelyn for about eighteen months. After a year they had gone on holiday together. Lounging on a sunny beach in Spain they had reached a tentative understanding that they were both looking for a long term relationship. Since then they had drifted on for another six months, until he had finally decided to ask her to marry him. It was more a case of suggesting that the time was right; it never crossed his mind that she might turn him down. Having bought a diamond ring that cost him more than a month's salary, he had been waiting for the perfect moment to propose. With the small black box safely stowed away in his pocket, he had booked a table in the window of an expensive restaurant with a view of Clifford's Tower. He knew she didn't like heights. She had refused to go up on the wall before. But it wouldn't have killed her to have made a bit of an effort to have a romantic walk on the old city wall. He had intended to propose to her looking out over the city, but she had ruined that idea with her stupid flapping.

* * *

He had hoped the evening would improve once they reached the restaurant. If anything it had deteriorated. Jocelyn had sat opposite him with such a long face, he hadn't felt inclined to propose to her right then. On the contrary, he had begun to think he had made a mistake in wanting to marry her at all. Doggedly he had focused on his food. He was paying for it, after all, and it wasn't cheap. It was hard to believe she hadn't realised why he had brought her there. Expecting her to cheer up, he was taken aback when she leapt out of her chair and left the restaurant. Quickly finishing his wine, he paid the bill without adding a tip, doing his best to look as though nothing was wrong. A diminutive Asian waitress smiled anxiously and dipped her head as she held the door for him, as though she knew what had happened. It wasn't difficult to work out. Shortly after leaving the restaurant he caught sight of Jocelyn crossing the park on her way back to Skeldergate, and had to run to catch up with her. He soon regretted having followed her.

Rain was falling steadily as he walked away, along deserted pavements. No one driving past gave him a second glance as he strode along, hurrying to get out of the rain. Approaching the entrance to his block of flats he forced himself to slow down. He was soaking wet, trembling, and gasping for breath. Shocked by the way the evening had turned out, he was determined to carry on as though nothing had happened. There was no reason why this setback should ruin the rest of his life. At least the months of uncertainty were over. He was never going to marry her. It was impossible now. A neighbour passed him in the doorway. Ignoring her friendly nod, he hurried to the lift, impatient to reach his room and take off his wet clothes. Stripping off, he chucked his clothes in the laundry basket and lay his leather gloves on the radiator.

Lying in a hot bath, he tried to analyse his turbulent feelings. More than anything else, he felt ashamed of an overwhelming sense of relief. It was a pity, because in many ways their relationship had worked very well. But he could never have trusted her again. His cheeks still felt hot when he remembered her walking out on him. He had wasted nearly two years of his life on her. If she had seen the huge diamond in his pocket her attitude would doubtless have been very different, but it was too late. She would never see it now. Barefoot and wrapped in a towel, he flipped open the lid of the little black box and gazed at the stone, sparkling and mysterious. He had no use for it any more. He wondered whether he should try to sell it, but he wouldn't know where to start to make sure he got a good price, and it wasn't the kind of item he could auction on eBay.

He leaned back on the sofa and held the ring high in the air above him. He had been having doubts about his relationship with Jocelyn for some time, but had never expected she would be the one to end it. The memory of her rejection rankled, as shocking now as it had been earlier in the park when she had told him it was over between them. The more he thought about it, the more obvious it became that she had been the cause of all their problems, with her constant anxieties and whining. But now he was left feeling guilty. His head felt heavy. He was afraid he might have caught a chill walking around in the cold wet night air. From the other side of the wall he could hear a television blaring, without being able to distinguish a single word. Worn out from the emotions of the evening, he dozed off. He woke up much later, shivering, and sprawled uncomfortably on top of the bed. It was three o'clock in the morning and he was alone.

Three o'clock. He sat up and tried to decide what to do. Four hours had passed since he had last seen Jocelyn. He wondered if most people would have called the police by now to report her missing, or whether it would be normal to wait until morning on the assumption she had found accommodation for the night and would show up the next day. It was too late to call her parents or her best friend, to ask if she had gone to stay with them. On the other hand, if anyone asked, they might consider it strange he had made no attempt to find her when she hadn't come home. On balance, he decided to wait. She had said quite clearly that she didn't want to see him again. Of course she wasn't going to come crawling back to him straight away. After all, if he hadn't woken up he wouldn't have known she was missing. All he had to do was say he hadn't noticed she had never come back that night, and no one would be able to disprove it. He climbed into bed but couldn't sleep, remembering how he had left her out there, alone, in the dark.

CHAPTER 27

Freddy crossed Skeldergate Bridge and carried on down towards Bishopsgate Street. Approaching a derelict Victorian warehouse at the water's edge, he noticed a bundle of clothes lying on the steps leading down to the river. He nearly didn't bother to take a closer look because it had been raining over night. Even if there was something there worth pilfering, it would be soaking wet. But he might find a decent belt, or a pair of shoes, or maybe even a wad of cash. However tough things were, he never lost hope. Winter was over for another year, someone had slipped him a fiver the night before, and he had bought himself a proper breakfast, for once. It made a change from the Salvation Army slop. He never complained. They were decent people. If they pitied him, they never let it show. What bugged him was how they were always so relentlessly cheerful. They said it was a pleasure to welcome him to their drop-in centres. Some pleasure! The better off people were, the more bullshit they spouted. It was all right for them. At the end of the day, they had their own homes to go to. But he kept his feelings to himself.

He shuffled down the steps and poked the bundle with the toe of his boot. It didn't surprise him to see a hand sticking out from a sleeve. He had stumbled on plenty of drunks and worse, lying unconscious in the street, and it wouldn't be the first time he'd come across a stiff either. If the woman at his feet was dead, at least she couldn't leap up and attack him. He moved round to lean against the old brick building where he would be less visible from the road. He wasn't sure, but he thought it might be a crime to steal from the dead. At any rate, he wasn't taking any chances. The ground floor windows behind him were boarded up and the building was abandoned. No one would be watching him from there. Across the river a row of bright orange hire boats bobbed about, too far away for anyone to spy on him from there. He glanced up at the intricate wrought iron bridge. No one was standing there looking down at the river, able to glance in his direction. Behind him, away from the river, on the far side of the road, was a patch of grass and steps leading up onto the bridge. Both were deserted. The only way he might be observed was if someone driving past happened to look out towards the river as went by. He would risk it.

★　★　★

He knelt down beside the body just as a cyclist went past, shoulders hunched, facing the road in front of him. Freddy ducked his head, but the cyclist raced on without looking round. He returned his attention to the body. He had to work fast. Every second he spent investigating increased his chances of being spotted. One phone call to the police from an interfering passer-by and Freddy could find himself facing a murder charge. It happened. A mate of his had gone down for no reason other than that he had been caught with a wallet he had nicked off a stiff.

'I never done, it, Freddy,' his mate had told him, with tears in his eyes, 'I never touched the geezer.'

Freddy wasn't sure whether he believed him or not. He was a vicious brute. All the same, it served as a chilling warning not to be caught fencing gear lifted from a murder victim – or worse, found with his hands on the body.

The first thing he noticed close up was that the hand was very small. His spirits sank. Children weren't likely to be carrying much cash. A closer look revealed that his initial impression had been correct. It was a woman's hand, with painted nails and a ring with a blue gem. The stone probably wouldn't be worth much. Still, he twisted it off her finger in case. It wasn't easy grabbing hold of it with his woolly gloves, but he wasn't stupid enough to touch her with his bare hands. Carefully he brushed back the hair that had fallen over her face and studied her profile. She was pretty, with light brown eyes and a turned up nose. He guessed she was in her twenties. Even after lying out on the dirty ground in the rain, she looked too clean and well dressed to be living on the street. Lucky for him. Noticing a row of pearls round her neck, he fiddled with the catch but couldn't undo it. Rashly, he pulled and the string broke. Pearls scattered like hail around him, bouncing on the stone step. Quickly he scooped up as many as he could, and stuffed them into his coat pocket, the one that didn't have a hole in it. They'd be worth a few drinks if they were genuine.

He turned his attention to the handbag on her shoulder. Ripping the zip open, he delved inside. Discarding a make up bag, he pulled out a purse. Fifty quid in notes and some change. Not bad. He stuffed the notes in his pocket and looked to see what else was in there. Credit cards, debit card, receipts. Slipping the coins in his pocket, he left the rest. One more rummage in the bag produced a phone, which he pocketed, and various useless items: a comb, a mirror, a diary and a few pens. He felt slightly uncomfortable groping in her coat pockets, but there was a chance she might have something valuable hidden on her. All he found was a packet of chewing gum and a hair band. He left those and clambered to his feet, wincing at the pain in his knees and back as he straightened up. Hesitating, he dropped the phone. They had ways of tracing them these days. It wasn't worth the risk for a few quid. A moment later, he was scurrying beneath the bridge, putting some distance between himself and the dead woman. He hadn't even noticed the name on her plastic. It made no difference to him – or to her now, come to that.

CHAPTER 28

On Monday Ian arrived at work to learn that the body of a young woman had been found near Skeldergate Bridge early that morning. Eileen was away at a meeting in Harrogate. Ian was the senior officer in York most experienced in dealing with murder investigations. It didn't take him long to reach a decision. So far they had made no progress with the investigation into Adrian's death. On the contrary, the investigation seemed to be going backwards. They had started out with a suspect kicking his heels in a cell. Since they had let Harry go for lack of evidence, they hadn't made any progress. A team was following up all the witnesses who had been at the races the previous Saturday, and they were waiting for the search team to complete their examination of the site. There was nothing needing Ian's urgent attention, so instead of sitting at his desk rereading statements he decided to take a look at the new case himself. He always preferred to be out and about doing something, rather than sitting around waiting.

★   ★   ★

The doctor who had been summoned to certify death had alerted the police to suspicious circumstances straight away. Ian studied the brief medical report before he set off. The victim had been strangled. Her body had been discovered beside the river by a postman on his early round. There was no question they were dealing with a murder. It appeared to be straightforward. With luck, Ian would be able to arrest the killer before the team at the racecourse had even finished their search for evidence. His first investigation in his new post was off to a frustrating start. So far it had done nothing to establish his position with his colleagues in York and there was a chance it might never be solved. If he could achieve a quick result in this second murder case it would certainly help to shore up his reputation. Whistling, he drove down to the river. After a hard winter there was finally a feeling of spring in the air; a lightness in the sky.

From the bottom of the steps leading up onto Skeldergate Bridge, the road had been cordoned off. A forensic tent was in place. A team of scene of crime officers were chatting as they packed up their gear. Were it not for the telltale signs of a recent fatality, it would have been a pleasant scene. The street was still wet after overnight rain; now the sun was out everything looked fresh and shiny. The ironwork on the bridge was attractive Victorian design at its best, the rippling water of the river sparkled in the morning sunshine, and bright red boats bobbed up and down on the far bank. From the other side of the river they looked like children's toys. Ian turned back and squinted at the forensic tent.

He nodded at a young constable who was manning the cordon.

'How's it going?'

'Sir?'

'Have SOCOs found anything?'

'Not as far as I know, sir.'

The body had been taken to the mortuary where a post mortem was being carried out that morning. Much as he hated viewing corpses, Ian was impatient to hear the pathologist's findings. He was keen to gain Eileen's approval by showing her how quickly he could achieve a result.

'What do we know?' he pressed the young officer.

'A young woman's been strangled, sir.'

The constable wasn't very forthcoming so, after a quick look around at the river and the bridge, Ian slipped inside the forensic tent to see if the scene of crime officers in there had any more information to give him.

'The body's only just gone off,' a female officer told him. 'Still, it hardly needs a pathologist to tell us what happened.'

'Go on.'

'Well, the doctor placed the time of death at around eleven on Friday night. She was strangled.

We think she was killed here, but there were indications the body had been disturbed by the time we arrived. She'd been shifted over onto her side after rigor set in, probably so someone could get to her pockets. Her bag was lying over there, open. A purse was inside the bag, also open. There was no cash, but her credit card and a debit card weren't taken, and her phone was lying on the top step.'

'All of which suggests this was a mugging that went too far?'

'Possibly, although like I said we think she was moved some hours after she died, so it's possible someone discovered her lying here and robbed her after she'd been killed.'

Above her mask she screwed up her eyes in a grimace of disgust.

The victim had lived just five minutes' walk from the spot where her body had been found, in a flat belonging to a man called James Newman. Ian wondered if she had been killed at home. It wouldn't have been very difficult to carry a body such a short distance after dark, without being seen. He put the idea to the scene of crime officer. She shook her head and told him the woman had been killed on the steps where she had been found. It was raining and the dead woman was soaking wet, but patches of ground beneath her body had been relatively dry when she was found.

'You don't think it is possible she was killed elsewhere and her body dumped here?'

'It's possible, but it started raining soon after eleven.'

Ian frowned. If they could find evidence of a struggle in her flat, the list of suspects would be short. Possibly only one name would appear on the list. A murder committed on the street might be more difficult to pin on anyone.

Driving towards the hospital Ian put his foot down, keen to get through the visit as quickly as possible. After speaking to the pathologist, he was going to question the victim's boyfriend. Hopefully James Newman would confess, and Ian would have at least one success notched up in York. He felt guilty that he was pleased about this second case turning up just when they were struggling to make sense of the death at the races. A young woman had been violently murdered. He should be focused on seeking justice for her, and punishing her killer. Although he was ambitious, he didn't want to turn into a career officer who prized his own advancement over a desire to see justice done. In his determination to prove his worth in his new job, he had to keep his perspective. His job was about taking a moral stand against violence and injustice in an increasingly vicious and chaotic society. His individual career was incidental. Yet just for a moment he had welcomed the discovery of a woman's body as an opportunity to showcase his professionalism. Ashamed, he pulled into the hospital car park.

He was turning into the kind of police officer he had always despised. Even the prospect of seeing the attractive young anatomical pathology technician failed to cheer him up.

CHAPTER 29

Approaching the back entrance to the mortuary, Ian tried to remember the name of the technician. He had no difficulty recalling the names of witnesses however briefly they touched on the case, even if he had only met them in passing, or come across their name on a statement. But although he had engaged in a conversation with the smiling young blonde, her name escaped him. He knew it was something short and simple. As he was raising his hand to announce his presence, her name popped into his mind: Avril. Smiling at having remembered it, he pressed the buzzer. A few seconds later he was inside, chatting to her. He noticed she wasn't wearing a wedding ring. While her relationship status made no difference to him personally, years of training and experience in observation meant he couldn't help noticing such details about people.

The home office forensic pathologist was in the examination room peeling off his gloves.

'You caught me,' he said as he caught sight of Ian in the doorway. 'I was just leaving.'

'Lucky me,' Ian muttered.

He avoided meeting the other man's eye, afraid that Jonah's sharp gaze would penetrate his facade of equanimity in the presence of death. The pathologist smiled warmly at him, like a host greeting a dinner guest. His turned up nose and twinkling eyes gave him a comic appearance so that Ian couldn't help relaxing, in spite of his queasiness. Jonah jerked his head in the direction of the corpse.

'Young woman. Not much over twenty from the looks of her.'

'She was twenty-two.'

Ian fixed his eyes on a point straight ahead, so the body on the table lay just below the line of his vision.

Jonah nodded impatiently. 'I know, I know, I know how old she was, we've both read the notes. I'm talking about what secrets the cadaver reveals, not about facts we already know. I don't need to tell you any of that, do I? That's not why you're here. You want to find out what *she* can tell us.'

He gestured towards the body as he spoke. Ian gave a non-committal grunt. He wasn't quite sure what secrets the pathologist was talking about.

'Go on,' he said. 'I'm listening.'

'Interesting case,' Jonah said.

Ian lowered his gaze until he was looking directly at the body.

'Interesting in what way? She was strangled, wasn't she?'

'Yes.'

Ian stared at the dead girl who lay on her back, with her arms straight down by her sides. Her eyes were closed and she had a blank expression on her face. Livid bruising was visible around her neck. It was somehow more shocking because her skin was so pale, apart from a mottled purplish patch on the right side of her face which was also pitted and scratched from lying on uneven ground.

'She suffocated,' the pathologist concurred, 'but there's something that doesn't quite add up.'

'What do you mean?'

Jonah heaved a sigh. 'Something's not right.'

Ian frowned. He was thinking along similar lines himself, for a different reason. Under normal circumstances he would be intrigued by a murder that baffled a forensic pathologist. He remembered discussing such cases with his former detective inspector, puzzling over possibilities, and weighing up probabilities. They had always uncovered the truth in the end, however well a killer had tried to cover his or her tracks. Unravelling the puzzle to expose the truth had been absorbing, even though it had often been hard. He sometimes likened his work to that of the code breakers during the war. But right now he already had one complicated murder case on his hands. He wasn't sure he could cope with a second one. At the same time, he was determined not to admit he was out of his depth. New to the area, he couldn't afford to show Eileen he was struggling before he had even had a chance to establish himself with the local team.

'What do you mean, not right?' he asked.

The two men stood for a moment gazing at a dainty face tinged with blue and scored with tiny scratches and grazes. Apart from that, the features were delicate and perfect as a face painted on a china doll. The pathologist shrugged his rounded shoulders.

'I don't know. I just have a feeling . . .'

Ian hoped the man wasn't going to prove flaky.

Jonah lifted his eyes to look at Ian. 'Don't you ever get a feeling that something isn't right, even though you can't put your finger on what it is?'

As it happened, Ian knew exactly what Jonah meant, despite years of training that had drummed into him not to trust anything but evidence able to withstand scrutiny in a court of law. With a sheepish smile, he admitted that he had followed the occasional hunch.

'Only there's nothing to look into here,' the pathologist went on. He sounded exasperated. 'It's a perfectly straightforward case. She was strangled and asphyxiated as a consequence. The cause of death couldn't be more obvious. So why do I get this feeling I'm missing something? Anyway, there it is. I'll get my report done, and then all you have to do is find out who killed her. Some people have it easy.'

He chuckled, and Ian couldn't help smiling.

'And now, if you'll excuse me, you're welcome to stay if you find you really can't tear yourself away from here, but I need to go. I'm under strict instructions from the wife not to be late.'

Ian realised he hadn't even registered the other man was wearing a wedding ring. So much for his training in noticing details about other people.

CHAPTER 30

Ian was desperate to wrap up the new investigation. It would be a hideous coincidence if a second difficult case landed on his desk before he had made any headway with the first one. Although not a superstitious man, he couldn't believe fate would treat him so unkindly when he had only just been promoted to inspector. So, with no reason other than a dogged determination to remain optimistic, he more or less convinced himself he was about to nail Jocelyn's killer. He knew he was clutching at straws. With no evidence to support his suspicion that James was guilty, he had to follow up the possibility. If he was right, James would be locked in the custody suite before the day was out. Previously, senior officers had been quick to praise Ian's results. Before long, Eileen would follow suit. So far she had only seen him floundering. That was about to change.

He parked along Bishopsgate, where Jocelyn had lived with her boyfriend, not far from where her body had been found. Impatient for a rapid outcome, he strode swiftly past the side wall of the derelict warehouse, its ground floor windows bricked up, its paintwork filthy and cracked, its pipes and guttering rusting and discoloured, and stopped outside a smart new block of apartments, its new red and yellow brickwork and stylish dark brown window frames forming a marked contrast with the abandoned warehouse. It was a pleasant location by the river, a short walk from the city centre. Having recently moved to the area, Ian couldn't help speculating how much a flat there would cost. He dismissed the thought and focused his attention on what he was going to ask Jocelyn's boyfriend.

He wasn't sure if James would be at home, but the door was opened almost at once by a tall dark-haired man. He looked utterly miserable, his eyes inflamed from crying and his long nose red from repeated wiping. His shoulders drooped as though he lacked the energy to stand up straight.

'James Newman?'

The other man's head fell forward in acknowledgement. He didn't speak. Ian introduced himself.

'I know. They told me.'

'I'm not here to tell you what happened. I'd like to ask you a few questions.'

Wordlessly James led him into a room furnished with a dark green leather sofa and matching armchairs arranged in a semi circle around a low wooden table. Opposite the door a large flat screen television hung from the wall. The furniture looked expensive but was too large for the room which felt uncomfortably crowded.

Ian took a seat on the armchair and James sat diagonally opposite, on the sofa.

'When did you last see Jocelyn?'

For answer, James dropped his head in his hands. Ian waited. After a minute, James sat up.

'We were planning to get married,' he said. 'I bought her a ring. Look.'

He drew a small black jewellery box from the pocket of his jeans and opened it to display a large diamond that winked up at them. Ian wondered why he hadn't given the ring to Jocelyn. He might have offered it to her and been turned down. Such a rejection could conceivably provoke a man into a rash fit of violence, especially if he had been drinking. Quietly Ian repeated his question.

This time, James seemed to register the words.

'We went out for dinner on Friday. I was going to ask her to marry me then. I had the ring in my pocket all the time. Only . . .'

'What happened?

'We went, that is I took her, to an expensive restaurant, right by Clifford's Tower. Only before I could ask her, you know, if she was ready to get married, we – well, we had a row, not even a row really, a tiff, you know. It didn't mean anything. I mean, I can see how it must look.'

'How must it look?'

162

James shrugged. 'I wasn't angry with her or anything like that. It was her. She left. Walked out. Said she was going home.'

'What time was that?'

'I don't know. About ten, I guess. Maybe half past.'

'What was the argument about?'

'Nothing really.'

'Nothing?'

James heaved a sigh that shook his shoulders.

'I took her for a walk along the wall. Everyone goes up there. It's very safe. But she's afraid of heights and made a stupid fuss about it.'

Ian thought he sounded inappropriately angry, considering he was talking about the woman he had wanted to marry, a woman who had been murdered two days earlier. At the same time, he didn't strike Ian as a stupid man. If he really had killed his girlfriend in a fit of rage, as seemed likely, Ian wouldn't have expected him to speak aggressively about her. And he noticed that James still referred to her in the present tense.

'What happened in the restaurant?' Ian asked.

'She was in a foul mood all evening because I'd taken her up on the wall. To be honest, if I'd known how she was going to react, I never would have taken her up there, but I'd never realised how bad she was.'

'Bad?'

'Yes, with the vertigo. I had no idea it was that

bad. But it wasn't my fault. She shouldn't have gone up there if she was that nervous.'

'What wasn't your fault?'

'Her vertigo. She should have said she didn't want to go up there. How was I supposed to know? I'm not a bloody mind reader.'

'So you were arguing on the wall, and when you reached the restaurant the row continued. Have I got that right?'

'That's right, more or less. Although it wasn't really a row as such. More a bad atmosphere. I took her to this really nice restaurant. It cost enough. But by then she was in one of her moods and that was that. In the end she just got up and left, without a word of explanation. If I'd gone after her, it would never have happened.'

'What time did you leave the restaurant?'

'I don't know.' James was suddenly reluctant to continue his account. 'Inspector, I've just lost my fiancée. I can't cope with any more questions. I just want to be left alone.'

He put his head in his hands once more. This time, Ian could see his shoulders shaking with sobs.

CHAPTER 31

Keen to focus on a case where they could achieve a quick result on a minimal budget, Eileen encouraged Ian to pursue James. Despite all the manpower and forensics they had thrown at the investigation into the death at the races, they were making no progress with it. Once the search team had finished, they would have to review their strategy if no new evidence had come to light. Vivien and Charles had returned to London. They remained under suspicion and a constable was still researching their circumstances. In the meantime, while they were waiting for the results of the searching and researching, Ian was glad to turn his attention to a less challenging target. Despite the fact that the outcome looked like a foregone conclusion, before apprehending James he wanted to gather as much evidence as possible. Even when arresting officers had been confident of gaining a conviction, suspects had been known to walk free for lack of proof. Some cases didn't even make it to court. He had to present Eileen with watertight evidence; he knew who would be blamed if a suspect escaped trial.

It was late morning by the time he went to the restaurant where James and Jocelyn had gone on the night she died. A notice on the door said the restaurant didn't open until midday. Peering through the window, he could see a small Asian man fiddling around behind the bar, wiping glasses and putting them away. Ian tapped on the window and, after several attempts, succeeded in attracting his attention. The man introduced himself as the manager of the restaurant.

'How can I be of assistance to you, sir?' he enquired in the formal tones of a non-native speaker.

'I'd like to speak to any staff who were working here on Friday evening.'

'Friday evening? Is there a problem, sir?'

'No, no problem,' Ian replied.

'A complaint then?'

Ian reassured him that the police enquiry had nothing to do with the restaurant and the man hurried away to check his rosters and summon the relevant people.

While he waited, Ian took a seat at a corner table and looked around the open plan dining room. Tastefully kitted out in pine and bamboo, with framed silk paintings on the walls, it had a calm atmosphere. He thought Bev would like it there.

As he gazed at the view out of the window, he heard footsteps and muttering and turned to see the manager accompanied by four serving staff and two white-coated chefs, all young slender Asians. Every one of them had been working there on Friday. After briefly questioning the kitchen staff, Ian dismissed them. He showed the waiting staff a photograph of James and Jocelyn sitting on a beach in the sun, laughing. One by one the staff stepped forward to look. One by one they stepped back, shaking their heads, until the final waitress nodded. She looked at Ian with frightened eyes.

'I remember this lady,' she whispered.

Ian thanked the rest of the staff and said he wouldn't need them any longer.

He invited the waitress who had recognised Jocelyn to join him at his table. At a nod from the manager, she sat down. Ian smiled encouragingly at her and she lowered her eyes.

'What can you tell me about these two people?' he asked, tapping the photograph with one finger.

'I do not see them before,' she replied, speaking slowly and awkwardly. 'I do not know them.'

'Anything you can remember about them might help us in our enquiry, anything at all.'

The young waitress shook her head. Her glossy black hair glinted in the light streaming in through the window. When she glanced anxiously at Ian, her huge black eyes reminded him of Geraldine Steel, his detective inspector when he had been a sergeant. Geraldine had often warned him not to be impatient. Her advice had been justified. He always expected a quick outcome to problems, even though he knew from experience that pursuing a false lead could set an investigation back weeks. Still, he was fairly sure he was on the right track now in suspecting James of killing his girlfriend.

He leaned forward and repeated his question.

'This is very important,' he added solemnly.

The girl glanced apprehensively in the direction of the bar, where the manager was busily polishing glasses, and lowered her voice until Ian could barely hear her.

'This is not good man. He is not kind to this woman.'

The waitress touched Jocelyn's face with the tip of a delicate finger. Smiling up at them from the photograph, the dead girl looked full of life. With a pang, Ian recalled the mottled skin and pale flesh he had seen that morning. It was hard to believe that raddled bundle of white skin and bone and the vibrant woman in the photograph were the same person.

'He is angry,' the waitress said softly. 'He shout at woman. She go away.'

She waved a slim hand towards the street.

'What time did she leave the restaurant?'

The girl shook her head. She didn't know.

'What did he do when she left?'

She looked thoughtful.

'He drink wine. He pay bill. And he leave. That is all.'

'How did he pay?'

When it was clear she didn't understand the question, Ian called the manager over to check his records. He confirmed that James had paid his bill with a credit card at ten forty-five. James had quarrelled with his girlfriend at the restaurant. She had left, by herself, at about half past ten. Fifteen minutes later James had settled the bill and followed her. Within half an hour of his following her out of the restaurant, she had been brutally murdered. It was time to question James again and see if he could remember any more about the night Jocelyn was murdered.

CHAPTER 32

That Monday Bev woke early. Ian had already left for work. She chose her outfit with care: a dark blue trouser suit, white shirt, navy shoes and matching bag, professional but not too smart. Feeling slightly sick with nerves, she forced herself to eat breakfast before setting off for her first day in her new job. The buses ran regularly, and she only had to wait for about five minutes. Even so, she was shivering by the time the bus arrived. Across the aisle, a stout woman was talking volubly to a very thin man. Bev tried to ignore her noisy monologue and focus on the day ahead. She breathed deeply to remain calm, telling herself it didn't really matter. She didn't intend to stay in her new job for long. Basically she would be working as a dogsbody for the human resources manager, Danielle. By the time she had quit her last post, Bev had been in charge of a team of four colleagues. Now she was a junior member of staff, answerable to a line manager younger and less experienced than herself.

★　★　★

Bev arrived early. She entered the code on the keypad and went through to the rooms at the back of the store, but her own office was locked. No one else was around, so after a few minutes she returned to the supermarket floor. Danielle arrived just before nine. Without smiling she said, 'You're not due in till nine.' The absence of any greeting made the statement sound like an accusation. Bev tried to smile cheerfully, as though she didn't mind being kept waiting.

'Hi Danielle. I'm glad you're here. I haven't got a key, and I couldn't find anyone to ask to let me in to the office.'

'You don't need a key. You're not due in till nine, and I'm always here by then.'

'What if you don't come in one day?'

'Let's deal with that when we come to it. I'm not planning a holiday any time soon.'

'But—'

Ignoring Bev's protestations, Danielle opened the door and marched in, signalling the conversation was over.

Bev's day didn't improve. Danielle was in and out of the office all morning, speaking to people working along the corridor and on the shop floor, leaving Bev sitting at her desk in their cramped office, entering data. By eleven o'clock she was desperate for a break. As if that wasn't sufficiently aggravating, Danielle picked up a few errors she had made with figures.

'Sorry, it's hard to concentrate for so long without a break.'

Danielle sniffed. 'No one said you're not allowed a break.'

She added a comment under her breath that Bev couldn't hear. It sounded like 'bleating.'

At half past eleven Danielle announced she was going to a meeting. Left on her own, Bev stared out of the small dirty window. She felt like crying. Her disappointment was all the more acute because she had been so pleased to have a job. It had seemed too good to be true. Granted the money wasn't great, but with Ian's promotion they weren't exactly hard up.

It wouldn't have been so bad if Ian had worked regular hours, but she never knew when he was going to come home once he was on a case.

'You might as well live in a hotel,' she had complained, but he had told her he was too tired to argue.

Now instead of being left to her own devices in a lovely house, she was stuck by herself in a drab little office. Hearing the door open, she turned back to her monitor and resumed typing. When she glanced up, the store manager was standing in the doorway, smiling at her.

'Hello, I just popped by to see how you're getting on.'

She smiled back and he came over to her desk. She hesitated to ask him for a key, since

Danielle had already turned down the same request. Before she could make up her mind whether to mention it, Danielle walked in.

'Everything's fine, thank you,' Bev promptly lied, and the manager smiled at her.

On the bus home, Bev reviewed her day. On balance she decided the job might not turn out to be so bad after all. Danielle was desperate to establish her own authority but the manager, Bev's real boss, seemed easygoing, and pleased to have her there. The work itself wasn't taxing, which suited her for a while. And best of all, Danielle didn't seem to want to spend much time in the office. It looked as though the position might be fine in the short term, at least until she had sorted out the house and felt settled in York.

CHAPTER 33

Before moving in with James, Jocelyn had lived with her mother in Bulmer, not far from Castle Howard. Leaving York, Ian drove a short way out of town along the A64 north towards Scarborough. It was a pleasant drive with open fields on either side of the road. Turning off, he passed through gentle rolling Howardian Hills, designated an area of outstanding natural beauty. A solitary road on the sat nav screen led him between high hedges, past a tall folly, before he turned off to Bulmer, a pretty village of yellow sandstone cottages where a large farmhouse advertised 'B and B'. If he hadn't been engaged on such a grim mission, Ian would have enjoyed the journey.

A short round-faced woman opened the front door.

'Mrs Sands?'

'No, no,' the woman replied, her taut face relaxing for an instant. 'I'm Jocelyn's aunt. I *was* Jocelyn's aunt,' she corrected herself. 'I'm Jill. Moira's my sister. She's taken it terribly hard. It's a terrible business, Inspector, a terrible business. Jocelyn was an only child. Not that it would have been any less of a tragedy if she'd been one of a dozen. Only now my sister's got no one.'

'She's got you.'

'Yes, but I'm not local. I'm only here for a few days. I can't stay long. I've got family of my own to see to, and my youngest is only fifteen. I've left him with his father, God help him.' It wasn't clear whether she was invoking divine aid for her son or his father. 'Do you know who did it?'

'We're working on several lines of enquiry,' Ian muttered.

Mrs Sands was sitting on a chair, arms wrapped round her chest, rocking gently backwards and forwards. As Ian drew closer he could hear her moaning softly to herself. He glanced up at her sister who merely shrugged.

'She goes on like this for hours,' Jill said.

At the sound of her sister's voice, Moira stirred. Jill leaned down and said very slowly, 'Moira, there's a policeman here to see you.'

The bereaved mother shook her head and resumed her rocking.

Ian stepped forward. 'Mrs Sands? Moira?'

She didn't answer or even look up at him. Ian pressed on, regardless.

'I want to ask you a few questions about Jocelyn's boyfriend, James Newman. Do you know him?'

*　　*　　*

It was quickly apparent that he wasn't going to get much response from Jocelyn's mother.

'It's the drugs,' her sister said sadly. 'They put her on these drugs to calm her down and help her sleep, but they've turned her into a zombie. I don't know how she's going to manage when I've gone.'

Ian made sympathetic noises and accepted a cup of tea before proceeding to question Jocelyn's aunt. He learned that Mr Sands had died when Jocelyn was seven. Ian had already concluded that the visit had been a waste of time but he pressed on nonetheless, in case Jocelyn's aunt knew something that might help incriminate James.

'Jocelyn changed when she met him,' she said.

'In what way?'

'He didn't make her happy. She used to be such a cheerful girl, in spite of everything.'

'Everything? What do you mean in spite of everything?'

'My sister was never the same after Jocelyn's father died. It wasn't an easy end.' She sighed, remembering. 'Jocelyn was only a child, but she was wonderful with Moira. The two of them were really close. You can imagine, it being just the two of them for so long. But then she started going with that young man, and she changed. Moira used to be on the phone to me, complaining about him, for hours on end. She was so upset about it.'

Jill explained that Moira hardly saw her daughter after she had moved in with James.

'She never called round to see her, and she hardly ever phoned. They virtually stopped talking. When she was younger Jocelyn used to tell her mother everything. They were that close. Moira was really cut up about it. She said she wouldn't have minded if she thought Jocelyn was happy, but she wasn't. When Moira did see her, Jocelyn was really quiet. Moira said she thought Jocelyn was afraid of him.'

'Afraid?'

'Yes, afraid of saying something he wouldn't like.'

Ian tried to suppress his disappointment. Jocelyn's aunt was anything but reliable as a character witness. For a start, what she had told him was hearsay. Not only that, her statement was based on the words of a woman who had reason to resent James. Realising he was wasting his time with Jocelyn's family, he thanked her aunt and took his leave. On his way out he handed her a card and asked her to be sure to call him if anything occurred to her that might help them with their enquiries.

'I'm sure you want to see Jocelyn's killer arrested,' he said as he was leaving.

He felt a fleeting sympathy for the suspect, struggling to remove his girlfriend from her mother's influence. Ian knew what that felt like. He and Bev had lived in Kent for several years, only a few miles from Bev's parents who had never missed an opportunity to denigrate him with subtle digs.

Bev dismissed his complaints as unfounded paranoia, but Ian knew her parents disliked him.

His final visit was to Jocelyn's work place, a hair salon a short drive from the city centre. Behind its dingy facade the salon was brightly decorated in tacky pink and silver. When the manager heard that Jocelyn had been killed, she launched into a eulogy of her dead employee.

'I knew something was wrong. It wasn't like her not to come in, and she hadn't even phoned. She had appointments in the book. The other girls had to cover.' She told Ian that Jocelyn had been one of the most talented stylists she had ever known.

'It's a tragedy,' she said, her face twisted in disbelief. 'I can't believe she's dead. The place will never be the same without her. It's going to be hard for me to keep going. We were very close. She was like a daughter to me.'

But when Ian asked what she could tell him about James, she didn't even know who he was.

CHAPTER 34

It would be virtually impossible to find DNA evidence to assist them in convicting James. He had been in close contact with his girlfriend anyway on the night she died. Apart from her killer, the waitress had probably been the last person to see the victim alive. She had witnessed Jocelyn arguing with James and walking out of the restaurant, shortly before her death. James hadn't helped his own case by admitting he had bought his girlfriend an engagement ring. He claimed he hadn't proposed yet, on account of their argument, but it was equally likely the row had erupted because she had rejected him. Ian discussed the situation with Eileen who agreed they needed to question James again urgently. He must have seen more on the night Jocelyn died than he had yet divulged. The likelihood was that he had blocked out all recollection of that night, because it was still too raw. But it was possible he had killed Jocelyn. Either way, it was time to jog his memory.

Taking Ted with him, Ian drove back to Bishopsgate. On the way he thought about the best way to approach James. He could have brought him in earlier for questioning, while he had the opportunity. In the hours he had spent running around speaking to people who knew him, he had given James a chance to gather his thoughts. But if he had interrogated him in the first place, he would have had to waste valuable hours talking to other people and might not have had enough time to put James under any sort of pressure before they had to let him go. Ian had to be sure he had enough information to convince James to confess, giving them the quick and sure result Ian's reputation needed. The criticisms levelled by Jocelyn's aunt didn't carry much weight, but Ian hoped a statement from the waitress would be enough to put pressure on James. At least she was an independent observer. Unconsciously, he put his foot down and the car leaped forward.

Leaving the car outside the block of flats, they ran up the stairs to the entrance. The light was on in James' front room but there was no response when Ian pressed the buzzer. He pressed it again. As they stood waiting another resident arrived, a middle-aged woman who scowled anxiously at Ian when he stepped forward to introduce himself. He could understand her apprehension when accosted by two strange men loitering on her doorstep, considering a woman had been murdered three days earlier, just a few minutes' walk away. Before agreeing to let them in, she called the police station to check their credentials. Ian sent Ted to watch the back exit to the building while he waited impatiently at the front. There were no other cars outside. Ian was alone on the doorstep. If James was out and came home, he would see nothing to suggest he was under suspicion. The more relaxed he was, the more likely he was to incriminate himself when Ian read out the waitress' statement.

At last the neighbour was satisfied and allowed Ian to follow her into a narrow hallway. Ignoring the doors to ground floor flats, he raced up the stairs, phone in hand. Ted answered at once.

'I'm inside,' Ian panted. 'Wait out the front. I'll bring him down that way.'

'OK, guv, but are you sure you don't want me in there with you?'

Ian hesitated before answering. He was outside James' flat, only a locked wooden door between him and the man they wanted to question. James could become violent. This was no time for bravado.

'Yes, you'd better come on up.'

Before Ted arrived, James' door flew open. He looked as though he had been asleep. His eyes were glazed and his face was flushed.

'I thought I heard—'

Recognising Ian, he broke off, suddenly alert. His shoulders dropped again almost at once, while his eyes continuously darted from side to side, checking to see if Ian was alone.

'What do you want?' he asked curtly.

His words were slightly slurred and he swayed. When he took a step closer Ian wasn't surprised to catch a whiff of alcohol.

'We'd like to ask you a few questions,' Ian said quietly.

'Well, ask me then. What do you want to know?'

'I'd like you to accompany me down to the police station.'

'No thanks. I'm not going anywhere.'

James glared belligerently at him, more drunk than Ian had first realised. He spoke slowly and clearly.

'Mr Newman, I'm sure you want to co-operate with us in finding out who killed your girlfriend. Now, if you'd like to come with me—'

Instead of answering, James leaped backwards in a panic and tried to slam the door. Ian rushed forward. Before he could reach the other man, James stuck out his foot to trip him up. As Ian struggled to maintain his balance, James landed a punch on the side of his head. Reaching out to save himself, Ian lunged at James, grabbing him by the arm and shoving him backwards. James let out an angry roar as his head banged against the wall. There was an unmistakable smell of whisky. Ian could see fine red capillaries in his bloodshot eyes, and heard his chest wheezing as he pressed his forearm against his assailant's neck, pinning him against the wall. Desperately, James pummelled Ian's arms with his fists.

'Don't be a fool. There's no point trying to resist. You'll only get yourself in more trouble. There are police officers surrounding the building.'

Choking for breath, James grew limp, all the fight drained out of him.

'That's better,' Ian said. 'There's no point in resisting. You'd never get away from here, even if you managed to get away from me.'

Ian worked quickly to secure his wrists, snapping the handcuffs closed with grim satisfaction.

'You're not helping yourself by refusing to come quietly, you know.'

'I'm innocent,' James protested. 'I never touched her. We were going to get married.'

'Save your breath. Now come on, there's a car waiting for us downstairs.'

James insisted he wanted to change his clothes, but Ian refused to release him from the handcuffs.

'Where you're going, you won't be needing any of your own clothes.'

'I'm telling you, I'm innocent. You're arresting the wrong person. It wasn't me.'

'Well, if you're innocent, like you say you are, you'll be home soon and then you can change your clothes as many times as you like. Now come on. You've wasted enough police time for one evening.'

★ ★ ★

They met Ted on the doorstep outside.

'What happened to you?'

Ted looked sheepish. 'I couldn't get in, sir. I called for back up—'

They heard a siren approaching.

'Who's wasting police time now?' James called out, as they bundled him into the car.

CHAPTER 35

There was no way James could be questioned before the following morning. Any information they managed to obtain from him in his present state would be thrown out by any court, if it even reached a prosecution. He laughed loudly as Ian led him along to the custody suite.

'You want to ask me questions,' he shouted suddenly, his speech slurred. 'Go ahead. Ask your questions and be damned.'

He flapped his manacled hands in front of him.

'Come along, sir,' Ian said doggedly. 'This way. Mind you don't touch the strip on the wall. It sets off an alarm.'

He regretted his words as soon as he mentioned the smart strip on the wall, but James didn't deliberately fall against it as some people did when they were drunk, just because they had been warned not to.

Ian steered him towards the custody sergeant's desk, relieved to hand over responsibility for his charge. The sergeant looked up and greeted them with a cheerful grin. He had seen it all before, many times.

'Come along, sir,' he called out. 'Let's get through the formalities and relieve you of those uncomfortable shoes, and whatever you've got in your pockets, and then you can go and have a nice long sleep. You'll feel better than ever in the morning.'

As if it wasn't bad enough having to wait for James to sleep off his intoxication, Eileen was shirty with Ian, although he had done nothing wrong.

'We need to get this out of the way,' she snapped, as though it was Ian's fault the suspect was drunk.

'I'll be onto it first thing in the morning, ma'am.'

Checking on the investigation into the death at the races, Ian felt as though he was stepping back in time. In the Visual Identification Images Detection Office a team of constables was still checking CCTV footage. Ian paused for a brief word with a friendly constable he had spoken to before.

'Bugger all so far, sir, if you'll pardon my French.'

Meanwhile the search team were going over the site once again. They had made no progress. There was nothing more Ian could do, so he decided he might as well go home. Before leaving, he wrote up his decision log carefully. He had a feeling he would need to be meticulous in keeping his records up to date, in case his motives were challenged at some future date. He wasn't sure Eileen would go out of her way to support him, if there was ever any query over his conduct. Of course there was no reason to expect her to stick her neck out for him, but even so it wasn't a comfortable feeling.

Bev was sitting in the kitchen when he got home. Grabbing a beer from the fridge, he flung himself down on a chair and took a long swig before asking for her news. Noticing her smart navy suit, he recalled that she had started her job that day. He sat up in his chair and smiled expectantly at her, signifying his interest, and felt a pang of guilt at seeing how pleased she was. He tried to concentrate as she began to tell him all about her irritating line manager.

'She's only about twenty-five, although she looks nearer forty, and she's a real bitch. You know she refused to give me a key to the office. I used to *run* an office bigger than that, and the stupid cow doesn't trust me with a key. It's bloody ridiculous. Talk about controlling! What if she's not there, how the hell am I supposed to get in then?'

'You should discuss it with her.'

'I did, at least I tried to, but she's impossible.'

'It's early days,' Ian said. 'She probably just wants to make sure she can trust you, like an unofficial probationary period.'

Bev muttered darkly under her breath.

★   ★   ★

Ian yawned and took another swig of beer.

'Well, if she's ever *not* there, you can come home and have a day off.'

Too late he realised his words could be construed as tactless, given that she had just started a new job. Immediately she started to vent her irritation on him. He tried to look contrite, while doing his best to block out her words as she complained he never valued her work.

'I know what I do is pointless, it doesn't matter if I'm there or not, does it? But you can't be spared from your important job, even on a Sunday, or a Saturday night. You're so bloody needed at work. But I can just take a day off any time, and it wouldn't make any difference to anything.'

Ian wasn't sure what she wanted him to say.

'If you hate it there so much, you can always leave,' he ventured tentatively.

He expected her to jump on his words with another tirade about the insignificance of what she did. To his surprise she responded mildly, telling him that apart from her immediate boss, the job wasn't too bad. With a smile, Ian stood up and pulled her close, wrapping his arms around her and leaning down to kiss her. For all his training in interrogation and judging whether people's responses were truthful or not, he hadn't the faintest idea what went on inside his wife's head. But right now, he wasn't thinking about her mind.

'Stop it,' she protested half heartedly, 'I'm wearing a work suit. You'll get it all creased.'

'Let's go upstairs and take it off then,' he answered, hoping she wouldn't laugh at his clumsy words.

He couldn't think of anything else to say, so he lifted her off her feet. She threw her arms around his neck as he carried her into the living room.

'Not on the settee, Ian,' she laughed.

He took no notice.

CHAPTER 36

Emma left early on Sunday. That night Richard slept well for the first time in weeks. He woke feeling pumped and ready for action. With Emma out of the house, the phone calls were no longer such a worry, at least for the time being. More importantly, Emma was out of harm's way. The next time he received a call, he would insist on meeting his tormentor. However extortionate the blackmailer's demands might be, at least Richard would know what he was dealing with. It would be futile for anyone to try and squeeze him for more than he was able to pay. He had just over five thousand pounds in a savings account. At a pinch he could scrape together another five thousand. With a loan and an overdraft, he might stretch to twenty thousand. Although nothing had really changed, having calculated his limit he felt he had regained some control over the situation. Once Emma heard about his sexual encounters it would no longer be possible to blackmail him and so he was confident his secret wouldn't be exposed before he had a chance to negotiate terms. He would tell the blackmailer he couldn't afford more than ten thousand, and take it from there. Having resigned himself to the fact that he would have to part with a substantial sum, he accepted that paying up might not be the end of it. But for the time being, the priority was to fend off immediate trouble. After that, as long as he remained a source of income for his blackmailer, he would be safe and Emma would be protected.

After work on Monday, he dropped the car at the garage. It saved him having to get up really early the next morning to drive there before work. Instead of catching the bus he strolled back across town, enjoying the mild weather. There was a slight breeze, but it wasn't cold. Out in the fresh air, he felt a sense of wellbeing. Emma was safe with her parents, and he was ready to buy his way out of his tricky situation before she returned. As he approached the town centre, the pavements became congested. He passed several groups of women, chattering and laughing. Their youth and exuberance made him horny. With no particular destination in mind he wandered around until he found himself down by the river. He didn't feel like going home yet. He climbed the stairs up onto Skeldergate Bridge. Leaning on the ornate metal railing, he stared down at the fuzzy reflection of the sky in the rippling water. Against the evening skyline the tower of the Minster rose tall and square. Past that, Clifford's Tower was indiscernible, concealed behind trees and bushes. Down below, a line of red hire boats lay moored along the far bank.

With a shudder he recalled seeing that same scene on the local news, with a headline screaming: 'York Killer Strikes Again'. Not for the first time, he wondered if he was withholding information that might help the police discover the identity of the killer. If he *was* going to report his nuisance calls, he ought to do it while Emma was away. But he wasn't confident the police would respect his request for discretion. It would be crazy to lose his girlfriend because some stupid plod shot his mouth off. On balance he decided it was best not to risk it. The police could do their job just as well without his help. It wasn't as if he had any useful information that might point them in the right direction. He couldn't even remember what the voice on the phone sounded like, although he would recognise it if he heard it again.

The sky grew darker and the breeze turned chilly. Feeling hungry, he set off back into town. Trotting down the steps at the end of the bridge, he glanced over his shoulder and glimpsed a hooded figure at the top of the stairs. With one leg extended, the man appeared poised to descend. Apart from that lone figure, there was no one else in sight. As Richard watched, the figure swivelled round and disappeared. Shoving his hands into his coat pockets, Richard walked rapidly into town. Street lamps flickered on up ahead. Around him shadows darkened. Glancing back, he noticed a hooded figure walking behind him. Turning off, he looked back over his shoulder. The other pedestrian had rounded the corner behind him, apparently following him. He walked faster. Although there was no reason to feel nervous, he was relieved when he reached the main road. The nuisance calls had made him jumpy.

He passed several restaurants, breathing in tantalising aromas. Passing a Chinese restaurant off the main road with a sign advertising an 'All You Can Eat Buffet', he dithered on the pavement for a few seconds. He wasn't sure what it would be like, but the menu was cheap and he was starving. He went in. Everything had been deep fried in batter, and tasted greasy. Washed down with beer, the fatty food lay heavily in his guts. It wasn't long before he regretted having wolfed it down so quickly. Feeling bloated but relaxed, he set off for home, his confidence restored. He hoped he would see someone following him so he could beat the crap out of the bastard for scaring him, but there was no one behind him now. His anxiety over the nuisance phone calls had faded. Whenever Emma went away, which wasn't often, he would eat out and meet other women. He had managed the first, at any rate.

★   ★   ★

Without warning he was almost dragged off his feet as a bony arm was flung around his throat, constricting his breathing. He had been mugged before. Still fairly sober, he kept his presence of mind.

'Take my cash,' he rasped, struggling to speak. 'I've got over sixty quid on me, but you don't want to bother with my phone. It's packing up anyway—'

The lie sounded pathetic but he had to try. It would be a nuisance if his phone was lifted, especially with Emma away. He wasn't sure he knew her number. A sour smell of alcohol engulfed him, making him feel sick. Inside his ear someone giggled.

'I don't want your phone.'

Richard froze, recognising the voice.

'We've chatted enough on the phone. I thought it was time we met, in the flesh.'

At the word 'flesh,' Richard felt the grip around his throat tighten. Another chuckle bubbled out of his assailant's throat. It sounded as though he was gargling.

Richard jolted to his senses, realising he had allowed his assailant to terrify him into submission. There were occasions when it was stupid to resist an attack, but this was no violent mugger. He was being throttled by a man who had threatened to kill him. He wasn't about to die without at least attempting to defend himself. As he tensed to fight back, the other man suddenly let go. No longer supported from behind, Richard staggered backwards. Regaining his balance, he spun round and started forward, but his legs were shaking. There was no way he would catch up with his assailant, who was sprinting down the road. Frantically Richard pulled out his phone and took several photos of the figure as it raced away. It was no use. All he could see was the back of a hooded figure in a grey track suit, disappearing into the darkness. The stranger looked fit, and was probably quite tall, but beyond that he had no visible discernible characteristics. It occurred to Richard that he might have missed his only opportunity to end the nightmare once and for all. He might not have a second chance.

Cursing himself for letting his stalker go, he staggered home, dizzy and disorientated. His legs felt weak as he kicked off his shoes and glanced in the hall mirror. Black marks on his neck turned dark purple when he switched on the light. The bruises could be concealed beneath a scarf. He couldn't hide them from Emma and would have to come up with some excuse to satisfy her curiosity. But right now he faced a more serious problem. His hands shook as he poured himself a tumbler of whisky. The stalker's threats had changed from verbal to physical. In Richard's heightened state of terror, he had been incapable of resisting an attack which could have proved lethal. Only when he calmed down did he realise that, despite having issued death threats, his assailant hadn't killed him when he had the chance. The stalker was just trying to scare him. He poured himself another whisky. His life wasn't in danger at all. This was all about money.

CHAPTER 37

By the time the suspect had been woken and fed the following morning, and given all the care to which he was entitled, the duty solicitor had arrived and they were ready to start the interview. Ian knew it was counterproductive to cut corners in the treatment of a suspect. Apart from the Police and Criminal Investigations Act that safeguarded the rights of suspects in custody, there was the threat of violation of human rights the newspapers loved to invoke, when it suited them. Allegations of police brutality were easily concocted. The damage such stories caused could be devastating, both to the public perception of the force as a whole, and to individual officer's careers, even where the complaint subsequently proved to be a complete fabrication. Apart from all of that, failure to follow the rules to the letter meant they risked compromising a carefully constructed case.

Satisfied they had adhered to the guidelines, Ian began. The solicitor looked uncomfortable in a tweed suit that was too tight for her plump figure. Her wild curly hair sprang out crazily in all directions, bobbing around distractingly when she moved her head, while she sounded so breathless whenever she spoke he wondered if she was asthmatic.

'Don't you worry,' she addressed her client in a wheezy undertone, 'we'll soon have you out of here.'

She threw a defiant glance at Ian who ignored her naive tactics. James visibly relaxed. Ian had been intending to put pressure on him, in the hope that he would crack. The solicitor's opening gambit seemed to have put paid to that idea, for the time being at least. Perhaps she wasn't as inexperienced as she looked. On the other hand, it might help if Ian could catch the suspect off guard. The solicitor's reassurance might not prove a hindrance after all.

'Tell me, in your own words, what happened on Friday night.'

'I've already told you.'

'I'd like to hear it again.'

'I don't think I can remember everything—'

'Tell me what you *can* remember.'

James shrugged and glanced sideways at his brief who smiled encouragingly at him.

'I was a bit drunk.'

'What else can you remember?' Ian repeated.

Haltingly, James gave an account of his movements on the night his fiancée was killed.

'You said she was your fiancée?'

'That's right. We were planning to get married.'

'She wasn't wearing an engagement ring.'

'No. I hadn't given it to her yet.'

'But you had bought her a ring?'

'Yes. I showed it to you.'

'That looked like a very expensive engagement ring. It must have set you back a fair bit.'

When James didn't answer, Ian pressed his point home. 'You must have been pretty sure she'd agree to marry you.'

'I knew she would. We'd already agreed. We'd been discussing it for months.'

'So you spent a small fortune on an expensive engagement ring for her?'

'Yes. I wanted her to have the best of everything.'

'It must have made you angry when, after all that, she rejected you?'

'What?'

James turned to his solicitor and began talking very fast. He spoke so quietly Ian couldn't make out what he was saying. Ian stared straight ahead, hoping his face betrayed nothing of his satisfaction at having riled James.

At last the solicitor turned to Ian. 'My client has already told you they were planning to get married.'

'Then why wasn't she wearing the engagement ring he bought her?'

'My client has already answered that,' the solicitor said firmly. She swung round in her chair. 'You don't have to answer that again, Mr Newman. And,' she added, turning back to Ian, 'it's perfectly clear what happened. My client was planning to propose when he took her out for dinner on Friday. Go on.'

James nodded at her. He turned back to Ian. He looked like a trapped animal.

'I took her to a nice restaurant, so I could propose,' he began.

All at once he sounded slightly hysterical and his cheeks were flushed.

'You said you had already agreed to get married.'

'In principle, yes, but we hadn't made it official yet, we hadn't fixed a date or anything. I wanted to get engaged so we could start making plans. We both did.'

James sounded close to tears. His lips twitched.

'Why did Jocelyn run out of the restaurant? Be careful what you say. We have independent witnesses who saw what happened that night in the restaurant. There's no point in trying to hide it, James. She turned you down and you lost your temper, didn't you?'

James denied the allegation vigorously. 'I didn't lose my temper. I'm not like that.'

'That's not what we've been told.'

'Whoever you spoke to, they're lying. It's her family, isn't it? Spreading lies about me. They never thought I was good enough for her.'

'But you admit you were angry on Friday evening?'

James nodded, wordlessly.

'And when you're angry, you get violent. Isn't that the case?'

'No. That's not true. I'm not a violent man.'

'You were quick enough to pick a fight with me when I came to see you.'

'That's different. I was drunk.'

'Is that why you tried to hit me?'

'Yes, no – I didn't know what I was doing. I told you, I was drunk.'

The solicitor turned and stared at James.

'Is that what you do, James, hit people when you're drunk?' Ian asked.

'No, no.'

'You were drunk on Friday evening, at the restaurant with Jocelyn.'

'No – that is, I'd been drinking. Who doesn't have a few glasses of wine when they go out for dinner?'

'And when you're drunk you become violent, isn't that the case? Like you did with me.'

'Look, you threatened me and I reacted. I felt intimidated. I would never have hurt Jocelyn. I loved her. I told you, I wanted to marry her.'

The solicitor broke in.

'When did this alleged assault against you take place, Inspector? I'm not aware that any charge has been levelled against my client. Do you have any witnesses for this alleged assault? Independent witnesses, that is.'

Ignoring her interruption, Ian pressed on.

'Why did Jocelyn leave the restaurant without you?'

'Because – because we'd had an argument. It had nothing to do with getting married. I hadn't even got round to asking her. She wouldn't have said no.' He heaved a deep sigh. 'If I'd asked her, she wouldn't have gone running off like that and . . .'

'Why didn't you ask her?'

'I've already told you, I was annoyed because she was in a mood. It just wasn't the right moment to propose.'

'Why was she in a mood? What had you done to upset her?'

There was a knock at the door. Frowning at the interruption, Ian looked up to see Ted beckoning him vigorously. Out in the corridor, Ted spoke in a rapid whisper. The team searching James' records had discovered a credit card payment for two tickets to the races the previous Saturday. Ian nodded and they returned to the interview room together.

'What were you doing at the races last Saturday?' Ian demanded.

James raised his eyebrows. 'At the races?' he repeated. He glanced at his brief who sat stony-faced, waiting.

'What were you doing there?' Ian repeated.

James shrugged. 'Watching the horses. Having a flutter. What does anyone do there?'

'Was anyone else with you?'

'Jocelyn.' James' face crumpled, but he rallied. 'She was feeling rough so we left early. She never could hold her drink,' he added morosely. 'Spoiled a perfectly good day out.'

'What were you wearing?'

James looked surprised at the question. 'Oh shit, I don't know. Jeans and a jumper. A blue jumper, I think.'

Ian frowned at Ted who nodded. It didn't sound as though James had been dressed for the county stand where Adrian was killed. Ian paused the interview while Ted went to check. He confirmed James had bought tickets for the grandstand.

'James, this is very important. What time did you leave the races?'

'I told you, I don't know. I'd been drinking, all right? I didn't look at the time.'

Ted put a photograph on the table in front of James. 'Do you recognise this man?'

James stared at it for a few seconds. 'Yes.'

Doing his best to keep his voice steady, Ian asked how James had known him.

'I didn't know him. I've seen his face in the paper, that's all. He's the man who – oh my God—' He broke off suddenly recollecting where he had seen Adrian's picture before. 'I never said I knew him.' He turned to the solicitor in a panic.

'You recognised him straight away,' Ian pointed out, but it was too late.

'I need to speak to my client,' the lawyer interrupted firmly.

CHAPTER 38

While they had been talking to James, Ted had left a constable looking into James' visit to the races. They already knew he had paid for his tickets by credit card, booking the grandstand, not the county stand where Adrian had been killed.

'And take a look at this, sir,' the constable added. 'It was taken last Saturday.'

He held out a mobile phone. Ian scrolled through several photographs taken at the Knavesmire. Most were of Jocelyn, laughing and pulling faces. Only one showed James with his arm around her shoulders. He was wearing a dark blue jumper.

'Is it easy to move between the two?' Ian asked.

'Almost impossible,' Ted replied. 'Otherwise everyone would try it on. The county stand tickets are more expensive and it's a more comfortable experience altogether than watching from the grandstand.'

'Almost impossible?' Ian seized on the phrase. 'Would it have been possible for a man in a green blazer?'

'Who would then have a motive for wanting to silence the only witness able to tell us what happened that day at the races,' Ted added, with growing excitement.

Ian shook his head. That was the problem. If James had gone to the races intending to kill Adrian, he wouldn't have risked discovery by paying for his tickets by credit card. He'd have been even less likely to take a companion with him who might become suspicious, and say something indiscreet. Ted wasn't deterred by Ian's reservations.

'What if he had never intended to kill Adrian, but only to talk to him, maybe confront him about something – or maybe he didn't even know him and they fell into an argument. It could have been a spur of the moment attack, sir. We know he's prone to violence when he's drunk, and there's a lot of drinking goes on at the races.'

Ian shook his head again. 'No. Adrian's murder was carefully planned. There's no way it was an unpremeditated drunken assault. The killer had worked out his movements in advance. He was really careful to leave no trace. James booked his tickets on his credit card and he took his girlfriend with him. And anyway, he wasn't wearing a green blazer in the photo, and he's not carrying a bag. Where did he put his disguise?'

'He could have hidden the blazer and the

moustache and glasses somewhere on site before-hand,' Ted suggested, but he no longer sounded convinced.

'He was at the races on Saturday, but so were thousands of other people, ma'am. We can't find anything to link him to Adrian, but he hasn't got an alibi for the time of Jocelyn's murder.'

'Has he confessed?' Eileen wanted to know.

'Not yet. I'm working on it.'

She looked closely at him. 'You're not in any doubt he killed her, are you?'

'Everything points to him,' Ian answered carefully.

He didn't want to sound indecisive, but the truth was he couldn't make up his mind about James. He didn't like him. He had possibly treated Jocelyn quite cruelly. At best he had been insensitive towards her. But that didn't mean he was a murderer. If every man who was unkind to his wife or girlfriend was convicted as a criminal, there wouldn't be many men left on the streets.

'Good. Let's get this one wrapped up then so you can get back to the races case. We seem to be going nowhere fast with that one. It's a shame we can't put James in the frame for both.'

Eileen sounded as exasperated as Ian felt.

He had left Ted in charge of the search team which was still looking for evidence at the racetrack. They seemed to be casting around fruitlessly. It could take weeks or even months to discover the truth. In the meantime, pressure was mounting for a result. It was unfortunate that Adrian had been murdered so spectacularly, in such a public place. Not only were there hundreds of witnesses – none of whom had seen anything that might help the police find the killer – but the media had been thrown into a frenzy over it. 'Death at the Races', the headlines screamed, 'Death Plunge', and many more in a similar vein. The atmosphere at the police station was growing more tense every day, with journalists regularly accosting officers outside the entrance to the building, all eager to be first with any new development. Even the nationals were following the story. It was impossible to step outside the station without being approached by a reporter gagging for a scoop.

With the furore over Adrian's murder, Ian was as keen as Eileen to get a result over Jocelyn's case. At least they could tie that one up quickly. After lunch, Ian interviewed James again. This time he adopted a more aggressive approach.

'Can you account for your movements after you left the restaurant at ten twenty?' He paused briefly, staring straight at James. 'That was about ten minutes before your girlfriend was murdered, about five minutes' walk from the restaurant. You might as well make this easy for yourself and tell us the truth. The sooner you confess, the easier it will be for you. It's pointless wasting any more police time. We all know what happened.'

James spoke loudly and firmly, looking askance at his lawyer as he spoke.

'I didn't kill her.'

The lawyer gave a brief nod. Ian looked away from her smug face and stared at James.

'What happened after you left the restaurant?'

'I went home.'

Ian sat forward. He had studied the route.

'Did you go via the bridge?'

'What?'

'You must have crossed Skeldergate Bridge on your way home.'

'Yes.'

'So you walked past Jocelyn.'

'No.' James rubbed his forehead, as though he wanted to erase his frown. 'That is, I didn't see her.'

'You didn't see her?'

'No. That is, I don't remember seeing her. I was drunk.'

'So you don't remember what happened?'

The lawyer interrupted sharply. 'I'd like a moment alone with my client.'

Ian ignored her. 'What happened while you were walking home, James? What do you remember?'

James shook his head, staring wildly at Ian.

'I don't remember anything,' he cried out suddenly. 'I don't remember anything.'

Ian sat back in his chair and spoke softly.

'You and Jocelyn argued in the restaurant, didn't you?'

James nodded dumbly.

'You were angry. There's no point in denying it, James. We have a witness who heard you shouting at her. Jocelyn walked out and that made you even more angry, didn't it? It's understandable. You'd spent nearly two thousand pounds on an engagement ring. You'd taken her to an expensive restaurant. And she walked out on you. That was outrageous, wasn't it? You were justifiably angry.'

'You can't say that—' the solicitor interrupted anxiously.

'It's the truth, isn't it, James?'

'Yes, yes, it's the truth.'

'You were walking home and you saw her walking ahead of you.' Ian paused, aware of how important his next words were. 'You followed her.' He swallowed. 'You were in a rage and you lost control. That's right, isn't it?' James didn't answer. 'You never meant to kill her, did you?'

For a few seconds no one spoke. A clock ticked in the room. Somewhere, far away, a door banged. Ian watched James' face closely. The suspect's resolve was visibly crumbling. His lips were quivering, and he looked as though he was going to burst into tears. It was fantastic. Ian struggled to sit still. He wanted to jump up and yell at the man to confess. 'We know you did it. Just say the words, James. You'll feel so much better. We know anyway. Say the words.' But he kept quiet, waiting patiently for James to surrender the truth. Finally, his lips moved soundlessly.

Ian leaned forward. 'What did you say?'

'I can't remember,' James whispered. 'I can't remember.'

At his side, the solicitor sniffed disapprovingly. 'You don't have to say any more, James.'

'We were in the restaurant together. She was in a mood and left. I finished my wine and paid the bill. I walked home. The next thing I remember is waking up with a hangover. That's all I remember.'

It was enough. Eileen convened a press conference straight away. Within an hour she was addressing the assembled reporters.

'A man has been arrested in connection with the murder of Jocelyn Sands—' she announced solemnly.

'What about the murder at the races?'

'Is it the same man who killed Adrian Curtis?'

Eileen held up one hand.

'Jocelyn Sands was only twenty-two when she was killed by Skeldergate Bridge,' she continued with her prepared speech.

Ian had to hand it to her that she handled the

situation well. As soon as she mentioned the victim's age, her audience fell silent.

As Ian stood listening, a constable approached him.

'There's a call I think you should take, sir.'

'Is it about James?'

'I don't think so, sir. It's Dr Hetherington. He's on the line now.'

With a grunt, Ian went to his office and picked up the phone.

'I don't know if you're going to like this,' Jonah said straight away. 'It's about Jocelyn Sands.'

'Go on.'

'You might not like this.'

'You've already said that.'

'Traces of Pentaketaphine were found in her blood, and metabolites, or breakdown products, similar to the toxicology results from Adrian Curtis.'

'You mean they were killed by the same person?'

'That's not for me to say, but off the record, it would be quite a coincidence if the two deaths weren't related, don't you think?'

CHAPTER 39

The whole team was excited to hear about the apparent connection between the two murders. Word had spread quickly so that, by the time Eileen convened a meeting, everyone at the station seemed to know about the results of the toxicology report on Jocelyn. Ian gazed around the Major Incident Room that had been set up in the station for the investigation into Adrian's death. Apart from Ted and Eileen, there were a couple of sergeants who had been supervising searches, both online and physical. They had been looking into the crime scenes, victims and suspects. Several constables were in charge of teams questioning witnesses. The work was still going on.

'We need to find a link between Adrian and James,' Eileen said, 'or else a link between Adrian and Jocelyn. Somehow there's a connection there. Did Adrian come to York to see Jocelyn?'

An excited buzz of conversation greeted this suggestion. It opened up new possibilities.

'Do you think Adrian and Jocelyn were having an affair?' someone suggested.

'And James found out and killed them both in a fit of jealousy,' another voice added eagerly.

'Before we start speculating, let's find our evidence,' Eileen said. 'We have to find the link between the two victims, any evidence they were ever in the same place at the same time. Check everything.'

Even the prospect of hours trawling through bank statements, travel records, hotel bookings, and everything else they could think of didn't dampen the team's enthusiasm. Once Eileen had finished speaking, there was an immediate bustle of activity. While the research teams were galvanised by the new information, Ian made his way back to the mortuary.

'She was strangled—' Jonah began, pointing to the dead girl's neck where the marks made by her killer were visible.

'After she was drugged,' Ian finished the sentence.

Jonah shook his head.

'That's what I wanted to see you about,' he said. 'I didn't want to try and explain this over the phone because frankly – well, it's very odd.'

Ian waited, but the pathologist just frowned at the body without speaking.

Ian shifted impatiently, and the portly pathologist seemed to shake himself out of a reverie.

'Defence wounds,' he announced.

Jonah lifted one of the dead girl's hands and Ian noticed the nails were chipped, the knuckles grazed.

'There are indications she tried to fight her attacker off.'

A surge of adrenaline coursed through Ian. He was so excited, he struggled to breathe normally as he asked whether any blood or skin had been found under her nails. But Jonah shook his head.

'Nothing from anyone else, I'm afraid. The killer was wearing gloves, leather gloves by the look of the bruising on her neck, and he kept himself out of her reach.'

'But he strangled her,' Ian protested, feeling cheated.

Ignoring Ian's plaintive tone, Jonah continued briskly. 'Her killer dragged her down the steps while she was still alive and mobile. I think he covered her mouth with one hand, to prevent her crying out for help. Can you see the faint bruising here, round the mouth and chin? She managed to reach out. Chips of her nail polish, with traces of nail still attached, were found on the wall beside the steps where she was killed, along with minute scraps of skin from her knuckles.'

'But nothing under her nails from the killer?'

'Nothing from him,' Jonah concurred gravely.

Ian was disappointed. 'This tells us nothing at all about the killer, then.'

He wondered why the pathologist had insisted on seeing him.

*   *   *

Jonah shook his head. 'I don't think you appreciate the significance of the defence wounds. I'm not sure I understand it myself. There were scraps of skin under her nails that came from her own neck. And look—' he pointed at a couple of scratches on the victim's neck. 'Those are from finger nails, but the killer was wearing gloves.'

Ian frowned.

'All this indicates she was trying to fight her attacker off while he was strangling her,' Jonah went on. 'Yet she'd been injected with Pentaketaphine, which begins to take effect almost straight away. How did she manage to struggle against her killer while he was dragging her down the steps, and still be struggling while he was strangling her, if she had been injected with the drug?'

Ian was confused. He wasn't sure what the pathologist was telling him, but Jonah hadn't finished.

'There's more. Not only did she continue to be mobile right up to her death, but the tox lab reported traces of the drug in her system. But enzymes in the blood begin to break the drug down almost immediately. There was no way I'd expect the drug to be evident in her blood, anywhere, after death.'

'So she must have been injected very shortly before she died?'

'While her killer was holding her down with one hand and strangling her with the other?'

It was a rhetorical question.

*　　*　　*

'I missed the puncture mark at first because she was injected here, look, right in the centre of this tiny mole in her neck. The wound's barely visible even under strong magnification. I only found it because I was looking specifically for a puncture wound that didn't appear to be there. Hitting that exact spot would have been tricky if she was moving, even to someone with a steady hand.'

'I'm sorry, I'm not sure I understand what you're trying to tell me.'

Jonah shrugged. 'I can't claim to understand it myself, but it's not my job to make sense of the facts. My job is just to report them. And what I'm telling you is that she appears to have been injected post mortem. There is no other explanation for the facts.'

When Ian arrived back at the station, Eileen summoned him. He hurried along the corridor to her office, hoping to hear new evidence had come to light that would move them forward. The news was disappointing. A constable watching CCTV footage of the turnstile had spotted James and Jocelyn leaving the races. He was able to pinpoint the exact time. It was just over an hour before the time of Adrian's death. Less than half an hour later, the couple were recorded on a close circuit camera on a bus travelling back into town. It was conclusive. James could not be implicated in Adrian's murder.

'But he remains a suspect for Jocelyn's death,' Eileen added.

Ian told her what he had learned at the pathology lab.

She frowned. 'So he's telling us we're looking for one killer?'

'What he said was, it would be a coincidence if the two deaths weren't related.'

Eileen's frown deepened. 'Don't like coincidences,' she said tersely.

'Me neither, ma'am.'

She sighed. 'OK, we'd better release James, for now.'

Ian nodded. 'I'll make sure he doesn't go far,' he said.

'We've wasted a lot of time on him already.'

Ian wasn't sure if that was a criticism. He left her office without answering. They were both disappointed to discover they were investigating a double murder, with no leads to the killer.

Discussing the toxicology report with Ted, Ian agreed it suggested that whoever had killed Jocelyn had also killed Adrian. But the sequence of events surrounding Jocelyn's death was unclear. The presence of the drug in her blood stream was problematic.

'Why would the killer want to incapacitate her after killing her?' Ian asked.

'To make sure she wouldn't recover?'

It seemed to be the only possible explanation, although it didn't make much sense.

'Do you think there could have been two people there, one to kill her, the other administering the drug?' Ted suggested, but that didn't make much sense either.

Two killers wouldn't have needed to incapacitate the victim. They could have simply overpowered her. But why anyone would want to inject a dead body with a drug that caused instant paralysis was a mystery.

'It doesn't make any sense,' Ted sighed. 'Oh well, I suppose all killers are crazy when it comes down to it. This one's just a bit kookier than some.'

If he hadn't been so tired, Ian thought he would have perceived the killer's motive straight away. As it was, the obvious answer didn't occur to him until he was driving home. For reasons they might never fathom, the killer *wanted* the police to know the murders of Adrian and Jocelyn were connected. The more Ian thought about it, the more convinced he became that he was right. There was no other explanation for the presence of Pentaketaphine in Jocelyn's blood stream. He called Ted.

'It's the same killer,' he blurted out. 'He wants to make sure we know. That's why he used Pentaketaphine on both victims. He needed it to immobilise Adrian, but in Jocelyn's case he wanted the forensic lab to detect the drug. That's why he used it on her after she was dead, so if she wasn't found straight away, the drug would still be present in her blood stream. He injected her after she died, to make sure not that she was really dead, but that her death would be linked to Adrian's.'

There was a pause. He could almost hear Ted thinking at the other end of the line.

'Why?'

'Perhaps he's using it as his signature. He waited deliberately until Jocelyn was dead so the drug wouldn't decompose after he injected her.'

'But why would he want us to link the two victims? Surely that doubles the chance he'll be caught.'

Ian shrugged, although Ted wasn't there to see the gesture. 'I've no idea what game he's playing.'

'Cocky bastard thinks we'll never find him. Do you think he's doing it to taunt us?'

Ian didn't answer. He had a horrible feeling the killer was playing a more dangerous game than either he or Ted could imagine.

CHAPTER 40

The mortgage was paid off with Adrian's death so the house belonged to her now. She would be responsible for paying all the household bills, and taking care of the property when things went wrong. She blinked, sniffing furiously.

'Are you all right?'

She grunted, flicking her head so that her hair fell forward over her eyes. She wished Charles would go away and leave her alone.

'I've got to call in at my office this afternoon,' he went on, 'but I'll be back as soon as I can.'

She nodded, unsmiling. She hated the way he spoke to her, yet much as she resented his patronising tone, she wasn't sure she could cope by herself. The prospect of living on her own terrified her.

'You don't need to worry about anything,' he continued. 'I'm here to take care of you. I owe that much to Adrian, at least.'

She had a panicky feeling he was never going to leave her in peace, and couldn't contain her irritation any longer.

'You don't need to be with me all the time,' she burst out. 'Give me some space, will you? I feel like I can't breathe without you standing over me.'

If he was taken aback by her outburst, he kept his feelings to himself.

'It's all right, I understand.'

'Understand what?'

'It must be hard for you, coming back here. Would you rather stay at my place for a while? I thought you'd feel more comfortable if we came here, but maybe I was wrong.'

As he leaned down to kiss her, she turned her head aside. He smiled to show he understood, and left, promising to be back very soon.

Through a gap in the curtain she watched him walk away down the front path. His powerful physique made her feel more vulnerable than ever. He belonged to a world of adults for whom life wasn't a source of constant anxiety. It seemed as though she was always worrying, only this time it was worse. She was afraid. Frowning, she turned away, feeling like an interloper in her own hushed home. A long hot shower made her feel better. Wrapping her dressing gown around her, she went into the kitchen and rummaged around. Unable to find anything she wanted to eat, she made a mug of tea and took it into the living room. At last she was alone, with time to think. One way or another she had to rid herself of Charles. The thought of him sickened her. She couldn't believe she had once found him attractive. Not only was she disturbed about what he had done to Adrian, she was frightened of what he might do to her. He had disappeared shortly before Adrian's dramatic fall from the balcony. Sooner or later he was going to realise she would work out where he had gone. The more she thought about it, the more obvious it seemed that he had thrown his brother off the balcony to pave the way for him to be with her. If she hadn't been seduced by her brother-in-law's smooth talking, Adrian would still be alive.

While she was crying, her phone rang. Recognising the number, she declined the call. He rang again. She ignored it. When he called for the third time, she answered. He said he wanted to reassure himself she was all right, but it seemed to her that he was calling to check up on her.

'I felt like a heel going off and leaving you alone. I should never have gone off like that.'

Vivien tried to remind him that she hadn't wanted him to stay, hadn't wanted him around her all the time, hadn't wanted him to come into the house, but she broke down again. Maddeningly, he assumed she was crying because she was grateful for his call.

'Obviously you're bound to be on a bit of an emotional roller coaster for a few days,' he went on, oblivious to her feeble objection, 'but that will pass. Now, I'll be round in an hour or so. Are you going to be all right?'

She was too upset to argue.

'I'll be fine,' she hiccupped. 'I just want to be left alone.'

But he had already hung up.

Sipping tepid tea, still tearful, she considered her options. The truth was, she didn't have anywhere else to go. Unless she ran off, leaving virtually everything she owned tied up in the house, she was stuck there. She felt guilty that she wasn't grieving for Adrian, but all she could think about was Charles. Her suspicion of him was too dreadful to contemplate, yet she couldn't get it out of her mind. With sudden resolution, she jumped up. He would be back soon. Whatever else happened, she didn't want to face him. If he realised that she suspected him of killing his own brother, there was no knowing what he might do. One conclusion was inescapable: she wouldn't be safe as long as he was in the house. She ran along the hall to the front door. Her fingers trembled as she slid the bolt across. It felt cold against her finger tips. She checked the back door and went round all the ground floor windows, making sure they were properly closed. Finally, she went upstairs.

As she reached the first floor landing, she heard a loud rattling downstairs. Charles had returned and was at the front door, trying to open it. The shrill summons of the bell startled her. Her legs were shaking so badly she could hardly stand. She stood on the stairs, clutching the banister, praying that he would go away. He knocked again and she heard him calling her name. Ignoring him wouldn't help. If anything, it was likely to fuel his passion. He had always been importunate about seeing her. Still, if she opened the door with the chain on, he wouldn't be able to get in. Whatever he said she would remain firm, resisting any show of affection from him. Letting him sleep in her marriage bed was completely out of the question. Her legs were still trembling as she went back downstairs. She reached out to open the door. Just thinking about what he had done made her feel physically sick. She hated him more than she had ever hated anyone before, and she was terrified of what he might do to her.

CHAPTER 41

Ian would be passing close to where his former detective inspector was working. On the off chance that she would be able to get away, he called her when he was half an hour from King's Cross station.

'Where are you now?'

'I'll be at Kings Cross in half an hour.'

'Perfect. Where do you need to get to?'

'I'm getting the Piccadilly line over to Acton Town—'

'Why don't I meet you at Kings Cross then?' she interrupted him. 'We can go for a coffee, or a bite to eat if you like.'

'Great.'

'I can't stay long.'

'Me neither.'

'Fine. See you in half an hour then, outside the station.'

Ian hung up, surprised by how excited he was at the prospect of seeing Geraldine again. They had worked closely together every day for years, but it was a while since he had last seen her. He wondered whether living in London would have changed her, although he couldn't imagine her being any different. Whatever the circumstances, she always maintained an outward composure, nothing like his volatile wife. He supposed it was the way they were trained to cope with extreme situations. Ian was one of the few people ever to have seen her let down her guard – perhaps the only person to have done so. Catching himself comparing his wife unfavourably to Geraldine, he pulled himself up sharply. It was hardly a fair comparison. He had never lived with Geraldine. All the same, their work had created a strong bond between them, as so often happened in the emergency services where colleagues might literally depend on each other for their survival.

He spotted Geraldine straight away. Although there was nothing particularly remarkable in her short black hair and large dark eyes, an air of self-assurance set her apart as a woman used to commanding authority. She took him to a pub round the corner from the station. They had a lot to talk about, having both moved on from the Kent constabulary where they had worked together. They gossiped about their former colleagues, and compared notes about their current stations. Tucking into pie and chips, Ian was pleased to hear that Geraldine was feeling more settled in London.

'What about you?' she asked. 'Not too quiet for you up North?'

Ian told her about the case he was working on, and she grinned.

'Oh my God, yes, I read about that. The death at the races. A bloke falling off a five-storey balcony in suspicious circumstances, wasn't it?'

Ian smiled. Geraldine's recall of detail had been legendary on the Kent constabulary. This wasn't even her case, yet she remembered Adrian had fallen five storeys. He wished she was working on the case with him.

Leaning forward and lowering his voice, he told her about the drug that had been used to incapacitate Adrian. Geraldine's eyes widened.

'And now we've got the same drug used on another victim,' he concluded. 'What are the chances of that being coincidence?'

'Not much, if you ask me. It sounds like the same killer. What's the connection between the victims?'

'That's the trouble. We can't find anything to link them. The second victim's a young woman.' He took a swig of coffee before continuing. 'We've looked, but we can't find any common ground between the two victims.'

Geraldine frowned. 'Look harder,' she said.

Ian nodded. She was right. The truth was always there somewhere. The problem was finding it.

'What do we know about the drug?' she asked after a pause. 'What was it called again?'

'Pentaketaphine.'

'That's got to be a good starting point. Drugs like that are strictly controlled, aren't they, and it's not that common. Who would have access to it? It can't go missing without leaving a trace.'

'We've checked all the suppliers, nationwide, and drawn a blank. No one has reported a break-in anywhere, or any supplies missing.'

'Maybe this is someone who controls the supply?'

Ian shook his head. 'Believe me, we've gone into it in detail.'

'I'm sorry,' she smiled. 'It's not my case, and it's not my place to tell you what to do. You're not my sergeant now, more's the pity.'

He returned her smile.

Genuinely interested, he asked her about life on the Met. She wasn't involved in a complex case and the conversation soon drifted back to his investigation.

'Your young victim might have been having an affair with the dead man,' Geraldine suggested.

'Well, yes, but there's no evidence they ever met.'

She smiled and repeated her advice to look harder and added, 'Did she stand to inherit shed-loads of money?'

'There's the house, but not much besides, and there's still a mortgage on that.'

For all the time they spent discussing his case, Ian was no further on when they left than he had been when he arrived.

'I haven't really helped at all, have I?' Geraldine said, when it was time to leave.

'It always helps to review a case, talk it through with someone else.'

She jumped on that. 'What are your colleagues like?'

'To be honest, the DCI's a bit pushy. I mean, she's all right, but she's clearly under pressure and passing it on. It's so wearing when you feel you have to prove yourself all the time. It's like I'm constantly under scrutiny, and nothing I do or say is ever good enough for her. She's so – dismissive.'

'Senior officers are often like that to begin with,' she sympathised. 'But don't take it to heart. She'll soon realise how lucky she is to have you on her team.'

Ian felt himself redden. He valued Geraldine's good opinion more than she could possibly appreciate.

'I've got a good sergeant,' he went on hastily, in an attempt to cover his embarrassment. 'He seems reliable and sensible. It's early days but I think he's going to be OK to work with.'

'How's your wife liking York?' she asked as they were leaving.

Ian felt a pang of guilt that Bev was only mentioned as an afterthought, raised by Geraldine. He should have mentioned her himself when he was talking about moving to York, but she hadn't even crossed his mind.

'She's fine. She's found herself a job and seems to be settling down really well.'

'That's good.'

She turned away. Suppressing an irrational impulse to run after her, he stood and watched her solitary figure melt into the busy London street.

CHAPTER 42

Ian made his way through the throng of people entering and leaving the station. He was lucky to find a seat on the train. As they jolted along he realised he was seeking a logical explanation for the actions of a madman, but he couldn't help puzzling over why the killer might have wanted Jocelyn's death linked to Adrian's. Perhaps Ted's first suggestion had been right, and James had injected Jocelyn with Pentaketaphine post mortem to make sure she was really dead. Probably no one would ever understand his behaviour. What they had yet to establish was why James would have murdered Adrian. It seemed reasonable to assume that the two victims had been having an affair, but Ian had enough experience to know that the obvious explanation wasn't necessarily the right one. It was essential to guard against being seduced into believing a theory before they had sufficient evidence to sustain it.

He found the street he was looking for quite easily. It was only about a quarter of a mile from Acton Town station. He walked quickly, partly because the sun had gone in and it was growing chilly, and partly because he had spent too long over lunch and needed to crack on. There was no response when he knocked at the front door. He waited a moment, then knocked again. There was still no response. It looked as though no one was in. He had come a long way to see Vivien. Irritated with himself for turning up on the off chance, he hammered on the door as loudly as he could. Just as he was about to give up, the door was opened on the chain and he saw Vivien peering out. Her eyes widened in surprise on seeing him.

'Oh, it's you! I thought it was . . . What do you want?'

'I'd like to come in.'

Her eyes were red and swollen from crying. She looked dreadful. Whatever part she may or may not have played in her husband's death, it must have been hard to return to the house where she had lived with him.

Vivien admitted him into a dimly lit small square hallway. He followed her into a living room, comfortably furnished with three large armchairs and a couple of coffee tables. She slumped in one of the armchairs, her arms wrapped around her chest, her head down. When Ian told her that a man had been arrested in connection with the murder of her husband, she sat up and looked at him, more animated than he had yet seen her.

Tears welled up in her eyes and she brushed them away with the back of her hand, smiling.

'You mean you know he did it?' she whispered.

'A man is helping us with our enquiries,' Ian replied carefully.

'Good.'

There was nothing untoward about her reaction, but it gave him a tingle of excitement nevertheless. He wasn't sure what made him suspect there was more behind her reply than simple satisfaction that her husband's killer had been caught.

'Is he in custody?' she asked eagerly. 'I mean, is he locked up?'

'For the time being, yes.'

'I can't tell you what a relief that is. I hope he never gets out. Thank you, thank you so much. I've been so worried. I didn't know what to do. He frightened me.'

He could understand that. No one was comfortable at the thought of a killer walking the streets, and she struck him as someone who was nervous at the best of times.

Dragging a coffee table forward, he laid out a few photographs in front of her.

'Have you seen this woman before?'

Vivien gazed down at the pictures and shook her head.

'No, I don't think so. That is, I don't recognise her.' She frowned. 'Who is she?'

'Her name was Jocelyn Sands.'

She looked up sharply. 'Was?'

She seemed more alert than when he had last seen her. He guessed she was no longer being medicated.

'Yes. She's dead. She lived in York.'

He studied her reaction. She looked more surprised to hear that Jocelyn had lived in York than that she was dead.

'What's she got to do with me? Why are you telling me about her?'

'She was killed by the same person who killed Adrian.'

'You mean – Adrian wasn't the only one he killed?'

Vivien appeared agitated when he explained there were strong indications both murders had been carried out by the same killer.

'But who was she? What did she have to do with Charles? He never mentioned anyone in York.'

Confused, Ian asked her to explain what she meant. He was taken aback to discover that she thought Charles had been arrested for murdering his brother.

'What gave you that idea?' he asked, keeping his tone level.

'But you said – you said—' she faltered and broke off, disconcerted.

Before Ian could press her further, she burst into tears. He couldn't hide his bewilderment any longer.

'Aren't you glad he hasn't been arrested?' he asked.

He had been under the impression she was close to her brother-in-law. For answer, she began crying in earnest. Ian wished he had a female officer with him. He wasn't quite sure how to handle the situation. He was intrigued to know why she had thought they would have arrested Adrian's brother. He wondered if there was more to Charles than he had supposed.

At last she calmed down enough to be able to answer his questions.

'Why did you think we'd arrested Charles?'

'You said—' she began, and broke off, flustered.

'I said we had arrested a man.'

'Yes.'

'So,' Ian repeated his question, 'what made you think it might be Charles? Why would you think we suspected him of killing his brother?'

'I was confused. I thought you said it was Charles.'

Remembering how pleased she had been when she thought her brother-in-law had been arrested, Ian pressed her to tell him about Charles, but she became reticent. After a minute, she put her head in her hands and sobbed hysterically.

When at last she grew calm enough to speak, it was difficult to make sense of her distraught speech.

'He did it because of me,' she kept repeating.

'Who did what?'

Finally he managed to understand. Not only had she lost sight of Charles at the races just at the time Adrian had gone up onto the balcony and fallen to his death, but she was convinced Charles had killed his brother so he could have her to himself.

'You told us you were with Charles when Adrian fell.'

'No, no, I didn't. I wasn't. I never said that. He might have told you he was with me, but it's not true. It's not true.' She broke off, sobbing hysterically again.

'Were you having an affair with Charles?'

She nodded, too distraught to speak.

'But if you wanted to be with Charles, why didn't you just leave Adrian?'

Vivien struggled to control her tears. 'I would never have left Adrian. I loved him.'

Ian was so startled he responded without thinking, 'You were having an affair with his brother.'

'You don't understand,' she replied wretchedly, 'it wasn't me. I mean, I didn't have any choice. It's impossible to say no to Charles.'

Vivien's accusation sounded far fetched, the ramblings of an emotional woman racked with guilt. All the same, her suspicion was just about feasible. James had a motive for attacking Jocelyn so they had been trying to find a connection between James and Adrian. Perhaps they had been looking in the wrong place all along. The connection they wanted might link Charles to Jocelyn.

CHAPTER 43

Charles worked at the pharmacy at Whittington Hospital, near Archway. The significance of his job hadn't been lost on the team investigating Adrian's murder. As a pharmacist, Charles would have been aware of the properties of Pentaketaphine. He would know how to administer it effectively, and where to find it. A thorough check carried out at the hospital where he worked had concluded there had been no irregularities with their stock. Besides, no one had yet taken Charles seriously as a suspect. They all thought he had been with his sister-in-law while Adrian was on the balcony.

Vivien's accusation changed everything.

As soon as he left Vivien, Ian phoned the police station to speak to Eileen. She wasn't available. Seeing as he was in London and not far from the hospital, he took the tube straight there, determined to find out what he could. After Vivien's unexpected revelation, it seemed her brother-in-law might be responsible for the deaths of Adrian and Jocelyn. All Ian had to establish was why Charles would have strangled Jocelyn. He wasn't going to return to York without questioning him. With luck he might catch him unawares. So far there was no reason for Charles to suspect he was in the frame. Nearly two weeks had elapsed since the death of his brother, and he had returned to work. He might no longer be on his guard. It could be a good time to question him.

The hospital was large. It took Ian nearly ten minutes to reach the pharmacy. An Asian woman looked up when he approached the counter.

'There's a waiting time of about forty-five minutes.'

She nodded at a row of people seated in a row against the wall behind him: a young woman flicking through a magazine, an old man staring dully at the clock, yet more patients gazing disconsolately at the floor, or reading magazines, all waiting for their prescription drugs. Ian pulled out his warrant card. He didn't have to wait long for Charles to appear.

'Inspector, how are you progressing? I mean,' he lowered his voice, 'have you found out who killed him?'

Watching the other man closely, Ian told him that a man had been arrested in connection with his brother's murder. Charles gave a grunt of satisfaction.

'Let's hope that calms Vivien down a bit,' he

said. 'She's taking it all very badly. Look, we can't talk here. Let's go into the office.'

He called to a colleague to cover for him before leading Ian behind the counter and into a small cramped room.

'Let's go over this again, Inspector,' Charles said when they were both seated.

Noting how Charles wanted to take control of the interview, Ian decided to let him have his head and see where the conversation led.

'So you've arrested the person who killed my brother. Good. Was it the race official?'

'I'm afraid I can't tell you that, sir.'

Charles sat forward in his chair, and went on eagerly. 'But why did he do it? Why? Why would anyone want to kill Adrian? I don't understand. He wasn't the sort of man to have enemies. I mean, for Christ's sake, there was nothing out of the ordinary about Adrian. I mean, Adrian of all people. It must have been some sort of random attack by someone who's mentally disturbed, or drunk, perhaps? An argument that got out of hand? But surely that would have attracted attention. I've been going over and over it in my mind, but I can't make any sense of it.'

He was thinking aloud, seeming irritated that he didn't know what had happened. Or he might have been doing his best to appear confused, in an attempt to mislead Ian.

'Adrian was a good man. He wasn't the sort of

person anyone would notice, let alone take against. I mean, he wasn't one of those aggressive types. He got on with people. He was the most inoffensive person you could wish to meet. No one would want to pick a fight with him. Not Adrian. Why did it happen?'

Ian shrugged helplessly. If he knew the answer to that question, he would know who had murdered Adrian.

He asked about Vivien, and Charles frowned.

'My sister-in-law? I'm afraid she's completely neurotic, and she's gone to pieces over this.'

'Her husband has just been murdered.'

'Yes, it's understandable. Still – well, all this has been very upsetting. Vivien's a lovely woman, but she's very fragile. It's good to hear you've caught him. I'm sure knowing that's going to help her a lot.'

'So are you going to be taking care of her now? Is that the plan?'

Charles hesitated. He looked uneasy, probably wondering if Ian knew he had been having an affair with his sister-in-law.

'I'm not sure what will happen now,' he replied cautiously. 'I don't think she knows what she wants to do yet. It's going to take time for her to come to herself.'

'Tell me about her,' Ian urged him.

'Vivien's a lovely woman,' Charles repeated.

'You've never been married yourself, have you?'

'No.'

All at once Charles sounded defensive. He scowled.

Annoyed with himself for risking putting the other man on his guard, Ian took out some pictures of Jocelyn and laid them out on the table.

'What can you tell me about this woman?' He paused to give Charles a chance to study them. 'How well did you know her?'

Charles shook his head, staring closely at the images.

'I've never seen her before. Who is she?'

His certainty was disappointing. He betrayed no signs of recognising the dead girl. Ian was encouraged when he added, 'Not that I can remember, anyway.' It suggested he might be worried he had been seen with Jocelyn. They could have been picked up on a CCTV camera somewhere. But so far there was nothing to connect Charles to Jocelyn. All Ian had was a faintly uneasy feeling based on what Vivien had told him about Charles. Meanwhile, he could only fish for information. He put the photograph away, mumbling that he must have been mistaken in thinking Charles knew her.

Charles glanced at his watch and stirred in his seat before saying he ought to return to his post.

'If that's all, Inspector?'

Ian nodded.

'Well, it was really very kind of you to come all

this way to tell me in person that you've caught the killer. It's a huge relief all round, and I know Vivien will be pleased. I'll let her know straight away.'

'There's no need. We've already spoken to her.'

Charles looked faintly put out, but he recovered his composure at once.

'I expect this is the last we'll be seeing of you then, Inspector?'

Ian didn't answer.

CHAPTER 44

Ian was pleased to hear Bev humming in the kitchen as he walked in. Kicking off his shoes, he stole across the hall and crept up behind her. Reaching out, he grabbed her by the shoulders and spun her round, making her screech, but she was laughing.

'I knew it was you.'

She gave him a passionate kiss. He was partly relieved when she pulled away from his embrace. His wife was the most attractive woman he had ever met, but all the same their sex life hadn't exactly been scintillating after the excitement of the move had faded. For a few weeks they had both been on a high, feeling as though they were on holiday in their new house. Now he was involved on a case, he was mentally and physically drained by the time he arrived home in the evenings. He barely had enough energy to collapse in front of the television and eat. And all the time, remembered statements and scenarios were rolling around in his mind, distracting him from anything else.

★ ★ ★

Bev was standing in front of him. She appeared to be waiting for something.

'Have you had a good day?' he asked, automatically.

She grinned.

'So, tell me, how's the job going?'

'Let's go and sit down and I'll tell you all about it.'

He hoped his interest didn't appear forced. All he wanted to do was sleep, but first he needed to review the notes he had made of his interview with Charles. It was hard to focus on Bev and her job with so many ideas spinning around in his head. Somewhere in all that seemingly random jumble of information were pieces that would make sense, if he could only make the right connections.

Slumped in an armchair, he found himself struggling to stay awake as he listened. Bev hadn't even been in the job for a week, and already she was complaining that her line manager was taking advantage of her. Wary of upsetting her, he stifled a yawn and nodded earnestly.

'So I was just sitting there, all by myself, for nearly the whole afternoon, while she was off gallivanting around the store. She didn't introduce me to any other staff. The only other person I saw all day was the store manager. At least he's a decent bloke.'

'You don't have to stay there, if you don't like it,' Ian said mildly.

'Let's wait and see. It's early days. So, how about your day?'

He shrugged. Bev frequently complained that he didn't tell her about his work, but there was usually nothing much to say. Today wasn't that different. He had been to London to question a possible suspect and then he had returned to York. A lot of his day had been spent travelling, and he was tired.

Wearily he began to talk.

'The thing is, we thought he had an alibi but it turns out he didn't.'

Bev frowned. 'You're saying you think this man's a killer, but you didn't check out his alibi until now?'

'It's not that simple. Of course we check up on what people tell us, if we think it might be necessary. Nothing's overlooked.'

'Then how come you thought he had an alibi and then found out that actually he didn't?'

Ian sighed. He really couldn't be bothered to try and explain why they had assumed Charles had been with Vivien at the time of Adrian's death.

'A woman who gave him an alibi has now admitted she was lying.'

'How do you know she isn't lying now?'

He sighed again. 'We don't. But now we have to check it out.'

'But if his alibi, or lack of one, depends on a woman who lies, how can you possibly find out the truth?'

'That's the problem. But don't worry, we'll get to the bottom of it, sooner or later. That's our job.'

He gave her a reassuring smile, wishing he felt the confidence his words implied.

Ian had checked through his notes on the train back from London. Charles had claimed that he and Vivien had been 'together the whole time' at the races. She had been sitting next to him when he said it, and she hadn't denied or queried his claim. He had repeated it, saying 'Vivien stuck with me.' Again she had confirmed his statement by her silence. Yet now she was insisting they hadn't been together when Adrian was on the balcony. Ian wasn't sure which of them was lying: Charles to give himself an alibi, or Vivien, confused about what had really happened and unhinged with guilt about her affair. He could see why she might have lied to begin with. Apart from the fact that she had been heavily medicated, she had been stupefied by guilt over her affair with her brother-in-law.

A voice penetrated his reverie. He woke up with a start and realised Bev was calling his name.

'You never listen to what I say.'

He stumbled over his words, in a panic to apologise. He could reduce grown men to snivelling children, but couldn't endure the displeasure of one woman.

'You never listen,' she repeated, her face flushed with irritation.

'I *was* listening,' he lied feebly.

He tried to recall what she had been saying. The last thing he could remember thinking about was Vivien, and whether he could believe a word she said. In giving himself an alibi Charles was also protecting Vivien, whom he clearly cared about. Charles might be seeking to cover his own back, or he could be aware that Vivien was the killer the police were looking for. Ian wondered whether Vivien could have killed Jocelyn. She and Charles were both plausible suspects, acting individually or together.

'What do you think then?' Bev asked.

Ian had been caught out like that before, half asleep and answering with the first thing that came into his head. This time he was careful.

'Well?' she pressed him.

'I think they're lucky to have you.'

His diplomacy was rewarded with a kiss, although he had a shrewd suspicion she knew he hadn't been listening to her.

'Let's get you some supper and then straight to bed. You look completely done in.'

He smiled gratefully, pleased to be home.

CHAPTER 45

Richard didn't feel like going home. It was boring there without Emma. He pulled his collar up and strode along the empty pavement, wondering how to spend the evening. When he had been much younger he had frequented seedy clubs in the centre of town, first with his mates and later alone. He had never had any difficulty picking up girls. After several years, the encounters had lost their allure. Moving in with Emma, he had resolved to give up other women altogether. Yet he still caught himself fantasising about casual meetings with strangers. Whenever Emma had gone away on a school trip, or to visit her parents, he had indulged his predilection for anonymous, uncomplicated sex. He had always found a willing partner. Everything felt different now someone else knew what he was doing. He had coped with the phone calls, but the physical encounter with his stalker had shaken him.

Passing an unfamiliar pub he had a sudden yen to unwind over a beer in a setting where he was unknown. The interior of the bar was even shabbier than its exterior, with a grimy patterned red carpet bordered by green lino, and chipped brown paint-work. A solitary barman was staring blankly straight ahead. He barely nodded at Richard before silently pulling him a pint. For the first time in weeks, Richard consciously relaxed. He breathed deeply. No one knew him there. Leaving a surreal waking nightmare, he had stepped into a welcome haven of normality. From now on, this was how his life was going to be, tranquil and dull. Any amount of visceral excitement wasn't worth the aggravation it caused. Pint in hand, he sloped over to a corner table that looked polished but felt sticky. The bar was nearly empty. Only a couple of young men in anoraks and hiking boots were engrossed in earnest discussion on the far side of the room.

After a couple of pints he was ready to go home when a girl came in and went to the bar. He couldn't help noticing the shape of her buttocks beneath her tight skirt, short enough to expose the length of her bare thighs. She sat down, raised her glass, and glanced around. Seeing him watching her she grinned and ran the tip of her tongue suggestively over her bottom lip. He watched, mesmerised by the dark pink wetness of her glistening tongue. He knew it was rash, but Emma would be home the next day. He might never have another opportunity to fuck a stranger. The knowledge that he had handed his stalker the power to control how he behaved suddenly made him angry. It didn't have to be like that. Anyway, no one would ever know what he got up to in this godforsaken place.

He slipped off his chair and approached the girl, empty glass in hand.

'Can I get you another one?'

Her clingy jumper showed off the shape of her breasts. He could see the outline of her nipples, and wondered if she was wearing a bra.

She smiled up at him. 'Vodka and orange.'

Returning with the drinks, he slid along the bench until his thigh was pressing against hers. Close up he could see her skin was faintly pitted with acne scars beneath her make up, but apart from that she wasn't bad looking.

'You're not married, are you?' she asked with sudden misgiving, as she picked up her glass.

For answer, he laid his left hand flat on the table.

She leaned towards him and confided she had just dumped her boyfriend.

'I'm sure he wasn't worth it. Not good enough for you.'

'Too bloody right there. He was only screwing my best mate. I caught them at it.'

She sounded outraged, but not upset. Feeling lightheaded he placed his hand on her leg and caressed her firm flesh.

'He must be mad not to want you.'

'Oh, he still wants me. He cried and everything

when I told him. But I told him I wasn't going to be his girlfriend no more. Not after that I wasn't.'

'Quite right.'

'There's plenty more fish in the sea, I told him. You're not the only bloke after me. I'll find someone who'll treat me right. I told him it wouldn't take me long to find someone else.'

With one swift movement she downed her vodka and turned to him, eyes bright with anticipation. She was asking for it.

'Come on then,' he said.

No one watched them leaving the bar. He led her round the back of the pub to a small garden screened by trees where they could only be observed from the car park through a gap in the hedge. The car park was empty. She smiled as he pushed her back against the wall.

'You're impatient. Where do you live then? I bet you got your own place.'

He drew back. The chilly night air had sobered him up and he felt uneasy.

'How old are you?'

She giggled. 'That would be telling, wouldn't it? Not as young as I look. How come a good looking bloke like you hasn't got a girlfriend? You been dumped and all then? D'you think it was fate brought us together like this?'

He wished she would shut up. Her callow flirting grated on his nerves.

★   ★   ★

He struggled to control an urge to slap her silly face and shout at her that he did have a girlfriend, a beautiful woman he was going to marry. He didn't need anyone else, certainly not a vulgar little tart like her. Breaking free of her grasping embrace, he turned and walked away. The sound of her voice, whining in protest, followed him all the way back to the street.

'What did I do wrong?'

If she hadn't been so pathetic he might have felt sorry for her. Still, she had no cause to complain. She'd cadged a free drink from him, and he had taken nothing in return. She would have no problem finding another bloke ready to string her along for a quick fuck.

As he hurried away, he heard footsteps. Vexed by her persistence, he walked faster.

CHAPTER 46

Ian was whistling as he drove to the police station the next morning. He had assumed his stress had been due to the move and the pressure of his new job. Now his wife had found a job and seemed content, he was beginning to feel like his usual cheerful self again. The sun was shining, and there was a feeling of spring in the air. Admittedly he was involved in a tricky murder investigation which was progressing slowly, but that didn't bother him. On the contrary, after a good night's sleep he relished the challenge. What was more, he had a feeling he might have cracked the case. It couldn't have been coincidence that Vivien and Charles had been in York at the time of both murders.

He was at his desk rereading statements from Vivien and Charles, wondering whether to have an early lunch, when Ted appeared at the door. He was breathing heavily and his face was flushed, as though he had been running.

'There's been another one,' he burst out, without waiting for Ian to ask what he wanted.

Ian looked up with a frown.

'Another what?'

'Another body. The DCI's on her way to see you. I passed her in the corridor.'

'*Another* one?'

'We won't know until the tox report's back, but it looks like the same MO. The doctor who signed the death certificate didn't spot any signs that he was drugged, but once the mortuary was alerted to the possibility, they confirmed there's a puncture wound in his neck.'

The Pentaketaphine killer had claimed his third victim.

Ian was on his feet as soon as the sergeant finished speaking. Before he could respond, Eileen entered. She was so terse, it was almost rude, but Ian didn't mind.

'We're on our way,' he replied, equally curt. 'Ted can tell me about it in the car. Is the body still at the crime scene?'

Ted shook his head. 'You know as much as I do now.'

'All I've got is the address,' Eileen said.

'Let's start there then.'

Their destination was a street of small new brick houses, round the corner from the station.

As Ted parked the car, they spotted the forensic tent. Pushing his way through onlookers who had gathered on the pavement outside the house, Ian overheard two women talking.

'Poor thing,' one of them said.

'Such a young girl,' the other one agreed.

'She wasn't that young.'

Passing the cordon, Ian intercepted the doctor who was about to leave having completed her initial examination.

'Can you tell us anything about her?'

'Who?'

'The victim.'

The doctor looked up at him in surprise. 'I'm not sure what victim you're referring to, Inspector, but this one's a man.'

'I thought—' he broke off, fleetingly confused. Clearly he had misunderstood the snippet of conversation he had overheard in the street. 'What can you tell us about him?'

The doctor spoke rapidly, in a hurry to get away. 'The victim was in his mid thirties. He died about nine hours ago, asphyxiated.'

'Was it the same drug as the one used on Adrian and Jocelyn?'

She shrugged. 'You'll have to wait for the tox report.'

Ian leaned forward confidentially. 'But off the record, Doctor, what's your opinion?'

'Off the record, I really couldn't say. Sorry.'

The victim had been taken away to the mortuary before Ian and Ted arrived. All the same, Ian wanted to stay around for a while, to hear what the scene of crime officers had found out. The dead man was called Richard Western. Aged thirty-three, he had been living in York for eight months, with his girlfriend, Emma Willerby. He had been killed just outside his house where his body had been discovered by his girlfriend. Ian found her seated in the living room, clutching a mug of tea. Her cup rattled precariously on its saucer but she gazed steadily at Ian as she assured him she was calm enough to answer his questions. He couldn't help admiring her quiet self-control. Emma was thirty-three, the same age as her boyfriend had been when he was killed. She was stunning, with delicate features set in a curiously square face, an imperfection that somehow added to her beauty. She reminded Ian of Bev. Lithe and blonde, she was built like a dancer, or an athlete. Tight jeans displayed long slim thighs, and a close-fitting T-shirt showed off her lean yet voluptuous body. Most women's looks would be ruined by eyes bloodshot from crying, but her red-rimmed eyes gave her a vulnerability that only added to her allure.

Reminding himself that she might be a callous killer putting on a decent pretence of grief, Ian pressed on with his questions.

'We were happy together,' she explained earnestly in a soft low voice. 'He would never have killed himself. I just don't understand it.'

She appeared genuinely baffled. It was hard to believe anyone could look so upset and yet remain so touchingly beautiful. Emma had known the victim for just over eight months.

'Do you believe in love at first sight?' she asked, opening her blue eyes wide, with a look of child-like innocence.

Ian grunted. His views weren't relevant.

'Do you?' he countered.

'I didn't until I met Richard, but then – well, we both knew right from the start.'

Emma was a teacher. She had been renting her small house in York for several years. Richard had moved in with her shortly after they met.

Ian couldn't imagine how terrible it must have been for her to stumble on her dead boyfriend lying in the front garden when she returned that morning from a visit to her parents, who lived in Surrey.

'Emma, we're investigating the possibility that Richard was murdered. If there's anything at all you can think of that might help us, now's the time to tell me. Was anything worrying him?'

She raised her tearful face to him and he waited patiently, while she gazed at him with earnest blue eyes, hesitating. He had the impression she was holding something back.

'I'm sorry,' she said at last. 'There's nothing. But I can't believe anyone would have wanted to harm him. He was a kind man. A good man.'

Ian couldn't help feeling protective towards her. He was pleased she had been away, and so couldn't be suspected of any involvement in her boyfriend's death.

'Are you going to be all right? It's best not to be by yourself.'

It must have shown in his face that he realised he had been tactless in his choice of phrase because she looked at him with a tearful smile and thanked him, assuring him she was fine. Reluctantly he left her to grieve alone. It was one of the hardest aspects of his job, abandoning the solitary bereaved. A generation before, a woman in her thirties would have been surrounded by infants, with her own mother and probably an elderly grandmother, and maybe an aunt, hovering in the background. Emma was alone. But there was nothing he could do to help her, other than find out who had killed her boyfriend.

CHAPTER 47

Richard's parents were both dead. He had one brother who lived in Cardiff. A message had been sent to him via his local police force, and he was going to travel to York over the weekend. Ian planned to speak to him as soon as he arrived. Meanwhile he went to see what he could find out at the victim's work place in Leeds. The dead man's boss was a stern-looking woman in her forties. Ian felt a flicker of sympathy for the victim who had been answerable to a controlling career woman. Supporting her staff seemed less important to her than asserting her own competence.

'It's shocking news,' she said as soon as Ian told her what had happened. 'Thank you for coming in personally to let us know.'

She stood up as though dismissing him, and expressed surprise when he said he wanted to ask her a few questions.

The furniture in her office looked brand new, the carpet grey, the windows concealed behind white slatted blinds. Everything was modern, combining to create an atmosphere that was tense rather than efficient.

'I don't know how I can help you. I know nothing about Richard Western's life outside the office. He worked for me. We didn't socialise. Now I need to get back to work, so if there's nothing else—'

She couldn't have made it clearer that she didn't want to talk to Ian, although he didn't get the impression that she had anything to hide. She simply had nothing to tell him, and considered herself too busy to waste any more time. It was a distasteful display of disdain from a self-important woman. Ian did his best to control his irritation.

'I appreciate how valuable your time is,' he began, 'but I'm sure you understand there are a few routine questions we need answered. It will save us both time if we can deal with this now, right here, and then hopefully we won't need to trouble you again.'

She sniffed and nodded once. She confirmed that the victim had been working for her for six months. As far as she was aware, he had found the job shortly after moving to York to live with his girlfriend. The company designed and maintained websites, and Richard had been employed as marketing manager. She was full of praise for his work, describing him as hard working and personable.

'I know it's a cliché, but he was a pleasure to work with.'

'I'd like to speak to his colleagues in the marketing department.'

'His job title was marketing manager, but actually he *was* the marketing department. We're a small company, Inspector. Richard helped out with maintaining the sites, as well as doing our marketing. He was good like that, a salesman who understood the technical side of things.' She looked genuinely sorry. 'He'll be a loss, that's for sure.'

Ian understood that wasn't a cliché either. Richard really had been a useful employee. But that was the extent of this rigid-faced woman's relationship with him, unless she was an extraordinarily good actress.

Ian spoke to each of Richard's colleagues in turn. It was striking how their responses seemed to be governed by their gender. The first woman he spoke to was in her early twenties, dark-haired and slim. She would have been pretty if her nose hadn't been disproportionately large. When she heard that Richard had been murdered, she burst into tears. Hiccupping and stuttering, she said she couldn't believe it.

Ian was slightly surprised by her extreme emotion. 'Were you very close?'

'No, no, it was nothing like that.' She blushed, still blubbering. 'I mean, we got on well, but it was only work. He was just really nice. He was—' she paused, trying to think of the right word. 'Nice,' she concluded feebly.

'You do know he was living with his girlfriend?'

'Yes,' she muttered.

He was pretty sure she was lying about that, but by now she was crying so hard he could barely understand a word she said. He assumed she had been infatuated with her colleague.

Ian's suspicions were confirmed when he questioned the other girl who worked there.

'Lulu was mad about Richard,' she said straight away.

Older than the other girl, Denise was also tearful, but at least she was coherent.

'You couldn't dislike Richard. He was just a really nice bloke, and really fit. I can't believe he's not coming back. It's unreal.'

'I'm afraid it is real. I'm sorry.'

Both of the girls seemed to have had a soft spot for Richard. According to them, Richard had been the sort of man who would always offer to help. He seemed to appreciate their company, taking them out for lunch regularly.

'Officially it was work,' Denise told him. 'But Richard was always being nice. It makes such a difference, working with people you get on with. Not everyone's like that.'

Ian wondered if she was thinking about her boss.

The sole remaining male employee peered short-sightedly at Ian, his long straight fringe brushing the top of his steel-rimmed spectacles. He looked like what he was: a techy geek. His account of working with Richard was very different to those of the three women in the office.

'He was full of bullshit,' he said simply. 'I hate to speak ill of the dead and all that, and of course it's shocking what's happened to him, perfectly reprehensible, but he was a salesman. Very good at what he did, but it was all talk. That's what you need in sales. He was fine as long as he kept to what he did best. He caused no end of trouble when he meddled with the websites. He thought he knew what he was doing.' He gave a rueful smile. 'So many people think because they can tinker a bit with the set ups, they know what they're doing. Everyone thinks they're an expert.'

'So you didn't get on with him?'

The IT technician looked thoughtful. 'It was mutual,' he said at last. 'He despised me, and I didn't like him much.'

'Why did he despise you?'

The young man shrugged carelessly. 'Women don't exactly find me attractive – which doesn't bother me – and he was an out-and-out charmer. You'd be forgiven for mistaking him for something special, the way the girls here ran round him, like flies round a dung heap.'

Ian watched his reaction to the next question carefully.

'That must have bugged you?'

The young man shook his head. 'Not really. He was quite nauseatingly good-looking and charming, but it was no skin off my nose. It's only work. I've got a life outside of this place. Us techy geeks do lead normal lives, you know. And I'm very happy with my girlfriend. So in case you're wondering, I'm not in love with either of our airhead girls here, and I didn't bump Richard off in a fit of jealousy because he was standing in the way of my getting the girl of my dreams. Sorry if that disappoints you, Inspector.'

Ian gave what he hoped looked like a sincere smile. 'The thought hadn't crossed my mind,' he lied.

He was open to suspecting everyone who had been in contact with Richard. So far they had no idea who had murdered him. If they could solve that riddle, they would also discover who had murdered Adrian and Jocelyn.

With three dead bodies to investigate in two weeks, Ian had to find the killer quickly. It was the hallmark of a civilised society that justice be accorded to all, the dead as well as the living. But the investigation had now shifted to a new level altogether. With three deaths, and no clue as to the identity of the killer, anyone could be at risk. It was no longer merely a question of seeking justice for the dead, important though that principle was. It was equally important to protect the living. That responsibility fell on Ian too, yet he was powerless.

There was no reason to suppose the killing would stop. He had brought his wife to a city where a killer was prowling the streets, and no one was safe.

CHAPTER 48

Ian wasn't sure whether Emma might be more likely to confide in a female constable, but she had come to the station and asked for him by name. If he hadn't found her so attractive, he probably would have gone to question her without a second thought. As it was, he hesitated. Afraid that it might seem churlish to refuse, he decided it was best to comply with her request. Through the window in the door of the interview room he observed her, head lowered, shoulders drooping, upper arms twitching almost imperceptibly as she fidgeted with her hands. She didn't seem to notice him enter the room but looked up with a nervous smile when he sat down opposite her. Her face was wan, but her eyes hadn't lost their lustre. He felt a rush of pity on seeing how grief had affected her beauty, and hoped one day her fortune would change, removing the grey pouches from beneath her eyes, and restoring a healthy glow to her face. There was something precious about the allure of beauty. It touched him on a deep level.

★   ★   ★

After a moment she cleared her throat nervously, but she didn't speak. Finally he prompted her gently.

'Is there something you want to tell us?'

'You said you thought he'd been murdered, and you asked if anything had been worrying him.'

Ian nodded.

'There were calls,' she stammered at last, so softly he could barely hear her.

'Do you mean phone calls?' he repeated when she fell silent again.

'Yes. Phone calls. Someone was calling him.'

Ian waited.

'Go on,' he said at last, unable to hide his impatience any longer.

'Richard hadn't been himself for a while. I knew there was something wrong. He kept telling me he was worried about a deal at work, but I knew it wasn't that. He'd only taken the job as a temporary stop-gap when he moved to York, just until he found something better. I knew it wasn't his job that was upsetting him. I was afraid he was having doubts about our relationship.'

She paused to blow her nose.

'I was renting the house when we met, and he moved in with me. The landline was in my name, and we never got around to changing it. No one ever calls that number anyway, apart from my parents. I don't think he'd even given the number to anyone. But recently he started getting calls on the landline, about the time he started behaving strangely.'

'Strangely?'

'Yes, he started snapping at me, as though he was really anxious about something. And he wasn't sleeping well, which was unusual for him. He didn't say anything about the calls, just told me it was a wrong number, but I overheard him a couple of times—' she broke off.

'What did he say?'

'It wasn't so much what he said, but I could tell he was upset, although he pretended everything was OK.'

Ian glanced up from his notebook.

'Can you remember anything at all about the conversations you overheard?'

'Yes. He said things like: "Who are you?" and "What do you want?" and one time he said: "You won't get away with this." But it wasn't just what he said, it was the way he said it. He was really jittery.' She paused before adding, 'and he was terrified every time the phone rang.'

'Do you think the caller was threatening him?'

'I don't know.'

'Did Richard say anything at all that might help us find the caller?'

She shook her head. 'He kept saying there was nothing wrong. But there was. I knew there was. And there was something weird about the caller's voice.'

★   ★   ★

Ian sat forward.

'Did you speak to the nuisance caller yourself?'

'Yes. At least, I assume that's who it was.'

'Tell me what happened. Think carefully. This could be important.'

'It was about a week ago. I answered the phone and it was him.'

'Who?'

'The caller, the one who had been upsetting Richard.'

'How did you know it was him?'

'Well, I didn't, not really. But I'm convinced it was because – well, it was odd.'

'Odd how? Can you remember any of the conversation? Anything at all?'

'I answered the phone. I said, "Hello", and he said "Hello Emma." When I asked who it was, he said he was calling to speak to Richard—' she broke off, frowning with the effort to remember. 'He said Richard had asked him to call. And then he said something to me.'

'What did he say?'

'I can't remember exactly.' She blushed, unexpectedly. 'He said something about Richard being a lucky bloke, something like that. When I told Richard the call was for him, he got really agitated.'

'What did they talk about?'

She shook her head. 'I don't know. I didn't hear.'

She was upset but Ian pressed on, aware this could be important.

'Can you describe the voice?'

'No.' She gazed at him in desperation. 'How do you describe a voice?'

'Was it a man or a woman?'

'I don't know.'

'You said "he".'

'Yes, I think it was a man, but it could have been a woman. I couldn't really tell because, whoever it was, he was trying to disguise his voice.'

'What makes you think that?'

'It sounded funny.'

'In what way funny?'

'Kind of forced and hoarse. It didn't sound natural. It was all on one tone, like a robot. Definitely not natural.'

There was nothing more she could tell him. She couldn't say exactly when the calls had been made, or how many there had been. Ian asked a constable to check phone records for the house. No doubt there would be a number of calls from withheld sources but even if they managed to find out where the calls had originated, the killer was unlikely to have used a phone that could be traced back to him. Instead he would have used public phones, in pubs or stations, or perhaps a stolen mobile phone. Ian had to check, just in case the caller had been careless. The likelihood was that they would find nothing more sinister than a time wasting nuisance caller, unconnected with the recent murders. All the same, Ian was going through the motions, careful to leave no stone unturned. They couldn't afford to overlook the slightest possibility of finding a lead to the elusive killer.

CHAPTER 49

A constable was checking Emma's telephone records, a team was looking through CCTV of the area where Jocelyn's body had been found, and another team was out asking questions door to door in Emma's street. Meanwhile Ian was sitting around kicking his heels on a Saturday while his wife was at home, lonely and bored. Besides any other considerations, he was too restless to do anything useful and needed to clear his head, so he went home early. As it turned out, that wasn't a good idea. Bev's pleasure at seeing him walk in the house was short lived. Sitting around with her was no more relaxing than sitting at his desk at work. Distracted by the investigation, he couldn't settle to anything. Several times he caught Bev scowling at him. Once or twice she challenged him.

'Are you listening to me?'

He did his best, but he was preoccupied by Emma's statement. Something about it bothered him, but he couldn't work out what it was. Feeling guilty, he offered to take his wife out to eat.

* * *

While Bev was upstairs getting ready, he scanned through Emma's statement once again, hoping to spot inconsistencies. There were none that he could see, beyond a confusion natural in the bereaved. He reread her words slowly. They had begun searching for a connection between the three victims, in a desperate attempt to make sense of the case. They hadn't yet looked into Emma's history. They knew about her association with Richard. If they found out if she was connected to Adrian and Jocelyn, or perhaps James as well, it was possible she might be able to lead them to the killer. He was considering what to do next when Bev came downstairs. She caught sight of him staring at his iPad and paused by the open door.

'Bloody hell, can't you forget about work for one day? It's Saturday for Christ's sake!'

He mumbled an apology and told her she looked gorgeous.

'Don't tell me, I look ravishing but you have to abandon me,' she said with a pout.

With a guilty twinge he assured her she had his full attention, and resolved to put the case out of his mind, for one evening at least. Emma could wait until the morning.

Eileen wasn't around when Ian arrived at the police station on Sunday, but he was relieved to find Ted there, on duty. Quickly, Ian outlined his theory. Ted was sceptical.

275

'I totally get that we have to follow up the nuisance caller, but I can't see how you make the jump from that to thinking Richard's girlfriend is somehow involved.'

Ian explained that while he didn't suspect Emma herself, he did want to investigate her to see if there was anything to link her to Adrian and Jocelyn.

'It's a possible lead, that's all. And God knows we need one.'

Ted went to arrange a search of Emma's contacts leaving Ian sitting at his desk thinking about Bev. The previous evening he had splashed out by taking her to an expensive restaurant, only to ruin the evening by his preoccupation with the case. Now he was at work, he couldn't stop thinking about his wife.

Plagued with regret, he was about to call Bev when Ted burst into his office brandishing a piece of paper.

'Don't tell me, you've won the lottery,' Ian greeted him. 'And has no one shown you how to knock at a door?'

For answer, Ted waved the paper with a tri-umphant air. He approached Ian's desk, gabbling in his excitement. When he heard what Ted had to tell him, Ian forgot about the sergeant's uncere-monious entrance. A constable had discovered that Emma had worked in London about fifteen years earlier. She had been briefly employed by the same small firm where Adrian Curtis had been working. They must have known one another.

Discovering that Emma and Adrian had known one another before he came to York opened up all sorts of possible reasons for his death. Perhaps he and Emma had met by chance at the races that day, and rekindled their earlier passion. Or she could have been the reason behind Adrian's visit in the first place. Richard might have got wind of what had happened, and set about killing Adrian in a fit of jealousy. That in turn might have provoked Emma to kill Richard. It was hard to guard against indulging in wild speculation. Ian jumped to his feet.

'We need to know more. Carry on ferreting around while I go and question her again, find out how much she knows.'

'More than she's letting on,' Ted agreed.

As he drove, Ian reviewed what little they knew about Emma. It was early Sunday evening so he was hopeful he would find her at home. Leaving the car in a small public car park off Leeman Road, he walked alongside the river towards the estate where she lived. On the way he passed several cyclists, a few people out walking their dogs, and an occasional jogger. A rowing boat glided past with an all women crew. He paused in his stride and turned to watch it slow down before it slipped out of sight under the railway bridge.

Looking up, he saw a group of youngsters gathered outside a boathouse on the opposite bank, probably up to no good. He walked on. The narrow footpath opened out into a road and soon after he turned off into Emma's street.

CHAPTER 50

So far the nights had been the worst. After work, Emma had always been ready to greet Richard with a cold beer, and the kettle on in case he preferred a cup of tea. Sometimes he had come home early, but more often than not he would be late, turning up full of excuses at half past seven, sometimes later.

'I know how hard you work,' she would reassure him, and he would kiss her and say something like, 'Working for our future.'

She had survived two days without him. It seemed to grow harder with every hour that passed, as the reality sank in. She had known all along that he was dead. She was the one who had found him, white-faced and staring, sprawled awkwardly across the front doorstep. Even then she hadn't believed he was never coming back. It was absurd how she hadn't believed it, although she had known it was true, as though her mind was operating in two different realities. The doctor had told her she needed to give herself time to come to terms with what had happened. She hadn't bothered to explain that she didn't want to accept it. He wouldn't understand.

She was being sensible, keeping off alcohol, remembering to eat at the right times, and taking the sleeping pills the doctor had given her, enough for a week. 'Just to tide you over,' he had told her, as though after a week her life would somehow revert to normal. During the day she had done her best to distract herself with anodyne programmes on the television. It was undemanding company of sorts. Richard had often been out during the day so she was used to being at home on her own. There had been moments when she had almost forgotten what had happened. Fleetingly, the image of his pale face had faded from her mind until she could no longer see his eyes fixed blindly on hers, while a static white line of dried saliva dribbled from the corner of lips that had kissed her so tenderly. Never again would she feel their gentle touch on her skin. During the day she tried to crowd it out of her mind but, after dark, memories overwhelmed her. When her mother phoned it seemed almost unbelievable that she didn't know what had happened. Richard had been dead for two days, and her mother was asking after him as usual. The conversation was surreal.

'Are you all right?' her mother asked. 'You sound terrible. What's wrong?'

She hadn't known what to say.

'How's Richard?'

'He's dead.'

There was a pause, and then her mother began questioning her. It seemed to go on forever. She knew her mother only wanted to be kind, but it didn't help.

Emma struggled to fend off her intrusive concern until, unable to think any longer, she fell back on the doctor's platitudes.

'I'm OK, really. I just need some time to myself, to come to terms with what happened.'

'You can't stay there by yourself. You must come home. Do you want us to come and get you?'

'No, no, I'm better off here, at home. I don't want to go anywhere.'

'Are you sure you're all right there on your own?'

'Yes, I'm fine really. I lived here by myself for years before Richard moved in.'

'Yes, but—'

'I'm OK, really.'

She only finally got off the phone by claiming to be really tired, and promising to call her mother in the morning.

'If you're sure you're all right.'

'I'm sure,' she lied.

It was stupid of her mother to ask such inane questions. She couldn't imagine ever feeling all right again.

She climbed into bed and picked up the bottle of sleeping pills. Annoyed and pleased when the phone rang again, she reached out to answer it. Clearly her mother didn't believe she was coping fine on her own.

'I told you I'm OK,' she said crossly, but she didn't really mind her mother's concern.

'I'm glad to hear it.'

With a shock she recognised the voice.

'Stop calling this number,' she snapped. 'Richard's not here.'

She was about to hang up, but his next words caught her attention.

'I know that. It's you I want to speak to,' he replied in a teasing sing song tone. 'You don't even know what I want yet.'

A sudden rush of anger shook her.

'I don't care what you want. If you don't stop calling this number I'll report you to the police.'

'Oh, I think the police have more important things to think about than a friendly chat on the phone, don't you? Like who killed Richard?'

'They might be interested to hear about a stalker who was harassing him before he killed himself.'

At the other end of the line the caller laughed.

'We both know it wasn't suicide.'

She was trembling with fury, making it difficult for her to speak. She took a deep breath. Before she could retort, he spoke again.

'But enough about Richard. He's done with. It's *you* I'm calling now.'

'What do you want? This is over. Everything's

over, do you understand? Richard's dead. Leave me alone.'

Petulantly she threw the phone across the room. It hit the wall with a soft thud and dropped to the carpet. Grief gripped her chest like a physical ache. Losing all restraint, she fell back on her pillow and wept. At last her fit of crying petered out leaving her with sore eyes and a pounding head. Wearily she got up and replaced the phone on its cradle before going to the kitchen to make a cup of tea. It felt like the middle of the night, although it was only six o'clock. While she waited for the kettle to boil, she wondered if it was safe to take aspirin with the sleeping pills. The phone rang again. She didn't answer but it rang again. And again. She ignored it, supposing it was her mother, anxious and fussing. When it rang for the fourth time she answered it. Her spirits sank because it was him.

'I thought you'd never answer. I was worried about you.'

'Leave me alone.'

'Are you sure you want to be alone? I would have thought that was the last thing you'd want right now.'

His intrusiveness was starting to unnerve her. She tried to speak firmly, as though to a child. She hoped he wouldn't hear her voice shaking.

'I don't want to hear from you again.'

'That's not very nice, is it?' His next words startled her. 'You know he wasn't good enough for you. He would never have made you happy. You should be grateful, after what I've done for you.'

'What do you mean? What do you want?'

His laughter made a horrible gurgling sound. She was beginning to feel scared.

'We both know what I want. You know I did it for you.'

'What do you mean? What exactly are you expecting from me?'

There was no answer. Automatically, she replaced the phone and went into the kitchen where the kettle was steaming. She poured her tea and sat down in the living room with his words ringing in her head: 'We both know what I want. You know I did it for you . . . we both know it wasn't suicide.'

The doorbell shrilled so suddenly she cried out in alarm. It could only be him. No one else would be visiting her at six thirty on a Sunday evening. He had been phoning and phoning, and now he was coming to see her, just as he had done with Richard. The bell rang again. Alone in the house she sat perfectly still, too terrified even to reach out and phone the police. The knocking grew insistent. He was desperate to get in. She sat, paralysed with fear, hardly daring to breathe.

CHAPTER 51

Danielle looked up with a bright smile when the manager put his head round the door of their tiny office. Bev couldn't be sure, but she thought Danielle blushed.

'Everything OK in here?'

'Yes, thanks, Mr Archer,' Danielle answered quickly.

He nodded at her and then looked at Bev as though waiting for an answer. She glanced back at Danielle before nodding in agreement.

'Excellent. I'd like a word with you in my office. Is now convenient?'

'Now's fine, Mr Archer.'

Danielle's chair made a scraping sound on the floor as she moved to get up. He raised his hand.

'Not you, Danielle. I'd like to speak to Beverley.'

At the periphery of her vision, Bev saw Danielle's chubby face scowling.

Bev followed the store manager along a draughty corridor to his own office. It was larger than the room she shared with Danielle but otherwise similar, with whitewashed walls, short pile grey carpet, and cheap white furniture. He gestured to her to take a seat.

'So, Beverley—'

'Everyone calls me Bev.'

He smiled. 'Bev then. And please, call me Dominic.' He leaned his elbows on his desk. 'I wanted to ask how you're settling down. How are you finding it here?'

She smiled uncertainly.

'You don't seem very happy. I know the job isn't quite what you're used to, but I don't expect you to remain working at your present level for long. We're a busy company, and people move around.'

She wondered if he was prompting her to complain about her colleague. He must be aware of Danielle's incompetence. It was hard not to speculate about her own job prospects if Danielle was out of the way. It hadn't escaped her notice that he had invited her to call him Dominic. He was Mr Archer to Danielle.

On balance she decided it was best to adopt a cautious approach.

'Everything's fine, thank you,' she said. 'Of course it's all new and still seems a bit strange, but that's inevitable to begin with. It's going to prove a good opportunity to develop my experience, once I get the hang of things here.'

Dominic relaxed back into his chair, still smiling. 'I'm pleased to hear you say that. I can speak freely can't I?'

She nodded, doing her best to conceal her excitement. If he made one criticism of Danielle, she was ready to take up the invitation to tell him exactly what she thought of her colleague.

'I think you're going to be a great asset to the team here. Of course it's early days and we need to ease you in gently, but I have plans for you, Bev.' He paused, leaning forward again. 'Tell me, are you ambitious?'

She felt her way cautiously. 'Yes, and I'm a lot more experienced than Danielle.'

Dominic backtracked. 'Yes, well, like you said, it's early days.'

'Of course, it's early days,' she echoed lamely. 'I'm still just learning the ropes.'

She was relieved when he changed the subject.

'And how are you liking York?'

'It's lovely.'

'I'm glad you think so. It's a great city with lots to recommend it. Have you been on any of the guided walks yet?'

'We haven't had time. Ian – my husband – works long hours when he's on a case.'

'Remind me what he does again. Is it the law?'

'He's a detective.'

'Oh yes.'

'A detective inspector.'

She was fairly sure she had told him that before. He pretended to be interested, but she noticed him glance surreptitiously at his watch.

'An inspector? So he wouldn't have time to sort out my parking ticket?' He laughed, not unkindly.

Bev smiled, but she was riled. He had no right to sneer at Ian's work.

'Nothing like that. He works on serious crime.'

'Serious crime, eh? Isn't all crime to be taken seriously?'

'Of course, but some crimes are more serious than others. He investigates murders.'

'Like the ones we keep hearing about on the local news?'

She nodded, sensing an opportunity to impress him. 'My husband's leading the investigation into all of them. The man who died at the races, the dead girl found by the river, and the man killed at the weekend. With three deaths, they're calling this a serial killer.'

She broke off, suddenly anxious that she had said too much. But she wasn't speaking out of turn. The papers were full of it.

'You won't tell anyone, will you? Only I'm not supposed to talk about my husband's work.'

His smile implied complicity. 'But you haven't told me anything I haven't already seen on the news. I imagine he's not allowed to tell you anything about what's happening, is he?'

Bev shrugged. Any prospect of promotion for her lay in Dominic's hands. Not only could he improve her position, but he could do so at Danielle's expense, which made the prospect even more attractive. Keen to maintain the camaraderie that seemed to have sprung up between them, she spoke softly.

'What do you want do know?'

Dominic was trustworthy. He was a supermarket manager. What harm could a little gossip do, as long as she kept to information that was readily available in the media. Ian never told her anything confidential. It wouldn't be difficult to curry favour with her boss without giving away any secrets, if she was clever about it.

'But you mustn't tell anyone,' she added.

He smiled. 'It will be our secret, if you ever want to talk.'

CHAPTER 52

Ian was in a good mood as he drove to the police station on Monday morning. Bev had insisted on making him breakfast. Now that she was working, and had to get up early, she said she wanted to spoil him, and chattered happily about taking him out for dinner at the weekend. He didn't point out that they might need her salary to pay towards their bills. Since they hadn't gone away after their wedding the previous year, he had booked a holiday before their move to York had been confirmed. It was intended to be a kind of belated honeymoon. Now, apart from the unforeseen expenses they had incurred in moving, he had to pay the balance of their holiday costs. Worse than the financial implications of the trip, he was anxious the case he was working on wouldn't be concluded before they were due to go away. At the rate they were progressing, they would be lucky to wrap it up before Christmas. From time to time murder investigations dragged on for years. He hoped this wouldn't turn out to be one of those cases.

★   ★   ★

He found Ted with a team of constables studying CCTV film from surveillance cameras filming the main roads near Richard's flat. Ted looked up and shook his head to signify nothing new had been discovered. It was a long and monotonous job. Ian was glad his own work life was more varied than that of his colleagues working in the Visual Images Identification and Detection Office. He led Ted back to his own room where they planned their movements for the day. Ian was happy to be working with the sergeant. An easy going guy, he knew his way around the town having lived in the area all his life. Although Ian had spent his childhood in Scarborough he hadn't often visited York itself, and had returned with only a vague recollection of the layout of the town. There would be times when Ted's company would prove invaluable. First of all they went to the mortuary to find out what Richard's post mortem had revealed. As this was a murder investigation, Ian hoped the toxicology report would already be there, although he appreciated the weekend had probably slowed the process down.

They found Jonah chatting to Avril in her small office.

'Oh get away with you,' she laughed, giving him a mock slap on the arm. 'You'll be the death of me, you and your daft jokes.'

Seeing the pair of them looking so relaxed reminded Ian of a couple he once knew who had met in similar circumstances, flirting over cadavers. It seemed a macabre place to begin a relationship, but of course Jonah and Avril wouldn't be fazed by the presence of a corpse. They worked with the dead like other people might work with plants, or legal documents, adopting a show of appropriate sobriety when mourners arrived to view the bodies. They both looked up when Ian entered. Avril had met Ted before and introduced him to Jonah.

'Come along in then,' Jonah greeted them cheerfully. 'He's waiting for you.'

'And I thought they were here for the pleasure of our company,' Avril grinned.

'Speak for yourself,' Jonah retorted and she gave him another playful slap on the arm.

'He's a good looking man. He looks like a Greek statue,' Avril said.

'She just can't stop talking about me,' Jonah added, and they both laughed.

Pulling on masks, Ian and Ted followed the tubby pathologist through purple and grey double doors. Richard's body looked very long and very white. His dark hair had been cropped short, presumably while he was still alive. Even closed, his eyes looked disproportionately large above his pinched nose. Taken all together, his features combined to give an effect of classic good looks. Ian remembered what Avril had said about looking like a Greek statue. It made sense, now they had seen the dead man.

★   ★   ★

Ian turned to Jonah and asked what he could tell them so far.

'The tox report's not back yet, but off the record I'd be surprised if we weren't looking at the same MO. He died from asphyxiation. There are no other physical symptoms. He seems to have collapsed and stopped breathing for no apparent reason. Pentaketaphine causes complete paralysis so that's definitely a possibility. To be frank, something like that would have occurred to me even without the previous deaths. Look at this.'

He pointed out a tiny red dot on the victim's neck.

'That puncture mark could have been caused by a small insect, but he could equally well have been injected with a drug like Pentaketaphine, just like the other victims. An insect wouldn't paralyse him like that. And look here.'

He indicated a faint white crust at the edge of the dead man's mouth.

'What is it?'

'Dried saliva. He was dribbling when he died. Of course none of this is conclusive. He could have looked very like this if he'd died of a stroke. But he appears to have been fit and healthy. I doubt he would have spontaneously collapsed and died on his front door step.' He squinted down at the tiny puncture mark. 'My money's on Pentaketaphine.'

*   *   *

Ian stared at the dumpy figure of the pathologist in silence. It was possible Jonah was wrong. He had said as much himself. He had been careful to make it clear that what he was suggesting was just a theory. Until proved, it remained just that. But if his assumption was correct, the media was right to speculate that one killer had committed three murders in three weeks. If the killing spree continued, they could expect another body to be discovered by the end of the week. And they still had no clues as to the murderer's identity.

CHAPTER 53

After their visit to the mortuary, Ian was keen to speak to Emma again. He had been to her house the previous evening at about six thirty, but she hadn't come to the door. After a brief discussion, he and Ted had concluded she must have taken a sedative and fallen asleep, oblivious to Ian standing on her doorstep, ringing the bell and knocking loudly. Ian was only too conscious of the fact that he hadn't questioned her about Adrian and Jocelyn. Time was passing. They needed to press her to tell them everything she knew that might have a bearing on the case. In failing to admit she had met Adrian, she had already kept back vital information. They could only speculate about what else she might be withholding. They had to persuade her to speak freely. If she did, there was a chance they might discover the identity of the killer before the end of the day. They drove to her house in a state of heightened expectation. This could be the break they had been searching for.

★　★　★

This time the door opened almost as soon as Ian rang the bell. He was taken aback to see how frail and grey Emma looked. All the vitality seemed to have drained out of her.

'We'd like to ask you a few questions, Emma.'

She nodded dumbly. It wasn't clear if she had understood his request.

'May we come in?'

For reply, she stepped aside to allow them to enter her comfortably furnished living room. Although it was small, a large window gave a spacious feeling to the room. They all sat down in silence. Emma stared miserably at her hands which lay in her lap, fingers tightly entwined.

'Why didn't you tell us you knew Adrian Curtis?' Ian began bluntly.

Her eyelids fluttered, but she didn't answer.

Ian leaned forward and spoke more gently. 'Emma, tell us what you know about Adrian Curtis.'

'Adrian Curtis,' she repeated dreamily. 'I met him years ago, when I was doing a holiday job in London. It wasn't very glamorous, just filing and making the tea, that sort of thing. I was very young. Adrian wasn't much older than me. He used to tease me for being a Northerner.' She paused, remembering. 'We had a bit of a fling, you know how it is. Everyone else there was much older than us, so we were thrown together, and one thing led to another. We were just kids. He was a sweet guy, but we both knew it was never going to last. He said he wanted to go on seeing me after the summer, but there was never any future in it. We kept in touch for a few weeks and then it just fizzled out the way things do when you're that age.' She broke off and looked up with a puzzled frown. 'Why are you asking about Adrian, after all this time? I haven't heard from him for about fifteen years.'

Her blue eyes met Ian's and he realised she had no idea what had happened to Adrian.

'I'm afraid Adrian's dead,' he told her.

Emma's eyes widened in surprise. 'Dead? Poor Adrian. But—' she looked helplessly from Ian to Ted and back at Ian again. 'I don't understand why you're telling me this.'

'We have reason to suspect Adrian and Richard were killed by the same person.'

'I don't understand,' she repeated.

'You must have read about the man killed at the races a couple of weeks ago?'

'Yes. And there was a woman as well, wasn't there?'

'The man killed at the races was Adrian Curtis.'

'Adrian? No!'

'I'm afraid so.'

'Oh my God. How terrible. Poor Adrian. I remember him as being such a nice guy. Why would anyone do that?'

'That's what we're trying to find out. We were hoping you could help us.'

'Me?'

'You knew both the victims.'

'Yes, but—'

'You said you'd had no contact with Adrian for about fifteen years. Think carefully before you answer my next question.'

Emma nodded, wide-eyed.

'Did you know he was coming to York two weeks ago?'

'No. I told you, we lost touch years ago.'

'You must have known about his death,' Ted said. 'It was all over the news.'

'The death at the races,' she said solemnly. 'Of course I heard about it, but I had no idea it was Adrian.'

'There was a picture of him in the paper, and on the local news.'

'If there was, I didn't recognise him. People change in fifteen years.'

'And you didn't recognise his name?' Ted persisted.

'They just talked about him as the man who was killed at the races. I suppose they mentioned his name but I didn't register who he was. Why would I? I only knew him for a couple of weeks, and it was a long time ago.'

Ian held out a passport photograph of Jocelyn Sands, taken about six months before she died.

'What can you tell us about this woman?'

'May I?'

Emma took the photograph from him and squinted at it. She shook her head with a faintly puzzled expression. Ian did his best to conceal his excitement as she hesitated before asking who the woman in the photograph was.

'Have you ever seen her before?'

'I don't know.'

Ian held his breath, willing her to admit she had known all three victims. Any minute now, the story behind three apparently unrelated murder victims might begin to unravel.

'She looks vaguely familiar, but I don't know who she is. Hang on – isn't this the woman who was murdered down by the river? Of course. That's where I've seen her before, on TV. No,' she added firmly, 'I'd never seen her before that.'

Disappointed, Ian returned to his original line of questioning, but the lead was going cold.

'How do you explain that two men you had relationships with have both been murdered in York within a couple of weeks of one another?' he asked.

Emma shrugged. 'I don't know,' she whispered. 'Maybe someone's out to get me.'

'What do you mean, out to get you?'

'What if I'm next?' She burst into tears.

Her fear appeared genuine, but when Ian tried to discover why she was afraid for her own safety she merely shook her head. He assumed she was overwrought by distress at her recent bereavement.

Recovering her composure, she told them she was thinking of going to stay with her mother for a few weeks.

'I have to get away from here,' she explained earnestly.

He made a note of her mother's contact details, and the two detectives left soon after, their investigation no further advanced.

'Do you think it was a coincidence, her knowing Adrian?' Ted asked as they walked back to the car.

'I don't know. It's a bit of a stretch to believe it's just chance, but then what about Jocelyn? How does she fit in? We know it can't be a copycat killer, because the details of Pentaketaphine weren't publicised anywhere. But—' he shrugged, nonplussed. 'Something about all this doesn't feel right, but I'm damned if I can say what it is.'

CHAPTER 54

'This is most unsatisfactory,' Eileen said.

She shifted in her chair without taking her eyes off Ian. Her thin lips seemed to disappear altogether between her pointed nose and strong chin, as though to emphasise her disapproval. Despite agreeing with her, Ian grew defensive.

'We're moving in the right direction—' he protested, but she broke in decisively.

'We're going round in circles, Ian. I grant you, we've discovered that Emma Willerby knew Adrian Curtis as well as Richard Western, but where has that got us? Unless she's lying, Richard's girlfriend didn't know Jocelyn Sands and we've established that the three victims were killed by the same person. Emma was on a train when Richard was being killed. Since she can't come up with any leads about who might have wanted to kill her boyfriend, she can't help us. We've found nothing to link Charles Curtis with any of this, apart from the fact that he was at the races when his brother was killed. But he too doesn't seem to have had any contact with Jocelyn Sands, which means he's not a suspect. And what's behind the anonymous phone calls Richard Western was receiving? Three weeks in and all we've done is eliminate suspects until there's no one left.'

'It's two and a half weeks, not three,' Ian pointed out.

'Don't quibble with me.'

Ian felt his face burning. He didn't suppose Eileen intended her comments as a reprimand but that was how it felt from where he was standing in front of her desk, like a naughty schoolboy who had been summoned to the head teacher for a telling off. He half expected her to ask him to account for having spent so much time questioning Emma the previous afternoon. Every time he thought about her he felt faintly guilty, because whenever he looked at Bev she reminded him of Emma. If they hadn't worn their hair differently, the resemblance would have been really striking.

'I was hoping Emma would know something that might help us,' he said, struggling not to feel undermined. 'She might have been able to put us on to any enemies Richard might have had, that kind of thing. If she'd given us a name of someone we could connect to Adrian . . .'

Eileen interrupted his babbling. 'She didn't.'

Leaving Eileen's office, Ian did the rounds of the teams looking into the victims' movements. He could have returned to his desk straight away, confident that he would have been notified of any developments, but he preferred to see for himself what was going on. It was a dispiriting tour.

'Nothing new, sir,' greeted him in every room.

Back at his desk he set to work scouring Emma's statements, hunting for any discrepancy that might suggest she had been lying. In the absence of any evidence, he hadn't mentioned to Eileen that he had the impression Emma was hiding something. He could imagine Eileen's scathing response. This was not how he had envisaged his first case as an inspector.

On his way out of the station at the end of a disheartening day, he bumped into Ted in the car park. There was a pub on the main road, just a few yards from the entrance to the police station, and they agreed to go for a quick pint before going home. It was a decent enough place that stocked a good selection of beers. The pub was almost empty at that hour, just a few people stopping for a drink on their way home. A couple of constables were seated at the bar, chatting to the landlord. After exchanging a cursory greeting, Ian and Ted settled at a table in a relatively quiet corner. They drank in silence for a few minutes.

'Nice to relax,' Ian remarked, and Ted grunted assent.

It wasn't long before they slipped into discussing the case.

'It's enough to drive you round the bloody bend,' Ted grumbled.

Ian agreed it was frustrating. 'Just when you think you're getting somewhere. It's one step forward, two steps back.'

'We're going round in circles,' Ted muttered into his pint.

Hearing the sergeant echo the detective chief inspector's words, Ian wondered if Eileen had been fishing for information behind his back. Ted had been working with her for a number of years. Apart from the possibility that he might have a sense of loyalty towards her, he was going to have to depend on her support if he put in for promotion. Ian would have to guard against expressing any criticism of Eileen in front of his young colleague.

'What did you make of Emma?' Ian asked after a pause, ready to do some fishing of his own.

'Well,' Ted put his glass down, considering the question. 'I don't see how she can be a suspect.'

Ian agreed. Richard had been killed around midnight on Thursday. CCTV footage confirmed Emma had arrived at the station in York at ten the following morning, after boarding a train at just after eight in London. She would have had to have travelled back to York on Thursday evening, killed her boyfriend some time before midnight, and then travelled back to London ready to turn around and leave for York again about five hours later.

'There's no way she could have killed him, even if we could find a motive, which seems improbable. She would have missed the last train back to London on Thursday night anyway. It's still possible – she might have hired a car – but where's the motive?' Ian said. 'He was her boyfriend. If she wanted to be rid of him, she could have thrown him out. The house was rented in her name. Although she has been clever enough to give herself an alibi, if it was her,' he added thoughtfully.

Ted looked down at his pint. His dark eyes disappeared beneath his overhanging brows. He seemed content to sit quietly, but Ian wanted to continue discussing the case. After a moment he brought up the other two victims.

'Emma didn't even know Jocelyn Sands.'

'True.'

'Unless she's lying about that as well.' Ian sighed. 'But I agree, she's not the killer. Whoever killed Adrian lifted his body over the high railing and she's not strong enough to do that by herself, at least not without considerable effort. Someone would have seen her. It had to be done quickly.'

'True,' Ted said again.

'So we're back to square one.'

They continued discussing Emma's possible involvement in the murders without getting anywhere. But they agreed it would be very strange if she had been involved in relationships with two out of the three victims purely by chance.

'Something doesn't add up,' Ian said.

Ted grunted again, gazing down at the dregs of his pint. Ian realised the sergeant was probably waiting to go home to his girlfriend.

'Oh well,' he said, 'this isn't getting us anywhere. I don't know about you, but I'm knackered. We'd best get off home.'

Ted was on his feet before Ian had finished speaking.

'Yes, Jenny'll be wondering where I am. See you tomorrow, sir.'

As he sat downing the last of his pint, Ian wished he felt equally excited about going home.

CHAPTER 55

Bev soon realised she had been naive in expecting the situation to improve. She had hoped her colleague would turn out to be shy rather than arrogant, but the more she saw of Danielle, the less she liked her. Danielle clearly thought Bev had been employed as her personal assistant, and seemed to relish the power that gave her to chivy her new colleague. If there had only been the two of them, Bev would have quit without giving the matter a second thought. Fortunately, Dominic's attitude was very different. A couple of times he had popped his head round the door to invite Bev to step into his office to chat about how she was settling in.

'Beverley's busy,' Danielle said when Dominic invited Bev to his office for the third time in a week. 'I'm free at the moment. Can I help?'

'Thanks, but I want to see Bev.'

Bev had hurried from the room, mortified for Danielle.

Seeing Danielle's crush on Dominic, Bev began to look at him in a different way. On reflection, she realised he was more attractive than she had first appreciated. She was flattered by his interest in her and wasn't averse to a little flirting, as long as it didn't develop into anything more significant than harmless office banter. Her previous boss had done his best to cajole her into having an affair with him, and his attentions had often livened up a dull day in the office for her. There was no reason why a similar lighthearted relationship might not develop between her and Dominic. At the very least it would be good to know she had an ally if she fell out with Danielle, which was on the cards. But when she confided to Dominic that she found Danielle difficult to work with, he cut her off.

'I'm sure you'll get used to our systems here.'

'Yes. I'm sure I will.'

When Bev discussed the situation with Ian, he advised her to tackle Danielle about it.

'She's just a bully,' he said. 'Don't let her push you around. You deserve more respect than that. No one should have to put up with that kind of treatment.'

She knew he was right. First thing Monday morning, she marched into the building ready to stand firm if Danielle tried to put her down again. The door to her office was locked. Fuming at being shut out, she stalked along the corridor to Dominic's room, determined not to hold back this time. Rapping smartly on the door she opened it and peered inside.

'Come in,' he called out cheerily. 'We were just talking about you. We've been discussing an idea Danielle had for streamlining the system you're using.'

Danielle looked round, smiling complacently. Both women knew she had appropriated an idea Bev had put forward, presenting it to Dominic as her own initiative. What made it all the more galling was her claim to be simplifying the system so Bev would be able to use it, as though Bev was stupid.

'I think you should talk to her,' Ian insisted when she told him about it later. 'Once you stand up to her the chances are she'll back off straight away. And even if she doesn't, what's the worst that can happen? When it comes down to it, you don't need that job. You can easily find another one.'

'You just don't get it, do you?' she snapped. 'Prospective employers look at your employment history when you apply for a job. I can't risk getting the sack.'

'They're not going to sack you. You've done nothing wrong. But if you're unhappy there, just quit. Let them manage without you.'

'Why should I lose a perfectly good job because of that bloody bitch?'

'I agree it doesn't seem fair, but it's not worth getting upset about. That's all I'm saying. You'll easily find another job. Either way, whatever you decide to do is fine with me.'

★ ★ ★

Of course he was right. She hadn't been there long. There was nothing to stop her walking out, apart from her determination not to give in. Danielle resented her because Dominic obviously preferred her. It was hardly surprising. Men found Bev attractive. Danielle was an ugly cow. That was why Danielle was trying so hard to browbeat her into leaving. That meant that if she caved in, Danielle would have won. On the plus side Dominic was proving decent, doing his best to help her settle in. He had already told her he had plans for her future advancement. She would be a fool not to stay and pursue any possible opportunity for promotion. He had as good as promised her she wouldn't be stuck in that tiny office with Danielle forever. As she rose through the ranks, she was going to enjoy watching Danielle get her comeuppance, one way or another, even if it meant encouraging Dominic's advances.

'It's not that bad,' she assured Ian, 'she's just annoying. I'm sure it'll be OK. It's nothing I can't handle. The boss is OK.'

CHAPTER 56

Charles was worried. Since he had brought Vivien back to London they had received just one visit from a police inspector who had implied that a man had been arrested for Adrian's murder. After that everything had gone quiet. According to the papers, the man who had been helping the police with their enquiries had been released. If the information reported in the media was accurate, no one was in custody any more. Charles telephoned the police station in York several times to ask what was happening, but each time they fobbed him off.

'I'm sorry, sir, but no further information is available at present. A press statement will be made shortly. It will be available online straight away to members of the public.'

'This isn't a public matter. Adrian Curtis was my brother. His widow and I would like to know what's going on.'

'I'm sorry, sir. I'll put you through to the press office.'

'No, don't put me through to the press office.

I'm not a ruddy journalist. I want to speak to the inspector who's running the investigation.'

But someone else was already on the line.

'You're through to the North Yorkshire Police press office. There's no one here to take your call right now.'

If Charles was deeply upset about his brother's death, he was even more anxious about his sister-in-law who had been behaving oddly ever since their return to London. She had become hostile, and was behaving so erratically he dreaded visiting her. He supposed it was part of the grieving process, compounded by sedatives the doctor had prescribed. As a pharmacist, Charles had been apprehensive about her taking such powerful pills. Not unreasonably, she had trusted the doctor.

'You shouldn't take those for too long,' Charles had warned her. 'They can become addictive.'

He didn't know if she was still taking them, she had become so secretive. He had been persistent in his visits, but since the weekend she had refused to see him. He still had a key to the front door, but she had bolted it so he couldn't open it.

Since their return to London he had seen her only a few times, and on each occasion his visit had been brief. He had noticed a steady deterioration in her appearance. Three days had elapsed since their last meeting. On that occasion, her hair had been greasy, her face oddly blotchy, and he had smelt alcohol on her stale breath.

'You need to look after yourself,' he had told her. To his consternation she had laughed loudly. 'Are you drunk?'

'Leave me alone.'

'Vivien, what's happened to you? What's happened to us?'

'Adrian!' she had shrieked with unexpected animation. 'Adrian happened. Or did *we* happen to *him*?'

By Thursday evening his patience had run out. He hammered loudly at her front door, and bent down to yell through the letterbox.

'Vivien! It's me! Charles! If you don't let me in I'm going to get the police to break the door down.'

This wasn't pique. He was genuinely concerned. Vivien could have taken an overdose of sleeping pills and be lying in the house unconscious, or worse. After what had happened to Adrian, it wouldn't surprise him to discover she was suicidal. He should never have listened to her when she had asked him to leave her alone. Convinced the worst had happened, he was startled to hear a faint scratching sound coming from inside the house. A bolt was sliding across. A second later, the door swung open.

Vivien looked ill. He stared at her glazed eyes and lanky hair, her gaunt face and bowed posture. But more frightening than any signs of physical degeneration was her malevolent expression when she registered his presence on the doorstep. Her bloodshot eyes glared, and her cracked dry lips began twitching in a wordless mumble.

'Vivien, you must stop taking those pills. They're messing with your mind. You have to let me take care of you. You're in a right old state.' He tried to smile. 'Don't worry, I'm here now. Just don't bolt the door again, please. It's dangerous, locking yourself in like that. I was worried about you.'

He thought she hadn't heard what he was saying, but she frowned.

'If you don't leave me alone, I'll tell everyone what you did.'

He took a step back, startled by her vehemence.

'What I did?' he repeated. 'What did I do? What are you talking about?'

'You know what you did.'

'Vivien, let me call a doctor. You're not well.'

She shook her head. 'Leave me alone. I don't want to see anyone, least of all you.'

As she moved to close the door, he advanced further to place one foot over the threshold and caught an odour of stale sweat. It wasn't only her hair that was badly in need of a wash.

'Get out, or I'll call the police,' she hissed.

She wasn't in her right mind. There was no knowing what she might do. While he hesitated, she repeated her threat.

'I'll tell them what you did.'

'Vivien, what are you talking about? You're not well. This is crazy talk. It's me, Charles. I want to look after you. I can help you get well again. It doesn't have to be like this.'

'Get away from me! You know what you did.'

'I don't know what you're talking about,' he insisted.

Her eyes narrowed to slits, staring at him with unnerving intensity.

'I know what you did,' she repeated.

She leaned forward and he took an involuntary step backward, almost losing his footing. Frantically, he grabbed at the doorframe to steady himself.

'What do you mean? Vivien?'

'I know what you did to Adrian, up there on the balcony.'

'I wasn't on the balcony. I was with you.' He broke off as the enormity of what she had said struck him. 'Vivien, you can't really believe I had anything to do with what happened to Adrian at the races? I didn't go anywhere near the balcony. I was getting champagne. I was with you—'

With a guttural cry she reached out with both hands and shoved him on the chest. He staggered backwards, surprised by her strength. Before he could recover, she slammed the door in his face.

CHAPTER 57

On Friday morning Ian went through his files one more time, searching for an elusive clue that might link all three victims. If they had only been investigating Adrian and Richard, there would have been several suspects to investigate. Jocelyn had thrown a spanner in the works. Teams of constables had spent a week researching the histories of everyone involved with the victims. They had found no one who might possibly be connected to all three of them. The man-hours involved had been costly. Eileen was grousing about squandering resources, and extravagant budgets. Ian knew she was only passing on pressure from higher up. If they had uncovered a useful lead, all the investment would have been considered worthwhile. The trouble was they hadn't. He could feel his eyelids beginning to droop and was thinking of packing it in and going to get some lunch, when the desk sergeant called him. Adrian's brother was at the front desk, demanding to speak to him. Ian suspected he had come to find out what the police were doing to find his brother's killer.

Still, there was a chance he might have some new information.

Charles looked up warily when Ian entered the interview room. After a cursory exchange of greetings, Ian asked him the purpose of his visit.

Charles was blunt. 'I want to know what you're doing to find the bastard who murdered my brother.'

Ian nodded, keeping his disappointment to himself. It was a fair enough question, one that Eileen had also asked.

'We're pursuing several leads,' he began.

'What you mean is, you're getting nowhere.'

'Not at all. We're pursuing several leads.'

'That doesn't tell me anything. I need specifics. What leads?'

'I'm afraid I can't say at this early stage in the investigation.'

Charles' face turned red with anger. 'Look here, Inspector, I'm a busy man. I've travelled all the way here from London because I can't get anything out of your people whenever I phone. They only put me onto the press office, who tell me nothing I can't read for myself in any newspaper. Now I'm here, I insist on being told exactly what progress you've made. I won't leave here until you tell me what's going on.'

'You can demand all you like, mate, you won't bully me into admitting that we're casting around helplessly,' Ian thought. Aloud, he said levelly: 'I'm sorry, sir, I'm not at liberty to pass on information to anyone.'

'Anyone? This is my brother we're talking about. Jesus, tell me who your suspects are, and I'll get a confession out of one of them myself.'

'I would strongly advise you not to try and take the law into your own hands. That will only land you in trouble. Leave the investigation to us. We'll find him. You can be sure of that.'

Charles's large square chin quivered. He rose to his feet and flapped his hands in agitation. Ian could only repeat his assurances that everything possible was being done to find whoever had pushed Adrian off the balcony. He stood up, signalling the interview was over, but Charles sat down heavily and put his head in his hands.

'Please, Inspector,' he mumbled. 'Please. You don't understand. I need your help.'

Ian sat down and waited to hear what Charles had to say. After a moment, Charles straightened up. His eyes looked moist, and he was clearly frightened.

'It's Vivien,' he said. His bombastic tone had evaporated and his words sounded tentative. 'She's gone crazy. The doctor put her on drugs – medication I should say – and it's affecting her mind. What with grief and shock at what happened to Adrian, she's – well, she's gone crazy. She thinks – she thinks it was me.'

★   ★   ★

He fell silent. Ian waited but Charles didn't continue.

'I'm not sure I follow you,' Ian said at last. 'She thinks what was you?'

Charles shook his head. 'It's difficult. It's so hard to explain. I don't want to give you the wrong impression.'

'About what?'

'About me.'

Ian waited.

All at once words poured out of Charles in a rush. 'The thing is, Vivien's got it into her head that I killed Adrian.' He raised anguished eyes to Ian.

Aware that he was conducting the interview by himself, without recording what was being said, Ian made the decision to press on regardless. He was reluctant to take a break and risk Charles changing his mind about speaking so freely. In his present state, it sounded as though he might be leading up to a confession.

'Why would she think that?'

Charles heaved a sigh that shook his upper body. 'I knew you'd ask that,' he said. 'I can see it looks bad, but you should see the state she's in, off her head with diazepam and alcohol, on top of what happened. If you saw her, you wouldn't take anything she says seriously. She's completely lost it. I'm telling you, if you go and see her, she'll accuse *you* of murdering her husband, that's how far gone she is. I need to get her to a doctor, but she won't speak to me. She won't even let me in the house. I don't know what to do.'

He jumped up and paced the small room in agitation.

'You've got to do something, Inspector.'

'What do you expect me to do? I'm not a doctor.'

'You have to help me sort her out, one way or another.'

'How am I supposed to do that?'

'You have to arrest someone. It doesn't matter who. You can let them go again afterwards if you've got the wrong person, once she's recovered. But you have to tell her you've arrested the killer, so she knows it wasn't me. If she doesn't get help soon, she'll go totally insane. Please, you have to help her get past this. She needs me to get her to a doctor. Without me, there's no one to make sure she's looked after. She's got to start trusting me again or she'll go totally insane. We have to make that our priority.'

'Your priority,' Ian thought, 'not mine.' He nodded circumspectly.

'We are as keen as you are to get to the bottom of this,' he said. 'But I can't see how talking to your sister-in-law will help us, unless she has some information we are not yet aware of.'

Ian knew he was being harsh, but he struggled to feel sympathy for a man who had been having an affair with his own brother's wife.

'Sit down.'

'Yes, I'm sorry.' Charles complied.

'We're doing all we can—'

'This is all my fault,' Charles blurted out abruptly. 'You don't understand, I have to look after her. I owe it to Adrian because – because it's my fault he's dead.'

Ian held his breath and gazed levelly at Charles' anguished face.

'What do you mean? Do you want to confess?' He sat very still and spoke softly. 'Did you kill your brother? Was it an accident? Tell me what happened. Did you get into an argument?'

'No, no, I didn't kill him. He was my brother. But it's my fault he's dead. It was my idea to go to the races. If I hadn't got the tickets, none of this would have happened.' He began to sob. 'It's all my fault.'

CHAPTER 58

Returning home from the local shop, Emma almost collapsed on the front door step, right on the spot where she had found Richard's body. She had slept badly the previous night, as she had done every night since his death. It was a struggle to keep her mind steady. Every time she started to feel calm her head began to spin and she felt sick. Closing the door behind her, she burst into tears. It was strange being on her own in the house. Wherever she looked, something reminded her of Richard. She deliberated over whether to take down the photograph on the mantelpiece. He looked so happy, she couldn't help smiling before she burst into tears again. It was no good. She had told her mother she was ready to return home, and now she had to get on with it. The photograph went into a drawer in the living room where she would keep it safely out of sight. She didn't want to keep it in her bedroom. It was difficult enough to put him out of her mind at night, in the dark, with nothing to distract her from her last memory of his white face and sightless eyes.

★   ★   ★

Sitting down, she saw her hands were trembling. Her mother had insisted it was too early for her to return to York, but when she had urged her to stay in Surrey for at least another week, Emma had remonstrated.

'There's no point in putting if off any longer. I can't delay going home indefinitely.'

'No one's suggesting you stay here with us indefinitely, but you're still in shock. It's bound to take time to recover, that's all I'm saying.'

Emma wasn't sure she wanted to recover. That implied acceptance of what had happened, and a readiness to move on and embrace a life without Richard. The prospect was unthinkable. They had intended to get married one day, although they hadn't even got engaged yet. For months she had been checking out rings in the local shop windows and browsing online, just looking, so that she would be prepared when he raised the subject. She knew exactly what she wanted, a princess cut solitaire on a white gold band, with a matching wedding ring.

By the evening she felt lightheaded and knew she ought to eat something. There wasn't much in the kitchen. She was too tired to go out, so she opened a tin of soup and took a slice of bread from the freezer and toasted it. Wine, she decided, was not a good idea. Once she started to eat, she discovered she was quite hungry after all. She enjoyed her simple meal all the more because she would never have been able to slob around like that while Richard was alive. He liked things to be done properly, even their evening meal, which they used to eat sitting at the table. Slouching comfortably in an armchair, with a tray on her lap and a light-hearted quiz show on television, for the first time since Richard's death she felt a flicker of confidence that her life might return to something resembling normality. She loathed herself for being disloyal, but she had lived without Richard before, and she could do so again. Unless she intended to kill herself, she had to get her life back on track.

Her mother wasn't alone in exhorting her to be strong. Richard wouldn't have wanted her to waste her life grieving for him. Horrible though it was to know that he would have made a new life for himself without her if she had died, it was also liberating. It wasn't going to be easy, but she would survive this. She owed it to him not to cave in. Feeling almost cheerful, she carried her tray into the kitchen. While Richard had lived with her she would never have left dirty dishes in the kitchen. Now she dumped them in the sink, taking care not to block the plughole in case the tap leaked. In some ways it was a relief that the police were still investigating Richard's death. It meant there was no need to fret about funeral arrangements yet. She tried not to think about the body, lying somewhere in the mortuary, perhaps stored in a refrigerated drawer. The Richard she had known was gone. That was the end of it. Thankfully she had been relieved of the gruesome responsibility of identifying the body. Richard had a brother in Wales who had done that. She had never met the brother and had chosen not to see him on this occasion, for fear he might resemble Richard.

She hoped Richard's brother would take care of the funeral too. As far as she knew, nothing had yet been discussed, but she really couldn't bear to be involved in making arrangements and inviting family and friends. It would be too complicated and painful. Meanwhile, the only pressing decision she faced was whether to return to work on Monday or take more time off. Initially the headmaster had been sympathetic, but his patience would soon wear thin. She had already been away for a week. The trouble was, she had no way of knowing if she would be able to go back on Monday. She would have to wait and see how she felt, and phone in to tell them if she didn't feel ready. It wasn't ideal from their point of view, but she didn't know what else to do. She didn't want to tell them in advance that she wouldn't go in, and then find she was fit to go back after all. Work might help to distract her from thinking about Richard. On the other hand, she didn't want to go in and embarrass herself and all her colleagues by falling apart. It was tricky. With a sigh she turned her attention to the television and tried not to think about anything.

★   ★   ★

The phone startled her out of a doze. Without thinking, she reached to answer it.

'Mum?'

'Hardly.'

It was the same strange gurgling sound she had heard before, as though his jaws were stuck together and he could only laugh in his throat. She was instantly alert.

'What do you want?'

'I just called to say welcome home.'

'Leave me alone.'

He laughed again.

'I'll hang up,' she blustered.

'We both know you won't, not yet, because you want to hear what I have to say.'

Infuriated, she hung up. Let him interpret her action as provocative. She refused to play stupid games with a psychopath. But she suspected he had only called to show he knew she was back. And if his intention had been to frighten her, he had succeeded.

CHAPTER 59

When Bev discovered Danielle was away for a few days, she felt as though she had been let out of prison. Dominic gave her a key to the office and left her to her own devices. At midday the door opened and he peered in.

'How's it going in here?'

She looked up and returned his smile. 'I think I can survive a few days without Danielle breathing down my neck.'

Although Dominic's smile didn't waver, his eyes glittered. She wondered if she had spoken out of turn. It didn't really matter, but there was no point in aggravating him.

'I was wondering if you fancy a spot of lunch?' he asked.

Bev had left Kent with a vague feeling of regret about the restraint she had exercised with her former boss. Although she had never succumbed to his flattery, she had enjoyed his attention. Now it seemed that her new boss was interested in her. She wasn't surprised. She had always been both gratified and unnerved by the attention she received from men. That was one of her reasons for marrying Ian. He made her feel safe.

With Ian engrossed in an investigation, Bev was bored, cut off from her friends and family. She couldn't help feeling pleased by Dominic's advances. The fact that he happened to be a reasonably attractive man was almost irrelevant. She had no intention of having an affair with him, but in her isolation she would have welcomed any overture of friendship.

'Lunch would be lovely,' she said brightly. 'Shall I just finish this?'

'How about we take a break in half an hour?'

'Fine.'

Dominic left and she hurried through her work to make sure she had time to check her make up before he returned.

They walked round the corner to a pub that served food at the bar. It was comfortable and spacious, and not too busy. While they were waiting for their food to arrive, Dominic filled her large wine glass. When she put her glass down after one sip, he looked at her anxiously.

'If you don't like it, we can order something else.'

'No, it's fine. I just don't usually drink at lunchtime,' Bev protested half-heartedly.

'While the cat's away,' he answered, laughing.

Assuming he was referring to Danielle, Bev heard herself laughing too loudly. Not wanting to offend him, or seem prissy, she drained her glass and watched him refill it.

'You're going to get me drunk,' she giggled, aware that she was already feeling tipsy.

Dominic was keen to hear about her move to York. He questioned her tactfully, and seemed to understand how she felt about being uprooted to follow her husband's career, after working her way up to manage the office in her previous post. It was understandable he would want to know all about her previous job. She hoped she didn't sound as though she was boasting when she told him she had been in charge of four girls. He was impressed.

'So you really were the manager?'

She nodded, noticing he must have refilled her glass. She took another sip, aware that she needed to slow down her drinking. She hadn't noticed him drinking much. He seemed to be more interested in listening to what she was saying.

'It must have been difficult for you, leaving your job after you'd worked so hard to make a success of it.'

'It was.'

Wary of revealing quite how drunk she was, she was relieved when the food finally arrived. They would be going back to work within an hour, and she was alone with her boss. Lunch was probably an informal kind of assessment of her aptitude for the job, although he was going out of his way to treat it like a social event. So much so that when he started talking again, he avoided mentioning work, chatting instead about York. The conversation drifted to the subject of his girlfriend.

'We've been together for five years,' he admitted sheepishly. 'We met just after I moved here. I think she'd like to make it official and get married, but—' he shrugged. 'I suppose we'll do it one day.'

She smiled sympathetically. 'It's a lot of hassle.'

'And expense.'

'Yes, there's that as well.'

After he had spoken so openly about his relationship with his girlfriend, it would be churlish of her to refuse to answer his questions about her husband. Besides, she was too drunk to control what she said. She heard herself boasting about Ian's promotion, and stifled a giggle.

Dominic agreed Ian's work was important.

'You must be very proud of him. But it must keep him busy. You said he deals with serious crime.'

'Yes.'

'So bank robberies? Things like that?'

She lowered her voice to a mutter. 'Murder.'

'Murder? You are kidding?'

She was miffed that he sounded sceptical. At the back of her mind she had a faint recollection they had been through this before. Clearly he hadn't really been listening. She leaned forward. This time she would spell it out for him. Through her drunken haze, she was convinced it mattered that Dominic believed Ian's work was important.

Complacently she watched him refill her glass.

'You must have read about the man who died at the races?' He nodded. She could see he was interested now, and she spoke more quickly, determined to make her point. 'He was murdered.'

'That's what the papers said.'

'It's a very complicated case for Ian. That man's connected to the woman who was murdered by the river, and there's been another murder. Do you see what I mean?'

'Surely it can't have been the same killer every time?'

She lowered her voice, aware that she was speaking too loudly in her excitement. 'The police don't want the papers to mention the words "serial killer" because then everyone panics, but that's what it is. A serial killer. And I'm married to the man who's in charge of the whole investigation.'

'Well, let's hope they get him then.'

'Ian will. He always does.'

She sat back with a grin. Around her the room spun gently at her movement.

It occurred to her fuzzily that Ian would be furious if he found out she had been boasting about his role in the investigation, but Ian wasn't there. He never was. And it wasn't as if she'd told Dominic anything that wasn't already in the news. Dominic was a kind man, taking her out for lunch and really caring that she was settling into her new job. If it wasn't for her job she would be totally isolated in York, friendless and alone. The thought made her want to cry.

'Are you all right?'

'I think I may have had a bit too much to drink,' she admitted.

'Why don't you take the afternoon off? Go home and sleep it off. I'm sure we can spare you for one afternoon.'

She smiled. He really was a very kind man. She was going to enjoy working for him. As for Danielle, one way or another that problem would resolve itself in time. Meanwhile, the silly cow was away.

'You go home now,' Dominic said. 'I'll see you in the morning.'

CHAPTER 60

Normally Ian was pleased to be summoned to speak to a witness or potential suspect. It was the most interesting part of his job, raising the possibility of discovering vital information to help them solve the case. But he was nervous about seeing Emma again. Dealing with tearful women was exhausting. Entering the interview room, he was relieved to see how much better she looked than at their previous meeting. Her eyes seemed to glow in her face, and her hair shone. Used to ruffling his wife's short hair, he wondered what it might feel like to stroke Emma's sleek head. Registering the warmth in her smile, he hesitated to mention how pleased he was to see she had recovered from her initial shock.

'You wanted to see me?' he asked as he sat down opposite her.

'Yes.'

She hesitated for a second, her face solemn. 'I thought it would stop now, but it hasn't.'

When she didn't continue, Ian asked her to explain.

'The phone calls.' She sighed, clearly finding it difficult to talk. 'When I first met Richard, he was so different. He wasn't afraid of anything. He was so full of life, and such fun to be with.' Her expression softened. 'We were really in love, you know. I mean, I knew him really well. I understood him. Sometimes I knew what he was thinking before he said anything.'

Her expression changed. Her eyes filled with tears but when she spoke her voice was firm.

'He changed really suddenly. Overnight. The thing is, I think he was scared. I thought he was concerned about our relationship and worried about making a commitment, but I can see now I was wrong. It started with the phone calls.'

'What else can you tell me about the phone calls?'

She shrugged. 'There's nothing more to say, really.'

'Were any calls made to his mobile?'

'I don't know.'

'As far as you can remember, when did they start?'

She shrugged again, wiping a tear from her cheek. 'I don't know. I think it had been going on for a while, but I can't say exactly when it started. All I know is, I noticed the change in him recently, around Easter.'

'So you noticed a change in Richard that you now suspect was the result of a series of nuisance phone calls that you think began around Easter?' Ian reiterated, keen to clarify her muddled account.

'Yes. I think so.'

Emma could be mistaken, but Ian had a feeling these calls might prove to be important.

'What did Richard say about the caller?'

'Nothing. He didn't say anything. I only found out because I answered the phone one evening and it was him, Richard's stalker.'

'How did you know who it was?'

'I could see it in Richard's face. It was about three weeks ago. The caller asked for Richard and when he took the phone and began to speak, he was scared. He sent me into the kitchen but I overheard him say something like, "You'll never get away with it. Wherever you are, I'll find you. You won't get away with this." When I asked Richard who it was, he said it was an old friend from work but I knew he was lying.'

She looked down and when she raised her eyes again Ian could see she was afraid.

'I didn't think it was important. I thought maybe he'd fallen out with someone. People do, don't they? I don't know why, but I thought he might have had a row with his brother. But a week ago his stalker called again, to speak to me.'

'Not to Richard?'

'No. He knew Richard was dead.' She stared at Ian.

'Why didn't you tell us about it straight away?'

'I panicked and went to stay with my parents.'

'Was it something the caller said that made you panic?'

'Yes. He told me it wasn't suicide. I thought he was threatening to kill me too. I should have come to you, but I was in a real state. I wasn't thinking clearly. When I came back yesterday, I felt better. I thought it was all over. Only then he phoned again, last night.' She broke off, trembling.

Seeing her face lose its colour, Ian pressed her to tell him what the stalker had said.

'He said he did it for me,' she whispered. 'He said Richard wasn't good enough for me and I should be grateful to him for what he'd done.'

Ian spoke as gently as he could. 'Are you saying the nuisance caller told you he killed Richard?'

'I don't know, I don't know, yes, yes, I think that's what he meant. He didn't say it in so many words, but I think he killed Richard.'

She was crying so hard now, she could no longer speak. Ian went to organise a cup of tea for her and when he returned, she had calmed down enough to insist she was ready to continue the interview.

'What did the caller mean when he said he did it for you?'

'I don't know. I don't know.'

★   ★   ★

336

Ian reassured her that they would find Richard's killer, but he was baffled. Once again he had a feeling he was missing something.

'And you can't remember anything distinctive about the way the caller spoke?'

Even with eyes glistening with tears she was touchingly beautiful. Her makeup was smudged. Somehow the flaw in her appearance seemed to highlight her loveliness.

'No. I'm sorry. He didn't have a stammer or an accent and he didn't speak with a lisp, or use an unusual turn of phrase.'

Ian smiled faintly. 'Would you recognise the voice, if you heard it again?'

'Yes, I think so.'

It wasn't much, but it was something. Ian thanked her for coming forward.

'It can't have been easy for you.'

She smiled at him through her tears and he made his escape, thankful that she had only broken down once.

CHAPTER 61

It wasn't easy deciding how far back to go, as Emma hadn't been able to give them a definite date when Richard's nuisance calls had begun. Ian directed a female constable to check all calls made to Emma's landline and Richard's mobile over the past three months. The officer he chose was a smart and hard working young woman called Meena. Making a rapid assessment of his instructions, she pointed out that he hadn't given her enough information to work on. All Ian could say was that she was to look out for a series of evening calls from a number that had only started contacting him recently. It was likely that the number had been withheld, in which case it might be relatively easy to spot and trace.

'So this caller didn't want to be identified,' Meena said, adding shrewdly, 'which means there may be no pattern to find.'

'That's right,' Ian agreed. 'He might not have called on the same day of the week, or at the same time.'

She gave a rueful smile. 'Or from the same number. Thanks, sir.'

★ ★ ★

A couple of hours later, Meena reported that she had come across a number of calls made from public telephones in pubs, bars and hotels, or on the street. None of the numbers had been used more than once. All had been evening calls made any time between seven and midnight. The two most recent coincided with the times Emma had been telephoned after Richard's death. They had been made from two different numbers. Ian studied the list. The telephones were all located in different areas in and around York. None were in the city centre. The list could be completely random and meaningless. On the other hand, there was a chance it might show them exactly where the stalker had been when he had made contact with Richard. Ian asked Meena to contact the venues and she returned after an hour to report that only a couple of the places she had been able to contact so far had surveillance cameras on site. The mystery caller had been careful to cover his tracks. Ian commended the constable's diligence. She shared his growing conviction that Richard's anonymous caller was also his killer.

Another constable joined Meena in checking CCTV film taken close to all the public telephones that had been used to contact the victim. A hooded figure was visible entering one of the telephone boxes seconds before a call had been made from there to Emma's landline, but however much the image was rotated and enhanced, the face was indistinguishable. None of the other surveillance cameras held any film relevant or useful to their search. Occasionally a figure moved across the screen in a blur, its face shrouded in a hood. It could have been the same person each time, but it was impossible to be sure. They might have been looking at several people, none of whom was their target. They focused their attention on the one figure they had sighted using a phone at the time Richard had been called from it, but failed to track the figure before and after its arrival at the phone box. The call had been paid for with a phone card that had been bought for cash. They had caught a killer on film, but were no closer to discovering his identity. All they had was a hazy image of a hooded figure flitting across the screen, its face concealed in shadows. It appeared at the phone box out of the darkness into which it vanished. The team nicknamed it The Ghost.

Ian couldn't help thinking of his former inspector, who had gained a reputation not only for being a workaholic, but for being incapable of delegating. Her insistence on wanting to check everything herself had made her unpopular with some of the less experienced officers, who felt she didn't trust them. Ian had never felt undermined by her. Despite her control issues, he had admired her single-minded determination to retain a clear over-view of every aspect of an investigation. He was convinced that had been a significant factor in her impressive record for wrapping up complicated cases in record time. He realised that he was beginning to behave like her, as he sat scanning the CCTV footage the team had already watched. He knew it was futile. He wasn't going to spot anything they had missed. But he stayed on late into the night staring at the screen until he dozed off and was woken by the duty sergeant.

Ian was pushing himself, but he was also under pressure from Eileen to achieve results. When he arrived at work on Tuesday morning he received a message that she was asking for him.

'Where have you been?' she demanded as soon as he opened her door.

Ian hesitated. He had only just arrived at work. Having stayed up late the previous night pointlessly staring at security films, he had overslept. Bev had already left for work by the time he woke up. He was annoyed with her for not waking him up. He decided to come clean and explain why he was in late.

'And did you find anything?'

'No.'

'That's three deaths in as many weeks,' she burst out, as though he was personally responsible for arranging the local murders to coincide with his move to the area.

He returned to his own office smarting from her implied reprimand. He knew she was only passing on her own stress, and was determined not to do the same. Shortly after that he snapped at Meena for having nothing to report, which was hardly fair, and was short with Ted who asked if there was any news. For the first time, he wondered if he had made the right decision in moving up North. York was a fascinating and beautiful city, but since his promotion he seemed to have lost his way. In Kent he had worked hard to establish his reputation at work. His colleagues had respected him, and he had mates there. They had worked as a team. He missed them. He didn't like to think what it must be like for Bev, torn away from everyone she knew so that he could pursue his selfish ambition. Now he had brought her to York, he wondered if his promotion was worth all the disruption.

Tired and dispirited, he went out for a breath of fresh air. As he stepped outside a cool light drizzle started, throwing a grey veil over the grass and trees. Behind him the square red brick and glass police station rose, uncompromisingly ugly. He felt a sharp sense of regret, remembering how hard he had worked for his promotion. He was afraid that he had been misguided, thinking he could cope with the responsibility that came with being a detective inspector. More than anything he wished he had stayed in Kent where Bev had been happy. He had let her down, but there was no going back. With an effort he shrugged off his gloomy musings. All that mattered now was the investigation. Three people had been killed. If he didn't track down their killer, he would fail them as well.

CHAPTER 62

Every time Vivien tried to sleep, dazzling points of white light darted around behind her eyelids. Despite overwhelming exhaustion, she was forced to open her eyes to stop the dizzying brilliance that was making her feel sick. With her eyes open, all she could see was a white blur. A woman's voice was calling her name. For a moment she thought it must be her mother. She blinked and a stranger's face appeared. Dark eyes framed in black rimmed spectacles gazed at her. Pink lips moved in a blur.

'Can you hear me? Vivien?'

Her throat was so dry it hurt to move her mouth. When she tried to answer all she could manage was a weak groan. She nodded her head, and felt her brain throb painfully with the movement. Keeping perfectly still, she forced out a rasping whisper.

'Who are you?'

'You're in hospital, Vivien. Vivien? Stay with me, Vivien.'

★　★　★

She wanted to drift back to sleep, but the soft voice continued relentlessly. Lights flashed when she closed her eyes.

'You had an accident. Do you remember what happened?'

She tried to shake her head but it wouldn't move. Her limbs ached and she became aware of a dull pain in her guts. Something was wrong with her, making her feel sick, but she didn't have the energy to worry about it. Instead, she succumbed to a blanket of sleep that filled her mind.

'Can you open your eyes?'

She grunted and forced herself to look up at the woman who was speaking to her.

'You had an accident, Vivien. Do you remember?'

She had the impression the woman wanted to be friendly, but she was too tired to remain conscious.

When she opened her eyes again, she couldn't see anyone else in the room. The first thing that struck her was a strong smell of disinfectant. Dimly she became aware of a humming noise, and distant scurrying. Somewhere far away an alarm was beeping. Every time she closed her eyes neon lights flared inside her head like silent fireworks, brilliant pink and green and white. She wondered whether she had suffered a severe case of flu. Every inch of her seemed to ache. But somehow she knew this wasn't a physical illness. There was something wrong with her thoughts, something that could never be cured. She opened her eyes to calm the bright lights, and looked around the room. Any sudden movement made her feel giddy so she swivelled her eyes gingerly. Everything was white. As the mist in front of her eyes cleared, she saw a man and woman looking down at her. The man spoke.

'Vivien, can you hear me?'

'Yes.'

He shone a light in her eyes and moved it slowly from side to side.

'Can you follow this? Look at the torch, Vivien. Good.' He nodded, satisfied. 'Well done.' He leaned forward, talking very slowly. 'You're in hospital because you took an overdose of sleeping pills. Do you remember what happened?'

She closed her eyes in an effort to forget and let sleep carry her away from his questions. It didn't matter what had happened, or why she was there. She was sick and tired, yet the man refused to leave her in peace until gradually, at his insistence, her brain began to function again. As her memories returned, so did the anguish she had attempted to leave behind. Tears tickled the sides of her face and she blinked.

'I want to die,' she whispered. 'I want Adrian.'

'We know about Adrian,' the woman's gentle voice said, 'we know what happened. You don't have to talk about him right now, if you don't want to. But you have to be strong, Vivien. There are people who can help you learn to cope with your loss.'

'No one can help me.'

'Believe me, it helps to talk to someone,' the woman assured her. 'It will help you deal with the pain. I know it will. And in time it will get better.'

'Time heals,' Vivien muttered bitterly.

The woman mistook her cynicism for positivity. 'Yes,' she agreed earnestly, 'time heals all wounds.'

With a groan, Vivien closed her eyes.

When she next woke up she felt lightheaded and nauseous, but stronger. The room was still humming and buzzing. Lights were flickering on a machine beside her bed. The mattress was hard, but not uncomfortable. Her head moved more easily than before, and she no longer ached all over. She breathed a shallow sigh of relief that the physical pain had faded. Noticing a beautiful scent, she looked to her left and saw a massive bouquet of lilies and roses.

'Thank God you're awake.'

She turned towards the voice. The man's face was familiar. It couldn't be Adrian. He was dead. She had seen him lying on the ground after his fatal accident – if it had been an accident. He had been surrounded by strangers milling about: race stewards, security guards, police. More and more of them had arrived until she hadn't even been able to see him. Remembering the scene, her head was filled with the noise of many people talking at once, a mixture of spectators eager to learn what had happened, officials barking orders, and somewhere a woman crying hysterically. Someone had brought her a chair. She had covered her face but she hadn't been able to shut out the mayhem beating in her ears.

The scent of lilies pervaded the room, strong and sweet.

'Don't worry,' Charles said. He sounded upset. 'I'm here now. I'm not going anywhere. You don't have to face this alone. Don't shut me out again. Let me help you. Vivien, look at me. I'm going to take care of you from now on.'

As he took her hand in his she whimpered, but she was too tired to withdraw it. He gently stroked her fingers and her eyes filled with tears. Hopelessly, she realised she would never be strong enough to break free of him. Adrian had gone. There was only Charles. And the pills.

CHAPTER 63

Ian's mood didn't improve when he went back inside, cold and damp, and heard that Eileen had been asking to see him.

'What is it this time?' he grumbled to the duty sergeant, a ruddy-faced man in his forties.

His colleague shrugged his shoulders. 'Search me.'

Eileen looked about as pleased as Ian felt when he entered her office.

'Ian,' she pitched in without any preamble, 'at last, you're here.'

He didn't answer. He knew her frustration was with the situation, not directed against him personally, even though it sometimes felt like that.

'We've been devoting a hell of a lot of manpower to this investigation. We've had search teams out for days at three deposition sites.'

'There *were* three bodies,' he muttered.

'We've interviewed hundreds of potential witnesses.'

Ian nodded. It had certainly proved a costly exercise looking into the death at the races.

'VIIDO teams are still occupied spending hours

and hours watching surveillance film. Well, of course all that has to be done, fine.' She leaned forward, speaking earnestly. 'There's no problem with throwing all these resources at the investigation. My problem is, I have to explain what's happening to the commander, so I need to understand the progress we've been making.'

Ian nodded again. He appreciated she was asking him to supply her with reasons to justify maintaining the budget for the investigation. In terms of finances and manpower, it was spiralling out of control. No one would quibble with the expense once they established they were making headway. The trouble was, they didn't seem to be getting anywhere, despite all the time and effort that had been devoted to the case.

'We can't continue at this level indefinitely. I'm sorry, Ian, but you're going to have to give me something. Do we have any suspects at all at this point in time?'

'Yes.'

She must have heard the hesitation in his voice, read it in his face.

'Who?'

Awkwardly, Ian told her about the anonymous hooded figure who had been recorded entering a phone box shortly before Richard had been contacted from that same phone. The phone box had been dusted for prints and finger searched, but they had found nothing that might help them identify the elusive killer. Ian refrained from telling her the VIIDO team's nickname for the target.

He didn't think he could cope with any more aggravation that evening, so he was relieved to hear Bev singing happily to herself when he arrived home. He found her busy in the kitchen. There was something different about her. He hadn't seen her looking so chirpy since their move to York. She greeted him with a bright smile.

'I thought I'd make a light supper,' she announced.

With her back to him she didn't see Ian pull a face. He was starving.

'How light?'

'A beer and a slice of cheese on toast would do me.'

'Or do you fancy a Chinese?' he suggested hopefully. 'We could go out?'

She shook her head.

'I couldn't. I went out for lunch. And I'm a bit tired, to be honest.'

'Out for lunch, eh?' He hoped he sounded pleased. 'On the piss?'

She gave a sheepish smile. 'Well, we did get through a bottle of wine,' she admitted.

'Each?' he laughed.

'No! There were two of us.'

Ian perched on a stool and smiled, pleased to see her looking so cheerful. It was ironic that she appeared to be so much happier in her new job than he was in his, although they had only moved on account of his promotion.

'Was this a bonding exercise with the girl you're working with, then?' he asked. 'It looks as though it worked.'

'What? Me and Danielle? Out for lunch? Hardly!' She laughed.

Pleased that she seemed to have made a friend he was nevertheless surprised, and a little curious.

'Who then?'

'Not Danielle,' she explained, 'she was off on some training day, so it was just me and the store manager.'

Ian felt a faint stab of jealousy. His knee jerk reaction dated back to when they had first met. All the boys at school had fancied her. As an adult, he had to accept that not every man who set eyes on her would try to get her into bed, especially now she was married. All the same, he couldn't help wondering why her boss would take her out for lunch, and throw in a bottle of wine. Bev had refused his offer of dinner, but had found time to go out for lunch with a relative stranger.

'The store manager?'

'He's a nice guy. You'd like him. We went for a working lunch.'

'I'm sure,' he muttered. Loudly he asked, 'Does he fancy you?'

'Of course not.'

'Why "of course" not?'

He struggled to control his anger. Somehow all his years of training counted for nothing in his relations with his wife. His hard-won objectivity melted away. He hated himself for overreacting, but he couldn't help it.

She was riled now.

'You know what your trouble is? It's got nothing to do with Dominic, or anyone else, and it's nothing to do with me. There's nothing wrong with the way I behave. It's you. You're the problem. You don't trust me, do you? Is that really what you think of me? That I'm some kind of slut who'll jump at any man who looks at me?' She waved her hands in the air in her agitation. 'How can you think so little of me, after everything we've been through? I gave up my job for you.' She was crying now. 'Why can't you trust me? How can you treat me like this?'

He hated himself for making her cry, despised her for being so easily upset, and detested her new boss for spending time with her. All at once he was sick of the whole situation and too worn out to deal with it. One way or another, it had to end. He grovelled shamelessly, desperate to stop her crying.

'I'm sorry. I was out of order. I'm just jealous that another man spent time with my girl. Come here, don't cry. I know you'd never do anything to hurt me. It's all my fault.'

'I've not done anything wrong,' she wept.

★   ★   ★

353

It took him the best part of an hour to pacify her, by which time he was ready to fall into bed and go to sleep. She went upstairs for a shower, leaving him to prepare a light supper he didn't even want any more, he was so tired. They were both exhausted after the move, and desperately needed some time together away from the strain of their everyday lives. He just hoped the current murder investigation would be over before they were due to fly to Greece. He didn't want an unresolved case hanging over him as he lay on a beach trying to relax in the sun – if he was even allowed to go. The way things were progressing, it seemed virtually impossible they would find the murderer in the next fortnight.

And there was no reason to suppose the killing would stop.

CHAPTER 64

Emma had been so stressed before going to stay with her mother that she had left without tidying the house. She hadn't even bothered to throw the rubbish out. She had returned to find a pile of dirty dishes and cutlery in the sink, and a stinking bottle of milk on the work top. By Thursday she had recovered her composure sufficiently to spend the morning clearing up the kitchen and changing her sheets. She was feeling almost back to normal when her school phoned. As soon as Emma assured the headmaster she was ready to return to work, he became reasonable.

'Why not take the rest of the week off?' he suggested kindly. 'You might as well come back fresh on Monday. We can manage without you until then.'

Emma had agreed at once, pleased to have an extra day at home. She still had to tackle Richard's wardrobe. His brother had cleared out all his tools, taking them away in Richard's old banger with a promise to send her a cheque once he had sold

355

the car. He had told her it wasn't worth much when they had spoken on the phone. At the time she had been grateful to him for relieving her of at least one chore. With hindsight she realised she had probably made a mistake handing over most of Richard's belongings so readily, and wondered if she would ever receive a cheque for the car, but there was nothing she could do about it. She had no legal claim on Richard's belongings anyway. It wasn't as if they had been married.

Including the weekend she had another three full days to herself before she went back to work, time to clear every trace of Richard out of the house, if she could psych herself up to do it. In some ways she was looking forward to returning to work. It would provide a distraction from her painful memories. It didn't help, being in the house where she had lived with Richard, cooking in the kitchen where they had prepared meals together, watching the television he had bought, sleeping in the bed they had shared. All the same, she liked her home. It had been her choice to move in there long before she met Richard, and she had been happy enough living there by herself once.

It was a sunny afternoon so she went to the super-market to stock up for the following week. It felt good to get out of the house. People she passed had no idea what had happened to Richard. They had never met him or even heard of him. The store wasn't busy. Wandering along the aisles, picking up milk and bread, she nearly didn't bother to answer her mobile. Only concern that her mother might worry made her pick up. She pushed her trolley over to one side of the aisle, beside the apples, allowing room for others to pass.

'Mum, I'm shopping.'

'I know.'

It wasn't her mother.

'The grapes are particularly nice just now.'

'What? I don't know what you mean.'

She rang off and began pushing her trolley hurriedly away from the trays of fruit beside her.

A moment later her phone rang again. She made a snap decision to deal with the stalker straight away. If she ignored him he would only call her again. Talking to him in the supermarket where she was surrounded by people was very different to receiving his calls when she was alone at home. Resolutely she manoeuvred her trolley over to one side of the aisle and snatched her phone out of her pocket.

'What do you want?'

'You forgot the grapes.' He didn't seem bothered by her hostility. If anything, he sounded amused. 'Why don't you get some? No one will mind if you go back.'

Nervously she glanced behind her. There was no one there. She looked all around but couldn't see anyone spying on her, and there were no security cameras in view. He was talking to her again.

'I mentioned the grapes because they're particularly nice right now.'

She hung up. He must have seen her entering the store and was standing out in the street somewhere, chancing his luck. It had been a coincidence that he had mentioned grapes just as she was standing beside them. He couldn't have known where she was. She walked on and paused by the fish counter. Even though she was half expecting to hear it, she was startled when her phone rang again. Tentatively, she answered.

'How about fresh mackerel? Oily fish is supposed to be very healthy.' He laughed. 'You see, I'm keeping an eye on you, watching what you eat.'

She glanced round. There was no doubt about it now. He was stalking her, completely out of control. If she wasn't careful, she could be his next victim. Her phone rang again. Driven by a horrid fascination she answered, unable to resist the shrill summons.

'Remember, I'm keeping an eye on you. You'll see.'

Before she turned her phone off, she heard him laughing.

A solitary man in a grey track suit brushed past her and she cried out. He paid her no attention. Whirling round she watched him stride along the aisle to vanish behind a stack of tins. An old woman tottered into the aisle. She peered anxiously at Emma, shaking her head and mumbling. She glared at the old woman, and watched her until she was out of sight. Trying not to think about what the caller had said, she pushed her trolley to the check out without stopping to make any more purchases. She needed to get home and lock her front door. She no longer felt safe out shopping. He might know where she was, he couldn't get in once she had double locked the front door and checked all the windows were shut. In the supermarket she felt exposed. He could be anywhere, watching her.

She told herself he couldn't possibly attack her in the presence of so many strangers. But hundreds of witnesses hadn't protected the man who had been murdered at the races. If Emma's caller was the same killer, she might not be safe anywhere. Abandoning her trolley, she hurried back to the car. It was a tense drive, but at last she reached home. After she had double locked the front door behind her, it occurred to her that she probably ought to have gone straight to the police station, rather than driving home. She shivered and hoped it wouldn't prove to be a fatal mistake.

CHAPTER 65

On Thursday morning Bev was keen to reach the office early. Turning her key, she was surprised to find the door unlocked. She had planned to be hard at work when Danielle arrived, but Danielle was already at her desk. On seeing Bev, her face twisted into a peculiar squint.

'Oh, it's you,' she said, raising her thin eyebrows and tilting her head back so she was literally looking down her nose at Bev. 'I wasn't expecting you in yet.'

Bev enquired politely how her course had gone. Danielle flapped her hand in the air as though to indicate Bev wouldn't understand.

'It was management training,' she said loftily. 'Now,' she went on, her tone suddenly brisk, 'I want to review everything you did while I was away.'

'Oh, hasn't Dominic spoken to you? I'm working on a project for him for a couple of weeks. I can't go into detail. It's to do with staff pay and conditions. I would tell you about it, only Dominic asked me not to tell anyone. It's all a bit hush hush for now.'

She smiled brightly, relishing Danielle's glowering silence.

In the end it had been quite simple to sort out her problem with Danielle, without the need to complain about her at all. It was Ian's idea to suggest she should ask to report directly to the manager, and she had a kind of now or never moment on Thursday, when Dominic had invited her to join him for lunch again. He had opened the way for her to speak freely.

'So, tell me, before Danielle comes back, how are the two of you getting on?'

'Do you want me to be honest?'

'Yes.'

He had totally understood the problem when she explained there really wasn't enough work to keep both her and Danielle busy.

'I hope I'm not talking myself out of a job here,' she had added quickly, 'only I was thinking it might be a good idea if I could report to you, if you've got anything I could help you with, that is.'

'You know, that's a very good idea,' he had replied with a broad smile. 'There are a few areas that need looking at, and you could be just the person to do it, with your management experience.'

At ten to one, Bev asked if Danielle would like to join her for lunch. She no longer harboured any animosity towards her colleague. Danielle was clearly too sore to respond favourably. It was a pity they still had to share a room, but with the problem of their working together resolved, Bev was beginning to enjoy the challenges of her new job. Certainly the store manager was a more amenable boss than Danielle, although there was a danger his congeniality could lead to problems if she wasn't careful. Not only had he flirted shamelessly with her the last time they had gone out for lunch, he had followed that up by loitering in her office at the end of the day like a lovelorn teenager. While the attention of an attractive man was always flattering, it could become awkward if he fell for her in a serious way. She hoped he had just been engaging in the casual banter she had enjoyed with her previous boss.

Bev had expected Dominic to be more circumspect about approaching her once Danielle was back so she was surprised to see him at the door of their office at twenty past five. He asked her to step along the corridor to his office to run through some figures with him.

'You might as well bring your things. Danielle can lock up here,' he added.

Danielle gave Bev a black look. They usually both left at five thirty.

'I won't keep you long,' Dominic added.

Bev quickly gathered up her coat and bag and left the room without a backward glance. She

362

didn't want Danielle to see she was flustered by Dominic's attention. After all, her relationship with her boss was strictly professional.

Dominic invited her to take a seat. Looking at his pale face, she noticed how his mouth turned up further on one side than the other when he smiled. She smiled back warily, suspecting he wasn't actually interested in how she was progressing with her work right then. She had been giving the situation some thought. When he invited her to go for a quick drink before going home, she was ready.

'Won't your girlfriend be expecting you at home?'

His mobile features flinched almost imperceptibly. 'She doesn't get in from work until about eight.'

'What does she do?'

He frowned and waved one hand in the air. 'She's in finance,' he replied vaguely.

'Finance?'

'Yes. To be honest, I don't really understand what it is she does, but she seems to enjoy it.' He leaned forward earnestly. 'But let's not talk about her. I'm interested in you.'

'It's just that—' she paused, uncertainly, then decided to be firm. 'I just wondered what she might make of our seeing one another like this—'

'Oh for goodness sake. We work together, don't we? You're working on a project for me, aren't you? It's hardly "seeing one another" if we talk about work. We could discuss it here, or over a drink in the pub. It's your choice, but I know which I'd prefer. Or if you like—'

Reaching under his desk he drew out a half bottle of whisky.

Watching his eyes as he glanced at the bottle, Bev relaxed. He wasn't trying to pull her by dragging her off to the pub. It was the alcohol he was after. No doubt he found it pleasanter to drink in the company of an attractive woman than by himself. Besides, her presence probably gave him an excuse to be there. Perhaps he kidded himself he was taking her to the pub to discuss work, rather than feeding his addiction. Drinking alone was an admission he had a problem. His insistence she join him now made perfect sense.

'One drink then,' she agreed. 'Shall I bring the files?'

He smiled. 'I don't think that'll be necessary, do you? It's just a quick drink. We can go over the figures in the morning.'

CHAPTER 66

Emma lay awake for hours, worrying. The more she thought about it, the less plausible it seemed. She had never been superstitious or even religious, believing only in the tangible world that she could see with her own eyes. Even as a teenager she had dismissed horoscopes, laughing at her friends who had gone through a phase of taking them seriously. The only logical explanation for what had happened was that Richard's killer had been watching her while she was shopping. There was no other way he could have known what she was doing.

Lying in bed in the darkness, alone, she tried to sleep. Hearing a clicking noise, she tensed with fear and held her breath, listening. Silence. She forced herself to breathe deeply. Obviously the sound had come from outside but she was so wound up, even the most harmless noise sounded menacing. A figure seemed to lurk in every shadow of her room. Fists clenched, body rigid, she closed her eyes, trying to control her rapid breathing. She reassured herself she was perfectly safe with the front door double locked, and all her windows closed. In the morning she would go to the police station and demand to speak to the good-looking inspector who had questioned her about Richard's death. She trusted him. Once she convinced him she was being stalked by a killer, he would have to arrange police protection for her. He would have no choice.

Waking up late the next morning, she was surprised that she had been able to sleep at all. In the bright light of a sunny morning, it was impossible to believe she had been spied on the previous evening. She must have misheard what had been said to her on the phone, or imagined it altogether. Her phone signal would have been unreliable inside the store. Probably her mother had called, and her own phone had cut out just as she answered. At the same time, she had over-heard a conversation going on somewhere in the store. Perhaps the man who had brushed past her had been speaking on a hands free phone, or there was someone else talking out of sight in another aisle. In her agitated state she had misinterpreted the conversation and mistakenly assumed it was directed at her. That was a logical explanation of the events that had upset her the previous day. There was nothing spooky about it at all. Having worked out what had happened she felt a lot better, although she was shocked at how easily she had fallen for such a crazy delusion. She had to regain her composure before she returned to work.

By the time she was up and dressed it was half past ten. She decided to have a leisurely breakfast and try to relax. Clearing out Richard's clothes could wait until the weekend. She had to allow herself time to adjust to life without him. The previous day she had felt her control slip away. It was a frightening feeling. She had to get a grip on herself, and return to some sort of normality. Having made coffee and poured cereal into a bowl, she opened the fridge and started back with a cry of horror. An involuntary jerk of her arm slammed the fridge door shut. Trembling, she opened it again and stared, transfixed with revulsion. A human eye stared back at her, nestling on a pink fleshy cushion. After a few seconds her initial disgust was swallowed up in fear. Richard's killer had told her he was keeping an eye on her. While she had been asleep, in the night, he had stolen into her house and left a sinister message.

A sudden crash woke her from her momentary stupor. At her feet lay the shards of a bowl, sprinkled with cereal. Automatically, she fetched a dustpan and brush, swept the floor, and tipped the detritus in the bin, her mind a blank all the while. A few moments later she found herself standing in the hall, phone in hand, dithering over whether to take a taxi to the station and board a train that would carry her as far away from York as possible, somewhere she would never be found. Scotland, Brighton, down to Dover and across the Channel to France. But she knew escape was impossible. Her pursuer seemed possessed of supernatural powers. There was no other explanation. He had succeeded in following her inside a supermarket without being seen, and had entered her house through a locked door. Nothing made sense any more. Still clutching her phone, she wandered giddily into the living room where she sat down and tried to breathe slowly. She would never be safe until the killer had been caught and locked up.

When the phone rang, vibrating in her hand, she shrieked out loud as she dropped it. Pulling herself together with an effort, she picked it up and called her mother.

'Hi mum, did you just ring me?'

'No. But I was going to call you later. How are you managing there? I've been talking it over with dad and we wondered if you'd like me to come and stay for a few days?'

'Thanks, but that's really not necessary. It's not as if it's the first time I've lived by myself. Stop fussing. Of course it's not easy, but I'm coping. I'm going back to work on Monday.'

★　★　★

She forced herself to chatter on, determined not to worry her parents. Since her father had suffered a minor coronary the previous year, the whole family had been going out of its way to avoid causing him stress. By the time she had finished reassuring her mother that everything was fine she felt perfectly calm, as though saying the words made it true. But as soon as she put the phone down, her composure crumbled. She wasn't in a fit state to go anywhere. The police inspector would have to come to her.

Her hand shook as she pressed the keys on her phone.

'Hello? I'd like to speak to Detective Inspector Peterson please.'

The voice at the other end asked her what she wanted.

'It's really urgent I speak to Inspector Peterson straight away,' she blurted out, giving way to panic again. 'Please tell him it's urgent. It's about Richard Western. My name's Emma Willerby and I've got some information for the inspector, only I don't want to discuss it on the phone and I can't come to the police station either. It might not be safe for me to leave the house.' She paused, aware she must sound crazy. 'I mean,' she added more slowly, 'it would be better if he could come here. Please tell him it's urgent.'

She rang off without waiting for an answer because she had started crying and shaking uncontrollably. She hoped the inspector would arrive before Richard's killer returned. Although he hadn't directly threatened her life yet, she had a feeling that was only a matter of time.

'Please hurry up,' she muttered, 'I'm scared.'

CHAPTER 67

Ian responded with alacrity when summoned to Emma's house. It wasn't as though he had any other pressing demands on his time, and the message that she had urgent information to pass on concerning Richard's killer raised his expectations. Trying to control his excitement, he drove fast. This could be the break they had been waiting for. His hopes were dashed when he rang the bell and there was no response. It was raining lightly and he didn't want to hang around there for long, with cold drops worming their way down the back of his collar. He was weighing up whether to turn away and try again later or summon back up and force an entry. Emma might have gone out, not expecting him to turn up so soon. On the other hand, she might have been calling for immediate assistance. She had asked to see him urgently, after all.

As he was deliberating what to do, he heard her call out.

'Who is it?'

She sounded apprehensive.

'It's DI Ian Peterson. You asked me to come here.'

'Stand where I can see you.'

She was definitely frightened. He stepped back and a moment later the door opened. With grey pouches under her bloodshot eyes, Emma looked so wan and haggard he thought she must be ill.

'Are you all right?' he asked.

'Come in,' she whispered, glancing quickly over his shoulder. 'Quickly.'

Seizing him by the arm she pulled him inside, slammed the door behind him and double locked it.

'Emma, answer me truthfully. Have you been drinking or taking any medication? Think before you answer.'

She gave a weak smile and shook her head. 'This is rational fear you're looking at, Inspector, not a drug-crazed delusion. I'm not mad. I'm not on medication and I'm not drunk. But what's happening is enough to drive anyone to drink,' she added miserably.

'Has your doctor prescribed any sedatives?'

'No, no. It's nothing like that. It's not safe for me here on my own.'

'I appreciate you're grieving, and—'

She interrupted him. 'This isn't about Richard's death, Inspector, it's about me. I'm in danger.'

She took him into the kitchen and put the kettle on.

'I'll make you a cup of tea, but I can't give you any milk,' she whispered.

'That's OK. I don't want any tea.'

Sitting down opposite him, she launched into a tearful account of how Richard's killer had continued his phone calls to her landline, followed her into a supermarket, and entered her house while it was locked.

'I double locked the front door but he still got in,' she concluded. 'There's no way he could have got in here, but he did. I double locked the front door,' she added plaintively, repeating herself several times in her agitation.

'When did this alleged trespass take place?'

'Last night. And it's not "alleged". It happened. I know it did.'

'Were you here at the time?' Ian interrupted her.

He leaned forward, wondering if there was a genuine concern for her safety, although he wasn't convinced she was talking sense. He needed to find out exactly what had happened.

With a visible effort to calm herself, she explained that she had been under the impression she had been followed into the supermarket the previous day. As a result she had taken care to check all her windows were closed, and had double locked her front door, when she arrived home.

'You thought you were pursued in the shop, or you were?'

She sighed. 'At the time I believed I'd been followed, but afterwards I thought I must have been mistaken. It's easy to jump to conclusions when you're upset. It's possible I overheard someone talking in the store and imagined they were talking to me.'

He nodded. So far she sounded lucid.

'But I'd been unnerved by it so I was extra careful to make sure the house was secure before I went to bed.' She raised a tearful face, losing control of her voice again. 'But he got in. He was here in the night.'

'Did he attack you?'

'No.'

'Did he threaten you?'

'No.'

'What did he say to you?'

'Nothing. I didn't see him. He was here while I was asleep.'

She was crying now, and finding it difficult to speak. Relentlessly, he pressed on. He was there at her request and he had to discover if there was any genuine reason for her suspicion.

'Emma, help me to understand. I need a clear answer. How do you know he was here?'

She looked up, her countenance rigid with terror.

'He left an eye in the fridge'.

For a moment, Ian thought he had misheard. Before he could say anything, she slipped off her chair and left the room, returning a moment later with a carrier bag. Peering inside it, Ian made out a fleshy blob inside a plastic bag. Carefully he drew it out. A closer look revealed an eye gazing lifelessly at him through its plastic shroud. The cornea was cloudy, with a grossly dilated pupil encased in whitish fatty tissue streaked with dried blood, below which a dark sphere resembled a small red onion. He focused on keeping his face impassive as he replaced the foul thing out of sight in the carrier bag.

'I put it in there in case there were any finger prints, and I was careful not to touch it.'

She shuddered.

Catching sight of his baffled countenance, she sat down and tried to explain.

'I know it sounds strange. I mean, why would anyone want to break into the house and leave this in the fridge? But he was giving me a message. He wanted me to know he'd been here. When he was talking to me in the supermarket, he said he was keeping an eye on me. This was to remind me he's watching me.'

'He said he was keeping an eye on you?'

'Yes. He said oily fish is healthy, and he's keeping an eye on me, and watching everything I eat. Something like that. It just sounded weird at the time. Afterwards, I thought I must have imagined hearing him on the phone in there, but then this appeared in the fridge.'

'You're absolutely sure you've never seen it before?'

She didn't bother to answer. It was hardly some-thing she was likely to forget.

★ ★ ★

What she was saying sounded crazy, but she didn't strike him as deluded. For one thing, she seemed to find the whole episode as bizarre and difficult to credit as he did. And then, there was the eye.

'I know it sounds weird,' she said at last.

She seemed very calm, until Ian asked how the intruder had got into her house.

She burst into tears. 'I don't know,' she stammered. She raised a tearful face and looked at him, appealing for protection. 'I'm so scared.'

Ian thought for a moment. If an intruder really had broken in during the night, he must have gained access somehow.

'I suppose he must have picked the locks,' she said. 'So maybe he's a known burglar?'

'Unless he had a key,' Ian replied. 'Who else has a key to your house?'

'Only Richard.'

'What happened to his key when he died?'

She shrugged. 'I guess the police kept it with his clothes.'

A phone call soon established that no key to the house had been found on Richard's body. Emma had a look around the house but it wasn't there. She called his brother who didn't think a key had been left in Richard's car.

'His brother says he emptied the car,' Emma said. 'But he might have missed it,' she added hopefully.

Either Richard had left his keys in his car, or

376

else they had disappeared at the time of his death. Emma's story of a mysterious intruder in the night was looking plausible.

'Emma,' he said quietly and paused, concerned not to frighten her any further. 'You should be perfectly safe once the lock's changed, but is there anyone who can stay with you until we sort all this out?'

She nodded. 'I can call my mother.'

'Would she come here?'

Emma's eyes widened, but she remained calm. 'She will if I ask her.'

'Make the call now, please.'

Before he left, Ian called a locksmith.

'We'll get a security lock fitted straight away, and a chain as well. Make sure you double lock the door behind you any time you go out, and put the chain on when you're home.'

'I don't think I'm allowed to do that. The land-lord has to give permission for any changes—'

'Don't worry about that. We'll speak to the landlord. The important thing now is to make sure you're safe from intruders. And we'll send this off to forensics to see if they can find any trace of prints or DNA on the – on it. This could be a real help,' he added, with an encouraging smile.

'You believe he was here last night?'

Ian shrugged. In all his years on the force he had never heard of anyone claiming an intruder had broken in to leave an eyeball in the fridge. The very absurdity of the story made it credible.

'I don't know,' he admitted. 'But I'm taking your claim seriously.'

He waited until the locksmith arrived and then left, warning her to keep her door locked. She nodded nervously and he hurried away, hoping it was safe to leave her on her own.

CHAPTER 68

Ian drove straight to the mortuary where Avril buzzed him in through the back door.

'I'm here on my own today,' she told him.

'It's you I came to see.'

'I'm flattered. It's nice to see a cheerful face around the place.'

'It's good to know I'm better company than a corpse,' he grinned.

'Well, it's stiff competition.'

They both laughed.

'So what can I do for you?'

He heaved a melodramatic sigh. 'You know I'm a married man . . .'

'Behave yourself!' she scolded, smiling. 'What is it then? Not another body?'

'No, not another body.'

'That's a relief.'

'I've brought you a small body part.'

'Sounds intriguing.'

Ian reached into his pocket for a cardboard box.

'I need some help identifying this, anything you can tell me about where it comes from. Once

379

you've established its origin, if you can, we'll try to find out who's been handling it, and how they got hold of it. After you've had a look we'll check for any prints, although it's probably too small for anything to show up. But we might get a partial.'

He knew the chances were slim. On his way to see Avril he had received confirmation that only Emma's, her mother's and Richard's prints had been found at her house. The killer had been careful enough to leave no trace of his break-in, other than what he had left in the fridge. He would almost certainly have worn gloves when he had handled the eye.

Ian handed over the box. He watched Avril withdraw the bag with practised delicacy. Frowning, she examined the macabre contents which were clearly visible through the plastic. She stood for a moment weighing the bag in the palm of one hand, before raising it up to her face and scrutinising its contents. A small blob of bloody tissue had become detached from the eye and had slid down into a corner of the plastic bag. Ian stared, wondering who could have gouged it from its natural resting place. After a moment Avril looked up at Ian, a puzzled expression on her face. She opened her mouth to speak then closed it and stared at the eye again, poking it gently through the plastic. Ian waited patiently.

'It could be human,' she said at last.

'I rather guessed it was. That is, I assumed . . .'

'Or it could be a sheep's eye,' she continued, ignoring the interruption, 'or even a dog.'

'Can't you tell the difference?'

'I'm almost certain it's not human. Give me twenty four hours and I'll be sure, one way or the other.'

She was curious.

'Where did you find it?'

He told her that Emma had found it in her fridge. Avril shook her head, looking perplexed. Ian explained that Emma had been living with Richard Western and she nodded.

'Of course. I remember the name now. So what was she doing with this in her fridge?'

'That's what we're trying to work out, but it looks as though Richard's killer left it there.'

'Why? It seems a bit random. It's not like it's his eye. It's not even the same colour.'

'We're working on the theory that this was left in her fridge as a message—'

'A chilling message.'

She grinned, and he couldn't help laughing.

Grotesque as it was, the thought that the eye could have been removed from an animal that was already dead made it seem far less disturbing.

'He could have come across a dead sheep that gave him the idea,' Ian began.

Avril interrupted him. 'This was planned.'

'We don't know where it came from, so how can

you be sure he didn't just find a sheep lying dead in a field somewhere. Sheep die, don't they?'

'Ask any farmer,' she replied. 'It doesn't take long for scavengers to find cadavers in the fields. Insects burrow into them, birds spot them from the air, and the eyes are the first to go. Crows sometimes take eyes from live lambs because they're an easy target.'

Walking back to the car, he called Emma to tell her what he had discovered. She was initially relieved when he told her the eye probably wasn't human.

'I'm sending it to forensics,' he added.

He hoped she wouldn't realise the futility of that routine. The finger print dusters hadn't found any prints at Emma's house apart from her own and her mother's, and those of her dead boyfriend. He did his best to reassure her, but they both knew she was in danger. The origin of the eye didn't alter the terrifying fact that a psychopath had gained entry to her house while she had been in bed asleep.

Ian returned to the police station to file his report. There had been no progress in his absence. Disappointed but not surprised, he summoned Ted and they went along to the canteen. Although he hadn't known the sergeant for long, Ian felt comfortable in his company. Ted hadn't yet seen Ian's latest report. Over tea Ian brought him up to speed. Ted put his mug down and sat forward with an audible intake of breath.

'An eyeball?' he repeated.

Ian nodded. 'Attached to some blobs of pink tissue.'

'And it was in her fridge? Jesus, I can just imagine what Jenny would say if she found an eyeball in our fridge!' He narrowed his eyes speculatively beneath his heavy brows. 'I wonder if she can claim for a new fridge off her insurance? I suppose those tight bastards would say it's a kind of animal product, and everyone keeps meat in the fridge.'

Ian couldn't help smiling at his sergeant's practical response, but he was slightly exasperated all the same. Ted was missing the point. Emma was at risk from some psychopathic maniac, and it was down to them to protect her.

Ian steered the conversation away from the hygiene aspect of the issue, and back to the mysterious intruder.

'It looks as though the intruder had managed to get his hands on Richard's keys which suggests Emma's intruder and Richard's killer may be one and the same person,' Ian said.

'Yes, presumably he took the keys when he bumped him off,' Ted agreed. 'Richard would have had them in his pocket.'

'He might have had his keys in his hand, ready to let himself in, because he was killed right outside his front door.'

'That's true. If he'd been holding the keys, and dropped them at the scene, the killer could have just picked them up. It wasn't necessarily all premeditated.'

'But having found them, he decided to use them to threaten Emma.'

'Yes,' Ted nodded. 'It's a blatant show of power. Look what I can do. Next time I'll come back and kill you.'

'He must realise she'd change her locks once we worked out he had her key, but it was certainly enough to scare her. Was that his intention?'

Ted shook his head.

'Who knows what was going through his mind when he planted the eye in her fridge.'

'He'd told her he was keeping an eye on her. It was a message. Wherever you are, I'm watching you.'

'No wonder she freaked out. I wonder where he got it?'

Ian shrugged. 'I don't know. If it's a sheep's eye, which Avril thought most likely, then it wouldn't have been that difficult to come by. He might have got it from an abattoir, or he could have driven out into the countryside and sourced it himself.'

'Killed a sheep, you mean?' Ted sounded shocked.

'Why not? He's killed three people.'

CHAPTER 69

'Come on,' Bev said. 'We agreed to clear out the garage this afternoon.'

Ian groaned. 'Give me a break. It's Sunday. I've just been working six days on the trot.'

'That's all well and good, but you'll be the first to complain when you want to find something that's buried at the bottom of a box out in the garage.'

When they had moved in they had dumped several packing cases in the garage full of random possessions from their old house, all the things they were undecided about whether to keep or throw away. They had promised one another they would sort through the contents of the boxes at the first opportunity. It would take time to go through deciding what they wanted to keep, and what to throw away. Somehow, their first few weeks in York had passed without a spare moment to start on the garage. By the time they were beginning to feel settled in the house, Ian had become embroiled in an all-consuming investigation, and a few more weeks had flown by.

★　★　★

'You're not the only one who's tired from a week's work,' she went on. 'The way you carry on, you'd think you were the only one who ever does anything around here. My job isn't exactly a walk in the park, you know. I'm tired too.'

He breathed slowly, blanking out the sound of her voice droning on and on. Tired didn't begin to describe how he was feeling. He was shattered. It was physically and mentally exhausting forcing himself to carry on, day after day, pursuing one futile line of enquiry after another, while constantly motivating his team to maintain their efforts and their morale. Bev had no idea of the pressure he was under. It wasn't the threat of danger from violent criminals that wore him down, but the interminable daily grind: keeping track, taking stock, recording data, asking pointless questions of potential witnesses who knew nothing pertinent to the case. It would be different if he felt they were making progress.

The first packing case was full of random wedding presents they had never asked for. Many were china or glass, individually protected in tissue paper. Ian remembered watching Bev wrap them all up. He had asked her at the time why she was bothering to take such care with gifts they didn't want, but she had been determined to take everything with them.

'Once we're in the new house we'll have time to consider what to keep and what to get rid of,' she had said.

As it turned out, they seemed to have less free time in York than they had in Kent.

'Why don't we just chuck the whole lot away?' Ian suggested, but Bev insisted on going through the contents, 'just in case.'

'In case of what?'

'In case there's something in there we want to keep.'

There wasn't. Ian lifted the items out one by one, Bev unwrapped them, and they spent a couple of hours rummaging through a host of objects they didn't want. Everything ended up back in the case, ready to be taken to a charity shop. Although the whole exercise had been a complete waste of time, Bev was pleased.

'At least we know we don't want any of it,' she said. 'And that's one packing case out of the way.'

Ian gazed disconsolately at the remaining half dozen packing cases. It was going to take them hours to work their way through all of them.

Ian was ready to call it a day, but Bev was keen to press on. They tackled the second case.

'Who the hell gave us this?' she asked, holding up a grotesque African mask and laughing.

Ian grinned. 'That wasn't a wedding present. I brought that back from Kenya, years ago.'

The mask was made of a dark wood, and life sized. Still giggling, she held it in front of her face and adopted a weird deep voice, waving her free hand in a circular motion in front of his eyes.

'Ian Peterson,' she chanted, 'you want to make your wife a cup of tea. You want to make your wife a cup of tea.'

Listening to her voice, which was unrecognisable, Ian had a sudden insight into what had been bothering him about Emma's nuisance phone calls. Without a word, he turned and dashed inside.

'Wait,' Bev called after him. 'I'm not that desperate for a cup of tea.'

Ignoring her cries, he ran to his screen and scanned through his notes. Bev followed him.

'Not work again,' she whined. 'Not now. Ian, we're in the middle of something.'

Paying no attention to her protest, he carried on searching until he found what he was looking for. Emma hadn't been sure if the caller was a man or a woman, but she had made a curious comment.

'Whoever it was, he was trying to disguise his voice. It sounded funny, kind of forced and hoarse. It didn't sound natural. It was all on one tone, like a robot. Definitely not natural.'

Hardly able to contain his excitement, he looked up.

'Why would a man disguise his voice?'

'So he wouldn't be recognised. Ian, what's this about? Are you making the tea or not?'

'So whoever he's talking to must know him. Why else would he bother to try and disguise his voice?'

'Who's disguising his voice? What are you talking about?' she asked again, but he barely heard her.

He was stunned by his own stupidity. He should have seen straight away that, although she hadn't yet realised it, Emma knew Richard's killer.

He grabbed Bev by the shoulders and planted a kiss on her lips.

'I ought to put on a mask more often,' she giggled, but he was already turning away.

'I have to go to work.'

'No, Ian, it's your day off.'

'I'll be back as soon as I can. I'm sorry, but this is important. It could be really important.'

'More important than spending time with me?'

He hated to disappoint her, but he had no choice. He would make it up to her somehow. Meanwhile, he attempted a brief explanation of why he suddenly had to rush off.

'I've just come across a way of finding this killer we've been looking for, or at least of narrowing down the search.'

'How could you possibly come across anything to do with that in the garage?' she asked, but he didn't have time to explain.

'I'll tell you later,' he called back over his shoulder as he hurried towards the front door. 'Don't wait up. I might be late.'

CHAPTER 70

Eileen wasn't in her office when Ian arrived at the police station. He didn't think she would be back until Monday. If anything, he was relieved. It would be better to pursue his new line of enquiry on his own initiative without her bothering him for explanations. All he had was a reasonable supposition, and a gut feeling that he was onto something. It might not be enough to convince Eileen he was right. The duty sergeant confirmed that the detective chief inspector had the day off. It was now just after four, leaving the rest of the afternoon and evening for Ian to find evidence to establish the killer's identity. He hoped to have something concrete to show Eileen when she arrived on Monday morning, something that would show her she could have confidence in him.

The woman who came to the door was obviously Emma's mother. With the same expressive blue eyes and perfectly proportioned features, her face was lined but still beautiful, her figure lithe and trim. She opened the door on the chain at first and peered out anxiously, even though Ian had introduced himself and shown her his warrant card over the intercom. When he asked to see her daughter she shook her head and told him it was impossible. Emma was asleep.

'I made her go to bed and take a sleeping pill. Hopefully she'll sleep through to the morning. She was completely exhausted. She couldn't have gone on like that, pretending she was coping by herself. I'm sorry, Inspector, but you'll have to come back tomorrow. But not too early. Let's leave her to sleep as long as possible.'

She agreed to call Ian as soon as Emma woke up, and he had to be satisfied with that.

He was back outside her house at half past eight the following day. Once again Emma's mother came to the door.

'Show me your identity card please,' she said sharply.

Behind her, Ian heard Emma's voice protesting. 'Don't be daft, Mum, you can see it's him.'

Her mother grunted as she opened the door. 'You can't be too careful.' She turned back to Ian. 'Inspector, maybe you can talk some sense into her. I don't understand why she won't come home with me.'

'You think he wouldn't be able to find me there?' Emma replied. 'That would just put all of us at risk.'

'I don't feel exactly safe here,' her mother muttered.

★   ★   ★

They went through to the living room. Ian saw at a glance that it had been tidied since his last visit, not that it had been untidy then, but where previously a few magazines had been carelessly strewn on the table, and several books had fallen over on a shelf, now there were no magazines in sight and the books all stood neatly perpendicular. A plant that had been withering on the window sill stood erect and healthy-looking. They sat down and Emma sent her mother to the kitchen to make tea while Ian explained his theory.

'I should have realised straight away that the caller was probably someone you knew well enough for him to be concerned to disguise his voice, in case you recognised it,' he concluded apologetically.

'I should have thought of that myself,' she replied, relief evident in her countenance. She leaned forward and placed her hand gently on his. 'Thank goodness you were clever enough to work it out.'

Ian felt his face redden as her face glowed with admiration.

'The important thing is that this narrows down our search,' he went on, slowly withdrawing his hand. 'We managed to catch a glimpse of your nuisance caller on CCTV, but it's impossible to get a clear view of his face. All the same, I'd like you to take a look at it and see if it reminds you of anyone. And then we'll need a comprehensive list of all the men you've been in contact with, anyone who might have become obsessed with you, with or without your knowledge. Past boyfriends, work colleagues, everyone.'

Returning with a tray of tea things, Emma's mother caught the tail end of the conversation.

'That's going to be a long list,' she said.

'Mum!'

'I mean, she's had a number of jobs,' Mrs Willerby added hurriedly.

'There was that weird boy at university,' Emma said thoughtfully, as she handed Ian a mug of tea. 'What was his name? You know, the one who turned up at the house that Christmas.'

'Oh yes,' her mother replied. 'He was certainly very odd.' She turned to Ian. 'He was obsessed with Emma. But that was a long time ago.' She screwed up her face, thinking. 'Nick, that was his name, wasn't it?

'Yes, that was it.' Emma turned to Ian. 'We never went out or anything. He just had a thing about me.'

'A thing?' Ian understood perfectly what she meant, but wanted to hear an explanation in her own words. 'Tell me about him.'

'It's hardly relevant after all this time.'

'Anything might be important,' Ian insisted.

Several years might have elapsed since Emma had known the admirer she was talking about, but she and her mother both remembered him. Ian needed to find out more, even if it was only to eliminate the name from their enquiries.

'What was his surname?'

'Oh God, I don't know. I can't remember. He was just someone I met at uni, you know. We weren't friends or anything. He was just there and he had this thing about me. It sounds cruel – it was cruel I suppose – but it became a bit of a joke with the rest of us. When you're young you don't realise the implications of these things.'

'Implications?' Ian queried.

Emma gave a nervous laugh. 'If someone stalked me like that now, I'd be terrified.'

Ian looked up from his notes.

'Did you say he stalked you?'

She shrugged. 'Well, maybe not stalked exactly, but he wouldn't leave me alone.'

'Was he in your year?'

'Yes. I think he was studying maths, or physics, or something like that. Not English anyway.'

It wasn't much to go on, but it would be simple enough to obtain a list of the names of all the boys in Emma's year at university. Ian stepped into the hall and made a quick phone call to the police station before returning his attention to Emma.

She sighed. 'We weren't very nice to him. He wasn't all there, if you know what I mean. Some people thought drugs had messed him up and some of us thought there must have been something wrong with him long before he tried LSD.' She glanced at her mother. 'Some of the students used to mess about with drugs – not me, but there was a group of them who did. One of the girls was on my corridor in hall and we became friends. That's how I met him. He was one of the crowd she hung out with. Well, not exactly one of the crowd, more of a hanger on. He had this crazy idea that he had seen me in a vision before he arrived at university, and we were destined to be together. He became fixated on me. It was weird. He followed me home one Christmas. You remember him, don't you?'

'How could I forget?' her mother answered. She explained to Ian, 'He spent the entire Christmas Day lying underneath the dining room table.'

Emma smiled miserably. 'He wasn't all there.'

Abandoning the tea, Ian returned to the station accompanied by Emma. She was subdued, but Ian was wired. Eager to pursue this new line of enquiry, he continued questioning her in the car.

'Think carefully, Emma. The voice on the phone. Could it have been him?'

'I don't know.' She sounded distressed. 'It was more than ten years ago. Do you really think he could have killed Richard? Because of me?'

Ian hesitated. He understood that could be a heavy burden for her if it were true.

'I don't know,' he admitted at last. 'If someone you met at university is stalking you, then we need to find him urgently. But if he's involved in Richard's murder, then quite clearly he's insane. You can't take any responsibility for his behaviour. There's no way you could have predicted what he was going to do.'

He heard her crying quietly beside him. Unsure what to say, he drove the rest of the way without asking any more questions.

Ian concealed his disappointment when Emma didn't recognise the shadowy figure in the surveillance film. It was hardly surprising. Beneath his hood, the features of the figure nicknamed The Ghost were virtually invisible.

'What about his gait, or the way he holds himself? Is there anything familiar about him? Anything at all?'

She shook her head. 'I'm not sure. I know he was tall.'

'What else can you remember about him?' Ian pressed her. 'Anything at all might help.'

'Apart from the fact that he was crazy?' Emma replied.

Now that they were following up a lead, however tenuous, she had recovered her composure, and seemed pleased to be doing something to help track down Richard's killer.

CHAPTER 71

As Bev was leaving work on Monday after-noon, she ran into Dominic by the exit. It was no surprise when he invited her to join him for a drink. She wondered if he had been watching out for her. She laughed uncomfortably, not sure how to refuse without putting him out. She had no objection to joining him for an occa-sional drink, but he seemed to want to see her after work every day.

'This is getting to be a bit of a habit,' she mumbled awkwardly.

'We're only talking about a drink.'

Somehow his invitations no longer seemed so casual.

'I'd like to sit down together and mull over your figures, but it's difficult to find the time during the day. I'm always so busy. Let's go for a drink and discuss it, and then I can drop you home afterwards if you like?'

Wondering how to refuse politely, she glanced at her watch.

'Thanks, but I really ought to get home.'

'Let me give you a lift then. My car's just outside.'

★　　★　　★

She hesitated. It would be nice not to have to hang around waiting at the bus stop. Besides, the sky was overcast, and she hadn't brought an umbrella.

'If you're sure it's not out of your way.'

'That depends on where you live.'

She told him her address and he grinned. 'Yes, of course, I should have remembered. It's not far in the car. Come on. Let's go.'

She thanked him again. With luck, she might wangle a lift home every day. She smiled at him, wondering what she had been worrying about. He was just being friendly. He knew she was married, and anyway he had a girlfriend.

She appreciated having the car door opened for her. Ian never treated her with such old-fashioned courtesy. But once they drove off, Dominic seemed preoccupied. She didn't like to say anything when they left the city wall behind them, although she wasn't sure if he was going towards her house. She had a feeling he had turned away from the town too soon, but he lived in York. He must know where he was going. They followed a bus route past a Premier Inn and an old cinema she didn't recognise. When they crossed an unfamiliar bridge over the railway she stared uneasily up at the massive grey metal struts spanning the road, bolted together with huge rivets.

'Where are we going?'

He didn't answer.

'I think we might be going the wrong way.'

He turned to her then, with a taut smile.

'I thought the idea was that I'd give you a lift so you'd have time for a quick drink on the way home?' When she frowned, he went on. 'I'm taking you to a really nice pub I know. It's only about half a mile out of town. We can turn round if you like, if your husband will be waiting for you.'

Bev snorted. That would be a first.

She didn't tell Dominic Ian was bound to be home late. It didn't take her long to make up her mind. She had the choice of going for a drink with an attentive colleague after work or going home to sit by herself waiting for her husband to show up. Ian would never find out she had been out with Dominic, unless she chose to tell him. She smiled. History was repeating itself, with her boss taking her out.

'A drink sounds great.'

They drove in silence. Bev leaned back in her seat and closed her eyes.

At last they slowed down and pulled up at the end of a row of terraced houses. Although there were curtains in the windows, it looked derelict. She glanced around. There was no sign of a pub.

'Where are we?'

'This is where my aunt lives.'

'Your aunt?'

'Yes. She's an invalid and I help out where I can, doing chores and running errands for her. She's all on her own now. She never had children of her own so she helped to bring me up. She was like a second mother to me. There's something I said I'd deliver to her on my way home. It won't take a minute. Tell you what,' he added as a thought occurred to him, 'why don't you come in with me? She spends a lot of time on her own, and she'd love it if you came in to say hello.'

Bev felt a flash of annoyance with him for dragging her along to see his aunt without asking her first, but it was fleeting. She could hardly censure him for visiting a lonely invalid. It only confirmed what she had already suspected, that he was kind-hearted. She was flattered that he wanted to spend time with her, which was more than could be said for Ian when he was busy with an investigation. In any case Dominic was her boss. It would be tactless as well as mean to refuse to even say hello to his invalid aunt. Feeling slightly awkward, she climbed out of the car and followed him up the path to the front door where, instead of ringing the bell, he took out a key and opened the door. Inside the house it was very quiet. She wondered whether his aunt had a full-time carer or lived there on her own. Before she could ask, Dominic broke the silence.

'This way,' he said softly. 'Let's see if she's awake.'
Dutifully, she followed him up the stairs.

The house had a musty, disused smell. The stairs creaked beneath threadbare carpet as they ascended.

'This way,' he repeated. His voice was oddly harsh as though he was struggling to hide his excitement.

He glanced back over his shoulder. His eyes were bright with anticipation. It was sweet that he was so excited about introducing her. Bev hoped his invalid aunt would be equally pleased to see her. At the top of the stairs he tapped at one of the doors. Bev didn't hear any response, but he looked back at her with a broad smile.

'Come on,' he said. 'Aunty's awake.'

Flinging the door open, he stepped to one side, taking her by the elbow as he did so. Swiftly he propelled her inside and pulled the door closed behind them.

The curtains were closed. Gradually her squinting eyes grew accustomed to the darkness and she made out the shape of a bed. It looked empty. She spun round, perplexed. In the dim light from the window only the right side of her companion's face was faintly visible. One eye seemed to glare wildly at her from the shadows.

'She's not here.'

'You like stating the obvious, don't you?' he replied.

His contemptuous tone made her uneasy. For the first time it occurred to her that she had followed him upstairs in a strange house. They had only worked together for a few weeks. She didn't really know much about him at all.

'I'd like to leave now,' she said firmly, mustering what confidence she could.

'What about my aunt?'

'She's not here.'

'No, but you are.' He took a step closer. 'Don't you think you ought to wait and see her, now you've come all this way.'

Without warning, he lunged at her and seized her round the waist, pinning her arms to her sides. She tried to kick out, and lost her balance. Together they fell backwards against the edge of the bed. She was screaming now, in the desperate hope that his aunt could hear the commotion. There might be a carer somewhere in the house who would come to her rescue. She was terrified he was going to rape her as he lifted her bodily and thrust her fully onto the bed, still kicking and writhing with all her strength. With brutal force he shoved her flat on her back and knelt on her chest, crushing her ribs. One of her legs twisted awkwardly as she fell backwards on the bed but she couldn't straighten it. Trapped beneath his weight she smelt his acrid sweat, and felt the heat of his body on top of hers. With one hand he whipped a length of cord from beneath the pillow, bound her hands together tightly, and attached them to the metal grid of the headboard. The rough cord chafed painfully against her flesh.

Sick with a visceral terror, it took all her energy to force herself to speak. Her teeth chattered uncontrollably and her whole body trembled with shock.

'Your aunt's going to find me—'

'I haven't got an aunt, you idiot.'

'You'll never get away with this—'

For answer he slapped her savagely across her face. Her nose stung and she tasted blood on her lips, salty and oddly comforting.

CHAPTER 72

O n Monday morning, Avril had called to
confirm that Ian had handed her a sheep's
eye. Ian set a constable to investigate
whether there had been any reports of dead or
mutilated sheep from farms in the area. Another
constable was contacting local abattoirs and
butchers in the vicinity to enquire whether any of
their carcasses had been tampered with. There was
a slim chance they would discover a sheep killed
somewhere out in the countryside being rapidly
destroyed by feral predators. Exposed to the
elements, any trace of the thief who had taken the
eye would have been obliterated, but, if they could
narrow down where and when the sheep had been
mutilated, they could examine CCTV of main
roads leading to the field, and trace vehicles which
had driven there at the relevant time. Security
cameras at abattoirs and butchers might yield
more specific information. Either way it was a long
shot, and time consuming, but they had to try. As
well as helping them identify the killer, they might
turn up enough evidence to convict him.

★   ★   ★

Once he had dealt with the information received from the mortuary, Ian went to fetch Emma so they could investigate her information. He was hopeful of tracing her acquaintance from her student days. Although he was expecting to eliminate the guy she had known, he had to follow up any possible lead. There was always a chance it might be significant. Settling her in an interview room, he frowned as he studied the information a constable had painstakingly gathered. Finally, he stared closely at Emma then glanced at his watch. Bev would be on her way home from work, and he would soon be finished. It had turned out to be yet another useless line of enquiry.

'We've checked all the students who were in your year at university,' he said. 'There's only one called Nicholas on the list, and he's in Canada. There's no record of his returning to the UK, but we're double checking,' he added wearily.

'Nicholas?' she repeated. 'Who's that?'

'You told me the boy who was obsessed with you was called Nick.'

'Yes, that's right. It's short for Dominic.'

Ian sent for the complete list so he and Emma could check through it together. It only took a few seconds for the information to come through, but it felt longer as Ian waited with growing anticipation. He had been disappointed before, but he couldn't suppress a feeling that they were closing in on the killer. Emma recognised the name

405

straight away, but in any case there was only one Dominic on the list.

'Dominic Archer, that was it!'

It didn't take long to discover that the new suspect lived in York. With growing excitement, Ian summoned a team to accompany him to the address in Bedern, a residential area round the corner from The Shambles. With the property surrounded, Dominic wouldn't be able to escape. Ian rang the bell and waited. This was it, the culmination of weeks of sleepless nights and days slogging through statements and records. There was no answer. He knocked loudly. Still no one came to the door. At last a window opened above Ian's head and a woman peered out.

'What's all that racket about? What do you want?'

Ian called up to her that he was looking for Dominic Archer.

'He lives next door,' she shouted back.

'I know that, but he's not answering the bell.'

'Must be out then,' she replied and disappeared, slamming the window behind her.

There was no landline listed for Dominic Archer. A constable had managed to get hold of his landlord who had passed on a mobile phone number. Ian rang it and waited impatiently. There was no answer. He tried again. When he rang for the third time, a man's voice came on the line.

'Hello?' He spoke very softly.

'Am I speaking to Dominic Archer?'

'Who wants to know?'

'This is Detective Inspector Ian Peterson of the North Yorkshire Police. We're conducting an investigation, and we think you might be able to help us.'

'I know who you are,' the man replied in an even tone, as calmly as though they were discussing the weather. 'I know who you are, and I know what you've done. I've been waiting for you to call. You can't keep her.'

Ian was puzzled. 'What do you mean?'

'I'm talking about Emma, of course. You've got Emma.'

'What?'

'You've got Emma,' Dominic repeated. A note of petulance crept into his voice. 'Don't try to pretend you haven't. I saw you take her away in a police car. I know your game, but you can't have her. Here's the deal, Inspector,' the voice went on, unnaturally calm again. 'You let Emma go, and you get your wife back alive. What do you say? Do we have a deal?'

Ian opened his mouth to respond but the line went dead.

'Are you all right?' Ted asked. 'What's wrong?'

Ian half turned on his seat. 'He's bluffing,' he said.

'What do you mean?'

Without stopping to explain, Ian rang Bev's

mobile. After a few rings an automated message informed him that her phone number was not in use. When he tried to locate the handset, a similar message came up on his screen.

'What's going on?' Ted asked. 'Are you all right?'

Ian couldn't speak. He was thinking about his wife spending evening after evening on her own, waiting for him to come home. His work had always impacted on her life, but never directly. Until now. He might already be too late to save her life.

Suddenly decisive, he jumped out of the car without stopping to explain.

'We need to get in the house. Come on! The killer's in there, and he says he's got my wife.'

When Dominic didn't come to the door, they smashed it in. As soon as it flew open, Ian rushed in. The house was silent. In the hallway dust settled slowly, disturbed by the falling of the door. Somewhere a pipe creaked. Leaving his colleagues to search the ground floor, Ian took the stairs two at a time. Several doors led off the landing. He raced from one to another but they were all empty. A pair of uniformed constables had made their way up into the loft. That was empty too.

Ian raced back downstairs where a search of the house and the garden had so far drawn a blank.

'Look again!' he exhorted his colleagues. 'Keep looking. The killer's here somewhere, with a hostage. Don't give up until you find them. They have to be here somewhere.'

'There's no one here, sir. We've looked everywhere.'

'They must be here. Look again.' He knew he sounded frantic, but he was desperate. 'You have to find them before he kills her—' His voice broke and he turned away. 'They have to be here,' he insisted softly. 'We have to find them. They have to be here.'

Finally Ian had to accept that Dominic had taken Bev somewhere else. With shaking fingers he dialled Dominic's number again. No one answered. Leaving a team of constables standing guard in case Dominic returned home, he hurried to the store where Bev worked. On the way he tried to recall everything she had told him about her boss. She liked him, that much he remembered. He wished he had paid more attention to her when she had told him about her new job, but either she hadn't said much about Dominic, or else he hadn't been listening. She had complained about a colleague named Danielle, but other than that he couldn't remember much of what she had said. He was close to tears. He had paid his wife such scant attention. She deserved so much more. Approaching his destination, he promised himself he would treat her better in future. But first, he had to find her.

★   ★   ★

The supermarket was cordoned off, with uniformed constables guarding all access points to the building. Nearby a small crowd of evacuated shoppers and passersby were craning their necks to watch the police activity from behind a line of uniformed police officers. Abandoning his car, Ian manoeuvred his way through the throng, doing his best to ignore their chattering. A woman peering through binoculars was giving a running commentary to her neighbours, but in truth there wasn't much to see. Everyone was waiting with anticipation that was almost tangible; he could virtually smell the excitement emanating from the spectators.

'Why don't they do something?' a man grumbled.

'Yes, let's see some action,' another voice agreed.

Ian was genuinely shocked to see the fate of a human being transformed into a source of entertainment, as though the crowd had gathered to watch an action film.

Inside, the offices had been stormed and a team was busy searching the premises. Dominic was dangerous, and there was a possibility he might be armed. The rapid response unit was in place surrounding the building. Ian tried not to imagine a homicidal maniac running out, holding Bev in front of him as a human shield. It crossed his mind that he would have quite enjoyed the drama of the occasion if it had been anyone other than Bev taken captive. He had always tried to show understanding towards families of victims. He now realised his expressions of sympathy had been no more than crass lip service to previously unimagined horrors.

Although none of his colleagues mentioned Bev's name, Ian could see in their faces that they knew what had happened. He tried to behave as though this was like any other investigation, but it was impossible to detach himself from the circumstances. Bev might be injured, or dying, and all he could do was bark out orders and run along gloomy corridors, banging doors open and looking inside rooms that had already been searched. He heard himself calling her name out loud, over and over again, bordering on hysteria. A sign on one of the doors read: 'Danielle Roberts' and beneath it, handwritten on a piece of card, 'Beverley Peterson'. His heart hammered in his chest as he saw her name. This was her office. If she hadn't taken his name, she would never have come here. He had searched through personal belongings in any number of people's homes without compunction, yet he felt like an intruder as he pushed open the door.

The interior was disappointing. Two work stations were crammed into the small room, with two cheap grey plastic chairs. A schedule displayed on a large white board on the wall was covered in scribbled notes, mostly unintelligible acronyms. He felt a stab of guilt that Bev, who loved to surround herself with beautiful objects, should have worked in such an ugly office. When he found her, he would take her away from this hideous place. Struggling not to break down in tears, he hurried from the room. His only focus right now was to find his wife and bring her safely home. But it was nearly midnight, and there was still no sign of Dominic or Bev.

Ian was on the point of collapse when his phone rang. His heart hammered as he recognised the voice.

'Where are you?' he blurted out.

Dominic greeted his question with laughter.

'I don't believe you've got my wife with you,' Ian blustered. 'If you want to convince me, you'll have to tell me where you are so I can see her, and then I'll know you're telling the truth.'

It was a stupid suggestion, but he couldn't think of anything better on the spur of the moment. In the background he could hear muffled voices. A few seconds later he felt as though the ground was swaying beneath his feet as he heard Bev's tearful voice.

'Ian, help me.'

'I'm coming to get you,' he gabbled, but the line was already dead.

CHAPTER 73

Bev lay perfectly still, trying to think. Her latest bout of crying had subsided, leaving her with a pounding headache. She was sure she must be dehydrated but there was nothing she could do about that. Her priority now was to keep a clear head and think of a way out of her predicament. Crying only made her feel worse, and it wouldn't help her devise a plan. There were only two ways of escaping this hellish situation. One was to make so much noise that someone outside heard her and alerted the police. The other was to persuade her captor to release her. The trouble was that she knew his identity. It would be impossible for her to convince him that she wouldn't give his name to the police. To make matters worse, he knew that her husband was a detective. Her best option was to devote all her energy to attracting attention to her plight. The police must be looking for her by now. She had no idea how long she had been tied up in the bedroom, but it felt like days. Ian knew she was missing and would be organising search teams to scour the city for her.

All she had to do was yell loudly enough, and they would find her.

The only light in the room came through the curtains. She could make use of that information, because she knew where the window was. If she could find something to throw, she might be able to shatter a pane. The smashed glass alone might attract attention. And with a broken window, it was more likely her screams would be heard from outside. But she had nothing to throw and, in any case, her hands were too tightly bound to move them. The chances of hurling a missile with her feet were negligible. Nevertheless, she kicked out as strongly as she could. One of her shoes flew across the room to hit the floor beneath the window with a futile thud. The other shoe fared no better. With nothing else to throw, she had to abandon that possibility. It had been a stupid idea anyway. Despair overwhelmed her and she dissolved in tears once more.

After a while she pulled herself together and began resolutely bending and stretching her legs and rotating her shoulders and head. Lying completely still was making her painfully stiff. Still sobbing, she forced herself to keep moving. Her shoulders hurt from the awkward position of her arms, but other than that the bed was not uncomfortable. It was damp, but there was nothing she could do about that. Dominic had pointed out the en suite, allegedly there for her use, but she couldn't get up to use it. Desperately, she resorted to screaming again until her throat felt raw and her voice came out in a feeble croak.

What had happened was bewildering, but she had to try and understand her situation. Dominic was insane. That much was clear. She would have to try and work on him, and convince him that she was his friend. She shuddered, trying to control her loathing. It was important to hide her reactions. She had read somewhere that mad people could be very sensitive to other people's feelings. But she couldn't understand what he wanted with her. Not knowing made her situation even more terrifying. Tying her to a bed suggested he intended to assault her sexually. She was encouraged by the fact that he hadn't done so yet. She shut her eyes, trying to remember the sequence of events that had brought her here. He had been banging on about his old aunt, only admitting that the aunt didn't exist after Bev was securely fastened to the bed. Then he had slapped her, hard, and left. If his motive wasn't sexual, what did he want?

She seemed to have been lying on the bed for days, alternately dozing and feeling sick, when he returned. Even though he had abducted her and tied her up, she was pleased to hear the door open and see him enter. He had brought her some water but refused to let her get up to go to the toilet.

'You'll have to wait,' he snapped.

'What do you want with me?'

He laughed at that. 'I don't want *you*. You don't really believe I could be interested in a slut like you? Married to a policeman.' He made it sound as though Ian's career was disgusting.

'I don't understand. What am I doing here?'

'You're my hostage, stupid.'

'Why do you want a hostage?'

'So we can get away, of course.'

'We?'

'Not you, stupid. God, how many times do I have to tell you, I don't want *you*. It's her I want. I always have done.' His eyes glowed with a crazy fervour. 'We were meant to be together.'

Bev stared at him, puzzled.

'You *are* together. You said you've been together for five years—' Seeing his expression, she faltered before continuing more firmly. 'You haven't got a girlfriend, have you? You never had a girlfriend. You made that up, didn't you? Just like you invented your aunt.'

He grinned but the wild expression in his eyes terrified her.

'I'm not a liar.'

'I didn't mean . . .'

'My aunt lived here for as long as I knew her.' He waved his hands in the air. 'She died in this bed. And my girlfriend's waiting for me.' His voice softened as he spoke about her. 'I don't need to

416

make anything up. We're going away together as soon as this is all over. She promised. "Do this for me and we can be together," that's what she said. And now it's happening, just like we planned.'

Bev managed to prop herself on one elbow while he held a water bottle to her lips.

'You obviously love her very much,' she said when she had drunk enough. 'What's her name?'

He didn't answer.

'If you love her, why don't you just go away with her, if that's what you want? What's it got to do with me?'

'God you're so stupid. They won't just let us go away, will they? Not after all this.' He waved his hand in the air in a vague circular motion. 'Not after everything that's happened.'

Bev felt a thrill of fear. Although he was crazy, his thoughts followed a certain logic. By kidnapping her, he had destroyed his own chance of escape. The more desperate his situation, the less likely her chance of survival became.

'If you let me go, my husband will make sure—' she began.

'Shut up and let me think.'

He paced the room for a moment then took out his phone. 'We need to get her out of there.'

'Out of where?'

'The police cell where they've locked her up, of course. Where do you think? If they don't let her go—' he drew a line across his throat with his finger.

'That's ridiculous. The police don't kill people.'

'Not the police, stupid. Of course they won't kill her. If they don't release her, you're the one who's going to die.'

CHAPTER 74

Ian didn't sleep that night. He went to bed for a while but there was no point lying there in the darkness. All he could do was think about Bev. He was better off being up and active, even if there was nothing he could do to help find her. He spent hours scanning through every record he could access for Dominic Archer. He read his work emails, hunting for clues, and studied his phone records, looking for patterns. He read through documents until he could no longer remember what he was looking for. Dominic's parents had both died when he was a teenager, after which he had been brought up by an aunt who lived in York. Apart from going away to university, he had lived in York ever since. It was past midnight by the time Ian found the records relating to Dominic's family circumstances. It was too late to go calling on the aunt, although she only lived a few miles away. He decided to speak to her first thing in the morning. Just as he had made up his mind not to wait that long but to wake the aunt up without further delay, he came across a copy of her will and discovered she had died a few years earlier. Dominic had been left with no living relations.

Bev's work colleagues had already been questioned. Ian had intended to speak to Danielle himself as she and Bev shared an office, but in the end he had withdrawn from the process. He wasn't confident he would be able to remain appropriately detached. Although Bev had only ever been critical of Danielle, he remembered her animation when she had talked about her colleague. When it came to it, he couldn't trust himself to cope with his memories. It was different now that he was on his own. If his eyes occasionally filled with tears, there was no one there to see. Eventually he lay down and tried to sleep. It was impossible. He dialled Bev's number for the hundredth time, but there was no response. He got up and brewed a pot of coffee. He had to think. Trawling through the paperwork, he studied the will Dominic's aunt had left. She had left everything to her nephew, but there was no trace of her property being sold. No significant sum of money had appeared in her nephew's bank account, and he still rented the flat where he had been living before. Studying the records, it raised the obvious question of what had happened to the old lady's house. With growing excitement, Ian called the station to see who was on night duty and arranged for any available officers to meet him at the aunt's address. Bev had to be there, but he wasn't going to rush round there on his own. Precipitate action like that would put his wife's life at risk as well as his own. There was no point in taking any chances with a serial killer.

Dominic's aunt had lived in a small end of terrace house along Holgate Road. To the right of the row of brick properties was a patch of grass. The street light immediately outside the house wasn't working. Ian took out his torch and made his way carefully up a short path bordered on both sides by tall weeds. Half a dozen uniformed officers followed him. Sending four of his companions to watch the back exit, he led the other two up to the small porch at the front door. The house looked abandoned, with windows so dirty it was impossible to see in. There was one large bay window on the ground floor and two small windows upstairs. He decided to risk breaking in and accept the consequences if he was wrong. Crouching down, he picked at the lock in silence. One of the constables muttered to a colleague. Ian swivelled round and hushed them furiously. It might prove crucial to their success that they effected an entry without alerting anyone inside. He turned back to the lock and continued gently rotating his key until with a loud click the door swung inwards. Ian straightened up and stepped over the threshold into darkness. Bev was in there somewhere. He could sense her presence.

* * *

421

The house smelt damp and musty. Torches in hand, they spread out to search. Ian stole upstairs. The first door he opened was a bathroom. It was empty. All the porcelain was covered in a thick film of dust. The second room he tried was a box room packed with cardboard boxes. There was nowhere anyone could be concealed in there. He came to the main bedroom. The beam of light from his torch trembled as he shone it around the room. It was empty. Entering, he thought he detected a faint scent of familiar perfume and felt his heart hammering in his chest. He examined the bed. It stank of urine. With growing disappointment he checked inside the wooden wardrobe, which smelled of mothballs and was stuffed with women's clothes: tweed skirts, cotton flower print dresses, and cardigans. There was nothing under the bed. There was no point in looking behind the curtains because they stopped at waist level.

As he glanced around, something caught his eye. He moved closer. The beam from his torch illuminated a navy and white court shoe. The breath caught at the back of his throat as he recognised it. Bev had recently bought an identical pair. Searching the carpet with his torch, he spotted its partner lying nearby. They were Bev's size. With trembling fingers he slipped them into a plastic bag. Either they belonged to Bev or by a strange coincidence a pair like hers had been left there by someone else. He could easily check at home to see if hers were missing. In the meantime, she wasn't there now. He ran downstairs. There was no one in any of the ground floor rooms. The officers who had accompanied him had checked the loft, the tiny patch of garden, and anywhere else that one or two people could be hiding. The place was deserted.

Ian was distraught. He had been so sure they would find her there. The disappointment was almost too harsh to bear. With no idea where to look next, he hurried home where he confirmed that Bev's navy and white shoes were missing. He couldn't be sure that she had been wearing them that day, but there seemed little doubt the shoes they had found that night were hers. He returned to the police station where Visual Image Identification Officers officers were searching CCTV footage trying to track where Dominic's car had gone. From his workplace he had driven across town in the direction of the aunt's house. They had lost sight of the car a few miles away from the house. Bev must have been there, but they had no idea where she was now.

CHAPTER 75

I an managed to doze for a few hours when he got home. He woke up feeling surprisingly fresh, and ready to renew his efforts to find his wife. Everything possible was being done to gather information about Dominic Archer. There was a nationwide alert to look out for Ian's missing wife, her kidnapper, and his car which hadn't been found. Meanwhile Emma was their only link to Dominic, apart from his work colleagues who didn't seem to know much about their boss. The officer posted outside Emma's block nodded at Ian. A second officer stood on guard outside her own front door. With so much security in place, he was pleased to see that she looked more relaxed than before, with colour restored to her cheeks, and her eyes no longer swollen from crying.

'I'm sorry about your wife,' she said with a gentle smile, 'but at least you know who you're looking for. That must make it easier.'

Ian thanked her.

'There's something that's been puzzling me,' he

told her. 'What did he mean when he said he would release Bev if we let you go?'

Emma shrugged.

'That puzzled me too,' she admitted. 'But I wouldn't waste your time worrying about anything he says. He's crazy. I suppose he didn't like my being taken to the police station. He was always very possessive. I guess that's why he killed Richard.'

She shifted uncomfortably on her seat. Ian couldn't help noticing that she seemed uneasy.

'You have to find him and lock him up,' she burst out suddenly. 'You ought never to have let him get away. He killed Adrian at the races, he killed some random woman, and he killed Richard right here on my doorstep. Every time he's getting closer. Next time it could be me. You can't let him get away with it. You have to find him and stop him.'

'Emma,' Ian said urgently, 'believe me, I want him found as much as you do. He's got my wife. If you know anything that might help us find him, you have to tell me.'

'I don't know,' she said softly, her beautiful eyes filling with tears. 'I wish I could help you.'

'I know,' Ian assured her.

Her smile seemed to lift his spirits. Somehow, he would find Bev.

With renewed determination, Ian returned to his desk and searched first through Dominic's records, then his aunt's. He noticed she had made regular payments for an allotment. It wasn't mentioned in her will but a little research disclosed the allotment had been purchased by her nephew, about a year before her death. It was possible Dominic was hiding Bev there. Ian raced along the corridor to Eileen's office. She didn't remonstrate when he barged in without knocking. As he blurted out his suspicion, he faltered, afraid he was clutching at straws, but Eileen leaped to her feet.

'Dominic rented an allotment? Why didn't anyone spot that? What are you waiting for? Go and check it out at once. I'll mobilise the rapid response unit right away and keep teams here hunting through his records and searching CCTV on the roads. Wherever he is, he won't get far.'

Ian stammered his thanks.

'Don't stand there blathering, get going!'

A fleet of cars turned off Blossom Street and drove silently over the railway bridge and past the train depot towards the allotments. Ian had issued strict instructions that no sirens or blue lights were to be used. He realised it was probably a futile hope, but he wanted to seize the initiative and catch Bev's captor off guard, if he was there. Instead of turning into the uneven driveway that led straight into the allotments, he parked out on the road, and signalled to the accompanying cars to do the same. While an officer unlocked the double gates, Ian deployed his team around the metal fence.

Satisfied the area was surrounded, he slipped through the gate to observe the allotments more closely. Only the trees made any sound, their leaves rustling in a light breeze that bore the smell of freshly cut grass, mingling with the familiar aroma of a herb he couldn't identify.

The area was divided into plots, overlooked on three sides by houses that were too far away for the residents to see what happened there among the sheds and bushes. Ian gazed around at large blue rain water bins, wooden sheds, some painted green, and an abundance of shrubs, flowers, vegetables and grasses. Many of the plots were open, but the one Dominic rented was in a corner of the area, partitioned off from the others by a low fence. Tucked into a far corner against the high wooden boundary fence, a small green shed was shielded from view on two sides by high trees.

Ian's legs felt weak. As a rule, he lived for this kind of action. It made the usual drudgery of his working life tolerable: the hours spent sitting at his desk, skimming documents and painstakingly writing up dull reports. The instinctive rush of adrenaline when they closed in on a suspect was the highlight of any investigation. Men had always experienced a visceral thrill from combat, from prehistoric man battling beasts for survival, through centuries of warfare, to the present day. Fighting for justice against vicious criminals was Ian's own hunting ground. But this was different. Fear gripped him in a way he had never experienced before. Even when his own life was at risk, his training helped him retain the ability to think clearly. With Bev's life in danger he struggled to focus on the job. It took a conscious effort of will not to dash for the shed and smash it down with his bare hands, screaming out Bev's name. Life without her was unimaginable. With a start, he realised his eyes were watering. Quickly he wiped his face, before any of his fellow officers noticed his tears. They were all too focused on the allotment to pay any attention to him.

The wooden shed looked unremarkable. Blinking furiously, Ian studied it. Someone handed him a pair of binoculars. Closer inspection revealed a brand new padlock on the door. There was no window. With luck they would be able to surprise the killer in his hideout before he had any inkling of their presence. While the preparations were under way, Ian fretted, physically shaking with impatience. So much fuss, and they might already be too late to save Bev's life. This was no longer about catching a serial killer. It was solely about rescuing her. Nothing else mattered. They could let Dominic go for all Ian cared. He just wanted Bev to be safe.

The detective chief inspector gave a signal to the armed response unit and Ian saw a flash of metal flicker around the perimeter fence. As far as they knew, their target was unarmed, but they were prepared for any eventuality. Dominic would not slip through their grasp again. With a roar, a helicopter appeared and hovered overhead. They couldn't keep their presence secret for much longer. The assembled officers waited. Ian closed his eyes, scarcely able to tolerate the suspense. Finally an amplified voice rang out.

'Dominic Archer. Your shed is surrounded by armed officers. Come out, with your hands raised.'

There was no response. Ian was afraid he would pass out. He was shaking uncontrollably.

'Come out with your hands raised,' the voice commanded again. 'You are surrounded.'

The door opened. Ian's breath came in short shallow bursts until he felt lightheaded. Forcing himself to breathe deeply, he watched as Bev appeared in the doorway.

She was close enough for him to see her eyes were bloodshot and inflamed, her face a mess of smudged mascara. But she was alive. Ian started forward. Before he could reach her, an arm seized her around the upper arms and chest and she was pushed out of the shed by a figure concealed behind her. Like some four legged beast they staggered forwards. Ian waited for her to fling herself sideways, out of his grasp, but she stood, quivering, her eyes wide with terror. A tremor ran through him, like an electric shock. Her captor was holding a gun at the side of her head, the barrel pressed against her temple.

'Let the woman go,' the amplified voice said calmly. 'You're making things worse for yourself.'

Ian couldn't bear it any longer. He ran forwards.

'Let her go and we'll take you to Emma,' he bellowed. 'Emma's waiting for you. You can see her, but only if you let your hostage go.'

It was a desperate ploy. He had probably thrown his entire career away, breaking protocol like that, but he didn't care.

'Let Bev go and we'll take you to Emma!' he shouted.

As if in slow motion, Bev swivelled round to face him, propelled by her captor.

'Where's Emma?' Dominic called back. 'I want to see her.'

'She's waiting for you.'

'I don't believe you.'

'She knows what you did for her,' Ian repeated. 'You have to believe me, you have to.' He was almost crying.

'Let me see her,' Dominic insisted.

Ian stared at Bev. Her eyes were fixed on his. She looked on the point of collapse. Trembling, she reached out a hand towards him. At her gesture, he felt a shutter snap shut in his mind. All at once he was in control of his emotions again, ready to deal with the situation. It was the only way he could save her life. Ignoring her pleading expression, he took a step backwards.

'Wait here,' he snapped.

With an almost unbearable wrench, he turned away.

CHAPTER 76

If Emma was surprised to see Ian at her door, she hid her feelings well behind a welcoming smile. Without any make up her skin looked unhealthily pale, and her huge blue eyes seemed to glow at him in the soft light that fell on her from the street. Her evident pleasure at seeing him vanished when he brusquely interrupted her.

'I'm going to have to ask you to accompany me—'

'Do I have to? I'm so tired. Can't this wait till tomorrow—'

He interrupted her again. 'No, it can't wait. We have to go right now.'

'Are you arresting me?' she asked with a nervous smile.

'No, of course not. You have to come to the Holgate Road allotments with me right now.'

'Allotments? Why? What's going on?'

Quickly Ian explained that Dominic was there, and he had taken a hostage. 'So you have to come with me. You're the only one who can persuade him to let her go.'

⋆　⋆　⋆

Emma took a step back, shaking her head. 'No, I can't come with you. I won't see him. Don't ask me to see him. He frightens me. Just go away and leave me alone.'

For answer, Ian reached out and seized her arm. 'You have to come with me. You have to do this. He's got my wife. You have to help her.'

'I'm sorry, really I am. But I don't see what you expect me to do about it.'

Ian struggled to keep his voice steady as he gave her further details of the situation, and promised to protect her. Although Emma was reluctant to accompany him, she could hardly refuse once he had persuaded her that a woman's life was at stake. His wife's.

'There's a team of officers in place, watching, so you'll be quite safe. I'll make sure nothing happens to you. I give you my word. Please. My wife's life depends on your help.'

He didn't mention that Dominic had a gun.

'All right, I'll go. I'll do it for you.'

In the car on the way he coached her in what to say. When she protested once more, he struggled to keep his temper.

'Tell him he won't be allowed near you until he lets her go. That's all you have to say. He'll believe you. He'll believe anything you say. Tell him you'll be waiting for him but he has to let her go first.'

He was babbling desperately.

'What do you mean, I'll be waiting for him? Waiting for him to be locked up, more like.'

'Look, it's quite simple. You have to tell him you've negotiated a deal with us and we'll let you both go if he releases Bev unharmed, but if he doesn't let her go, we'll lock you up and he'll never see you again.'

'But—'

'I know it's not true. For Christ's sake, Emma, that doesn't matter. Say anything you like, as long as you persuade him to let her go. Saving her is all that matters right now. Otherwise he's going to kill her.'

They turned off after the station and sped along Holgate Road over the bridge, and past the railway depot. There was no need to hide their presence any longer, so he drove right up to the gate in the metal fence. The sun was rising and there was a crisp wind blowing as they climbed out of the car and followed the grassy track between allotments towards the low fence that marked the entrance to Dominic's plot. Reaching the gate, Ian turned to look at Emma. With wild eyes, her hair blowing in the wind, she looked curiously animated, exhilarated rather than anxious.

'Are you all right?' he asked.

She nodded without speaking. He turned back to the shed and called out.

'Dominic! Dominic! Emma's here!'

There was no response. He shouted again and

434

stopped, listening. He hoped no one else had noticed the desperation in his voice.

Eileen came and stood beside him. She reached out and touched his shoulder.

'Ian,' she said gently. Surprised by the softness in her voice, he turned his head to look at her. 'Leave this to the negotiator. Go back to your car and wait there. You've brought Emma. You can't do any more.'

He shook his head. 'No—'

'That's an order, Ian. Go back to your car now.'

There was a sudden disturbance in the far corner of the allotment as the door swung open and banged against the side of the shed. Bev appeared, framed in the doorway, crying hysterically.

'Where is she?' Dominic's voice rang out.

He pushed Bev forwards. She stumbled but he held her up, supporting her with his hand under one of her arms while the other pointed the gun at the side of her head. At his side, Ian heard Emma gasp. She had seen the gun. Ian held his breath, afraid she would pull back and insist on leaving, but she didn't move. For a moment they stood mutely in a row, Eileen, Ian and Emma. Then Bev cried out and Ian started forward.

'Emma's here,' he yelled. 'Let Bev go and you can speak to her.'

Dominic responded without loosening his grip

435

on his hostage. He sounded drunk and seemed to sway slightly as he spoke.

'Where's Emma? I want to see Emma!'

Before Ian could react, Emma stepped forward.

'I'm here!' she shouted.

'What are you doing?' Ian hissed. He grabbed hold of her arm and pulled her back.

She turned to look at him. She seemed unnaturally calm. 'I'll go over there. Once he sees me coming, he'll let her go. Don't worry. He won't hurt me.'

Eileen intervened. 'I'm sorry, but there's no way we can put you at risk like that. The man's unstable, and he has a gun. He might shoot you. Ian, take her back to the car right now and you can both wait there.'

'He won't hurt me,' Emma repeated. 'He worships me, he always has done. He'd do anything for me. I'll go over to him, and he'll send your wife back to you. As soon as she's no longer shielding him, I'll throw myself on the ground and you can shoot him, and this will all be over.'

'But—'

'You'll be able to get a clear shot at him.'

'We don't want to shoot him unless we have to,' Eileen pointed out.

'You have to kill him,' Emma said firmly. 'He's insane. Just shoot him and it will all be over.'

The next few seconds were chaotic. Before Eileen could protest again, Emma dashed forward calling out to Dominic to let his hostage go. With a sweep of his arm he flung Bev aside. No longer supported, she fell to her knees, swaying and wailing. At the same time, Emma threw herself forward onto the ground. In the confusion, Dominic's gun appeared to explode in his hand. As soon as the shot rang out, the three characters acting out the macabre scene seemed to freeze. Ian felt a bolt of terror. Barely aware of Eileen barking at him to stay back, he sprinted towards Bev who held out her arms towards him. She was sobbing, but as far as he could see, she was uninjured. As he reached her, he noticed Dominic was writhing on the ground, groaning, while blood seeped into the earth from a flesh wound in his thigh. A centimetre further over and he would have severed an artery. As Ian registered what had happened, Emma lunged forward and seized the gun. She pointed it at Dominic. Her hand was trembling so much the gun was a blur. Ian sprang to his feet. Seeing him, Emma hurled the gun away. It skittered across the dry earth and came to rest in a patch of long grass.

'He's not armed!' she yelled, throwing herself down on the ground once more. 'You can shoot him now. Shoot him, please, shoot him!'

CHAPTER 77

'Don't go.'

Ian smiled at her.

'You're crying,' she whispered.

He shook his head. 'No, I'm not.'

She giggled, then her expression grew solemn again. 'Please don't go.'

'I'll be back before you know it. You're safe now.'

'You want to go, don't you?'

'I have to do this, Bev. I promise I'll be back soon. Just rest and concentrate on getting fit. Don't forget, we're off on holiday soon.'

His chair made a nasty scraping sound on the floor as he stood up.

'I'll tell the nurse I'm off so they can keep an eye on you in case you want anything. You'll be well looked after here.'

'I keep telling you, there's nothing wrong with me.'

Although physically unharmed, apart from some nasty scratches and bruises, Ian was keen for her to see a counsellor while she was in hospital under observation.

'It's over now,' she insisted. 'I don't want to talk

about it. I just want to go home. And to know that he's locked up.'

'He killed three people. There's no way he'll be let out. And if he ever is,' he added, leaning over the bed so she could hear him talking under his breath, 'I'll go after him myself. I'll kill the bastard before I let him put a finger on you again.'

She must have realised it was only bluster but she smiled anyway, and her pale face relaxed.

Eileen was reluctant to allow Ian to question Dominic himself. On the face of it he was the obvious person to conduct the interview. He had orchestrated the eventual arrest, and knew more about the investigation than anyone else. When Eileen expressed concern about his emotional involvement with the case, he had to work hard to persuade her that his professionalism outweighed his personal feelings.

'It's what we train for. Please, ma'am, I really want to see it through. I need to do this.'

'That's what's worrying me,' she replied. 'You're too eager.'

Despite the assurances he had given the detective chief inspector, he felt a burst of rage as he sat down opposite the man who had kidnapped Bev, causing her unimaginable terror. For a few seconds he struggled against an urge to leap across the table and grab the other man round the neck, squeezing all the breath out of his lungs. But he sat immobile, his face impassive as he went through the procedure.

★   ★   ★

Dominic had refused to have a solicitor present, claiming it would 'mess with his head', so, once the preliminaries were over, Ian asked point blank where he had been on the afternoon of Adrian's death. Dominic ignored the question and stared at his bandaged leg, injured when his gun had accidentally gone off.

'Where's Emma?' he demanded at last. 'You said she'd be waiting for me.'

'Emma doesn't want anything to do with a maniac like you,' Ian said softly. 'She said she hopes we lock you up and throw away the key.'

'You're lying.'

Dominic's eyes darted around the room, as though he thought Emma might be hidden in there.

'Where is she?' he repeated. 'I won't say another word until I see her. And not here. She said you'd let us go so we can be together. We're meant to be together.' He dropped his voice and whispered across the table. 'There's no one else here so you can switch that machine off and take me to her. No one will know it was you. No one will know we've gone. We'll be discreet. We'll just disappear, go abroad, and never be found. Where is she?'

'Dominic, we'll discuss your relationship with Emma when you've answered my questions.'

'I want to see her now.'

He sat back in his chair and closed his eyes.

★   ★   ★

Ted was sitting stolidly beside Ian, arms crossed, staring at Dominic.

'You've been arrested on three counts of murder and one of abduction,' Ian said. 'So you'd better start playing by the rules. There's no chance you'll see Emma again before you've answered my questions.' He paused. 'And no chance after that either,' he thought to himself.

Dominic scowled. Ian suddenly felt a wave of exhaustion. He almost regretted having insisted on interviewing Dominic himself. At his side, he heard Ted stir.

'Now, let's get on with it,' Ian resumed briskly. 'We know you're responsible for the deaths of Adrian Curtis, Jocelyn Sands and Richard Western. Confirm that's the case, and it will be all the better for you. Tell us why you killed them. Come on, Dominic, the quicker we get through this, the easier it will be for you, and the sooner you'll get to see Emma.'

Dominic opened his eyes. He stared directly at Ian and gave a careless shrug.

'Just for the record, tell me why you killed them,' Ian repeated patiently.

Without answering, Dominic shut his eyes again.

'How did you get hold of the drug? Did you steal it?'

'I'm not a common thief. As manager I had access to all the store records. It wasn't hard to add it to the order for the pharmacy. The pharmacist never saw it because I removed the stock

441

as soon as it was delivered, and deleted it from the records before anyone could spot it on the list. It was easy enough to cover up the cost. You'd be surprised how much food gets thrown away every day in a store that size.'

'Why Pentaketaphine?'

'It's fast acting and completely paralyses the patient. They use it in operations to prevent involuntary movement. All I had to do was wait a few seconds after injecting them, and they were helpless. I could do what I wanted with them. It was easy.'

Ian relaxed at the admission, but he still had questions. 'You could have left them after injecting them. They would have died anyway.'

'I had to make sure.'

'You must have enjoyed the power it gave you, when they were helpless to defend themselves against you.'

Dominic shook his head. 'That wasn't it. I just had to kill them,' he said simply.

Ian sat forward. 'Why?'

'Because of what they did to Emma. After the way they treated her, they had to go.'

His matter-of-fact tone was chilling.

'Did Emma want you to kill them?'

'Of course not. I did it for her, but it was nothing to do with her. She doesn't know I killed them.'

All at once Dominic seemed alert. His eyes darted rapidly round the room. Ian noticed the change in his demeanour but made no comment.

'What about Jocelyn?'

'Who?'

'The woman you killed.'

Dominic smiled. 'That one was my idea,' he said. 'It was a stroke of genius, killing a random woman. If it wasn't for her, you might have suspected the other two deaths were linked to Emma. I had to protect her.' He passed one hand across his face, with an anxious expression. 'Where is she? I want to see her.'

'What do you mean, that one was your idea?' Ian asked.

Dominic gazed at the ceiling and refused to answer any more questions.

Taking a break from the interview, Ian went back to his own office and sat at his desk, pondering. Emma had described Dominic's second victim as a 'random woman' as well. It might have been coincidence that she and Dominic had used exactly the same phrase, but Ian wondered if he had been too ready to accept what Emma had told him. Perhaps she knew more about the murders than she was letting on. Emma had pointed the gun at Dominic, dropping it only when she had noticed Ian watching her. Had she threatened to shoot Dominic in the panic of the moment, or had she intended to seize the opportunity to silence him?

Emma had divulged Dominic's name, information that had led to his arrest. It was possible she had persuaded Dominic to kill Adrian and Richard. At the allotment, she had begged the police to shoot him. What had appeared to be a momentary panic now seemed open to a more sinister interpretation. She had failed to silence Dominic herself, or to persuade the police to eliminate him for her. After that she had reverted to her original plan of having Dominic arrested, convinced he would be convicted. If he tried to implicate her in the murders, she could be confident no one was going to take his accusations seriously.

Quickly he checked through Emma's statements until he found the sentence he was looking for.

'He killed Adrian at the races, he killed some random woman he'd followed, and he killed Richard right on my doorstep.'

Emma had warned Ian not to believe anything Dominic said. He glanced down at his notes again.

'I wouldn't waste your time worrying about anything he says. He's crazy.'

What Ian hadn't considered before was that some of Dominic's ravings might be true. According to Dominic, he and Emma were going to be together. Ian might have been too quick to dismiss his words as mere delusional fantasising. Perhaps Emma had promised she would run away with Dominic if he killed the two men who had betrayed her. It sounded crazy, but it was possible.

CHAPTER 78

Dominic refused to discuss Emma, but Ian hoped he might not be able to resist boasting about what he had done.

'Tell us about Jocelyn, your second victim. You said that was a stroke of genius, and I have to admit you were clever there. How did you find her?'

'It was easy. She was on her own. I followed her across the park opposite Clifford's Tower and down the steps from Skeldergate Bridge to the river. There was no one else around.'

'You killed them all to impress Emma, didn't you? She knew what you were doing, didn't she?' he asked bluntly. 'Did it work? Was she pleased with you?'

Dominic didn't answer.

'Oh come on, Dominic. You've been co-operating so far. Why hold back now? Don't tell me you still think you're protecting her. We all know exactly what happened. But there's something you don't know.' He leaned forward, staring Dominic in the eye. 'Emma betrayed you. She gave us your name. She wanted us to find you.'

★   ★   ★

Dominic shook his head. He looked anxious. 'That's a lie.'

'How do you think we found you? Come on, Dominic, wise up. She used you to kill her ex, and her current boyfriend, and now she's letting you take the blame all by yourself. Why did she want you to do it? Was it revenge?'

Dominic didn't answer.

'She handed you to us. She used you, Dominic. You mean nothing to her. You never did. She doesn't want to see you. Didn't you hear her calling out to us to shoot you? Emma never wants to see you again. You did all this for her, didn't you? And she wants to see you dead.'

Dominic shook his head again.

'Just admit that Emma talked you into doing it. Everyone will understand you did it for love. Or was there another reason why you killed those people? Did you have reasons of your own? Did you get off on it? Come on, Dominic, if you can convince a jury you were persuaded to kill them, you'll be treated more leniently. Don't be a fool. You're protecting a woman who deliberately talked you into committing murder so you could take the punishment for it, when the whole thing was her idea. You were just her puppet. But you'll go down for life if you don't tell the truth, and she'll get off scot free. She's walking away and laughing at you for being an idiot.'

Dominic's eyes sparkled darkly, but however much Ian pressed him, he refused to answer.

Emma looked surprised to see Ian and Ted on her doorstep.

'You have got Dominic behind bars, haven't you?'

'Yes. Don't worry. There are just a few more points we'd like to clear up, and we think you can help us.'

Ian tried to give her a reassuring smile, but it was difficult. Looking at her fragile beauty, he almost bottled it. But three people had died. He couldn't walk away.

'Can we come in?'

'I'm kind of busy.'

'Busy?'

'Yes.'

'Is your mother still here?'

'No. She went home. I'm on my own.'

She looked at Ian, her full lips curved in an almost imperceptible smile, as though an intimacy had developed between them. He couldn't help smiling back.

As soon as they were all seated, Ian began.

'Dominic's told us everything.'

'That's a good thing, isn't it?' Her voice sounded artificially cheerful.

'I mean he's told us *everything*,' Ian repeated, placing careful emphasis on the last word.

She looked outwardly composed but her fists clenched in her lap until her knuckles protruded.

Ted stared at her blankly. Ian knew his sharp eyes missed nothing.

'Poor Dominic. He's completely mad, isn't he?' She gazed sadly from Ian to Ted and back again. 'I told you, he's a complete fantasist. You can't believe anything he says.'

Ian sat forward.

'Dominic confessed to killing three people.'

She nodded. 'I knew it!' There was a note of triumph in her voice, although her expression remained steadfastly sombre.

'He says you've known what was happening all along.'

She smiled incredulously. 'How could I have known? I haven't spoken to Dominic for over ten years, unless you count his anonymous calls, stalking Richard and then me—'

Ian stared closely at her. 'He told us you knew how Adrian was going to be murdered before it happened.'

'What? How could I possibly have known—'

'Dominic told us you put him up to it.'

She jerked upright at that. If Ian had slapped her in the face she couldn't have looked more startled.

'What are you talking about?'

Ian studied her face. Her mouth didn't move but her eyes narrowed, watching him, and her hands trembled in her lap. She was frightened.

'Is something wrong? Surely you're not bothered by the accusation of a fantasist?' Ian paused and glanced at Ted. 'Unless Dominic's telling us the truth.'

'Poor Dominic,' she replied, recovering her composure. 'You can't take anything he says seriously. I already told you, I haven't spoken to him for years.'

'He accused you of asking him to murder three people.'

'That's a ridiculous allegation.'

She stared at Ian, wide-eyed, the picture of innocence. But he couldn't shrug off the suspicion that she had exploited Dominic's obsession, just as she had beguiled Ian himself into neglecting to treat her as a potential suspect all along. She gave him a sad smile. She must be aware that a jury was unlikely to convict her on the basis of his flimsy hunch. Unless Dominic was prepared to accuse her of complicity in the murders, there was no evidence to suggest she had been an accessory. Ian wavered. She might be innocent as she claimed. Even now, she seemed more concerned about Dominic than worried for herself.

'He's not right in the head,' she said with a rueful expression. 'You can't believe anything he says.'

Ian nodded, noticing her hands had begun writhing in her lap again.

'I don't think there's anything more I can tell you. You can believe the ramblings of a nutter if you like, but it's my word against his that I knew anything about this insanity. I don't think I'll have too much trouble persuading a jury of my innocence.'

Ian couldn't help but admire the careless grace with which she rose to her feet.

'I'd like you to leave now.'

Ian didn't budge. He was convinced that Emma knew more than she was prepared to admit.

'Why do you think he told us it was all your idea, and that you wanted to be revenged on Adrian and Richard? You'll make it harder for yourself if you refuse to co-operate.'

She sat down again.

'I told you, I haven't spoken to Dominic for years.'

'What possible motive could he have had for killing those three people?'

She shook her head. 'I'm sorry. I really can't help you.'

'OK.' Ian shrugged and glanced at Ted as though to signify they were finished there. 'I'm sorry about that, Emma, but we had to follow up Dominic's crazy accusation. You're right, he really is a piece of work, isn't he? But don't worry. You're safe now. The one thing I don't understand,' he added, 'is why he killed Jocelyn. She doesn't seem to fit. Why did he kill her?'

'You'll have to ask him.'

Ian turned to Ted who was watching Emma closely.

'He said he killed her to throw us off the scent. Don't you find that a bit odd, Sergeant? I mean, how lucky to stumble across a woman, just when he was looking for someone to kill. It sounds like a bit of a coincidence. I mean, something just doesn't add up. Do you think he knew her?'

'She was a stranger,' Emma replied. 'Surely that was the point. He must have thought you would never track him down if he killed someone who couldn't possibly be connected to him.'

'Then how did he find her?'

'He just followed her from the park by Clifford's Tower across Skeldergate Bridge and down the steps to the river,' she said promptly. 'It's pretty deserted along there at night.'

Ian stood up.

'We'll leave now, Emma.'

'I'll see you out.'

'I'm afraid we'll need you to come with us.'

'What?'

'Emma Willerby, I'm arresting you on suspicion of being an accessory to murder—'

'You can't be serious.'

With a sigh, Ian explained that Emma couldn't possibly have known how Dominic had followed his intended victim across the park and down the steps from Skeldergate Bridge unless Dominic had told her. Jocelyn's route across the park had never been mentioned in the media because it hadn't been known. Ian had only discovered the details himself when questioning Dominic less than an hour earlier.

'I didn't know that's what happened, I was just guessing,' Emma blustered.

The slump of her shoulders revealed that she knew the game was up. Her hands lay perfectly still in her lap.

She fell silent and dropped her head in her hands. Ian waited a moment before pressing her once again for an account of her role in the murders. Her voice was flat as she replied.

'You know it all anyway. It's like he told you. I asked Dominic to kill them and I'd do it again. It was no more than they deserved.'

Ian didn't retort that no one deserved to die like that.

'They betrayed me, both of them. Adrian and me weren't together long, but we were happy and we could've stayed that way, only then he met Vivien and dumped me for her! No one treats me like that and gets away with it. No one!' Even with her face contorted in fury, she was beautiful. 'As for Richard, he was living with me and screwing other women every chance he got. Did he really think I'd never find out? They were scum, both of them. Look at me. I'm thirty-three. I've wasted the best years of my life on men and you're all liars and cheats. Well, those two had it coming to them. Death was too good for them. And they weren't the only ones. There would have been more, if you hadn't interfered. I was going to pay them back for the way they treated me, all of them. Dominic thought he had the upper hand. He tried to frighten me – he did frighten me – but two can play that game. After all, he was the one who killed them, not me. But he would have come round, and done whatever I told him to do. He always did.'

Ian struggled to speak. 'You used Dominic because you knew you could persuade him to do anything for you.'

She smiled. 'That was what gave me my chance, bumping into him again. I knew he'd help me get rid of Richard. All I had to do was ask. And then when Adrian got in touch and told me he was coming to York, it was too good an opportunity to miss. Adrian suggested we all meet up – him and his wife and me. As if I'd want to see them again! I knew they wouldn't be here in York for long so I got onto Dominic, and he did the job for me straight away. He knew how to do things without getting caught. He was always clever like that. It was so easy. All I had to do was promise I'd go away with him afterwards. I told him once Adrian and Richard were out of the way, there'd be nothing to prevent us being together. As if I'd ever go away with him!' She laughed harshly before her lovely features twisted with disappointment. 'Now he's betrayed me too.'

She looked so crestfallen, Ian was tempted to admit that Dominic had remained faithful to the end, but he was silent.

EPILOGUE

As soon as he stepped off the plane, hot air enveloped him, filling his lungs and making his skin prickle. His head began to pound. Despite his need to escape into the shade, he could only move slowly. They were both relieved to enter the air conditioned airport.

'Stuff the bus,' Ian said when they finally reached the exit, 'let's get a taxi. How much can it cost?'

'Enough. Don't go mad. We're not made of money.'

'Nothing's too good for you,' he replied cheerfully. 'Remember, this is the honeymoon we never had.'

She smiled and they made their way to the waiting taxis, trailing their cases behind them.

Exploring the island later, they climbed an uneven path that wound between low whitewashed buildings. He felt a fleeting sadness that so many people would never witness the glory of bougainvillea, a blaze of magenta against a wide white wall. Seeing Bev take out her camera, he thought how a photo would never capture the delicate trembling of petals, moved by a touch of air he couldn't feel. He wondered what else he was missing. Strolling on up the hill, they climbed a stone staircase to the terrace of a cafe that looked out over the sea. A small white dog lay in the shade, lazily observing their approach. Up here the cooling breeze was a relief. Staring down at the lightly criss crossed surface of the ocean far below, his job, the move, everything slipped away until his life seemed as distant as the swimmers, reduced to mere dots in the ocean.

'Ian?'

'Hmm?'

'Will you do something for me?'

He smiled. 'What is it?'

'Promise me you'll leave the police. Get a normal job.'

He gazed at his beautiful wife, remembering how close he had come to losing her. Being a detective not only threatened to ruin his relationship with her, it had nearly cost her life. He leaned down to kiss her lightly on the lips.

'Ian?'

She was waiting for an answer.